Charlotte Nash was born in England and grew up in the Redland Shire of Brisbane with a love for horses and heavy machinery, later studying both engineering and medicine (some of which on an army base). She subsequently worked for the CSIRO and for private industry, which included building rockets and visiting mine sites and ports across Australia. These days, she is a technical writer and fiction author, and teaches creative writing at the University of Queensland and in the community. *The Horseman* is her fourth novel.

Web: charlottenash.net
Twitter: @CharlotteNash79
Facebook: AuthorCharlotteNash

Also by Charlotte Nash

Ryders Ridge
Iron Junction
Crystal Creek

The
Horseman
CHARLOTTE NASH

hachette
AUSTRALIA

hachette
AUSTRALIA

Published in Australia and New Zealand in 2016
by Hachette Australia
(an imprint of Hachette Australia Pty Limited)
Level 17, 207 Kent Street, Sydney NSW 2000
www.hachette.com.au

10 9 8 7 6 5 4 3 2 1

National Library of Australia
Cataloguing-in-Publication data:

Nash, Charlotte, author.
The horseman/Charlotte Nash.

ISBN 978 0 7336 3424 6 (pbk.)

Women physicians – Australia – Fiction.
Love stories, Australian.

A823.4

Cover design by Nada Backovic
Cover photographs courtesy of Getty Images and Trevillion
Author photo: Jen Dainer, Industrial Arc Photography
Text design by Bookhouse, Sydney
Typeset in 11.9/16.7 pt Sabon LT Pro
Printed and bound in Australia by Griffin Press, Adelaide, an Accredited ISO AS/NZS 14001:2009
Environmental Management System printer

For Dellah, the bestest most magical horse a girl could have wished for

Chapter 1

January, somewhere in the Wonnangatta National Park

Peta Woodward froze on the leafy trail the moment she heard the hoof beats.

Motionless, her pack pulled on her hips, and the last tendrils of mist that lingered like smoke between the towering trunks condensed on her cheeks. She scanned the forest silence, straining to hear. Was that a horse? Or just a memory come to haunt her?

She reached for her necklace.

The phantom gallop became reality. A horse erupted from the foggy morning, nostrils flared, ears flapping backwards, an empty saddle on its back and reins dancing dangerously under its hooves.

Peta lurched in surprise, and the weight of her pack dragged her backwards. She landed, turtled, on the uphill slope amidst the ferns and shrubs, her heart crashing against her ribs.

The horse gave a snort and shied, tossing leaves at the trail edge as it thundered past.

Peta arched her neck to follow the brown-and-white rump. It wasn't a wild horse. And that meant—

'Patch!' A plaintive human call, coarse and distant, bled through the fog.

Oh, no. *People.*

Peta unclipped the pack and wriggled out of the shoulder straps, strode over to the nearest tree and hid behind it, taking stock. At least she hadn't gone off the other side, where the spur plunged down towards one of the creeks that cut this side of the mountain. Her stomach muscles ached – she'd probably tensed as she was falling – but patting herself down she found no other damage, just a scrape on the side of her knee below her shorts. She peered around the trunk, breathing quietly.

A woman soon appeared, huffing misty breaths along with a man. No, a boy, probably fifteen or so. The woman was perhaps in her forties, with blonde hair rumpled from sleep, her legs clad in blue jodhpurs and a quilted waistcoat covering her long-sleeved hiking shirt. The boy was lanky and looked cold in just a t-shirt and jeans, his hands tucked under his arms.

Peta pressed her back into the trunk. She hadn't seen or heard another human for two weeks, since she'd taken a long leave of absence from her job in emergency at Royal Melbourne Hospital, and she wanted to keep it that way. But there was no place to remain properly hidden.

'Oh, hello!' the woman exclaimed. 'Did you see a horse?'

Peta nodded and pointed off down the trail. 'That way.' Her voice was rough with disuse.

'God, I hope he hasn't gone far. Patch!' the woman called, but made no move to walk past, as if unsure of the social protocol for meeting another hiker.

Peta deliberated. This part of the trail was remote, and if Patch was hard to catch, they could probably use another pair of hands.

Soon, they were all searching up the trail. The woman seemed eager to chat. Her name was Linda, and she and Toby were doing the whole national trail to Cairns with Toby's parents, who were back at the camp with their other horses.

Toby was on his gap year; they'd planned to be through the Alps before the end of summer.

'At least he's easy to track,' Linda said, pausing to inspect hoofmarks in the soft earth. 'The rotter. He's quiet as a mouse at home but get him up here and everything's new and different. A wombat spooked him this morning. A wombat! Toby was in the middle of packing him up.'

Peta glanced at Toby, whose hands were still jammed under his armpits, his hunched shoulders full of teenage reluctance. Peta wondered whose idea the trip had been. However much she loved being out here, it was clear he didn't. When Linda struck off again, Peta fell in beside Toby, appreciating the silence, while Linda ploughed on ahead, drowning out the bush sounds with her patter. By the time they rounded a sharp bend, Peta had heard their entire trip itinerary.

'There you are, you bugger,' Linda announced a moment later.

Patch had ended his run in a sweet siding off the trail, where the grass was thick and glimpses of the rolling mountains appeared through a break in the trees. Peta studied the horse with the experience of a girl who'd grown up on a stud. The horse seemed calm and peaceful, but he had one eye on Linda as he pulled at the grass, and his pack girth hung on by one buckle, in danger of ending up around his flanks. Peta put out a hand to stop Linda.

'He's going to run again. Just wait.'

'Oh, he's thinking about it,' she said, 'but I have the magic.' She reached into her pocket and produced a bright orange carrot.

Patch's nostrils quivered, betraying greedy interest.

'See, I know what you like,' said Linda.

A moment later Patch was munching on the carrot while Linda extracted a halter rope from the pack, ignoring the precariously placed girth.

'Let me just fix this,' Peta said, inching in. Patch was too busy with the carrot to care, his flanks heated from his run, and the horse scent flooded through her, drawing a wave of memory. This is what every morning of her childhood had smelled like. Her fingers fumbled with the buckle before she managed to heft the pack higher and redo both straps.

'There,' she said, stepping away quickly.

'You must be a horsey girl yourself,' observed Linda.

'My parents had a stud,' Peta said. Now the crisis was over, she was looking for escape.

'Is that right? Whereabouts? Here, Toby, take him.'

Toby hesitated in a way that caught Peta's professional eye, noting how he protected his right hand.

'You hurt yourself?' Peta asked.

'Patch gave him a little rope burn when he pulled away,' explained Linda, with little sympathy.

'Can I take a look?' Peta moved towards Toby, as though he were a frightened animal. 'I'm a doctor.'

Toby drew his eyebrows down, but unfurled his hand and tilted it towards Peta. The palm was marked with an angry red scuff, with curls of dead skin where the surface had been stripped across his fingers.

'I bet that's sore,' she said, evaluating. The abrasions looked shallow but dirt streaked the undamaged skin. 'How about you come back to my pack and let me have a better look? I've got a torch and some saline.'

Gently, she coaxed him while Linda followed, leading Patch and firing off questions – where did Peta work? How long had she been walking? What were her plans? Peta did her best to shut this out and when they reached her pack, she concentrated on finding her first-aid kit.

'Ropes are fairly dirty, so we should definitely flush this clean,' she explained. 'When was your last tetanus shot?'

'Before we left,' he mumbled.

'We've got more water back at camp,' offered Linda. 'No need to waste your kit.'

'If it's trail water, it's not sterile and you shouldn't use it for this,' Peta said, twisting the cap off the saline. 'Sorry if this stings,' she said to Toby.

He made it through the cleaning with minimal flinching, and soon Peta had the wound dressed in gauze and a bandage, stark white against the earthy browns, sage and grey of the leaves fallen on the trail.

'Now, you need to keep it clean,' she told him. 'And have it looked at as soon as you get to a town. You don't want an infection out here.'

'It's four days to Omeo, but we've got travellers' antibiotics,' said Linda.

Peta nodded. He would be uncomfortable for all that time. 'Make sure you see a doctor there, and if it's looking infected – red, sore, swollen, hot, any of those – don't leave again until it's better.' Peta repacked her kit into its pouch. 'In the meantime, do you have gloves?'

He nodded.

'Good, use them. And don't put any pressure on your hand. Someone else needs to do the leading.'

'Thanks,' said Toby, who had perked up the moment Peta had mentioned stopping in Omeo.

Linda seemed put out, making noises about whether that was really necessary. 'Why don't you walk with us?' she then suggested, as if this solved everything. 'If it becomes a problem, we'd have you along. Must be lonely doing this by yourself. What do you say?'

With a shot of panic, Peta righted her pack, avoiding eye contact. 'No thanks, really.' Helping out was one thing. Getting stuck in a big party, especially with horses, was quite another.

'Well at least come and eat with us – you look half-starved. Billy's already boiled.'

Peta pretended to consider, but there was no way she was going back. She couldn't. She wouldn't tell them that her father had just died, or try to explain the complexities of her relationship with him. That both of them had been tangled in the grief of what had happened to Stacey and that they had never managed more than a perfunctory conversation in the fourteen years since. Or that, despite this, he'd now left behind a massive and unexpected debt, one that charged Peta with an impossible decision. No. Peta had already tried to unsnarl her feelings and decide what to do amidst the pressure of her job in emergency medicine, and it had been impossible. She needed space, and the clarity of physical exertion. It was how she'd learned to deal with everything, and she wouldn't be waylaid now.

She swung her pack expertly over her head and lifted the weight onto her hips. 'I need to keep moving,' she said, with a curt nod. 'Look after yourselves.'

'Oh, nice necklace,' said Linda in a last ditch effort to engage her. 'I used to have one just like it. Who's the beau?'

Peta snatched at the pendant, brushing the half-heart's jagged edge as she tucked it back in her shirt. 'No one,' she said.

But it was not the truth. The necklace was her reminder of Stacey. And she would carry it silently far beyond the end of the trail.

—

Peta pushed on for an hour, stretching the distance between herself and Linda's party, but she knew that on the horses they'd catch up. So she stopped under a snow gum, her skin steaming and a crescent of sweat at her shirt front, to gulp from her canteen and inspect her maps.

She pulled out her compass and estimated her position from the nearby peaks and creeks. A whipbird called as she traced her intended route, all the way to Omeo – the same route that Linda's party would most likely take. But just ahead, if the map was right, she'd find a branching trail that swept north and met another called the Ridgeback, before eventually rejoining her intended route much closer to Omeo. Peta smiled – the detour was marked as walkers only. She could let Linda and co. overtake her.

She found the new trail easily, and by mid-afternoon she had broken out of the tree cover and onto the Ridgeback, a bald spur that rolled across the roof of the mountains. On either side, the high country was green peak after empty green peak, each with a bristling coat of dead snow gums. A similar row of blanched trunks also lined the edge of the Ridgeback. It was all fire damage, which was hard to imagine this year, when a wet summer had produced so much new growth. Overhead, the huge sky was blue and clear, the sun hot, even through the chill wind.

Peta kept walking as she unzipped her jacket and let the air cool her skin. Toil helped her focus. She stared ahead and asked the same question. *What should I do?*

Still, no answer. But one would come. She had to keep going.

By the time her feet were aching in the early evening, she had met no one else and the morning's incident seemed a month ago. She chose a little hollow to camp in and swung the pack down. Tomorrow, she'd reach the end of the Ridgeback and the next day, rejoin the trail to Omeo.

Her end-of-day routine was soothingly mechanical: strip socks, dress any blisters (today: left heel), set tent, shake out sleeping bag. Prepare a freeze-dried meal with canteen water, scratch the day's distance in her notebook, plan the next, then sit and watch the land change colour. In all this, her fatigue was a relief, an assurance of sleep. So when the sun sank, painting the mountains in a red glow that promised tomorrow's delights, Peta looked forward to a good day.

She was badly misled.

In fact, Peta woke to find the sweeping views swallowed in thick fog. Only ghostly limbs of the dead snow gums were visible, like a misty soup of broken bones. The air was sticky cold, the light dim and grey, so much so that she'd slept an hour past normal.

She made fast work of breakfast with a pack of oats and dried fruit soaked in water, and broke her camp. She would need to take extra care with navigation to avoid delays, and was scrutinising the map when the first raindrops spattered down.

Peta pulled her hood up, huddling over the laminated sheet. A hut was marked just over a kilometre down the path. She'd head for that; if the weather turned really bad, she could ride it out there.

But ten minutes later, bad didn't quite describe it. Peta knew alpine weather was notoriously mercurial, but now it seemed belligerent in proving the point. The wind whipped over the ridge and sent her stumbling, the rain drove up under her hood. Peta cursed, losing count of her steps. The hut couldn't be far now. She leaned her shoulder into the storm and blinked water from her eyelashes.

All she could see was the path itself, a rocky furrow between clumps of grass and tiny alpine flowers. Beyond it, in the fog, she knew there were little flat plateaus before the land fell away into steep valleys. If the hut wasn't right on the track, she could miss it.

The rain was relentless. By the time she'd reached where she reckoned the hut should be, her hair was soaked and water was running down her back. The pack straps were rubbing her skin raw. She kept walking while she tried adjusting them, lost the path, and abruptly found herself above a steep drop.

Peta's body thrilled with fear. She backed up, knees trembling, and nearly fell over a charred, fallen branch. Taking greater care, she circled the area, searching slowly for ten minutes, before realisation dawned and she retraced her steps. It wasn't a branch. It was a post.

The hut she'd been looking for was gone, except for the beams lying in the grass, and a slumped iron fire-pit. Peta tripped on it as the wind buffeted her pack. It must have burned down in the last fire. She couldn't go on; she would have to hunker down until the storm passed, and find somewhere less exposed to do it, or she'd never hope to put her tent up.

With stiff hands, she wedged the pack against the old fire-pit and began a scouting pattern, radiating out and back from the fire-pit, looking for a rocky outcrop, a hollow or tree clump, anything to provide some cover. Without the pack's weight, her steps were light and easy, her trail shoes gripping on rocks in the grass. On her third journey out, she spied something ahead – was that a furrow in the grass?

She realised her mistake too late; her left foot was already over the edge. Cold fingers of undiluted terror dragged her as she fell. Her hip met the edge with a thud and she slid on mud and water. Her back jostled over rocks, her body flipping over before she crashed to a stop. The wind seemed to have stopped. She blinked up, panting and shaking. She hadn't fallen quite as far as she'd imagined; the lip of some kind of gully was still visible, maybe two metres above, over which cascaded a thin stream of water. Behind, though, was a cliff that gave her vertigo, the land far below just visible through the floor of the fog. She must have landed in a landslip, right on the edge of the mountain.

Jesus, that was close.

Peta took several breaths to calm down and look around. The gully's walls were earth and rock. She should be able to climb out.

'Ow, shit!' She fell back, her left foot a tight ball of pain. She stretched her leg out with a hiss. The ankle was swelling inside her boot. She hadn't broken it, had she?

Had she?

Please, no. She refused to think it. She'd only slipped. It was just a sprain. She would get out of this gully, ride out the storm with the foot elevated in the cold wind. By tomorrow, it would be mostly better. A light day's walking would loosen it up, and then she'd be fine again.

That was when she noticed the blood running down her right calf. Pulling the skin around, she discovered a shard of pale wood gouging the skin. She probed around it. It wasn't too deep, not a deal breaker. She silenced the voice in her head that asked *are you insane?* She was a doctor. She could handle it. She just had to get out of here, clean it up and dress it.

And the first part was getting out.

Peta set her jaw, looking for rocks to use as handholds. Sticking the injured foot in the air behind her and using her knee, she rapidly discovered how wrong she was about this landslip. The walls weren't just earth, they were *mud*. And the rocks were covered in a green slime. The first time her hand skidded, she told herself it was unlucky; she'd be more careful. But the second time, she had to acknowledge how stupid she was being. What if she fell again? She could slide right off the edge of the mountain.

At least she was out of the wind down here. Her jacket and shirt were wet, but her gear was meant for alpine use. She wasn't too cold – at least not yet. She had plenty of water, and half a trail bar in her pocket. Once the storm passed, the walls of the gully would dry out. She could climb out then.

The voice of reason tried to remind her that she was out here alone, that no one was waiting for her. Well, except the lawyers. And they wouldn't be sending a search party. She had to face it: she, Dr Peta Woodward, originally from Adelaide but lately of Melbourne, could die out here on this lonely trail. Of exposure. Or sepsis. Or something else she'd once seen on that *I Shouldn't Be Alive* show the interns watched late at night.

Peta tamped these thoughts down with the force of her will, and tucked herself against the wall, prepared to wait. She dislodged the wood shard, washed out the gash with handfuls of rainwater, dressed the wound with a wad of tissues, strapped it down with the lace from her left boot and elevated her injured ankle. She had things to resolve, so she would simply have to get out of here. And she would, when the storm passed.

Then she'd be right back on track, and no one would ever know.

Chapter 2

The sun was just clearing the horizon as Craig Munroe pulled his second-best stock saddle from the tack room and dropped it on the yard railing. After yesterday's thundering rain, the sky had dried into a soft powder grey, only waiting on the rising day to turn it blue again. Later, the only evidence would be the horses, wearing muddy boots past their fetlocks, and Craig's own prints showing his path from the cottage across the feed-shed floor.

Candle, Craig's bay gelding, flicked his ears, sidling over to claim a pat before the day's work. Craig was happy to oblige, running a rope-calloused hand over his velvet muzzle. The attention brought a whicker from Buck, a tall grey in the next yard with a threadbare mane, who liked his share. Craig chuckled under his breath, the thrill of their response to him never growing old, as he looked over his shoulder.

'You going to come looking, too?' This he addressed to the creamy mare in the loose box, whose liquid eyes were calmly watching him, ears softly pricked in his direction. Bel was the tranquil centre of the yard, and echo for the serene blushing dawn that turned the trees up the rise into silhouettes. The air was still and fragrant and full of expectant bird song, and the

Yarraman River cut a dark mark through the pasture down the hill.

Craig took the time to run a hand down Bel's neck. In answer, she nudged him, a gentle reproach because she wouldn't be the one carrying him up the mountain this time.

'Should only be gone a night if I have to stay out,' he told her. 'Gotta go find Charlie's cows. So be good and keep Buck in line.'

He was turning back to Candle when a flashlight beam fell on his face.

'Oh, it's only you,' came a female voice beyond the glare.

'Jeez, Gem, out of my eyes. Who else would it be?'

Craig blinked the light-blindness away to find his sister, Gemma, ten years his junior, standing in the doorway of the feed shed. She was wearing an old pair of trackpants and a faded red t-shirt that served as pyjamas, her long fawn hair twisted into a scrappy knot.

'Don't know. Diane was telling me Old Charlie's had some herd nicked. I was making sure you weren't the rustlers.'

'They're missing, not nicked,' Craig said, slipping through the railing and throwing the saddle blanket over Candle's back. 'I'm heading up across the back fences now. The others are checking down the valley.'

Gemma leaned on the railing. 'How was the meeting?'

The question was out of character. Usually, the weekly gathering of the property owners in the Yarraman Valley didn't register her interest. After all, Harry, Old Charlie, the Rusty brothers, Evelyn and Erica weren't exactly a party – they met because it made business sense to help each other out, especially in the bad years. Gemma could be serious about running their small herd and keeping the farm ticking over, but she was a hands-on girl. Meetings were torture, and therefore never asked about.

But one piece of information might make her interested in last night's meeting. Craig experienced a flash of irritation, like hot pepper up his nose. 'It was fine,' he said, avoiding her eye.

'Anything exciting?'

'Nope.'

A long pause.

'Erica didn't mention anything of interest?'

Erica was the local vet, who, being slender and petite, had been dismissed initially as unsuitable for a large-animal practitioner, until she proved everyone wrong with her skill. When she'd first arrived in town, Craig was instantly drawn to her, and it should have been a match made in heaven – they both loved animals, and could talk shop for hours. She was direct and spoke her mind, which he found uncomplicated. But it had become rapidly apparent that there was no chemistry between them. Erica had straight out admitted she was relieved; she was too busy for relationships, and her candour had removed any awkwardness. She and Craig now got along like old mates. Last night she'd come back after the meeting to look in on Bel's new foal, and had brought the news that Gemma was clearly now fishing for.

Craig cinched Candle's girth to the first hole and glanced at Gemma over the pommel. 'Gossip doesn't become you, Gem.'

'Diane said she'd heard some big announcement coming at the festival, too,' Gemma pushed on. 'She said she didn't know the details though.'

'Well, that's a first.'

Gemma put her hands on her hips, clearly annoyed he wouldn't confirm anything. The return of a prodigal son was big news for a small community, even if that son was Wade bloody Masters. Craig's eyes involuntarily sought Bel, making sure she was still there.

'Come on, tell me.'

Craig grunted. 'Look, Gem, how about just staying away from the festival.' The instant he said it, he knew he'd made the wrong move. After all, she was twenty, not twelve.

She narrowed her eyes. 'Do you mean you're not going either? You wouldn't miss the race – everyone comes to see you!'

'I'm going to find these cows. If that takes a few days, the race isn't that important,' he said.

'Now I know something's up,' she said. 'Is this still about the fight?'

Craig ignored her. He strapped his pack roll behind Candle's saddle and grabbed the bridle. Candle nudged him before accepting the bit. The act broke the tension stretched between Craig's ribs. Masters brought out the temper Craig both hated and feared, the one he identified with his father. After the last time he and Masters had met, Craig worried what might happen if he had to see the man again. Knowing Masters would be in the race was reason enough to avoid it.

He pushed the gate open, crammed his akubra on his head and, with a dry swoosh of his oilskin, swung himself up onto Candle. But when he looked down again at Gemma, her big blue eyes implored him. His mother had those same eyes, and he couldn't deny either of them.

'Won't you tell me?' she asked.

Craig sighed as, with a tiny shift of his weight, Candle moved off. 'Yes, Wade Masters is back,' he said.

⟶

Wade bloody Masters. Craig shook his head as Candle pulled with enthusiasm, eager to be heading out. They skirted the big house as rays of sunshine broke through the trees and turned the field of dewdrops into sparkles. Craig sucked in the fresh air and focused on Candle. He could feel every minute shift in the horse's stride, from when he picked a hoof up higher to clear

a grass tussock, to the bend in his neck as he paid attention
to movements in the undergrowth. His grandmother had been
the one who taught Craig how to attune to a horse, to love
and understand them, and he had taken that teaching into his
soul. Now, the partnership quieted his breaths and soothed
his angst until he could be more objective, even about Wade.

The Masters family had a farm in the next valley, but it had
been a while since any of them lived there. Wade's father had
started a heavy machinery company that diversified and had
gone multinational when Craig and Wade were still teenagers.
The business had taken Wade's parents away, and now they
rarely returned, preferring private jets and business meetings
to their family farm. And while Wade had initially stayed and
run the property, four years ago he too had left, to pursue
business interests down in Melbourne.

Craig had been very glad about that, not only because of
their disastrous last argument, but because Gemma had had
a crush on Wade. Still, Craig had kept an eye on what Wade
had been doing. In the last two years, that had been a lot of
buying up struggling farms, aggregating them into large soulless
enterprises. Craig hadn't imagined he'd come back.

Craig cast a protective glance over his shoulder. His cabin
beside the yards was dark, its shingle roof silver in the oblique
light. Higher on the rise, a single window was lit in the big
house, nearest the chimney that was a sooty block against the
sky. The rest of the Munroe property stretched along one side
of the Yarraman River, which carved down the valley from
the highlands, sustaining every farm and household until it
met the Buckland River down on the flats. Nestled in one of
those bends was the tiny Yarraman Falls village. It was cattle
and horse country for the most part, with occasional sheep,
alpaca and orchard ventures. The falls themselves were on
the Munroe property, formed where a branch of the river had

been diverted by pioneering miners, and now they cascaded over the edge of an old gold excavation.

Craig headed for the rugged four-wheel-drive track that joined the end of the drive. One direction led down into town, the other, seldom used, up into the mountains. After last week's rain and yesterday's storm, the ground was soft. If it was like this here, the festival ground would be mud two feet deep, and the Rusty brothers would have a lot of work unbogging cars. But the rain had also washed the air clean, so that each bush scent came to him crisp and clear – gum resin, lemony wattle and damp ash – and each lungful further dissolved the tension Craig had felt since Erica mentioned Wade Masters.

He was about to turn Candle uphill when an engine sounded, followed by headlights coming up from the village.

'Easy,' he murmured to Candle as a four-wheel drive appeared, bristling with antennas and a strobe rack, 'POLICE' printed across the bonnet. The vehicle pulled to a stop and dropped the window, revealing an officer whose sandy hair was flat on one side, a telltale sign of a fast wake-up. Otherwise, Senior Constable Ash Drummond carried the quiet command of the small-town policeman who had to rely on himself and make judgements he could stand by.

'Craig,' said Ash, 'I was just coming to see you.'

'That sounds like bad news this early.'

Ash nodded. 'You have any trouble up here last night? Harry lost some stockyards. Looks like someone lifted them clean out of his shed.'

'The portable ones?' Craig knew all about those stockyards. They were equipment for rounding up wild horses, and supposed to go out for use further north in a few weeks' time.

'That's them. Could have been any time since lunch yesterday, but my money's on during the evening. Harry said you had a meeting.'

Craig grunted. 'Yeah, every Wednesday.'

Ash nodded. 'That's why I wanted to check with everyone who was there.'

'No issues here. Erica came up to look at Bel after the meeting, so I'd have noticed if anything was gone. Gem didn't mention hearing anything this morning.'

'Right-o.' A flush spread over Ash's cheeks, which was predictable whenever Gem was mentioned. Craig didn't know whether to play the older brother and warn him off, or roll his eyes, knowing Ash would never act on his attraction. Besides, today he had bigger problems.

Craig reined Candle around. 'You think the yards will turn up?'

'Never know, but they wouldn't be hard to move on. If we can't get a lead today, odds aren't too good. You heading bush?'

'Going to find Charlie's cows. Gemma's convinced they've been rustled.'

Ash raised his eyebrows. 'Well, wouldn't be the first time. A backhoe disappeared two valleys over last month, too, and then it turned up on the roadside. Probably realised it wasn't much of a getaway vehicle, top speed being twenty clicks.'

Craig snorted. 'Probably some kids up from the lowlands for holiday camping, drunk and bored without TV.'

'Probably. Clever enough to wipe it down for prints, though. And these yards look like a slick job.'

'I guess they won't be dumb enough to flog them down at the festival then.'

'Won't get that lucky. You racing on Saturday? I heard that Masters is coming back, and he's entered.'

Craig experienced a stab in his chest like a hot poker, but shrugged, non-committal.

'Not going to have any issues, are we?' Ash went on. The tone was friendly, but Craig knew this was a warning. Ash had pulled Craig off Masters outside the pub four years ago. While ashamed of his behaviour, Craig's chest still felt strapped in the tight bands of unfinished business, and he worried about what he might do should a similar situation arise. His temper could get the better of him. No doubt Ash, with his policeman's radar, would be all too aware. But Craig had no desire to give Ash work.

'No issues.'

'Good. Let me know if you need me to put out the word about the cows.'

'Thanks, mate.'

Ash waved and pulled away, and Craig turned Candle towards the trail, his thoughts firmly on the lost cows. Old Charlie's wife had split more than ten years ago for a sea change in Queensland, and his grandson, who'd been so enthusiastic about the property a few years ago, had now decided to head for university instead. Craig didn't blame him – you had to want to do this work – but it had left Charlie short of help. Already hard of hearing, Charlie had spent much of the meeting last night nursing a beer and concentrating on what everyone was saying. He'd already exhausted himself checking the property for the stock, and had enough to do without looking further.

Craig sniffed the air like a bloodhound. He was going to find those damn cows.

For the first few k's Craig wound uphill, through tall gum forest and dense undergrowth, droplets cascading off his hat and chaps. He knew the way so well he could do it blindfolded, and Candle enjoyed himself, deliberately tossing the occasional low-hanging branch to send water scattering into the sky, and shaking beads out of the fine hairs on his ears.

'Knock that off,' Craig said gently, but he couldn't help smiling, especially when Candle flicked his ears backwards to hear better. He might deal in a little mischief, but Candle was a superb endurance horse, and had the most sensitive touch of all the horses Craig had worked with. Craig barely had to think what he wanted, and Candle had it done. More than that, he was bombproof: even when a pair of rabbits streaked across the path ahead, Candle only pricked his ears and watched. Craig frowned. Rabbits were a pain, eating out the native regrowth after the last fire. Was probably time for some marksmanship. He put it on his mental job list.

If only it was so easy to know how to deal with Wade Masters.

As the path became steeper, the tall forest gave way to stunted snow gums and open pasture. Craig found the corner of Old Charlie's property fence ten minutes later. He rode along it for twenty minutes, and all appeared intact. He was starting to think one of the others would find the cattle, when just near an old gate, he spied dung.

Craig could tell without dismounting that it was about two days old. He swung around in the saddle with a creak of leather. No sign of cows now, but the pockets of shaggy snow gums would provide hiding spots. He aimed for an attractive patch of pasture in the distance. Sure enough, not far away was more dung, and tracks in a boggy patch of earth. The evidence rushed Craig's blood, and with a shift of weight, Candle surged forward.

He followed the signs uphill for the next half-hour, through a stand of forest, and then out into open pasture. Something must have spooked the cows, because the dung spread out. And the higher he climbed, the deeper Craig's concern – he was now into the national park, which was illegal for grazing. He'd better find them soon.

Before he knew it, the spine of the Ridgeback trail was in sight, and there was a clutch of fat happy cattle tucked into a hill, half of them lying and chewing cud, floppy ears lazily attending at Candle's approach, as if they had no idea what the fuss was about.

'Stolen, my arse,' Craig muttered, pulling Candle up for a quick headcount. He'd be able to drive them back down to Charlie's, then ride out the remainder of the fence. They must have come through it somewhere. But a few head were missing.

Leaving the cows, he followed fresh tracks up a muddy goat-trail that climbed up to the top of the Ridgeback. Craig had ridden the length of it a few times, twenty kilometres of exposed country above the tree line that eventually plunged into a deep valley. When the dry winds came, the Ridgeback would dry out and be vulnerable to fire again, but for the moment it was a grass-filled paradise.

Unsurprisingly, he soon spotted two more cows basking in the sun. Craig paused, appreciating the view as he pulled a canteen from his saddlebag. He could see the mountains all the way to Kosciuszko, pale blue in the distance. Still short two cows, he pushed on past a stand of perished trees, their trunks now fallen down the mountainside. And there were the charred remains of an old cattleman's hut, lost in the last big fire. Craig huffed a sigh; with mountain grazing now illegal, the hut would likely stay that way, decades of history lost.

He climbed down and paced around, thinking how long it would take to rebuild, when he was brought to pause by a bright blue shape by the iron fire-pit.

It was a hiking pack, well used, its top faded from sun exposure, and one clip at the back different to the others – probably a replacement. Water had pooled on the waterproof material, so it had been here at least since yesterday. Craig hefted the straps, feeling the weight. Heavy, but the grass underneath was still green, so it hadn't been here too long.

He straightened, looking around. The trail ran north–south here. He'd come up from the west on a path he knew wasn't marked on maps. The few campers that came through Yarraman took the four-wheel-drive road further south, where the national park entry made access easier. Besides, he hadn't seen any human tracks that way, and there were none here either, in or out. That narrowed the time of the pack's deposit here to before the storm yesterday.

Or during it.

Craig left Candle and crested the next rocky high point on foot, where he could see the path meandering down the next ridge. He loosed a ringing whistle that bounced off the hillside, followed by a 'Hello?' that could have shattered glass.

He listened. Nothing.

He turned back, and that was when he saw Candle, ears pricked, picking his way towards a broken edge on the western side. It looked like an old wombat hole, eroded out into a gully.

And that was how Craig Munroe found Peta Woodward, still trapped inside.

Chapter 3

Peta woke stiff and sore, thinking she'd heard a whistle. Miserable and chilly, she had slept little overnight. She was practical enough to be glad it was summer, but by the time the sun had finally come up she had been more than ready to get out. Trouble was, the gully faced west so its sides remained in shadow, and looked just as slippery as yesterday.

Still, she was determined. Using her bum as the main hold, she had managed to make it halfway up, dragging her bad leg and ignoring the ache in her injured calf. But her backside was bruised from being wedged on the rocks, and the side was too steep. She'd resolved to try again after a rest but, damp and muddy, her ankle now badly swollen, she had instead slept through pure exhaustion.

Now, she eased to standing on her good foot, wondering if she'd dreamed the sound. But then came a cry, a man calling hello. Peta's hopes surged, tempered with remembering there were plenty of lyrebirds around here, and the buggers were pretty good at imitating things they'd heard.

A snuffle sounded right over her head, and she glanced up to find a big horse face peering down at her.

'Jesus!'

Peta nearly toppled over. Frantically, she scrabbled, grabbed a rock in her fingertips and steadied herself. When she looked up again, the horse was still there, its big inquisitive nostrils blowing, one rein trailing down. She wondered if Linda's party had found her after all, but then a man's face appeared, capped with a beaten akubra.

'You okay down there?' he asked.

Peta experienced relief like a hot shower over her skin. 'Busted ankle,' she answered. 'I can't get out.'

'Hold on then.'

He disappeared, and a moment later the horse moved away. Then she could hear the slap of leather straps, and the jingle of a buckle. When he came back into view, he held a long length of rope.

'Can you climb up if I give you a rope?'

'Send it,' she shot back.

It wasn't dignified enough to be called climbing, but the rope gave her a handhold as she inched her way upwards on her backside, using her stronger leg as a prop. When she was near the top, he reached over and they grabbed arms in a monkey-grip. Peta felt every callus in that powerful grip, his forearms solid muscle under her fingers.

Next thing she was sprawled on the grass, gratefully sucking in air and blinking in the sunlight. She could smell her own rank sweat. Her jacket and skin were caked in mud, and from the way her cheek pulled, mud was drying on her face, too. But she was out.

The man offered a battered water canteen. 'Here.'

She sat up and gulped, then tipped some water into her hand, trying to wash the worst off her face. Meanwhile, he sat on his heels, watching her with an unreadable expression. She squinted at him over the canteen. He was younger than she'd first assumed, maybe thirty, with a couple of days' golden stubble on his chin and fair hair under his hat. From his forearms and the way his shirt stretched over his shoulders, he did plenty of heavy lifting, and from the jeans, chaps and boots, he wasn't out for a hike. He looked like the kind of man who should be wielding an axe at a country show.

Peta lost her view of him as her vision swam. Her ankle throbbed, and with each beat her head felt mushy, as if she might faint. Getting off the ground seemed impossible.

'You by yourself?' he asked.

'Yes.' She weakly offered her hand in his direction. 'Peta Woodward.'

'Craig Munroe.' Peta awkwardly brushed dirt from her hand before they shook, his calloused hand engulfing hers. A moment later, those same calluses were feeling her legs. What the hell was he doing? She batted at his hands, but then realised she hadn't actually moved. Confused, Peta felt a fresh sweat break out above her lip.

'Ah, that's nasty,' Craig said, his fingers light on the hot tight skin of her ankle. Peta's head cleared. Oh, right, he'd seen her ankle.

With sure movements, he eased her boot tongue forward, and slipped it off. Peta hissed.

'Yick,' she said, inspecting the damage. Her sock was brown above the shoe line, and when he peeled it back, the foot was bruised and her toes swollen with damp. It looked like a plate from a pathology textbook. Next, Craig probed the damp, dirty mass of tissues held down with her bootstrap on her other calf. 'How bad is that?'

'Just a big splinter,' she said. 'Help me up. I need to get my tent.' She remembered that much was part of her plan.

'What do you mean, your tent?'

'So I can camp here for a bit.' This seemed entirely logical. What was his problem? Why was he looking at her like that?

'Don't be silly. I'll take you down to the valley, and drive you to the hospital in Wangaratta.'

Slowly, Peta processed what he was saying. She was dimly aware that her plan might be failing to account for something important, but he was missing the point. She *had* to finish the trail. She folded her arms. 'No way. I'm staying here.'

'That ankle looks bad. You need to see a doctor.'

'I *am* a doctor.'

He gave her a hard look. 'This is serious.'

'So am I. Now, thank you for your help, but I'm not going anywhere.'

He muttered something under his breath that sounded like a curse. Then he pulled off his hat and raked his fingers through his thick hair. 'You know where you are, right?'

She hesitated. She'd gone off her original path, so she didn't know this part of the map by heart, and she couldn't remember the name of the trail. Racetrack?

'Thought so. Well, Ms Woodward, you're on the Ridgeback trail. It's exposed up here when the weather comes in, as you found out, and it will come in again, believe me. If you think I'm leaving you up here, you're insane.'

'It's *Dr* Woodward,' she said, intensely irritated, 'and I'm not leaving. Now, help me up.'

He obliged, her body weightless in his strong hands. But as soon as she was vertical, and he let go, a searing pulse pounded in her ankle, and a bolt of pain shot up her leg.

'Ooof, no, down.'

Her stomach spun and her heart hammered for a good minute after he'd lowered her back down. She'd have to crawl to her tent. The ridiculousness of that idea finally broke through her mental fog, and reality streamed in. No, she couldn't stay here. She would need some treatment.

Craig was busy dragging dead branches over and lining them up beside her leg.

'What are you doing?'

'Measuring a splint. It'll help for the ride down. After that, like I said, I'll drive you to Wangaratta.'

'I don't need a splint and I'm not going to Wangaratta. What's the nearest town?'

'Yarraman Falls,' he said, standing to rummage in his saddlebag. He pulled out a black roll of electrical tape. 'But there's no hospital. And the only doc's a temporary one with a first-aid kit at the festival. You'd be better off in Wangaratta.'

Peta brightened. 'Take me to the doc at the festival.'

He stared at her, shaking his head. His eyes were very blue above the stubbled jawline, the kind of stare that saw through people. For a moment, she wondered what he was going to do with the tape.

'It's my decision,' she said stubbornly.

'Suit yourself. The ride will probably take a couple of hours. Candle's slower with two, especially downhill.' At this, the horse flicked his ears and bunted Craig in the chest. 'You done any riding before?'

Peta absorbed the question with a peal of nerves. She hadn't been on a horse in fourteen years, not since the accident. She hadn't wanted to ride again, and now it seemed she had no choice. 'Pity you don't have a helicopter,' she muttered.

'The trees make the landings a bit interesting,' he said dryly, busy hauling her pack over. 'The first bit's steep and churned, so I'll walk and Candle will take you. Further down when it shallows out, we'll double. Take whatever fits in that saddlebag or your pockets,' he said. 'The pack's too heavy to take.'

On this point, she couldn't bend him. So Peta stuffed her valuables and her only change of clothes into her tiny day-bag, but then some critical part of her motor functions shut down. She could only stare forlornly at the pack, which had accompanied her on so many journeys, leaning against the old fire-pit again as Craig led Candle over. She didn't resist when Craig lifted her into the saddle, but she didn't help either and she heard him grumble under his breath.

Rigid and defeated, she fixed on Candle's withers, too proud to admit that her head was spinning and her foot throbbed where it rubbed against the saddle. Her throat was suddenly tight, as if she was about to burst into tears.

Craig was rubbing Candle's neck and telling Peta she needed to relax. She found it impossible. This wasn't what was supposed to happen. But all she could do was sit, helpless, and let him lead her away.

The journey down was hell-punctuated purgatory. Peta's foot was a knot of pain, and she clamped her jaw so hard her whole face ached. She couldn't pay attention to anything Craig said, even when he tried to reassure her on the first part of the trail down, which was terrifying, as Candle's hooves slipped on muddy sections. But the horse always recovered, and when Craig climbed back on, he sat behind the saddle, and eventually she leaned back against him in exhaustion.

At one especially bad moment, Craig again mentioned taking her to a proper hospital, and Peta had sworn at him and tried to take the reins. Craig relented, his obscenities quite audible this time. Finally convinced he had listened, all Peta could do was count Candle's steps and focus on closing the distance to painkillers, bandages and ice.

Gradually, the snow gums transformed into a towering forest, and then into rolling hills, and they broke from the trail onto an unsealed road. Another kilometre and potholed bitumen kicked in, until Peta saw a few houses clustered around the street in the distance. A white-walled pub stood in the road bend, and opposite, a shop sported a single fuel pump, with several utes waiting in a queue. Craig turned down a side road just before the pub, and Candle's hooves clopped across the river bridge.

Beneath the wooden beams, the Yarraman River undulated with spots of foam, its colour a clean, cold green, its surface brushed with willow boughs. All Peta could think was how she wanted to plunge her foot in that water. 'How much further?'

'Not far.'

'Good. Need morphine.'

He grunted, in a way that told her it was on her own head. A few minutes later, when Craig reined Candle through a gate and up a churned driveway, a gust of fresh air caught Peta in the face, and she heard a distorted voice on a distant PA. They crested a rise, and Peta saw the festival: an impromptu showground on a sprawling pasture within steep hills.

From their elevated position, the sea of tents, two arenas, a mini fairground, and rows of floats and horse trucks made a rough grid. The road into the showground switch-backed down the hill and through the grid's centre, disappearing in places under huge mud puddles.

Clouds softened the glare, making every glass blade and tree glow emerald against the churned earth. Candle picked his way down the last slope and abruptly, Peta was amongst a mismatched crowd – horsemen in oilskins and akubras, bright-coated children clutching fairy floss and tornado potatoes, and adults seemingly unprepared for the elements, their jeans muddy to the knees.

Despite her frayed mental state, the first thing Peta noticed was the attention as every third person turned to stare. What, hadn't they ever seen anyone come in by horse ambulance before?

'Craig,' came the gruff acknowledgement from several men, who tipped their chins up as they passed, with questioning expressions reserved for Peta. Craig said nothing.

She was relieved when she spotted a red first-aid tent. A man in a grey t-shirt and running shorts was slumped in a folding chair inside, clutching a take-away coffee, a stethoscope stuffed into the pocket of his pants. A curling paper nametag read *Dr Randall*, though whoever had written it had run out of room, smudging the last three letters so it looked like *Dr Randy*. He looked up blearily as Craig pulled Candle to a stop.

'You the doc?' asked Craig.

'Guilty as charged.' The doctor noticed the improvised bandage on Peta's calf. 'Know you're in the country when a horse drops off the patients,' he said, stretching with a wince. Peta had enough clarity to decide he looked hungover, and with firm opinions against sloth, took an instant dislike to him.

Craig was already down off Candle and offering her his hand.

'I can do it,' she said, stupidly, given her two injured legs. But Craig had obviously had enough of her, taking her firmly by the waist and pulling her down with little grace. Maybe he thought she was going to abscond with his horse.

'You been in the mud wrestle?' Dr Randall asked Peta with too much amusement for her to tolerate.

She put all her weight on her better leg, and tried to summon the voice she used in the ED. 'I need analgesia, a ligament assessment, plus stitches and antibiotics,' she told him.

'Whoa, steady on, love. Let's not get ahead of ourselves.'

'I'm a doctor,' Peta said, bristling at the 'love' as she commandeered his chair and stuck her foot up on a nearby table. The relief was instant, and she let out a sigh. More of the fog lifted from her mind. 'Some ice would be good, too.'

She was aware of Craig watching from the side of the tent, his arms folded, Candle peering around from behind him with ears pricked. She ignored him, further irritated as Dr Randall refused to be hurried. He had an annoying habit of rubbing his nose, which Peta found disgusting, and he examined the cut on her calf as if he'd never seen one before. Peta thought any of her first-year interns could have done a better job.

'Right-o, I *guess* we'll do some stitches here. But for the ankle, I'm going to send you down to Wango. Needs an X-ray. The ambos are off getting lunch, but when they get back I'll send you.'

'I don't need an X-ray.'

'You might have a fracture.'

'It's not broken. I need some anti-inflammatories, a few days' rest and elevation, then a brace and early mobilisation. I'll rehab it myself and be back on track in two weeks, tops.'

Dr Randall stared at her. She could see him trying to formulate an argument, and from his bloodshot eyes, suspected the after-effects of a late night drinking were impairing his progress. Peta had no sympathy; she'd been doing nights on call for as long as she could remember, and you never drank if you had to be on shift. Dr Randall glanced at Craig, seeking support, and found nothing but a what-do-you-expect-me-to-do shrug. Peta's feelings towards Craig thawed just slightly.

'Can I get those stitches now?' she said. 'And some painkillers, please. I did just spend two hours on a horse.'

Peta was aware she was being difficult, even rude, but pain was winning over tact, and she was running on less than empty. Her eyelids felt as though they were lined with cement. She won the staring contest and the doctor went to rummage in the supply box. Tipping her head back in relief, she squeezed her necklace in her palm. The mud-caked edge of its split heart left a brown streak on her skin. She had to keep going; she knew she wouldn't be whole again until she finished the trail.

After the doctor had applied her ankle bandage incorrectly, Peta stripped it off and redid it, overlaying each wrap half on the last. Good at her job, and used to the decisiveness of the ED, when he hesitated with a suture pack, she made no move to hide her impatience.

'You want to do the stitches yourself, too?' he asked, a testy note in his voice.

'Yes, actually.'

The doctor threw his hands up, and when Craig still offered no support, he chucked the sterile glove packet down, picked up his coffee and stalked out of the tent. Peta reached for the instruments. She could do sutures in her sleep, could tie knots one-handed from all the dog bites, glass-cuts and home gardening or cooking accidents she'd seen over the years. At least the painkillers were starting to work.

'You just going to stand there and stare?' she said, narrowing her gritty eyes at Craig.

'Believe me, I have better things to do today.'

'Feel free to go do them, then.' Lord, she sounded like a complete bitch. But she didn't feel as bad when she caught him suppressing a smile. Fine, laugh. If she was really that entertaining.

She was saved from further scrutiny when a woman appeared across the tent. Her near-black hair had been staked behind her head with a pair of chopsticks, and she wore blue work pants, boots, and a green t-shirt with a design too faded to read. Her skin was pearlescent, her expression pinched. And when she spoke, her voice carried an edge. 'Craig. Good. I need a word.'

Peta turned back to her work, glad to be left alone. Three sutures would be enough. She started on the second knot, wishing this day would dissolve, and she could wake up on top of the ridge, and find she'd been dreaming the whole time.

⤙

Outside the tent, Craig regretted even more that he'd had to play rescuer. Not only was this crazy woman refusing to have proper medical attention, but now he was faced with Karen Waters.

'I heard Charlie's been grazing cattle in the national park,' she began, her eyes searching his face as though she could detect lies. Craig contained his surprise; this was the last thing he'd expected.

'Oh?'

'Do you know anything about it?'

Craig knew she was smart and dogged, which he respected, but her environmental agenda ran in the face of many of the valley's residents. Old Charlie would never have put his cows up there voluntarily. The farm was close to the wall as it was; he didn't need trouble from the law, too. Craig kept his face neutral.

'Nope. Who'd you hear it from?'

'Anonymous tip-off. Someone called the office this morning. I don't have to tell you it's illegal.'

'I'm well aware.'

Who the hell would have called Karen? He'd only just found the bloody cows himself. Karen's gaze was still searching his face, waiting.

'I'll look into it,' he said.

With a twitch of her lips, she nodded. 'Please do. You know I only care about the impact. It's not about punishing people.' And with that, she strode off, the chopsticks an X behind her head.

Craig cast his attention around the ground. He'd have to drive those cattle down, pronto. And then find where they'd come through the fence.

He glanced inside the tent where Peta was still bent over her leg. She looked frightful – her clothes streaked with mud, her choppy short brown hair matted, her thin face drawn and haggard. She was loopy, but clearly exhausted, too. Probably wasn't thinking straight. And it wasn't in him to leave business unfinished. He should try to convince her to go to a proper hospital.

He was just calculating how he might argue it when he spotted a man striding towards the tent. Foreboding prickled down Craig's neck. He had filled out since Craig had last seen him, now sporting a roundness about his middle as well as the unmistakable rugby shoulders, but even with a baseball cap pulled down on his hair, Craig would have recognised the smooth walk anywhere. Once, it had been the mark of a friend. Now, the skin across Craig's knuckles tightened.

Wade Masters.

Wade spotted him and broke into a smile that betrayed no discomfort. 'Craig Munroe,' he said, as if they were merely business associates. 'Been a long time.'

Not long enough. Craig stared, emotions thundering like hooves around his head.

'Festival's still a kicker. Scotty was even saying the numbers are up on last year, even with the rain.' Wade looked around, satisfied, as if he were personally responsible for this windfall. Then Wade's attention fell on Candle. 'Nice looking horse. New one?'

Craig's temper struck like the heavy end of a sledgehammer. 'Stay away from my horse.'

Wade arched surprised eyebrows and dropped his voice. 'Still touchy, then? Want to take another swing?'

Craig itched. 'You should have stayed in Melbourne.'

'And maybe you should have gone. You're small-town, Munroe.' Wade tossed it out easily, like a soft bowl.

And Craig swung. 'At least I know how to treat an animal.'

'Yeah, you enjoy the company of animals. That's what happens when you can't keep a woman,' Wade said softly. 'Even one that's got her arm up a cow's arse all day.'

Craig had the momentary awareness of nearly hurtling across that line, beyond which his temper became a thing of its own. Then he was shoved from behind, and found Candle nosing under his arm, wanting to know what was going on. Craig rested his hand on the smooth muzzle, his anger breaking into shimmering pieces.

Wade laughed. 'I do hope you're riding in the race. Can't deny the fans the chance of a famous rematch, can we? And it'll make such a great platform for my announcement later when I win.' He winked. 'Take care, buddy.'

A moment later, Craig was watching Wade's wide back depart for the event arena, stopping only to shake hands with people he recognised. Craig turned away, his jaw working, his blood hot and his stomach nauseated. Wade was an arse, but Craig hated the sticky feeling of almost losing his temper. More, he still felt a faint tickle of sadness for the friend Wade had once been. But it was only faint. He shouldn't have taken the bait.

That was when he noticed Peta staring at him through the tent flap. A neat bandage was now across her stitched calf, and her damaged ankle packed with ice. She'd probably seen the whole thing.

'You still bent on staying?' he asked.

She nodded.

'Suit yourself,' he said shortly. 'But the only accommodation is at the pub. I've got something to do, but I'll drop you there when I'm done.'

'Thanks, but I'd rather travel on four wheels this time.'

'I can borrow a car.' He ground the words out between his teeth.

'I'll save you the trouble,' she said. 'I can look after myself.'

Craig took one last look at this thin, muddy woman with the crazy ideas and thought, screw it. One less problem. He led Candle away. Now, all he had to do was find the Rusty brothers and ask them to go round up those damn cows, and check Old Charlie's fence.

Because Craig knew he wouldn't have enough time to do this himself – not now he was back in the race.

Chapter 4

After Craig left, Peta breathed out. Finally, she was back on her own. She didn't want to get in a car with him anyway. He might lock the doors and decide to drive her out of town. Plus he looked like he needed to walk it off after the conversation she'd witnessed.

'Good news,' said Dr Randall, who'd reappeared and sounded anything but enthused. 'Got a gift for you.'

He presented her with a dusty set of crutches. They were an old-school, under-the-arms pair, with some ratty sheepskin held down with electrical tape over the arm pads and a split in one of the feet.

'One of the competitors pulled them out of a float,' he said, confiscating the suturing equipment and putting the first-aid box out of Peta's reach.

Peta accepted them, pulling herself up to test her weight on her good ankle. The stitches pulled, but she could manage. 'Good. Just need to find a ride back to the pub.'

'They'll be full up,' said Dr Randall. 'Now, for the last time—'

Peta didn't let him finish. She shouldered her daypack and crutched awkwardly away from the tent. She'd bloody well hitch. As if the gods were finally on her side, she quickly found a woman in a dented ute who agreed without any questions to take her to the pub.

Ten minutes later, she stood in front of the white-walled building, which was flanked by two towering gums. Behind, a public park buffered the pub from the river, which crashed over a weir and then streamed through trailing willow boughs. The pub's tall, wood-framed windows reflected the sky, and large double doors promised a cool, dark interior. Through the glass, Peta could see patrons clustered around tables of pint glasses, with their checked shirts, jeans and beaten akubras at home beneath the soaring ceilings. A chipped sign announced accommodation was to be found at a split stable door near the end of the facade. But when she reached the door, another sign read *No Vacancy*.

Great. Peta looked down at her muddy clothes. Her body ached as the painkillers wore off. She wanted a shower. Any shower. She'd just hobbled down to the opposite end of the pub and was eyeing off the public toilets in the park when a voice called across the street.

'Yoo hoo!'

Peta twisted around. In the doorway of the shop, a woman in jeans and a bright red shirt was waving.

'Yes, you, with the gammy foot!' called the woman, beckoning.

Seeing no better options, Peta hobbled across the street, clearing the petrol pump and a phone box before nearly tripping inside.

The woman had retreated behind a counter that included a steaming bain-marie of pies, and assorted orange and yellow fried fare. The rest of the shop was stocked with ice-cream freezers, bakery shelves and a mini-supermarket. A ceiling-mounted television faced the counter, and when Peta peered up, Miss Marple's face looked back on pause.

'So, how was the ride with Craig Munroe?' asked the woman with a grin. Her hair fell in a grey bob, but her face was dominated by her eyes, which were unnaturally wide, making her seem permanently surprised.

'How did you—'

'Oh, I can see the road out the back window. Hear the horses coming from miles away. Saw him taking someone across the bridge earlier. Recognised your clothes. So what have you done to yourself?'

Peta recovered. 'Sprained my ankle up on the mountain.'

'Ah, hiker then? Where're you from?'

'Melbourne.'

The woman's eyes moved as if she were writing this down on her eyelids. 'Craig must have taken you out to that doc at the festival,' she surmised. 'That's not like Craig. I thought he'd have driven you down to Wanga'.'

Peta shifted her weight off her heel. 'He offered. I didn't want to go. I'm looking for a room.'

'Didn't he tell you that the pub's booked? And there's nowhere else, not in Yarraman Falls. You'd have to go down the highway to the next town to even have a chance.'

Peta bit her lip. The day was already too far advanced, even if she'd had the energy. She had no way of transporting herself down the highway, and all her gear was still up on the Ridgeback. She was dirty, hungry and fed up. One way or another, she was staying in town. She looked around the shop, with its deep crevices and nestled shelves. 'I don't suppose you sell tents? I've got one but I had to leave it up the mountain.'

The woman peered at Peta's crutches. 'You want to camp with a foot like that?'

'Doesn't look like I have much choice.'

'Hmmm.' The woman set her mouth, as if this was some kind of personal challenge. Then she rubbed her hands together and grabbed a plate, throwing on a pie, a scoop of floating peas, and a slug of gravy. She pushed it across the counter. 'Look, stay here and eat something. I'll be back in a minute.'

Peta collapsed in a steel chair near the front corner and poked at the pastry. She hated pies, but she was hungry enough for anything. Three weeks ago, she would only have wanted coffee. Good, strong coffee from her favourite barista across the road from the hospital. She rubbed the back of her neck, feeling the necklace against her skin, and sighed.

Next moment, a cold flat surface was pressed against her cheek, and someone was tapping her on the shoulder. Peta sat bolt upright, heart racing, and found the shopkeeper bent over her. All that was left of the pie was crumbs, and she'd left a muddy mark from her cheek on the table.

'You must be exhausted, poor thing.'

Embarrassed to have fallen asleep, Peta began to apologise.

'Forget about it. I have the solution,' said the woman, gleeful. 'There's one room in the pub that's being renovated, but no one's working on it during the festival. It's pretty rough, but it's yours if you want it.'

Maybe Peta's luck was turning. 'Thanks so much. I owe you.'

'I'm Diane,' said the woman with a broad smile.

'Peta Woodward.'

'Oh, I have a niece called Peta. How do you know Craig?'

'I don't. He just gave me a lift down.'

'Down from where exactly?'

'The Ridgeback. That's where I hurt my foot,' she said.

'Really? I wonder what Craig was doing up there. He didn't say, did he?'

Diane's eyes were working again, sucking in the details.

Peta shook her head.

'That's fine. Gemma will know. Anyway, go and get settled and have a shower. If you have trouble sleeping over there,

I have ear plugs and masks, and the best coffee right here in the morning.' She pointed at the espresso machine that to Peta looked old enough to be there under protest. 'Don't buy it from the pub bar. They specialise in beer for a reason. And you let me know if you need to see the doc again.'

'I am a doctor,' Peta said wearily, for the third time today.

'Are you really?' Diane said, with renewed enthusiasm. 'I don't suppose you could help me with—' then she gave Peta another quick appraisal. 'Look, when you're feeling better, you can repay that favour. I could take you out to the race on Saturday, too. Craig will be riding, and that draws a big crowd.'

Despite her exhaustion, Peta's curiosity tweaked. Now she remembered talk of a race in the confrontation she'd witnessed back at the festival.

'Why's that?' she asked.

'Man's a legend around here,' Diane said conspiratorially. 'Magic with horses, and he won by the largest margin ever a few years ago on Bel – beautiful mare. People still talk about it every year. And he can break a horse in faster than anyone's ever seen. Well worth watching, especially as you've met.'

'Sure,' Peta said, without any intention of taking her up on it. She only wanted to get back to the trail. Everything else was secondary.

Only when she'd closed herself into room fourteen of the pub and looked in the mirror did she realise how frightful she looked. Dirt was caught in the crease lines at the base of her neck, the silver chain around it dark as lead. Her hair was lank, her face all eyes and nose above her sunken cheeks. She'd always been a thin, sporty kind of girl, but the trip had dropped more weight. It brought back the memory of her mother, who'd been thin like that, too. But not Stacey. Stacey had been solid, and vibrant, full of something Peta lacked.

Wearily, Peta turned away and surveyed the room. The bed was a hasty re-installation – just a mattress on the floor, with the origami towel on top. She stuffed it through the crutches and crept into the hall. Time to find the shower – at least she could wash away the mud.

⟜

Craig arrived back at the farm less than an hour later, irritated. First, there was Wade Masters, the race, and the hangover of their confrontation. But there was also Peta Woodward. He'd felt dismissed, but to save his pride, he decided that whatever kind of nutcase she was, he felt bad for leaving her to fend for herself. It wasn't the kind of man he was.

The late afternoon sun was warm as Craig angled Candle for his cottage, and as he passed the big house, the front door flew open and Gemma appeared.

'Craig! What's this about you rescuing some woman from the mountain?'

Craig didn't stop, steering Candle into the yards while Gemma threw on her gumboots and came after him down the hill. She appeared in the feed-shed doorway as he was removing Candle's saddle.

'I thought you'd be doing the mail run,' he said pointedly.

'Nope. Filling orders.' She waved a small band of horsehair in front of his face.

'Must be a good month, then,' Craig said, taking a brush to the saddle mark on Candle's back. Gemma ran a horsehair jewellery business on the side of the farm, which had done surprisingly well. She had a keen eye for design, and fingers built for precision. Craig had watched her many times, in front of the fire in the big house, sorting, braiding and designing for hours, even when she was tired. It would have driven him bats, and he deeply admired both her persistence and her talent.

'Show me that?' he said, nodding at her hands. She passed across what he discovered was a bracelet, an elaborate, six-strand weave of Candle's rich chestnut mane and Bel's pale cream tail, the length set off with silver buckles.

'Lovely,' he said, appreciating the even, flawless braid. 'What else are you working on?'

'Matching rings for a wedding, if you can believe it. So fiddly. But what happened with the cows? This woman wasn't stealing them?'

'Found them up near the Ridgeback. And no, she'd fallen down a gully and done her ankle. Took her down to the doc at the festival.' He thought about it for a minute. 'Who told you about it?'

'Diane. Said she'd come to get a room at the pub. She's a doctor from Melbourne. And she's real skinny, like one of those fashion models. Diane said she must have been in the hole starving for a week.'

Craig gave Candle a pat and climbed through the rails, trying to remember. All he could see in his mind were Peta's defiant eyes under her choppy hair, and the long length of her fingers as she'd re-bandaged her ankle. He shook his head to clear the picture, then hefted the tack back into the shed. 'She'd only been there one night,' he said over his shoulder.

'And . . . ?' asked Gemma, waving her hand to keep him talking.

'And what?'

'You found the cattle. Does that mean you're back in the race?'

'Looks like it.'

Gemma grinned, satisfied. 'And what about Wade?'

Craig sucked the air in, and let it out slowly. He turned to the feed drums and began making up Bel's, plunging the scoop into the chaff and pellets with satisfying muscular effort. 'I saw him.'

'He's riding, too?'

Craig paused to look around. Gemma was leaning on the dividing wall between the feed shed and tack room, one gumboot casually crossed over the other. She looked absurdly young, and was doing a bad job of concealing her interest. 'He's bad news, Gem.'

'Because of the business thing?'

'That, and other things.'

'Like what? I still don't understand. You used to be friends.'

Craig's eyes found Bel again. She was standing at the railing outside the loose box, just watching him. The foal had folded up, asleep at her feet. 'I don't want to get into it.'

'You never do,' Gemma muttered. She made for the door, but then turned back. 'But I'm so glad you're back in the race!'

Craig put the tack away and went back to his cabin, glad he'd been able to divert Gemma. He needed to reassess the next few days. Jobs for the farm were mounting up, and he'd promised Jack Rusty he'd go down and take a look at a new horse who was giving him trouble. Plus, he needed to think about the demo he was giving in Bright in a few weeks. Craig knocked the mud from his boots at the cabin door and wrenched them off. He didn't like performing in front of people. But he believed in kindness with horses, that training them didn't have to be a battle of wills, and he wanted to show people that. He'd been trying to turn his hand to teaching for a while, running a few classes, but despite their popularity, he found reasons not to do more.

The cabin inside was simple: a single room with stone walls, and a wooden floor over packed earth. A small kitchen occupied one corner, a lounge and open fire opposite, and a bed that folded down from the wall. In his rush to get going this morning, he'd tipped it up unmade so that it looked like a monster's mouth full of sheets. A mug of yesterday's strong black tea rested on the sink. The mess bothered him; he'd clean it up right after he'd sorted his week out. He took a slug of the cold tea and picked up the phone.

'Craig, I was about to call you,' his mother answered a moment later.

Craig rubbed his forehead. 'Let me guess, Diane called you too?'

'She did. Even in Cairns, she thought I needed to know.' She laughed. 'So, who's the woman?'

Craig's lips pulled in a small smile. Since his mother had moved to Grant Dwyer's farm, she'd acquired a directness and confidence that was new, surprising, and to Craig, bittersweet. Grant was a good man, and the pair of them were now off on an around-Australia caravanning adventure while Grant's brother watched the farm. She deserved to be happy; she shouldn't have waited so long.

'She's a doctor from Melbourne. But that's not why I'm calling. How's things there?'

'Fine,' she said, and gave him a quick summary of the last week's travel, meandering up the highway from Rockhampton, where they'd stayed on a cattle property belonging to Grant's family. She sounded content. 'Gemma said Old Charlie lost some cows,' she finished.

'Found them up on the Ridgeback. That's where I found the doctor, stuck down a gully.'

'Ah, and how's Bel?'

'Better and better. Filly's perfect. Actually, that's kind of what I wanted to talk about.'

'Mmmm?'

Craig paused. 'Wade Masters is back.'

He looked out the window then, down the hill towards the river where the water began its long journey from the high country to the Murray. When he'd first come here as a boy, the family had been running away. He'd never imagined the place would become a home he would defend against drought and fire. Today, he felt like a leaf on that river, caught in a vast eddy that had brought the past circling back.

'You know, Craig, you're not like him,' his mother said when they were done talking. 'You have to remember that.'

Craig grunted. 'I know,' he said. But a part of him didn't believe it. He should try to be better. So when he put down the phone, he thought of Peta. She was bull-headed and loopy, but she was only a danger to herself. That was the difference between them.

—

The next afternoon, Thursday, Peta was reconsidering the wisdom of her plan. Her room at the pub was a small problem. All the boards had been sanded back to timber, leaving the smell of old paint in the air, and the light fixture was out of service, replaced by the dim bedside lamp. The mattress on the floor was large and the linen was clean, but with only a foot clearance to the wall, it was difficult to manoeuvre on crutches.

She resolved to work around it; she was strong from hauling her pack. The bigger problem was that Yarraman Pub had been built before anyone had heard of ensuites, and so every time Peta needed the shower or the bathroom, she had to negotiate an obstacle course.

Firstly, the step down from her room door, then the hall, whose floor appeared flat but which was actually a maze of uneven bumps and slopes. This was fine in the daylight, but twice in the night, bleary and exhausted, the split end of the crutches had caught on the carpet and Peta had crashed her shoulder into the wall. The second time, she'd forgotten and put her bad foot down, sending a plume of hot liquid pain into her hip, which had then kept her awake until dawn.

Secondly, there was the bathroom itself. Converted from a room of unknown past use, it involved a step up from the hall, and then a wriggle around a corner, avoiding towel rails, a sink, and grotty towels that the other residents left on the floor. The shower head was on a funny angle and the water supply appeared at the whim of some hot-and-cold god.

Lastly, there was the fact it was a pub, alive with activity until after midnight, with the noise from the bar leaking through until three in the morning. All this had cemented Peta's fatigue and feeling of being a prisoner as she kept her foot elevated.

Peta also discovered that her mobile, always flawlessly connected in Melbourne, had no reception in Yarraman no matter where she hobbled to, or how high she held the handset up to the sky. The bartender only shrugged when Peta asked about it.

'Not enough people and too many hills,' he said. 'Even the Telstra tower goes on the blink sometimes. There's a gold phone in the residents' hall or the call box across the street,' he added helpfully.

So with nothing to do as the rain came down again, she occupied the residents' lounge – a high-ceilinged room with free toast and cereal on a sideboard, a dozen curling paperbacks, and a television. Peta hadn't watched so much TV in years. On three occasions, a bleary-looking man in jeans, socks and an untucked shirt had wandered into the room, said g'day and asked her the cricket score.

Peta thought several times about giving up and finding a way back to Melbourne. But the thought of walking back into her old life – to the grind of twelve-hour shifts, coming home to an empty apartment, to her weekend running group where she met many people and yet knew no one – stopped her. She'd committed to the trail, to seeing it through for Stacey. This injury was just a minor inconvenience in the face of all that; it was not going to stand in her way.

So after another sleepless night, and a lacklustre lunch on Friday, she seized the crutches, hobbled to the hall and began, slowly and painfully, to put a little weight on her big toe. Four laps later, bolder, she escaped out the back of the pub, where a series of terraces led down to the river weir. Enthused in the fresh air, she stayed an hour, doggedly making laps on the path up and down the bank, even when the overcast sky began to spit again.

When she returned to her room she realised she'd overdone it. Her ankle was swelling again. Grimly, she repacked it with ice, and resigned herself to reading a tea-stained copy of *Bravo Two Zero*.

Later, a knock came when she was dozing in her room. Startled awake, Peta momentarily thought she was back on a night shift in the hospital. 'Who is it?'

'Diane.' A pause. 'I've brought you a roast.'

When Peta opened the door, Diane was clutching a foil-covered plate and shaking raindrops off a brown coat.

'Well, you look a bit better, I'd say,' said Diane, reminding Peta of a nurse as she deposited the plate down on the bedside table and fluffed up the pillow. 'I haven't seen you back across the road, so I figured you must be eating toast. You're not going to heal that way. You need meat.'

Peta could smell the delicious aroma wafting from the plate. 'That's very kind.'

Diane waved a hand to indicate it was nothing, then her roaming gaze fell on Peta's book. 'You enjoying that?'

'I'm just passing the time.'

'I can lend you something much better,' Diane said, crab-stepping round the bed to open the window. 'What about *Murder on the Orient Express*? That's a classic. Anyway, can't stay long, Charlene's minding the shop. I just came to find out if you want to see the race tomorrow, and when I could cash in that favour.'

'Um . . .' Peta had little interest in the festival, but for one attraction – the doctor and more medication. She was desperate for better painkillers than she could buy off the shelf in the store, but the favour sounded ominous. 'What sort of favour?'

'Research for a book I'm writing. I need some medical input.'

Peta relaxed; that should be easy. 'How early can we go?'

Diane grinned. 'I'll come by at seven. Now I'd better get back before Charlene short-changes me.'

Chapter 5

The festival ground was even more churned up than Peta remembered. As Diane sent her beat-up red Volvo boldly down the road, Peta could see the marshals had abandoned gumboots in favour of trout-fishing waders.

Diane sloshed into a park at the end of a row of utes and killed the engine. Through the windscreen, Peta could see a flagged-off area where stewards in hi-vis vests milled around with riders in Driza-bone oilskins. Horses were everywhere, some alert and anxious, others dozing with one back leg cocked and their lower lips hanging. Peta opened her door and instantly caught a lungful of horsehair and sweat – smells of a long-ago home. She hoped she could be done with the doctor quickly, convince him she needed something with codeine and some more anti-inflammatories, and then head back to town.

'Bit of a quagmire,' Diane said, stepping round the bonnet. 'We'll avoid it on the high ground. I'll get your sticks.'

Peta slotted the crutches under her arms and set her jaw. The red first-aid tent was only about a hundred metres away, but her crutches sank into the ground and her good foot slid, making her nervous.

'Bad as stilettos,' she muttered, as one crutch sucked out of the grass and she collapsed against a rail on the arena. The food stands and fairground across the paddock seemed miles away.

'You're sure you don't want help?' called Diane, who was heading for the edge of the marshalling area.

Peta plugged on, but when she finally reached the red first-aid tent, she didn't see Dr Randall, just a man in an ambulance uniform sitting in the chair with a plate on his lap.

'What can I do for you?' he asked, eyeing the bandage and crutches.

'I'm looking for the doctor.'

'Ah, you're the lady that was here on Thursday,' said the ambo, around a mouthful of bacon. 'Haven't seen the doc for a bit. Want to wait?'

Peta chewed her lip. She was tired and sore, her hands were bruised from the crutch handles, and desperation was setting in. A paramedic wouldn't do. She squinted back across at the marshalling area, and thought she spied Dr Randall leaning on the fence.

Before she'd made it very far, however, she realised she was wrong. Although Diane was there, talking to one of the riders through the fence.

'You're back,' she said, when Peta appeared.

'Have you seen the doctor? He wasn't at the tent.'

'Can't say I know what he looks like, but I'll help you find him as soon as the race starts. This is Seb, by the way. He might have a shot at second.'

'Thanks a lot, Diane.'

She gave him a cheeky smile, and Seb – who had curly black hair and a Roman nose – shook his head as he turned his grey back into the ring. Most of the riders were mounted now, a mixed lot in jeans and jodhpurs, akubras and helmets. Peta spotted a familiar chestnut with a warhorse's look, his powerful hindquarters relaxed, ears swivelling. Unmistakably Candle. And as he moved from behind the others, she saw Craig, broad in the shoulder but with hands as light as air on the reins, his gaze intent across the ring.

'Yoo hoo, Craig!' Diane called.

Craig looked around and caught Peta's eye first. His eyebrows curved in surprise; Peta supposed it would be surprising for anyone to have braved this ground on crutches. Without seeming to give the horse any direction at all, he wheeled around and approached the fence. A moment later, Candle was inspecting her with his whiskery nose as if they were old friends, and Craig was above her, still like a cattleman going to muster in his chaps and akubra.

'I've put money on you,' Diane said. 'How's Candle?'

'I'm a bad bet on a wet day. Wouldn't want to waste your money.' But he seemed distracted, glancing around.

'Jack Rusty did say he's pulled three cars out of the mud pool already,' Diane went on. 'Are you saying I should bet on Wade?'

Something dark crossed Craig's features. 'No.' Then he shook himself and shifted his attention to Peta. 'Still here, then? I give you points for persistence.'

Then he tipped his hat and Candle moved away.

Peta pressed her lips together, searching again for the doctor. 'Please tell me this is a fast race?'

'I did say it was endurance,' said Diane. 'The course is eighty k's.'

'Eight?' asked Peta, impressed.

'No, *eighty*, with check-in stations every twenty. First one back here with a horse in good health is the winner.'

Peta momentarily forgot her foot. That distance would take her nearly four days to travel on the trail, making good time.

'The winner will probably finish in five hours,' Diane was saying. 'The rest, could be up to eight. Everyone wants to get back before the festival launch, you see.'

Peta ran her eyes over these horses and riders with a quiet awe. She'd come into the world on a horse stud in the Adelaide Hills and learned to ride as soon as she could walk. She'd been in pony club, but later hack classes and dressage became her style. She didn't enjoy adrenaline thrills; that had been for her sister, who'd excelled in gymkhanas and barrel racing. Stacey had been the fearless one. Without thinking, Peta fingered the necklace through her shirt, her heart sick with the unchangeable past.

When she brought her attention back, she found a young woman with long fawn hair tied back in a plait and chap-covered jeans had leaned into the rail between her and Diane. 'Have you seen Wade?' the girl asked Diane. 'His horse is amazing.'

Wade, that name again. That was the man Craig had faced off with. Peta squinted at the riders, trying to remember what he looked like. 'Which one's Wade?'

'That's him, there on that black,' the girl said.

Peta looked. The riders were forming a line. Candle stood solid on the far end, Craig staring ahead. At the nearest end, a tall black gelding was dancing around, nostrils flared, small curved ears pricked. Peta had been away from her family stud for more than twelve years, but she could still see the quality bloodlines in the animal. And on his back was a man with thick shoulders, tousled dark hair, and an easy, laughing mouth.

'Oh, yeah that's him,' said Peta, recognising the face.

'You know him?' the young woman asked, with interest that had a protective edge.

'No, just saw him the other day, talking to Craig.'

'Really?' asked the woman, as if this was extremely interesting.

Now Diane came in. 'Wade's a local, but he's been away a few years, building companies down south. Just like his father – you heard of Greg Masters, Peta? Used to run a farm over the hill, but his company went gangbusters fifteen years ago and he's hardly ever back. Too many yachts, I reckon. Anyway, made a few people sore when Wade left, too. But he promised to come back and now he has. *And* there'll be a big announcement later on, according to Scotty.'

'I wonder what,' said the woman. 'I asked Craig but he said he didn't know. Then again, he doesn't like Wade very much. I don't understand it – they used to be friends. And I've had a crush on Wade since high school.' She sighed dramatically.

'Yes, something happened there,' Diane admitted, sounding upset not to know exactly what. 'But competition poisons friendships, sometimes. They used to compete together, but then Craig had his famous win on Bel. She used to be Wade's, so Wade's probably dirty Craig did better with her.'

Peta turned back to the riders. Craig's quiet intensity set him apart from all the others. Candle was alert and ready, but calm in a way the other horses weren't. The two of them moved as one unit, attentive to each other. Peta had never seen anything like it.

A marshal climbed up on a yard fence and blared something incomprehensible through a loudspeaker that spooked every horse but Candle. Although she was only catching every third word, Peta understood they were being reminded about the condition of the trail, to follow the rules and stop in at the checkpoints to see the vets. Then, a tiny pistol cracked.

Peta had expected that with eighty clicks to go, the start would be slow. But the riders took off at a gallop, the crowd cheering.

'They go around the ground once first!' Diane yelled.

Peta abandoned her crutches and, using her good leg and hands, hoisted herself up on the fence railing to see. The pack was stringing out, Wade's black taking an easy lead. Midway she spotted Candle, cruising with Craig barely moving in the saddle, hands soft, body supple. Peta had to admit, the man was a cool rider, unbothered by the others, finding his own space. By the time they'd circled the ground, he'd moved up into a position just back from the three in front, Candle's long strides floating across the ground. As they were finally lost in the trees, Peta found her heart thundering like the hoof beats, her cheeks warm in the cool mountain air. She wished she could see more, the pain of her ankle momentarily forgotten.

'They'll come through the valley in about a half-hour, and there are cameras set up in a few places – some bright spark put it on the internet this year. We can watch it down in the tents.' Diane pointed excitedly.

Peta eased down to reach for her crutches, and found the young woman already holding them out.

'Thanks,' she said, accepting the horrible agents of pain and looking across at the tents again. The girl stuck out her hand.

'I'm guessing you're Peta. I'm Gemma, Craig's sister.'

⟶

Once the pack left the festival ground behind and the trees closed in, Craig eased Candle back to a rolling canter.

'Miles and miles to go,' he murmured. But his heart surged to be striding out under these trees, the earthy scents of the forest like a call to come home. Candle was a hardy stockhorse with the Waler blood of a warhorse, and an old hand at this game. Craig knew he could sit on a decent pace through the easy country, while most of the other riders dropped back to a trot; just the three in front were still pushing on.

Craig saw only one of them. He wondered if this was how race jockeys felt, their attention narrowing down to a singular purpose. And even as they turned around the base of the hill, where the wildflowers carpeted the ground in glorious yellow and purple, he couldn't see the colour, only Candle, and the man in front.

The time to the first vet check-in blurred past, and before long, Candle was pulling up. Craig spotted Erica – diminutive amongst the horses, in a bright blue polo and drill pants, her dark hair pinned neatly behind her head. He was down in a moment and leading Candle around. Wade was nowhere to be seen; he must already be through. Seb and the other frontrunner were remounting, waiting for the green light to go.

'Good leg?' Erica asked, all business as she scrutinised Candle's trot out, his breathing already settling.

'Straightforward. Trail's not churned at the front,' Craig said, trying not to think about how far ahead Wade was. He reminded himself that Candle's welfare was what mattered, and for a moment, he calmed and caught the full glory of the land around him: the gentle curve of the hills, the vibrant greens and golds of grass and trees. He knew the trails like he knew Candle: with an intimacy that went beyond words, and he fiercely loved them both.

That didn't mean he didn't want to win.

'Looks good,' Erica said, after she'd counted Candle's heart rate.

Craig threw himself back up in the saddle, finding the stirrups as the horse sprang away at his lightest touch. He knew with Candle's quality, that he would catch Seb and the other rider before they went up into the third leg's hills. But Wade ... he could be a long way ahead indeed.

When Peta made it back to the first-aid tent, trailing both Diane and Gemma, there was still no sign of Dr Randy.

'What if someone was injured?' she asked in irritation.

'Hey, I don't think it's all right, either,' said the ambo.

'I'll put out a call on the PA,' said Diane, striding off towards some official-looking scaffolding.

Having suitably tempted the fates, a girl of about ten came running up two minutes later. 'Hey, someone's passed out over by the cattle yards!'

The ambo gave Peta a dirty look, as if this was *her* fault, and grabbed his partner and their kit, leaving Peta a vacant chair. She sat with relief, putting her foot up on a milk crate to wait. A minute later, the PA called Dr Randall to the cattle yards; she was going to have to wait a bit longer.

'They'll be at the second stage by now,' Diane said when she reappeared. 'Seems it's still Wade, Craig and Seb out front.'

'What's the second stage?' said Peta, eyeing off another first-aid box she could see stowed under the stretcher table.

'It's fairly flat,' Gemma said. 'Runs beside the river. But then it turns back into the hills. There's a real scramble in the middle of the third stage, then a ridge crossing, more climbing before they come down the spur to the last check-in. From there, it's a straight cut through the next valley back to us here.'

'The whole thing's based on a legendary mounted police chase, going after a gold thief,' said Diane.

Gemma snorted. 'That's made up.'

Diane looked indignant. 'Excuse me, but it *could* be true. My husband told me that story – he was the town policeman for many years, Peta. And the mine is a prime setting. It's on Gemma and Craig's property,' she added.

Gemma rolled her eyes. 'The only thing that mine is good for is occasionally tempting a tourist to brave the crappy road off the main highway.'

Diane laughed. 'Anything to bring them into the shop. I should tell that story more.'

Peta adjusted the bandage on her foot. What was taking everyone so long?

That was when she spotted the small crowd approaching the tent. At its centre were the two ambos, bearing a stretcher. And on the stretcher, slapped in a neck brace, was Dr Randall.

Chapter 6

'What the hell happened?'

Peta was up on her crutches in an instant, inspecting the doctor, who was covered in mud, and groaning. The tent was crowded with the two ambos, Gemma, Diane, several onlookers and three kids wearing dirty jeans and cowboy hats.

Adrenaline took care of the fatigue weighing down Peta's limbs and the crutches digging into the raw skin under her arms; she focused as only an emergency doc could.

'One of the kids found him on the ground by the cattle pens. GCS was thirteen when we got there,' said the ambo, quoting the scale, out of fifteen, used for consciousness. 'He was trying to sit up. One of his shoes is missing. Maybe he trapped a foot in the mud, tripped and knocked himself out.'

Dr Randy put in another soft moan. Peta ran a quick physical survey of the man. Heart and lungs functioning fine. Good pupil reflexes, eyes tracking, and no other focal neurological signs. That was reassuring. Peta put a hand on his shoulder.

'Dr Randall? It's Dr Woodward. You've been unconscious. Do you remember what happened?'

A vague shake of the head.

'Anything hurt?'

'No,' he croaked.

And through her subsequent questions, she established he remembered where he was, his birth date, and the prime minister.

'And I can count back from a hundred by sevens, too, I know the drill,' he finished, as if now remembering where he'd left his dignity. He tugged at the neck brace. 'Can I take this stupid contraption off now?'

'Nope. We don't know what happened, and I'm going to rule out any possibility of a spinal injury before I take it off. You know the drill.' She gave him a sweet smile.

He scowled. Peta lifted her eyes to the onlookers. 'Okay, I want whoever found him in here, everyone else out. Was it one of you kids?'

As the gawkers reluctantly departed, one boy of about seven timidly raised his hand.

'All right.' Dropping her crutches against the wall, Peta sat so she was at eye level with him. He looked absolutely terrified. Peta smiled kindly. 'Hey, I like your hat. You ride at the festival?'

Disarmed, the boy took a second to answer. 'No, but maybe next year,' he said hopefully.

'What's your name?'

'Alex.'

Peta smiled again, pushing down her natural impatience. 'Alex, can you tell me what happened when you found this man?'

Alex shrugged his shoulders in an exaggerated motion, his mouth curling down.

'Okay, I just need to know if he was moving or talking when you first saw him. Do you remember if he was?'

More fervent head-shaking.

Peta sighed. She hauled herself up on her good leg, the stitches in her cut tugging. 'That's okay. Thanks.'

The boy scuttled away. Peta was about to ask the ambos the whereabouts of the nearest X-ray machine when a small hand tugged at her shirt. A hazel-eyed girl, probably about eight, had snuck back in.

'I know what happened!' she hissed, looking around fearfully. Peta guessed she was looking for the two boys. She quickly stepped away from Dr Randall's earshot and leaned in with her best conspiratorial voice.

'Tell me quick!' encouraged Peta.

'Alex and Jacob were hiding in the truck. They dropped their toy spider on the man as he walked past. He jumped and slid in the mud, and hit his head on the yard fence.'

Peta pressed her fingers to her mouth to avoid an inappropriate laugh. But she couldn't shake the picture of Dr Randall, in full arachnoleptic fit. No wonder Alex was terrified. But she was only interested in one thing. 'And did he get up straightaway or did it take a while?'

'A while. I *told* Alex and Jacob they had to tell Dad, but they said not to dob.'

'You did the right thing. I won't tell. You can go.'

After the girl had run off, Peta got into a pow-wow with the ambos. As the rush of seeing a case wore off, she noticed her foot throbbing again, and a dull ache echoed it behind her eyeballs. Thankfully, the course of action was straightforward. This was a head injury, and there was no equipment here to rule out a spinal problem. The doctor would have to be shipped out.

Dr Randall wasn't happy about it. His car was here, he said, and he had a date tonight. Peta firmly resisted the wheedling – doctors could be the worst patients.

'You hypocrite,' he said finally in exasperation. 'You wouldn't listen to me two days ago!'

Peta had no mercy. '*I* have a sprained ankle. You might have a sprained *brain*, or a spinal instability. Don't be daft. You don't want a slow bleed missed. You're going.'

He muttered, but acquiesced and, after calls to the nearest district hospital, was soon loaded into the ambulance. Peta hobbled back into the seat, and pulled the first-aid kit in close, figuring she'd earnt a rummage. She peeled back her shirt to inspect the raw spot under her arm. Just the thought of crutching the distance back to the car park put her in a bad mood.

'Ooof, that looks awful. Those things rubbing you?' Gemma had materialised, clutching two lemonades.

Peta hastily dropped her shirt and took one gratefully. 'Thanks.'

'Bet the doc's glad you were here.'

'I don't think he really was,' she said. 'Besides, the ambos could have handled it.'

'How about I buy you lunch?'

Peta's stomach gave a grumble and just beyond the pain, she had a sudden hankering for a steak sandwich. 'That would be great, if you can wait a sec,' said Peta, digging in the kit. 'Pity I can't give myself morphine.'

～

As he expected, Craig overtook Seb and the other rider at the end of the second stage, then cleared the vet checkpoint for the long drive uphill in the third.

This was the worst part of the course, and Craig would get off and walk before he'd allow Candle to break himself over the rough parts. It would almost be worth slowing down – the view down off the ridge showed the whole valley, the Yarraman River a lush scribble along the floor, the bordering hills reaching up to touch the heavy sky. Home and heart, all in the one place.

Candle, however, showed no signs of tiring, bounding over the rises like a rabbit. By the time they peaked the ridge and were coasting along the spur, Craig was sure they must have made very good time. But the third checkpoint held a surprise.

Wade was there, his horse wearing a sweat blanket and being walked around in the shade. Craig only had to look at the lathered coat and flared nostrils to know what had happened: the vets had held him back.

Craig pulled his focus back to Candle. The horse's coat was wet through, but tension was rippling through him – Candle loved to race, and now, after two k's downhill, he was dancing to get going again. He waited for Craig's signal, trembling with anticipation. Craig could only rub his neck and chuckle.

'I know, I know, but you're not running into the ground for me. And I know you would.'

Candle gave a snort. The vets waved him through a few minutes later, just as Wade was being allowed to remount. Craig didn't even look; with less than half an hour along the river to the finish, he gave Candle his head. Wade was right behind him. And as the Ferris wheel finally became visible over the trees, the race got serious.

Craig heard Wade's horse behind: snorts syncopated with drumming hooves. He didn't look around, didn't need to. The shift of Candle's back told him that the black had drawn his nose level with Candle's rump. Craig could imagine Wade on his back, his body crouched forward, spurred heels tucked up in his horse's flanks, his gaze penetrating the back of Craig's skull.

Candle's body dipped as he stretched his stride, ears pinned against his neck. He hated losing. Craig could feel the effort the horse expended now, could see the tight curve of his nostril flared to grab more air. If it had been any further he would have pulled up . . . but there was the finish – a white banner rising from a thick crowd, a muddied path through the final straight.

A crack of leather, and Wade's black surged forward. Shoulder to shoulder now, Craig's heart struck against his ribs, his attention on the ground, watching for ditches or logs, ready to steer Candle to safer ground. Wade was a shadow in his periphery, a shadow that was, inch by inch, pulling away.

Then with fifty metres to go, a deep mud furrow appeared, disguised as a thick puddle. Craig had a split second to swing Candle across a shallow part, while Wade's black hit the thick mud with a slosh. As the horse pulled his legs free, he slowed just enough, and Candle did the rest. The mountain horse took the bit and thundered across the finish. The crowd were a roaring blur, camera flashes exploding as Wade crossed only just behind. Candle was so intent on pushing ahead that Craig had a job stopping him, calming him down, convincing him they'd won.

Craig also knew the race wasn't over. He still had to go through the final vet station, where Erica was now waiting. He could see the vet, gesticulating emphatically. Mistaking her intentions, he rode over, only to be waved away.

'Masters, over here!' she yelled past him.

Wade's black horse was being ushered in, his sides heaving, black coat lathered. Craig swung down and loosened Candle's girth, walking him around as Wade was asked to trot his horse out, and Erica listened with a stethoscope. Craig could see the horse still blowing hard, neck drooping. Erica's eyes met his across the field, the concern etched in her features. Ah, shit.

Craig knew it was Masters who'd ridden him, but Craig couldn't help feel responsible for the animal being run so hard. Candle was a seasoned campaigner, but Craig wondered if his grandmother would have disapproved of him not thinking about the others. The black was young and eager to give; Wade couldn't have had him long, and he was highly strung, just as Bel had been. Craig swallowed a wave of remorse. He hung around the exit of the vet station, holding off the congratulatory officials with a 'not-f-ing-now' look.

Wade finally appeared without the horse, a defiant glint in his eye.

'He all right?' Craig asked, concern for the horse momentarily trumping all that had gone between them.

Masters stopped. 'Doesn't really count when you win on a technicality, does it? I was fifteen minutes in front at that last gate. Could put in a protest.'

Craig watched Wade stalk away, but he didn't follow. Instead, he led Candle back to the screened vet area and stuck his head around the fence. Inside, Erica was supervising a drip into Wade's gelding. She knew about Wade's history with Bel, though he knew she'd be equally cautious with any horse.

'You need any help?' he asked.

She glanced up. 'No, you're good. Just hang around for fifteen minutes for a last recovery index. And congratulations.'

Craig stepped away, murmuring to Candle. But the image of Wade's gelding was heavy in his mind. He wouldn't see whip marks on that black coat, but he wondered if they were there. He blew his breath out, dropped his shoulders. The race was won, but the trust in Candle's generous brown eyes was what really mattered.

⟶

Peta watched the end of the race from a cosy stand position, her ankle more comfortable thanks to the anti-inflammatories she'd extracted from the replacement ambulance crew. After two hours watching riders cutting cows out of a herd to a time limit, a straw-bale-stacking competition and an obstacle course on horseback, she was jangling with bad coffee as Diane drifted back and forth, refilling her cup.

But she didn't need caffeine to ride the excitement after the finish.

'They'll be a while in the vet area,' Diane said, as the crowd dispersed. 'We should make a move on the main tent. The seats will fill for the official opening.'

And so Peta found herself again slipping through the mud towards a covered tent, furnished with plastic chairs, where a bush-poetry competition was packing up, the platform stage being set with a podium. Most chairs were already full, though with one look at her crutches, several seats were offered.

Ten minutes later, Peta watched an official-looking man in a blazer shuffling pages behind the microphone, while a group of similarly tailored men stood waiting.

'Who are they?' Peta asked.

'Sponsors,' said Gemma. 'And one of them will be a politician. They always show up here. The guy at the microphone is Scotty, the festival president.'

'I want to thank you all for your support,' Scotty began. 'Yarraman's a small place and this is our big event for the year. It means a lot to our community.'

The crowd clapped and cheered. Scotty went on with a great deal of guff about the quality of the competition, the contributions of all the local businesses, and the excitement of the Endurance Cup, the prize for which would follow the opening, so everyone would have to be patient. Then came the thanking of sponsors – a produce store, a stockman's outfitters – Peta missed the names.

'You'll perhaps notice the absence in our list this year of the local member,' Scotty went on. 'Everyone here knows that when it comes to politics, we're a long way from Melbourne. Our voices get drowned out in parliament. We've gone through a lot in the last ten years – closing of the mountain pastures, the cancelling of the scientific grazing study—' Scotty paused as boos echoed around the tent.

'What's that about?' Peta whispered to Gemma.

'Last government started a study about letting cattle graze in the alpine pastures. When the government changed, they cancelled it.' Gemma pursed her lips.

'—and some of the worst fires we've ever seen. All that, and we're still waiting for treated water in town, promised ten years ago. Well, for those of you tired of this story, I think you'll want to hear this. So I welcome to the stage our prodigal son, Wade Masters!'

Peta clapped along with the crowd's hearty cheers as a smiling Wade stepped up on stage. Peta had seen him finish the race; his mount looking wrung out and straggly compared to Candle's bounce, but Wade himself looked genuine and tough, still wearing his mud-spattered shirt and chaps, as though a reporter should be sticking a microphone in his face at the edge of a sportsground.

'Thanks Scotty,' he said, lifting a hand to the crowd. 'It's certainly wonderful to be home.'

The crowd replied with cheers of goodwill, which Wade lapped up with a grin.

'Now, I had hoped to be staying longer on this stage as the winner of the race, but sadly it wasn't to be.' He raised his hand philosophically. 'But I think you'll agree that there's a much more important race, and that one I intend to win. Everything Scotty says is true. Our voices in the mountains are drowned out in Melbourne. We've got latte-sipping greenies telling us we don't know how to care for this country, when we've been here a hundred and fifty years! Now, I know that people weren't impressed when I left to run businesses down south. I'll admit that. You all know who my father is. But that's not me. I'm back to make a difference. I've learned how things work in Melbourne, and that's a plus for us. I intend to be the voice that we've never had there. The election isn't much more than a year away, and we can't do another term like the last one. We need the water. We need investment. And we need a say in our own country. That's why I'm announcing my nomination for the district. I'm for a voice for the mountains. Are you with me?'

The crowd erupted in a deafening cheer, the program temporarily forgotten as a throng of people surged forward to shake Wade's hand. Peta glanced at Gemma, who seemed enraptured. But beyond, standing just outside the tent, she spied Craig's familiar profile. He looked as mud-spattered as Wade, but he wasn't smiling. His face was rigid, the masseter muscle slowly working in his jaw. Clearly brewing on something.

'Oh, what a great idea,' Gemma was saying. 'Wade's perfect for that, don't you think?'

'Certainly unexpected,' Diane ventured, sounding vexed she hadn't known in advance.

To Scotty's credit, the derailed proceedings were swiftly put back on schedule, and soon the prize was being presented for the Endurance Cup. Craig appeared on stage then, shaking Scotty's hand and accepting the cheers of the crowd in a retiring way, and he didn't make a speech, though the cheers for him were just as loud.

'Doesn't say much, does he?' Peta heard someone say behind her.

'Man's a legend. He don't need to say anything.'

But all the other conversations around her were about Wade's announcement.

When the official speeches ended, Peta hauled herself up. She'd been avoiding negotiating the toilet block – which was a truck-mounted bank of units up a steep flight of stairs and over a particularly deep puddle – for an hour and couldn't put it off any longer. Ten minutes later, after checking her crutch ends for toilet paper and wishing for hand sanitiser, Peta carefully descended the stairs. Pausing to adjust her grip, she was surprised to see Craig sitting on an upturned bucket at the end, meditatively staring towards the main tent and wiping his hands on a towel. It took her a moment of staring to realise his hand was bleeding.

Drawn by the injury, she sloshed, heedless, across the mud. 'What did you do?'

He glanced up in surprise, then noting who it was, turned back to wiping at the skin over his knuckles. She wondered if he was considering how to escape, but then he gave her a wry glance.

'This wall just jumped out at me.'

'Funny,' she said. 'How bad is it?'

'Not that bad.'

Peta could tell he wasn't bending his fingers. 'Let me make sure you don't have a fracture.'

With a shrug, he let her take his hand. Intent on examination, Peta initially noted only the perfect conformation: long, straight fingers; a broad palm; and the muscular forearm that had been so useful getting her out of the gully. She flicked the end of each long finger, then palpated each metacarpal. No local tenderness, a good sign. But then she became distracted, noting the sun-kissed skin, thick over the palm and smooth across the back, except where it was torn over the first two knuckles. The hand suited the rest of him: strong and outdoorsy, but rough around the edges. Then she realised what she was doing.

'Looks intact,' she said, dropping his hand, embarrassed.

He grunted, and in that moment seemed more approachable than he had a few days earlier. After seeing the race today, she was curious.

'You had a good win,' she said. 'I didn't think you'd have reasons to disagree with this . . . wall.'

He surveyed her with an expression she couldn't quite read.

'Or maybe it was this Wade Masters running for office thing?' she guessed.

His expression instantly guarded, he stood, replacing his hat. 'Sorry, Peta. I need to get back to Candle. Excuse me.'

Peta was left standing in the mud, her body swaying as the connection between them collapsed. She looked down at herself. Her bandaged foot was grubby, her folded-up pants leg wet through, both crutches crusted in mud. She had plenty of reasons to be prickly. But she didn't go around punching walls because her trip had suffered a setback. The man was clearly a loose cannon.

Tiredness flooded her, as if it had been accumulating in a mind cloud that chose that moment to rain. Maybe she should have gone straight to the hospital in Wangaratta two days ago. Then she wouldn't be standing here in the mud, feeling like a fool.

⟶

Overtired, Peta slept poorly, her dreams a strange mix of giant black spiders – for which she thanked the boys who'd brought down Dr Randall – and pale-as-moonlight horses. These apparitions were more familiar dreamscapes, but strangely now they all had riders. And each time it was Craig Munroe, who watched her with that steady, even gaze.

She woke, groggy and disoriented, on Sunday and spent the day gently massaging her elevated ankle between reading *Murder on the Orient Express*, which Diane had pushed under the door. This then led to Sunday-night dreams in which Peta left the highlands on a train. Craig Munroe always rode alongside, and she practised saying, *I do not like your face, Mr Munroe*, under her breath.

This was, quite frankly, ridiculous.

Monday morning came with relief. Today she could make a phone call. The pub was at its quietest as Peta limped from her room, leaving the crutches, which had rubbed her skin enough to form scabs. She checked her watch; half an hour to kill before nine when the office would be open. So Peta slotted in a batch of toast and started on a rehab plan. The ankle was past the acute phase – it would be time to begin exercise soon.

She kept one beady eye on the toaster, which had a habit of scorching bread in two seconds flat, setting off the smoke detector. When that happened, a lovely Filipino lady who spoke little English would rush down with both a fan on the end of a stick to wave at the detector, and a silent remonstration. Peta had earned this look twice already, and didn't want a third.

Right on nine, she limped down the hall to the residents' gold pay phone, stacked her coins on the table, sank into the hard wooden chair, and dialled the number by heart.

'Turner and Decon, how can I help?' answered the chirpy receptionist.

'It's Peta Woodward. I need to speak with Mr Turner, please.'

'One moment.'

Peta could hear the intrigue in the woman's tone.

Mr Turner picked up swiftly. 'Ms Woodward. I didn't expect to hear from you, yet.'

'I've had a change in plans,' she said quickly. 'I've injured myself, and I'm in a small town without mobile reception. I'm going to be here for a little while. It's just a bad sprain, but I can't walk at the moment.'

'So you're coming back early?'

'No. I'm just delayed.'

'I see. How delayed?'

She paused. 'Two weeks, maybe three.' To be honest, catering for the time to recover and complete the trip at a slower pace, that would be pushing it.

'Might it be longer?' Mr Turner asked in a neutral, lawyerly tone.

Peta bit her lip. 'Maybe.'

'Ms Woodward, can I offer you some advice? These circumstances must have been extremely draining for you. You don't have to accept the executor's position – we can make an application to appoint someone else.'

'No,' she said sharply. The last thing she wanted was someone else carving up her family's estate. She knew she wasn't objective, that she was still processing her father's death, but no one else could be trusted. Not when Stacey's memory depended on it.

'I respect your decision. But you must bear in mind that you need to act prudently. The estate has substantial debts. We've made the probate application and the due diligence won't be much longer. The creditors may complain about your conduct if you're off in the wilderness and taking no action to remedy the debts, especially when there's a good offer on the table.'

His tone transported Peta back to her high school classroom, being admonished by the principal. The fact Mr Turner was right had little to do with it; she resented anyone having an interest in the endless green fields of her family home.

'I don't want the property carved up into pieces,' she said.

'I understand. But you need to prepare yourself that otherwise, any sale would likely fall short of the debts. That could leave you in a difficult situation.'

Beeps sounded, and Peta fed a dollar in the slot with a shaky hand. 'How long do I have?'

'There's no prescribed time, as I've said before. But if you want to investigate other alternatives, you need to make active enquiries. I don't imagine that can be done from a mountain chalet.'

When Peta put down the phone, she slumped against the wall. The rough bricks scraped the backs of her arms, but all she could feel was her obligations and her mistakes, both lodged like splinters in her heart. Her mistakes she couldn't change, but her obligations she needed to fulfil, and she couldn't do that without walking the trail.

Chapter 7

Late the next morning, Peta was gingerly walking the hallway carpet, testing weight on her foot and trying to remember to lift her toe high over the lumps in the floor. So far she'd tripped three times, prompting reactions that would have required heavy investments in her family swear jar. Still, the ankle had improved. She'd need to start balance exercises soon to retrain the proprioception and help avoid injuring it again.

She'd just returned to her mattress and was inspecting her stitches when she heard a knock at the door. Expecting to find the cleaner, or Diane, she was instead taken aback to find Craig Munroe.

He wore a pair of jeans and brown leather chaps, a check shirt and his beaten akubra. The man looked straight out of a movie, except for the wear on the chaps and the faded shirt that said this outfit worked as hard as the body beneath.

'Diane told me where to find you,' he said by way of greeting. 'We need a doctor if you'll come. Harry's collapsed.'

'Harry?'

'Cattleman, runs a property three lots over from us. Ambulance is out of town, apparently. The call directs to our local copper but he's caught up down the valley.'

Peta was already looking for her shoe. 'How far is it? Do I need the crutches?'

'Unless you want to be carried, I'd recommend it.'

Any sign of rain had vanished and the sun glared down from the perfectly cloudless sky. Harry's place was high on the southern slope of the valley, and as they drove, Peta squinted out the windshield of Craig's old Land Rover, which rumbled like a tank.

'How long have you had this thing?' she said at one point, grabbing the arm rest when the engine made an alarming *thunk*.

'It was my grandmother's, before she passed away,' he said, with an inflection that told Peta the woman was greatly revered.

'Oh,' she said. 'Sorry.' So much for that avenue of conversation. 'You know, at this rate the town could really do with a medical centre.'

Craig glanced across at her. 'We had one, actually. Used to be staffed in the ski season to handle the traffic going up to the resorts. But one of the resorts closed, and it was used less and less when the highway around us was upgraded. It's been abandoned a few years.'

'Really? I don't suppose it would have better crutches?'

'No idea, sorry.'

When they arrived, Peta found Harry sitting in a chair on the verandah with another man – who, thanks to Diane's commentary at the festival, she recognised as Jack Rusty – pushing a grease-smeared water bottle on him.

'Here they are now, Harry.'

'I told you I don't need a doctor. I need the police. Where's Ash?'

'On his way,' Craig said. 'Why don't you let the doc check you out anyway?'

'What happened?' Peta asked.

'Nothing. I tripped,' Harry said.

Jack snorted. 'I found him up the paddock, making no damn sense, face as red as a beetroot. Was just lucky I went that way coming back from checking the front fences at Charlie's.'

'It's a hot day,' Peta murmured. Harry did seem fine, and denied that he'd had any chest pain. As she worked, Jack pulled Craig away and they spoke in low voices by the window.

'What were you doing up the field?' Peta asked as she took his pulse.

'Going after my damn cows.'

Craig looked around. 'You lose some, too, Harry?'

'Thirty head. Thought they might have gone down the back of the spur, out of the heat. 'Course, they weren't down there. But found something else. That's why I need Ash.'

'What'd you find?'

They heard a crunch from outside as a car pulled into the drive.

'Take Ash and look. There are tyre tracks down there, Craig.'

—

Craig and Ash drove as far as they could along the spur, then went the rest of the way on foot. At the bottom, a tiny tributary to the Yarraman River was only a trickle through the trees. Evidence of cattle was everywhere – hoof marks at an easy access to the stream, rub spots on the trees. But no actual cows. Craig followed the signs. The ground was drying out after last week, but there was still a discernible trail leading away from the water. Then, on a solid part of the meadow, he found it.

'Now I see why Harry's excited,' Ash said, squatting by a long mark in the grass. 'That's a tyre track.'

He pulled a camera from his pocket and snapped a few photos, circling around and then pulling back to squint at the surrounding trees. 'How old do you reckon?'

Craig pushed his thumb into the edge of the mark. 'Not fresh today, the edges have dried out. But damp in the deep parts. Maybe last night. Pretty big truck, too,' he said, pacing out the width of the tyres.

In silence, the two men followed the mark, Craig leading, until they emerged onto an old four-wheel-drive track through the trees.

'Where the hell does this go?' Ash asked.

'Winds down the next spur, then fords the creek before an old gate in the fence,' Craig said, seeing the whole thing in his head. 'But then it does this weird deviation along the edge of the valley, even though it's close to the road into town. Eventually comes out down the highway, up a steep incline.'

Ash grunted. 'Remind me to bring you along next time I need to go off-road.'

'I've ridden it a few times, just not for a while. I used to shortcut through the lower part to the town road sometimes if I'd been down at Seb's.' Craig leaned a hand against a tree, thinking. 'You know, that slope up to the highway is pretty steep for a cattle truck. And if I'm not mistaken, there's been a landslip through that lower road, too. Charlie was telling me about it a few months ago.'

Ash shook his head. 'You'd better show me where it comes out on the highway.'

Half an hour later, after Jack had promised to give Peta a lift back to the pub, Ash slowed on Craig's directions, and took an overgrown left hand turn off the highway. It wasn't far from the airstrip that serviced the valley; Craig could see the sign ahead: Yarraman Private Airfield, although someone had spray-painted *International* over 'private' as a joke. For the first time, Craig wondered about the vandals; maybe they'd been the ones who'd taken the backhoe Ash had mentioned last week. But it was hard to imagine the leap from that to cattle theft.

'Wouldn't even have picked there was a track here,' Ash said.

'Lots of abandoned trails in these hills.'

Maybe a kilometre in, they found a landslip where an old sheer-rock wall had punched out a pile of rocks, right across the road. Both men piled out.

'I guess that answers that,' Craig said, inspecting the fractured rocks. 'This is part of an old mine, I think, like the one around the falls.'

'Think I can drive around it, down the slope a bit?' Ash asked.

'Yeah, you might. But no one took a cattle truck out this way. They'd have rolled it. And a truck that size would have broken the overgrowth up at the highway end, too. We didn't see that. I've got another idea.'

So they drove around the landslip and kept going towards Harry's, until Craig told Ash to stop at a bend. Here was a gentle slope towards the town road that Craig had cut through years ago. It came out behind a lay-by where a town-information sign was fading in the sun. And there, where the grass met the gravel, Craig found two scuff marks on the bitumen.

'Same width as up at Harry's,' Craig said. 'This must be where they came out.'

Ash was taking more photos. 'Pretty slick operation,' he said. 'They must have planned it. Really knew their way around. And they probably waited for Harry to leave.'

Craig grunted. 'Seems like a lot of effort.' But the idea was unsettling: that someone might be lurking around, watching the farm, waiting for an opportunity. 'Makes me think about Charlie's cows last week, too.'

'But you found them, right?'

'Yeah, but in the national park. I figured they came through the fences somewhere but Jack Rusty's been down every one and he couldn't find a break. It's like someone opened the gate and let them out up there.'

—

The next night, Craig arrived for the pub meeting and caught himself parking on the accommodation side, and walking more slowly than normal to the bar doors, wondering if he'd run into Peta. Jack Rusty had relayed that she'd stayed a long time yesterday, supervising Harry's rehydration and Craig wanted to thank her. Or that's what he told himself.

He was trying not to dwell on the fact that he sometimes thought of her inspecting his hand at the festival. He'd be making a feed order, or checking a weather report, or working with one of the horses, and find himself thinking about those smooth, deft fingers on his skin.

But he saw no sign of her, and arrived at the meeting's usual corner table to find Old Charlie and Jack and Seb Rusty with fresh pint glasses. Wally had to be somewhere nearby, because his blue dog Sally was visible under the table, tolerated by the management because she was an institution. Erica was absent, sending word she was stuck with a possible tetanus case on a farm thirty k's away. No Harry. Craig slipped into his seat as Wally returned from the bar and handed him a glass.

'Guess it's going to be a grim week,' Wally said, sneaking a cracker to Sally under the table.

'You all heard what happened up at Harry's?' Craig asked.

There were nods around the table.

'Ash find anything yet?'

'Not as far as I know. But whoever it was did their homework,' Craig said. 'Ash's put the word out, and Diane's passing it through the CWA network, too.'

'Feel bad for Harry,' Old Charlie said, rotating his beer glass with a shaky hand, 'when I got mine back. And I want to thank you blokes for that. I heard that greenie girl Karen was sniffing around.'

Craig grunted, remembering Karen's approach at the festival. He was still wondering how she'd found out about it. It was as if someone had wanted Charlie to get in trouble with the government. 'No damage done this time. But we might need to see what we can do about security at Harry's. He also lost those stockyards.'

'A dog is what he needs,' Wally put in. 'Damn strange farm that doesn't have a dog.'

'Maybe he's got allergies,' Seb put in, then caught a look from Craig. 'Sorry. But you know that—hey, Harry!'

Craig twisted around to find Harry approaching the table, his face morose, as if he'd just come from a funeral. 'Didn't expect you to make it in this time.'

'No, I needed to come,' he said, sinking into a seat and chucking his hat under the table. He looked around them all. 'I've made a decision. I'm going to sell.'

Amongst the exclamations of surprise, Craig felt a weight on his chest. 'Is this about the stock and the yards? You'll recover. We can all help.'

'Yes, and no. Look, I've just had enough. It's been harder and harder, especially now I'm on my own. My eyesight's going. The thefts were just the last straw. Someone made a reasonable offer a while back, so I'm taking it.'

'Where are you going to go?'

Harry rubbed his mouth with a work-hardened hand before he answered. 'My daughter lives down in Melbourne. Said she'd put me up for a while, see if there's anything they can do about my sight. I'll take my time finding something else to buy into.'

The meeting continued on with a kind of stunned resignation. Everyone told Harry that if he reconsidered, they'd help him out. But Harry shook his head. For Craig, the cattleman's decision was understandable, but Harry was part of the fabric of Yarraman Falls. His departure would create a rent; there'd be a new owner to work with, or maybe Harry's offer was from a company, and another family farm would be gone. That had consequences beyond their meeting; loss of families meant the school could close, and the heart of the community would be gone forever.

Craig rubbed his face. Change was thick in the air. It had started the moment his mother had told him about her moving in with Grant Dwyer. And Craig wanted to know if it would end with Yarraman Falls still intact.

Chapter 8

The next morning, Peta was bored of reading in the pub. She was due to help Diane with her book research later that day, but the minutes passed with laboured slowness until finally, looking hatefully at her crutches, she decided to go on a mission. She found Diane pensive over a laptop behind the store's counter.

'Oh, Peta, you're early,' she said. 'I was still compiling my questions. Let me make you a coffee before we start.'

'Don't rush your questions,' Peta said hastily, having experienced Diane's coffee. 'I actually came to ask you about the medical clinic. Craig said the town has one.'

'Had. They closed the doors at the end of a ski season a few years back and never opened them again.'

To Peta, this sounded encouraging. 'So it still has equipment?'

Diane looked dubious. 'Maybe. Don't know what state it's in.'

'Where is it? I want to see if there are some better crutches I can borrow, and I need to remove my stitches.'

Diane gave a single nod. 'Two streets over from the pub,' she said. 'Ash keeps an eye on it, and he has the keys. Do you want a lift?'

But Peta was already hobbling for the door.

The Yarraman Falls Medical Centre was a squat building rendered in dirty white, and about the size of the other small houses on the street. *Medical Centre* was stencilled in faded red letters over a wide glass double door. The place was dark and empty inside, and some graffiti had been painted over, evidenced by lighter patches done with a roller on the external wall.

'Knock yourself out,' said Ash, as he pushed the door open with a shower of dust and handed her the key. 'I don't know what you'll find. Lock up and drop the keys back to me at the station when you're done.'

Inside, the stale air smelled of long-dried disinfectant. It was a far cry from the huge hospital Peta worked in, and smaller even than most of the tiny rural practices she vaguely remembered from her internship. Behind a screen, two emergency-style bays formed half of the front room, with a triage desk and some plastic chairs askew on the other side. As Peta moved down the short hall, her crutches left circles on the grimy lino. The back of the building held three rooms: a large storage space, what must have been a consulting room with a desk and exam couch, and another equipment room with a deep sink and a lumpy shape under a dust cover. Peta pulled open the high cupboards. They were mostly empty, but in one were a few rolls of plaster. Encouraged, she searched, but most of the stores had been cleared out. Certainly no crutches. Nor did she discover any in the storeroom.

What she did find was boxes of basic supplies – cannulas, saline, syringes, needle tips and bandages – hiding in a corner, plus a few sets of bed linens still crisp and clean in a laundry bag, and a cache of mops, brooms and half-empty cleaning products. Tearing open a suture remover, she made fast work taking out her stitches. The wound had healed well. When she was done, she pulled off the dust cover and found a slit lamp, which hummed to life when she flipped the switch. So, there was still power.

But there was a heap of junk, too: empty cardboard boxes, dead insect casings from industrious spiders, and dust, lots of dust.

While there were no crutches, the desk chair in the consulting room had wheels. Peta sank down on it. She didn't have much else to do besides balance exercises so, using the seat as an impromptu wheelchair and a mobile mop bucket as a rolling ottoman under her foot, she went to work cleaning up.

Later, not having remembered lying down, she woke suddenly on the couch in the exam room, her fingers chalky from cleaning products, her leg propped up on a folded towel. The room was dark now except for the splash of yellow light in the hall from the reception lights she'd turned on. She pushed herself up. Oops. Ash would be wondering where his keys were, and Diane might think she'd snubbed their appointment.

Then she heard a thumping, and a woman's muffled voice. 'Anybody in there?'

⟜

Peta emerged from the consulting room to see someone with long dark hair desperately knocking, her form smudged through the frosted glass. When Peta pulled open the door, she realised it was the same woman who'd approached Craig that first day at the festival. Peta had seen her once since, putting leaflets under windscreen wipers outside the pub. Now, her fine pale skin was bloodshot across her cheeks, and her frantic eyes were hung with dark circles. She was wearing stained trackpants and a multi-coloured top with one side falling off her shoulder.

'Oh, I thought you might be the doctor from the festival,' she said, her expression a reflection of her fallen hopes. She turned away.

'Wait. I am a doctor,' Peta called. 'I'm Peta Woodward. Dr Randall injured himself. Are you sick?'

The woman's expression transitioned from anxiety to relief in half a second. 'No, it's my son, Ned. I think he just had a seizure.'

As Peta crutched across the street a moment later, the woman – who quickly introduced herself as Karen – hastily filled Peta in. 'He had a runny nose today, but he didn't seem too bad, though he had a fever. I gave him some Panadol and he went to sleep. Then I went to check on him and he was jerking.' Her voice broke and she fumbled with her front door. 'I shouldn't have left him, but I saw the light on across the road. I wasn't thinking straight.'

Soon they'd reached a tiny room with a low child's bed, a lamp glowing softly. A Thomas toy was cast aside on the floor next to an open story book. Ned himself was tucked against the wall, chewing slowly on the ear of a pink elephant, his eyes droopy. Peta guessed he must be around three, maybe a little older, and had the same dark hair as his mother. Otherwise, Peta's deep medical sense was relieved at the sight of him: although Ned's nose was crusty and his cheeks dabbed with colour, he didn't seem very ill, at least not the kind of ill that would set nurses running in an emergency room. But she also knew looks could be deceiving, especially in children.

'What temperature was he running?' she asked.

'Thirty-eight and a half. It's still on the thermometer, here,' Karen said, reaching for a digital unit on the nearby drawers.

'I need to ask some questions,' Peta said, easing down onto the floor and speaking in a soft voice. 'Has he been awake like this since it happened?'

'He was groggy for a while afterwards,' Karen said, sinking down onto the bed.

Ned pulled the elephant out of his mouth and pressed himself against her leg, his breaths crackling through the dried crust in his nose.

'How long did it last, do you think?'

'Felt like an hour,' Karen said, with a soft laugh. 'But I don't know. I didn't see it start. What I did see must have been less than a minute.'

'Describe what he was doing?'

Karen tried, but in the end, she had to imitate, moving her legs and arms together, except the leg Ned was snuggled into. 'Like this,' she said. 'I have a cousin who has epilepsy. It looked like hers. I think they call it Grand Mal? That's why I'm so freaked out – she has to take so much medication, and she's hurt herself a few times.'

'You must have been terrified,' Peta said. 'I think from what you've told me I know what this is. But let's take a look at him first, okay?'

She asked Karen to pull Ned into her lap, and looked the little boy over. And while he whined, once Peta had examined him she could find no neurological signs at all. She re-took his temperature: high, right on thirty-eight. Peta pushed back onto her heels.

'Okay, have you heard of a febrile seizure before?'

'Um, maybe?'

'There's some indication of a genetic component to it, so you might find other family members had it when they were little. Your cousin – do they know why she has epilepsy?'

'After a car accident.'

Peta nodded. 'Well, that's a different story. A simple febrile seizure usually has no ongoing problems. And I think that's what Ned's had as I can't find any signs of infection or problems with his brain. Just be aware that if he gets another fever it might happen again. You can give him the paracetamol to bring the fever down, but that won't actually stop a seizure from happening.'

By now, Ned's eyelids were almost closed. Peta thought the poor boy must be exhausted. She pulled the story book towards her and flipped to the cover.

'*John Brown, Rose and the Midnight Cat*, oh, I loved this one,' she said. 'But I always felt bad for the cat.'

'Me, too,' Karen said. 'Ned just loves it. I think because he saw a sheepdog like in the story at the festival. Otherwise it's been Thomas every day for the last six months.'

Peta stayed while Karen read the story, but Ned only lasted a few pages before he was snuffily asleep.

Awkward on her crutches, Peta crept down to the kitchen, which was a single bench with bunches of herbs hanging to dry above the tiny sink. It smelled of rosemary and lavender.

Karen appeared a moment later. 'I think I remember you from the festival,' she said softly. 'You were in the first-aid tent with your foot.'

'Yes, I remember you, too. You came to talk to Craig – something about cows.'

A smile touched Karen's lips, but then she sighed. 'Yes, another day at the office. Someone left a message on the department phone about cattle in the national park. I didn't have time to hike up there this week. I thought Craig might know something about it.'

Peta leaned her hands on the back of a chair. 'Why's that?'

Karen shrugged. 'He's the big man around the place, so tends to have his finger on the pulse. Plus, he's not difficult like some of the others. Most of them wouldn't talk to me because of what I do. But Craig's never been like that, and he's also sweet with Ned.'

Peta found this assessment curious. 'Why don't I make you a cup of tea?' she said. 'And you can tell me about your work.'

'Oh, I'm sure you've better things to do . . .'

'I'll go if you want me to, but I know you're worried about Ned. You're probably going to be up the rest of the night looking in on him.'

Karen laughed. 'Right.'

'So, I'd feel happier knowing you're not on your own. Besides, my bed at the pub isn't exactly comfortable. Your couch looks okay. I'll just pretend I'm on-call, if you don't mind.'

Karen's smile was as warm as her red cheeks. 'I can't tell you how glad I am that you were across the road,' she said, taking down two mugs. 'I can see from here when the ambulance is away. I'd probably have put Ned in the car otherwise, and driven to Wangaratta myself.'

'I can't imagine not having a doctor around,' Peta said, fishing two tea bags out of a packet. 'So why don't people want to talk to you?'

'I'm an environmental scientist,' she said. 'A lot of my work here is monitoring water quality, because the town doesn't have any treatment.'

'It doesn't?'

'Nope. Water comes straight out of the river, all on private pumps. So, of course, when we have feral animals upstream or people swimming in it, or campers digging toilets near it, it's a pretty big issue. That's one of the reasons we don't want cattle up in the national park; or horses, for that matter. The cattle grazing's been stopped, but lots of people round here have been cattlemen for generations and they see it as a heritage issue. That's why they don't want to talk to me. I'm part of their problem. They didn't teach me about that in Melbourne.'

'That's where you studied?' Peta asked, as the kettle boiled.

'Oh yes. Marvellous time. But I always loved the idea of the high country. We used to come up here when I was a kid, so I took the job here. I wouldn't swap it for anything, even with the problems. The only thing I really miss is the coffee – Diane thinks she knows what she's doing, but she really doesn't.'

'God, yes,' Peta agreed. 'It's probably the worst coffee I've had anywhere. I've been missing the barista across from the hospital.'

For an hour, Peta and Karen swapped stories about Melbourne between checking on Ned. Karen felt like an old friend who Peta had simply not seen for a few years, and that was an odd feeling for Peta, who realised the barista across from the hospital was as close as she'd been to just about anyone in recent years. The tea was finished, and a fresh batch made. Karen moved on to the Yarraman River, how it began in the range above the Ridgeback, and wound down the mountain past the old mine on the Munroe property. There, a branch became a waterfall over the old high wall, and the river then ran through town and the rest of the valley.

'I do a lot of hiking up river with Ned in a backpack, collecting samples,' she said. 'He's getting heavy and I have thighs of iron now!'

Peta sat up straighter. 'You're a hiker, too? That's what I was doing when I hurt myself. I've done trails all over Australia.'

'Well, not really. I did a bit when I was at uni. It's mostly just for work.'

'You know, I remember now that man who's running for office – Wade Masters? – he said something about getting water treatment for the town.'

Karen made a face and shook her head, throwing the remains of her fourth tea into the sink. 'They've been lobbying for years. I wouldn't hold my breath. And it doesn't fix the broader problem upriver. We're also trying to keep a handle on rabbits, foxes and bloody deer. It's divisive. I have to be so careful and I still get people offside. I don't think a new politician is going to change that.'

Her voice was suddenly very tired. Peta checked her watch. Eleven pm.

'Do you think you might be able to sleep? I'll look in on Ned every fifteen minutes if you want to try.'

After Karen had gratefully turned in, Peta settled on the couch, twisting around to peruse the bookcase. Karen seemed to have a wide-ranging taste – a bunch of Penguin Classics sat beside well-handled copies of *Pride and Prejudice* and *Great Expectations*. But there was the whole series of The Wheel of Time, too, and a half-shelf of beautiful photographic coffee-table books. And then she found a whole shelf of Elyne Mitchell children's novels, their spines cracked, covers torn, pages gone brown with age.

The story was soon open in her lap, as familiar as it had been twenty years ago when she'd read the whole series obsessively. Thowra, the cunning brumby, and Bel Bel, his mother. And naturally that made Peta think of Craig's horse Bel, that Diane had mentioned in such reverent tones.

She closed the book and pushed it away to check on Ned, who was still sleeping. When she came back to the table, it was with *John Brown, Rose and the Midnight Cat*, a safe story with no horses to prompt memories or thoughts of Craig Munroe.

⤙

Karen managed to sleep until seven. Ned's fever had disappeared, so Peta went back to the pub with fatigue setting like concrete in her limbs. She moaned softly as she spied the un-slept-in bed, the pleasure of lying down sliding through her like fine wine. She remembered this sensation vividly from her early months on night shifts, before she became used to the routine. A whole night awake, plus adrenaline, plus vigilance equalled a complete mental shutdown.

Soon, the crutches were against the wall, and she'd closed her eyes. A construction crew could have jackhammered outside the window and she still could have slept.

She woke again in the evening with a dull headache, just as the last of the light was fading the sky to tarnished silver through the window. She needed to wash away the cobwebs, which meant another battle with the pub bathroom. Her ankle was better again, but she still banged her elbows in the small space. Sore and annoyed, at dinnertime she was hovering over the toaster with a threatening butterknife when she heard a knock down the hall. Curiosity and two quick hops got her to the doorway, and Peta peered out to find Gemma at her room door with a bulky bag under her arm.

The smoke alarm chose that moment to scream.

Peta whirled around to find the toaster happily smoking. Frantically hopping and cursing, she yanked the plug from the wall and snatched the tray under the bread loaves to wave ineffectually at the detector, which was high up in the colonial ceiling.

Gemma laughed behind her. 'That's quite a sight!'

'You could help,' Peta panted, bracing on the toes of her bad leg as she fanned. So Gemma yanked a cushion off the couch and joined her. But Peta could already hear footsteps overhead – no doubt the cleaner on her way with the stick-fan.

Mercifully, the alarm cut out, leaving Peta's ears ringing.

'Sorry!' she called towards the hall, then she gave up and collapsed onto the remaining couch cushion, absurdly on the verge of tears. She hoped Gemma would disappear quickly and let her get on with things, first of which might be taking revenge on the toaster.

'Well, that was exciting,' Gemma said brightly. 'I also heard you saved little Ned Waters last night.'

'How—?'

'Diane, of course. Charlene looks after Ned mornings for Karen, and she also works in the store, so . . .' Gemma shrugged. 'Diane also said you're re-opening the clinic, and that she understands you missing your meeting for such a worthy cause.'

'That's not true,' Peta said quickly. 'I was just looking for crutches.'

'Take it you didn't find any since you've still got those old ones . . . which is why I'm here. Wait a sec.'

She disappeared into the hall and came back with her bag and two modern aluminium crutches, the type that had a plastic ring on the forearm. From the bag she pulled an ankle brace and set it on the floor.

'I broke my foot when I was fifteen,' explained Gemma. 'I still have these. I'm not planning on needing them again.'

All Peta could do was stare at the generous padding. 'Oh, thank you,' she finally managed.

Gemma beamed. 'I also need to ask you something. You went up to Harry's place with Craig a few days ago, right?

'Yes.'

'He didn't mention anything about Wade Masters, did he?'

'No. Not that I recall.'

'And you didn't happen to say anything to him about what I said the other day, at the festival?'

Peta frowned. 'About Wade? No. Why?'

'Oh, no reason. It's just Craig doesn't like Wade very much.' Gemma gave Peta a grin that told her Gemma's crush was very much alive. 'Last time he was in town I was only sixteen, so he'd never have looked at me, but now . . .' She smiled again. 'Anyway, I'm sure Craig will come round, but in the meantime, he doesn't need to know.'

Peta remembered the exchange she'd witnessed at the festival and couldn't blame Gemma. She tactfully changed the subject. 'Does Craig breed his own horses?'

'Some of them. But others just come to him. Like Candle, he's a brumby, caught wild. The guy who had him couldn't do anything with him, but Craig did. Mostly he works with cattle horses though, breaking or working with the difficult ones.'

'Candle looks like a Waler.'

Gemma nodded slowly. 'Where'd you pick that up?'

Peta hesitated. 'I grew up on a stud in the Adelaide Hills.'

'Oh, really?' Gemma eyed the toaster. 'Listen, you know what? You should come to the farm for dinner tomorrow. You can tell us all about it.'

Peta considered. She wasn't sure she wanted to spend any time with Craig Munroe, but then her pack was still abandoned up the mountain. She needed to ask him about getting it back. Besides, after all the whispers, she almost wanted to see the Munroe farm and the mysterious Bel. She gave Gemma a cautious smile. 'All right.'

Chapter 9

The Munroe farm was at the end of a long four-wheel-drive track through the hills above the town. Twilight had set in as Gemma made the final turn, under a sky that had turned heavy and ominous. Peta watched a wooden sign go by, 'Munroe' burned shakily into the surface.

'We're still running a herd, but Craig spends most of his time with the horses, and my business is doing better – I've got a distributor interested now.'

Gemma had been chatting about her jewellery-making while Peta stared out the window, a lump against her breastbone at the sight of the fields and horses through the trees. It didn't look like home, but the feel was the same. Only when the trees gave way, revealing a neat timber house painted soft green, could she shake the associations. This, at least, was nothing like home. The neat verandah was bare except for a wrought-iron chair set, while an oversized brick chimney propped the house's northern end.

'Is this the cottage?' she asked.

Gemma laughed. 'No, this is the "big house". The cottage is down the field, next to the feed shed, see?'

Peta ran her eyes down the sloping meadow and saw the cluster of fenced yards topping larger paddocks, all converging on a large shingled shed. A stone cottage rested alongside with the same roof. In the fading light, Peta could see horses in the yards, noses in feed bins, ears swivelling as they heard the car.

Soon, she was crutching after Gemma down a bluestone pathway and through the door of the 'big house'. Wearing Gemma's space boot made it easy, stabilising the ankle so that she could put almost her full weight on it. Inside, a short hall ended at a polished wooden dining table, beside a kitchen that smelled of rich roasting meat. The view through the windows was straight down to the fields.

'I just have to stick the mash in to reheat. The shanks have been slow-cooking all day,' she said.

'I'm not much of a cook,' Peta admitted. 'Someone once told me I could burn water.'

Gemma laughed, but Peta didn't. That someone had been her sister, and many years ago. Gemma had her nose in the oven and didn't notice.

Then, abruptly, the back door opened and Craig appeared.

The petite house made him seem larger, even with his boots discarded outside and his sock feet silent on the stone floor. His shirt was undone two buttons showing his broad chest, and his rolled sleeves revealed fine blond hairs on his tanned arms. Seeing Peta, he paused in a way that suggested Gemma had failed to mention the dinner guest, but he quickly recovered, nodding a hello in her direction and absently raking at his work-ravaged hair.

'There you are,' Gemma said. 'We're probably still half an hour away. So you've got lots of time to do the fire.'

'Gem, it's only going to be nine degrees tonight. It's still summer.'

Gemma made a face. 'Nine degrees is cold. Plus I like it, and we have a guest.'

'Fine.'

'*And* take a shower.'

'What are you saying?' Craig asked, looking down at himself as though he was perfectly clean, then when Gemma made a face, he tossed his hat at her. Gemma ducked expertly. The flash of warm playfulness was such a surprise Peta found herself staring after him as he retreated to the cosy lounge space to set the fire.

'He's still missing Mum's cooking,' Gemma stage-whispered.

'I cook better than you,' Craig shot over his shoulder. 'Stop misrepresenting me to Dr Woodward.'

Gemma rolled her eyes, as if this was an argument they'd had many times before.

As soon as Craig had finished the fire and disappeared to the bathroom, Peta raised her eyebrows. 'Your mum?' Going off Gemma's tone, it seemed a safe question.

'She moved in with her fiancé a few months ago,' Gemma explained. 'He's a farmer two valleys over, and they've gone on a massive caravan trip. They're in Queensland right now. I miss her heaps, but she's having a blast.'

Gemma didn't offer any explanation of what had happened to her father, so Peta didn't pry. Gemma rummaged in a tin and held out a woven bracelet with a silver clasp.

'Here. What do you think?'

Peta turned it over in her fingers, wondering at the smooth work. It was fine strands of chestnut and pale cream in a complex plait – incredibly light, but lustrous. 'It's lovely. I can't believe it's horsehair.'

'It is quite fiddly. But they've become very popular. I get orders from everywhere, even some from overseas.'

Peta looked again, impressed by Gemma's skill. Every weave was even, as if done by machine. She was still inspecting the piece when Craig reappeared, transformed: his hair wet, skin scrubbed and wearing an old t-shirt and jeans. He began taking down plates and glasses.

'We'll eat in front of the fire. It's nicer than in here,' said Gemma. 'You go and sit, Peta, and put your foot up.'

The lounge was cosy with three mismatched couches clustered around the fire and a low table. Flames licked lazily over a solid stack of logs, promising heat and comfort for long into the night. Peta sighed and pulled off the space boot. The swelling was almost gone now, and she pointed the joint towards the heat.

'How's the foot?' Craig asked, as he laid knives and forks on the table.

'Better.'

The phone rang in the kitchen and Gemma answered it. Craig sat opposite Peta regarding her with those blue eyes before he spoke. 'I heard you helped out Karen Waters the other day. Her boy had some kind of fit?'

Peta noted the care in his words. 'Yes. Fortunately it doesn't look like anything serious. Some kids have fits when they have a fever.'

'Still, that's twice now you've been asked to help. Thank you, for Harry, too.'

'Three times if you count Dr Randy, which I'm not,' Peta added hastily.

Craig actually smiled. 'I'd forgotten about that.'

'I imagine you had other things on your mind,' Peta said, remembering finding him after Wade's announcement. 'Is your hand recovered?'

Craig flexed his fingers, showing her the skin had healed. 'Yeah, all good.' He held her eye a fraction longer than she thought necessary before he looked into the fire, and Peta wondered if he was still brooding on Masters. She was trying to think of a tactful way to bring it up when Gemma appeared.

'I've got to duck out,' she said brightly. 'Sorry, Peta.'

'What, now?' Craig said. 'Who was on the phone?'

'Just Charlene. But there's a rush order I forgot about, and I just remembered the clamp I need is over at Mum's place.'

'You'll be an hour going there and back. Can't it wait until tomorrow?'

Gemma was already digging for keys in the hall-table drawer and grabbing her jacket from the hook. 'I'll be fast as I can. Mine'll keep hot so don't wait for me.'

The next moment, the front door had closed and she was gone.

Craig shook his head. 'Sometimes, my sister is completely scatty.'

'Her work seems very good, though. She showed me a bracelet.'

'It is, for sure.'

A silence settled, as though they'd both registered they were alone and in front of a cosy fire. Peta couldn't help noticing the way his chest tapered into his jeans. He must be spectacularly fit from all the riding. Peta fished around for conversation to cover the awkwardness.

'So . . . has the farm been in the family a long time?'

'It was my grandmother's place,' Craig said, leaning back into the couch. 'We came here when I was ten.'

He seemed unlikely to offer anything more, then abruptly said, 'She was a natural horsewoman, my grandmother. She got me started, taught me a lot about training.'

His gaze flicked from the fire to Peta's face, and the way his eyes lingered on her tripped her pulse. Wait . . . no. He wasn't interested in her, was he? As though he'd caught the silliness of her thought, he abruptly stood and went to the kitchen, returning with two loaded plates. He settled back to eat, his expression closed. She must've been mistaken.

After a few minutes, he said, 'Gemma said you grew up on a stud.'

'I left a long time ago and haven't been back. Not much to say, really.' In fact, that was more than she wanted to say at all.

Craig was watching her again, not in that intense way he had a few days ago, or in the lingering way she must have imagined a moment ago, but quietly, with patience. Peta suspected he'd detected her reluctance, and now he changed the subject with the same light touch she'd seen in his hands as he rode Candle.

'What made you want to walk the trail by yourself? Most people up there are in teams.'

She responded with enthusiasm. 'Oh, I've done lots of solo trips. Milford Sound in New Zealand, the Overland Track in Tasmania. I've even done the northern part of this trail, Cooktown to Gunnawarra in Queensland.'

Peta paused with a sudden insight, thinking about all those trips, her fork poised over the mashed potato. She didn't mention that the Tasmanian trip had followed a break-up; he'd been a registrar she'd met at grand rounds, and who'd wanted things she didn't. Or that she'd taken off for Milford Sound after a particularly bad Christmas period at work one year. The truth was, she didn't feel alone on the trips; she felt relieved, decompressed, and she came back renewed, ready to go on. It was a healthy way to manage her stress. Listening now to the soft pops and crackles from the burning logs, her healing ankle soaking up the warmth, she was more satisfied than ever that she was right to stick it out and finish this trip, too.

'I always go back to Melbourne for the coffee, though,' she finally added, scooping up her potato, aware Craig was finished.

He smiled. 'Well, everyone needs a vice.'

'I hope Harry's doing all right?' she asked as she put down her fork.

'Not exactly. He's selling his place.'

'Oh, why?'

'He's getting on, eyesight's going, but the thefts pushed him over. He wants to take it easier. Can't exactly blame him.'

From such a big man, the consideration in his voice now surprised her. Then from outside came a rumble, and a moment later rain began drumming on the roof. Craig pushed his plate onto the table and tipped his head towards the ceiling.

'I was wondering when that was going to start.' He looked at his watch. 'I give her ten minutes.'

'Give who?'

'Gemma. She hates driving in the rain.'

And sure enough, after eight minutes, the phone in the kitchen rang again.

'Gemma's going to stay at Mum's,' Craig said, as he returned from the phone and sank back into the same spot. 'She scared herself driving down the track in a storm not long after she got her driver's licence. She hasn't got over it yet, and this rain's going to set in for the night.'

'Oh,' said Peta, thinking that now she really was imposing. 'Sorry to put you out.'

'You're not.' But he was watching her again, his gaze hooded.

Peta licked her lips and searched for something to say. 'Did I tell you how Dr Randy got hurt? Some kids dropped a fake spider on him. He freaked out, slipped and beaned himself on a fence. They were so scared they formed a ring of silence about it.'

Craig's still features broke into a grin. 'Cheeky buggers. Was it the Rusty kids? It sounds like them. How did you find out?'

'One of the little girls broke ranks and told. And now I've broken my promise not to blab.'

His laugh was a rumble from deep in his chest. The sound warmed the whole room, and Peta relaxed.

'It sounds like something Gemma would have done at that age,' Craig said. 'She's not very good at keeping secrets. You got any sisters?'

The question came so cleanly into the light mood that Peta answered before the darkness could worm its way back in.

'I did. She died. When we were teenagers.'

'I'm sorry,' he said quickly. 'That must have been awful.'

Peta's hand had gone to her neck automatically, and now she brought out the pendant: half a heart, a symbol implying that somewhere existed the other half. She held it up to the firelight. 'We were best friends. She had the other half of this, and I still wear mine. To remember her.'

Abruptly, she frowned and put the necklace away. She didn't know what had come over her; she never talked about Stacey, and wished she hadn't. She didn't want to get into it.

But Craig simply nodded, and said, 'I guess you weren't really walking alone, then.'

Peta stared at him in surprise; it was the last thing she'd expect him to say. As if to give her some space, he took the plates back to the kitchen. Over the drum of the rain, Peta heard him raiding the fridge, and when he came back he set down two bowls of ice-cream.

'Your parents still running the stud?' Craig asked, pushing a bowl towards her.

Peta poked at her dish, pushing down the complex wad of grief that threatened to choke her. 'Not anymore. Mum left years ago and my father just died last month. So ... yeah, there's no one there.'

She glanced at him, hating to appear dramatic. What would he care about it, anyway? She was just a house guest he'd been saddled with. But Craig was sitting forward with his elbows on his knees, his expression without pity or impatience, as if he was simply adding these dimensions to what he knew of her.

'I'm sorry. Again,' he added.

Peta didn't know what to make of him. They ate in silence while the rain continued outside and the logs crackled. Craig finally pushed his bowl away. 'Do you play cards?'

'Um, like poker?'

'Steady on, that's a bit serious.'

'What do you mean?'

'Poker,' said Craig, reaching for a deck of cards on the side table, 'is a game that's kind of boring, but still results in people getting competitive and losing their stuff.'

'I don't know how to play it anyway,' Peta admitted.

'Just as well. How about snap?'

She ghosted a smile. 'What are you, three years old?'

'Sometimes. Fine, you suggest one.' He began shuffling.

'Um, I don't really know any. Med's not a job that involves a lot of sitting around. Not that I'm sure yours does, either,' she added hastily.

'Nice save. Fine, I'll teach you Arsehole.'

Peta laughed. 'That's a game?'

'Sure. And before you make any jokes, yes, I know a few.'

Peta laughed again. 'You really don't have to,' she said. 'If it's not too much trouble, I'm just as happy to go back to the pub.'

Craig spun the deck between his fingers. The fire lit the fine hairs on his arms as his tone turned apologetic. 'Don't know if you noticed the road in was dirt,' he said. 'It gets really slick, and the rain's going to keep on. I'm exhausted already, and I think it's a bad idea to drive into town, not to mention you'll be out in it at the other end. That couch you're on is a sofa – you'll have the place to yourself. Gem or I can run you back in the morning. Now, let's see how many hands I can last before I get soaked going back down the hill.'

The next morning Peta woke when the light was still blue and the only sound was the soft click of the kitchen clock. The fire had become a pile of warm ash, and the air on her cheeks was cool again. No sign of Gemma; her jacket was still missing from the hall peg.

Peta limped to the kitchen, and looked out on the farm. The rain had stopped sometime in the deep night, leaving its dark kiss on the wooden fences and the cottage shingles. Far beyond, she could just see the path of the Yarraman River as a snaking smudge of riverbank trees, and either side of the paddocks, the thick forest.

A minute later, feeling fresh, she had her boot and crutches and was swinging herself down the slope through the damp grass in search of life. The cottage lay still and silent, and Peta turned for the shed, as if it held a long-forgotten tune that she was desperate to hear again.

The instant she stepped into the doorway, she felt at home. The air smelled of lucerne and molasses. How she loved that scent. It permeated her memories: of playing hide and seek around hay bales, of long hours cleaning saddles or simply sitting on the rails watching the horses. She could almost see those same memories playing out here – to her right, the wall held a giant blackboard with the horses' names down one side, and columns listing measures of each feed. *Candle* appeared near the top. And there was *Buck, Echo, Dolly* . . . and at the very bottom, *Bel.*

Next to the board, forty-four gallon drums with labels that read 'chaff', 'oats', and 'pellets' were raised on pallets and a rack of smaller containers held electrolytes and salt. From the sticky rim around one bucket, she figured she'd found the molasses.

She wondered if Craig and Gemma had ever chased each other around those drums, or climbed the hay bales stacked alongside. If they had, it must have been a long time ago.

Now, the place was in perfect order, carefully swept, not a cobweb in sight. A black-and-white stable cat watched her ruefully from the bales, then arched up to demand a scratch as she approached. Peta dug her fingers into the coarse fur, her eye roaming.

Down the centre of the shed was a dividing wall, and when Peta stepped around it, the smells shifted, becoming leather, saddle soap and neatsfoot oil. Here, the long wall was full of tack: saddles on racks, bridles hanging from the cantles. A cleaning station welded from tubular steel stood vacant in the centre, and underneath were the bars of saddle soap and the drum of oil.

Where the two-roomed shed would have had a back wall, it instead opened under a long awning, and it was here that each yard fence terminated, feed bins hanging from the rail. Several horses down in the field had spotted her and were walking up, ears pricked, probably hoping for breakfast.

Peta breathed out. So much like home. Then she caught a movement to her side, and twisted.

A creamy gold palomino mare stood in the doorway of a large loose box built into the corner of the last yard. Her thick mane and forelock were palest white and cascaded over her neck like a waterfall on long exposure.

Peta leaned against the rail, a thrill turning over in her chest. This horse was magnificent. From the perfect curve of her face, the smoothness of her coat, the width of her chest to the length of her neat legs. And it went beyond the physical: she had a deep calm in her eyes, a delicate flare of her nostrils as she reached her nose forward, sniffing, curious.

Peta reached out with shaking fingers. The mare's nose was velvet softness, and she blew hot air into her palm, twitching her whiskers and tasting Peta's skin with her tongue. Then, she lifted her head and the warm breath blew on Peta's neck.

Peta shuddered as great wells of emotion pushed up within her. This touch and smell . . . it was comfort she hadn't had since childhood. Tears pricked her eyes, but with them somehow came a settling, a sense she would find a solution to the problems she had.

Then the mare shifted her nose, and whickered with soft delight. Peta looked around, and started, her hand flying to her chest. 'You scared me.'

'Sorry.' In the next yard, Craig sat astride a tall grey with a sparse spiky mane and a white blaze. Fire burned into Peta's cheeks as her body registered the fact that she'd been caught snooping. Then she realised Craig's horse wasn't wearing a bridle. Or a saddle.

'Where did you come from?' she asked. The top of his akubra and shoulders were wet, as if he'd been riding under the dripping forest.

'Down the front paddock. River pump's packed up. I see you've met Bel.'

'This is Bel? Diane told me you had a famous win on her. The fastest race ever, or something.'

'Something like that,' Craig said. His eyes were moving carefully over Bel. 'She must like you. She doesn't let everyone get that close to the filly.'

'What?' Peta looked again, and this time she spotted a second set of legs, much finer and more spindly, hiding behind Bel's rump. A tiny chestnut face, marked with a ragged white star, peered around. Bel turned her head to give the foal a whicker, and it slunk forward, oversized ears timidly pricked. Peta hadn't seen a foal since she'd left home. The way the filly crept along Bel's side, sweetly trusting, made Peta's throat tremble.

'Oh, she's lovely,' she whispered. 'I'd guess maybe four weeks old?'

'Pretty close. We haven't given her a name yet, but I'm thinking of Timid.'

'You can't do that. You'll mark her for life!'

Craig leaned forward on his horse's withers, laughter in his eyes, his smile gently curving his lips. Peta realised he wasn't serious, but from the way he looked at the mare, Peta knew that Bel was something special to him. That they'd shared things he didn't share with other people. Peta knew what that felt like.

Then Craig's horse moved without any apparent signal, swinging around on his hind legs and heading for the gate to the next yard. Peta watched as Craig executed a perfect mounted pass through the gate, opening and closing it from the horse's back. Finally, they stopped at the rail closest to the feed shed, where the feed bin was painted with *Buck*. Craig swung himself off, patted the horse and slipped through the rail.

'How'd you do that?' Peta asked.

'Do what?'

'You know what. The no bridle, no saddle thing.'

'It's just riding by feel,' he said. 'Buck doesn't need much to know what I want.'

'I've never seen that before.'

Craig came to lean alongside her on the rail, accepting Bel's affections. 'If you're still here next week, I'm running a class. Come along if you like.'

Peta laughed, thinking he must be playing with her. 'Busted ankle, remember?'

'Might be better by then, rate you're going.'

Peta was suddenly aware of an unexpected warmth between them. Maybe it was simply that Craig was in his element, but somehow over the course of the night, through the many hands of cards, their initial animosity had grown through tolerance and into something respectful. Craig's shoulder was inches from her own. She snuck a glance at him and caught him looking at her, that same unreadable expression he'd had last night. She meant to look away, but all she could think was his iris was the colour of the alpine sky. They stayed like that, caught, for a long moment, as if neither of them could figure out how to break away.

'I'll run you back to town,' he said, finally straightening and adjusting his hat, as if he was embarrassed. 'Just give me ten minutes and I'll meet you back up at the house.'

He left without a backward glance. Peta stared after him, wondering what had just happened. That thrill had gone through her, just as it had last night, and then again, the next moment she was sure she was mistaken. She should have gone straight up to the house to collect her things, but instead, sobered, she turned back to Bel.

'You like me, huh?' Peta said, with a great sadness. Bel responded with another snuffling breath, smelling of clean grass and mountain water. Peta let the gentleness burrow inside her, turning over the places in her mind that hard questioning could never have reached. She sighed. No one was around. 'I wonder if you'd still like me,' she whispered, 'if you knew I'd killed my sister?'

Chapter 10

The next Wednesday night, Craig arrived at the pub for the meeting knowing his mind wasn't quite on the job. Normally, he paid attention to the road on the way down to town, noting any patches where holes had developed, and running his eye over the fence alongside. Tonight, he was aware he'd remembered none of it. His head was quite simply somewhere else.

And dammit if somewhere else wasn't that loopy doctor from Melbourne; though, he admitted now that judgement had been unfair. She had just lost the last of her family. Craig thought about Gemma and his mother. What would life be like if they weren't here anymore? It so easily could have happened all those years ago. Now, having been safe for so long, the idea was too awful to contemplate.

But it wasn't only sympathy that had occupied his thoughts. He'd found himself enjoying her company. Actually *laughing*. Craig hadn't done much of that his entire life, except when he'd first met Erica. Peta was skinny in a way that he wished she'd eat more, and her face tended to rest in an expression he'd have called stern. But the unfriendly impression he'd had from their first meeting had softened in knowing her better. In fact, he had been quite fascinated when she spoke, with how he could read the subtle shift in her expressions. And in doing so, he'd noticed the way her intelligence showed through her eyes, and how her cheeks creased when she laughed. And that had led him naturally to notice her lips, and be surprised at wanting to kiss her. And more surprising, that the idea hadn't vanished once the night was over. Never had any girl he'd met at a dance or a show over the years come close to the lingering interest he had now.

Craig sighed as he pushed through the pub doors. He was sure it would pass; all the more reason to focus on something else. So, the meeting should have been a relief, a chance to take stock after Harry's announcement. But then Craig rounded the corner and saw who was sitting at the table.

'Craig,' said Wade affably, his smile appearing genuine.

Craig noted that Wade was wearing a suit, though he'd discarded the jacket and tie. He was already two inches down a pint and clearly in easy conversation with the others. Charlie had his ear cupped to hear better. Wally was leaning forward across the table. Sally had her ears pricked. Even Harry, quiet after admitting the impending sale was to a company, was still listening, a thoughtful frown knotting his brows.

'Good news, Craig,' Wally said. 'Wade here decided to join us.'

Craig nodded, his tongue unresponsive. Tension filled the space between him and Wade like a dense cloud. He wondered if the others were thinking of the last time he and Wade had met at this pub. Craig tried to relax. He accepted the beer Charlie pushed across, and then the Rusty brothers were back from the bar and everyone was toasting to old neighbours. Craig finally recovered his voice.

'Your place giving you time enough to drop in here?' he asked.

It was a subtle jibe. The sprawling Masters property had been running under caretakers since Wade left four years ago, and they'd never shown any interest in pitching in with the other owners.

Wade was unruffled. 'We've cut back a lot. Too much going on with the campaign.' He tugged at his collar in a resigned way, as if he wore the suit under protest. 'But if I'm going to do the best job by everyone, I need to hear about issues right at the grassroots. That's why I'm here.'

The others were nodding. Only Craig felt as though someone had shoved a steel pole down his spine. He looked hard for the man he'd once called a friend, but he only saw glimpses. Occasionally, the way Wade smiled or tilted his head seemed familiar. Otherwise, what had happened with Bel had made him a stranger. If that wasn't bad enough, this politics routine was painful.

All through the meeting, Craig had fantasies of sinking his fist into that smug expression, which would just end up with Ash slapping cuffs on him. Craig wasn't so stupid. He wondered, though, if they had been alone and not in a well-patronised bar, if he'd be able to stop himself. The idea lurked, a demon in the back of his mind.

'It might be beneficial to do some kind of patrol,' Masters was saying now. 'Keep an eye on each other's places.'

Craig couldn't help himself. 'What good will that do?'

Masters milked the ensuing silence, before he spoke slowly and reasonably. 'If people are canvassing the farms, looking for stuff to knock off, we might spot them.'

The others were looking at Craig now with furrowed foreheads. They would want to know why Craig didn't think they should do something to protect their properties.

Craig spread his hands. 'Look, our places are all on four-wheel-drive tracks, and connected by other trails, some on the maps and many not. That's kilometres of road to cover. There are only a handful of us, and we have plenty to do as it is. I don't think it would make a meaningful difference.'

The glances swung back to Wade. 'Sure, but the chance of spotting something could still be worthwhile, and if we worked a roster, we could minimise the impact. Maybe we could hire some people, too.'

Craig didn't bother to answer that one. No one had money to spare.

'But everyone has to be in it,' Wade said firmly. 'We all help each other, agreed?'

Craig almost admired the masterful way Wade used the mutual goodwill of the group as a wedge. If Craig refused, Masters would assume the leadership. Craig could see it all turning on what he said next.

'We'd better talk about it with Ash,' he said. 'He's the copper. He might have some ideas, and better to let him know. We'd want to know what to do if we spotted anything.'

There it was – appealing to a higher power. Wade quickly moved on, and for the rest of the meeting Craig said little. But when everyone broke for the night, Craig took his time, until it was only Wade at the table, shaking out his jacket.

Craig drained the last of his beer. 'You better do what you say you're going to if you get in,' he said. 'No one would back you if they thought you were going to favour a multinational.'

Masters gave him a pained expression. 'Let's get this straight, Craig. I haven't done anything wrong here. I'm in this for the community.'

'You're in it for the opportunity, just like the company that's buying Harry's. How hard is it going to be for everyone when we can't work with the owner because they're some suit in Melbourne?'

'Harry was telling everyone at the festival how hard it's been for him. Did you want him to wait until he injures himself one day because he can't see what he's doing? Some friend you are. Maybe you should concentrate on your own little place.'

With that, Wade pushed past him and out the front doors. Craig remained, his hands clenched on the chair back. Yarraman Falls had always been too small for Wade, and he'd seen Craig as weak for caring about it. But Craig couldn't quite shake the feeling that Masters might be right – maybe he had to mind his own business. Harry would be better off.

Craig just wondered if everyone else would be, too.

The next morning found Peta on her knees in the medical centre's bathroom. The place still had running water, but mildew had bloomed around the caulking. With Gemma's boot, her ankle was much improved; in fact, she'd begun leaving the crutches behind when she was indoors on the flat surfaces. But it still ached in the mornings and Peta could never sleep in, so she had chosen practical distraction. Diane had probed her for details when she'd gone to purchase new cleaning products, but Ash had only shrugged when she'd asked for the key again, and told her to hang onto it for now.

Over several days, she'd spent her time putting the place to rights: throwing out the rubbish and testing the abandoned equipment. A defibrillator seemed to need a new battery, but the slit lamp worked, and so did an ECG machine she'd found stuffed in a box. She'd tried it on herself and laughed at the healthy trace – there was evidence she still had a heart; the machine just wasn't sensitive enough to show the breaks.

In between her efforts at the centre, she exercised her ankle, including balancing on one leg for as long as she could tolerate. Soon she'd try squats. She would begin walking outdoors again tomorrow, and soon she'd be on her way again. So it was odd that she found herself wishing she hadn't said anything about her family to Craig Munroe. She told herself she didn't have to see him again, then had remembered she'd completely forgotten to ask about her pack, still up on the Ridgeback.

Now, with her foot propped up behind her on the mop bucket, scrubbing a stubborn spot of mould with extra fervour, she thought about how to best approach that subject.

'Peta?'

Now she must be imagining things, because that sounded like Craig. She heard footsteps.

'Shit.' She tried to twist around, but her foot on the bucket caught, and a moment later she knew Craig Munroe had been greeted with the sight of her backside up in the air, her face red as a tomato with exertion and her hair slick with sweat.

'What are you doing?' were his first words.

'Cleaning,' she said indignantly, managing to right herself. Her cheeks flushed hot and her hair stuck across her forehead. There must be damp patches under her arms, too. Then she noticed Craig didn't look any better – there was a hat mark across his forehead, his hair dark with sweat and sticks of chaff were stuck in the collar of his shirt. But it was his expression that shoved away Peta's concerns. 'What's happened?'

'Ash called, said Charlie's been shot. Can you come?'

Ten minutes later, Peta was hanging onto the door handle as Craig's Land Rover bounced up another four-wheel-drive track. The surrounding forest was eerily dense here, different to the woods that surrounded the Munroe place.

'Why isn't he just in an ambulance?' she asked, still trying to tie the shoelaces on her good foot.

'Crew was at a call down the valley and they're still an hour away. Besides, Ash said Charlie's refusing to leave. He's pretty stubborn, even worse now his hearing's poor.'

'Who shot him?'

'No idea.'

Three minutes later they pulled alongside a brick and timber house centred in a clearing. Old Charlie turned out to be just as Peta had been picturing him in her mind – a man with a life-worn face, with grey hair and beard, in jeans and a beaten shirt, and teeth a pale yellow. He was perched on a hard chair in his kitchen, whose sink was stacked with dishes, and clutching what looked like an old rolled t-shirt to his left shoulder. Peta's first thought was at least he was conscious, and talking to Ash, who crouched in front of him.

'Bloody bastards, that's what they are,' Old Charlie was saying. 'Coming up here, thinking they can take what they like.'

'But you didn't see anything?'

'Like I said, I saw a light up in the trees. If you ask me, they were on the high trail, the old road up there.'

'Anything else?'

'Yeah, I got off a good few myself. So you go look for someone with shot in their tail-lights. Miserable bastards.'

Ash rubbed his face as Craig cleared his throat and raised his voice. 'Charlie, this is Peta Woodward. She's a doctor. She'll take a look at your shoulder.'

'I heard about you,' Charlie said, peering down at his own shoulder. 'Easy to spot on those crutches. Know what you're doing?'

'I've seen a few gunshots,' Peta said, trying to match Craig's volume so Charlie could hear. In fact, each of those cases was currently flashing through her mind, wounds that had come through her emergency room at different times of the night and often with police in tow. The only difference now was that she wasn't also managing other patients, and her own exhaustion. While this was serious, she could focus. Ash pushed an open first-aid kit towards her.

'Check this out then,' Charlie said, taking his hand off the t-shirt.

The shirt fabric was soaked in red, but underneath she saw a neat round wound, sporting a thin red rim. 'Probably the entry, fairly straight,' she muttered, then asked him to lean forward. Yes, there was another wound in the back of the shoulder, this one with no red rim. 'And that's most likely the exit. Did you want pictures?' she asked Ash.

'Guess you have seen a few before. Only looks small, maybe a twenty-two.'

But Peta wasn't paying attention to Ash, she was focused on Charlie, who was now complaining about the state of law and order in the high country, and that when Diane's husband had been the copper, this never would have happened. Ash took this all with remarkably good grace. Peta felt for Charlie's pulse. It was rapid, but Charlie wasn't a young man and he was excited. But it also seemed . . . thready. Peta remembered another patient who'd come in with facial injuries after a bicycle crash, only to discover later he also had a fractured arm. Everyone had been so intent on the obvious injury, they'd missed it. Luckily that hadn't been too serious, but it reminded her to check everywhere.

'Weren't hit anywhere else were you, Charlie?'

He was protesting he wasn't even as Peta pulled the shirt aside, looking. Nothing on his back or his side. But then lower on his flank was another red circle. A stream of blood had tracked down inside the shirt unnoticed, and into the waistband of Charlie's pants. Peta felt gooseflesh crawl up her body.

'How far away's your ambulance?' she asked Ash in a low voice, pointing to the wound. 'If it's more than twenty minutes, we'd better get him down to the med centre. At least there's some equipment down there. I can't find an exit for this one.'

Ash's clear green eyes met hers. 'I'll find out.'

Peta gave a curt nod and turned back to Charlie. 'Charlie, I need you to stop talking for a second. You've got another bullet wound here, all right? And the bullet might still be inside you. Now, how about you lie down? Maybe you're fine. But maybe things'll get a bit interesting and I'd like you horizontal and with a drip in if that happens. Yes?'

Charlie was genuinely amazed to find he'd been shot more than *once* and rapidly let go of the idea of staying where he was. Peta soon had a drip started and rechecked her survey, making sure there was nothing more to find. Worry chased her work; she wasn't a surgeon, and had no idea how much damage had been done. She'd seen young, healthy people die from such injuries, and Charlie wasn't young.

Between Ash and Craig, they had him back down to the med centre in fifteen minutes and installed on one of the gurneys. Peta rechecked his vitals. His blood pressure seemed stable for now, but she wanted him on his way to a hospital as fast as possible. She wasn't equipped for resuscitation. After twenty more tense minutes, the ambulance finally arrived and Charlie was loaded, still yelling instructions, though with less volume.

'Tell Craig I stashed the rifle in the pantry!' was his parting volley.

Ash left to escort them down the valley, telling Craig to leave the place alone until he could come back in the daylight to look for evidence. This left Peta with Craig in the med centre's reception, watching the departing tail-lights.

'You know, coming from Melbourne I don't think of the high country as somewhere thieves shoot you at dawn,' she said as she stripped the sheets from the gurney.

Craig made a sound in his throat. 'There are problems up here like anywhere else, but this doesn't sound like theft. We've got illegal hunting that goes on.'

'You think that's what this was? Someone out hunting?'

Craig chewed his lip. 'Could be. But it's a bit odd to get hit twice. And shots looked too small for someone after deer.' Craig shook his head. 'Stubborn old bastard. If you hadn't been here, he might have sat up there insisting he'd be fine until he keeled over.'

'He was lucky,' Peta said. 'That second bullet must have missed every important structure for him to have been fine for so long. It can't have hit a major artery. But it's the first rule of emergency – you look everywhere, otherwise you might miss something.'

'Thanks, yet again,' Craig said, and he put a hand on Peta's shoulder. Peta felt the shock of contact – he was so warm, and it had been a long time since someone had touched her with warmth and affection. Even at her father's funeral, her stony face had held off all but the most determined huggers, and they had found her stiff and unresponsive. Now, she allowed herself to accept it.

Only when he removed his hand did she realise she was holding her breath.

'I like seeing this place back in working order again,' Craig said, glancing around, 'even if it is only temporary.'

This part he said with a kind of longing that made Peta drag her eyes up to his. The look on his face was difficult to read – two parts approval, one of apprehension. The moment seemed to stretch until it made some kind of path, one that led the two of them away from here and into something else.

A knock on the door, and the path vanished.

Karen Waters stood outside the glass, Ned on her hip, waving.

'You said to get him checked over when he was well again, and I saw the ambulance go, so I was hoping you'd be here,' she said. Then she noticed Craig. 'Oh, I didn't know you were busy.'

'I'm not, come in,' Peta said firmly, holding the door open. For Karen seemed far from her usual self – her eyes wide and shadowed, her mouth drawn down. It might simply be lack of sleep, but Peta's emergency-doctor radar tripped. Karen seemed rattled. When Craig made to leave, Peta shot him a quick look that asked him to stay.

'Put Ned down there,' Peta said, indicating the gurney. She spent five minutes looking the boy over, who seemed thoroughly recovered and who looked fetching in a pair of blue overalls. But Karen was still obviously distressed. Peta could hear her trying to control her breathing. In the end, Peta pulled her aside.

'Has something happened?' she asked in a low voice. 'Ned's fine, but I can tell you're not all right.'

Karen made a face. 'Oh, it's nothing,' she tried first, then when Peta gave her a pull-the-other-one look, said, 'Fine, it's just something stupid.'

'Stupid enough that you're upset. What is it?'

Karen glanced outside, then at Ned on the gurney. Craig had sat beside the little boy and was entertaining him with his akubra, trying to balance it on Ned's tiny head. Giggles were coming from under the brim.

'Craig, can you watch him for just a sec?' Karen said, then she pulled Peta outside and across the street to her house. At first, Peta had no idea what Karen was doing when she stopped in the front yard – all she could see was the narrow front garden, and the bins along the wall. Then Karen pulled a bin out.

'There,' she said.

Peta looked. Someone had graffitied the wall in bright red paint, the five letters large and jagged. 'Hawer?' she asked, confused. Then she got it. 'Oh! That's horrible. Who the hell would do this?'

'Someone who needs another spelling bee,' Karen said wryly, shaking her head. But Peta could see the joke was covering a deeper hurt. 'Probably some kids out for a lark. My big grey wall was probably too good to miss. They did the med centre a while ago, too, and the airfield sign a while back.'

'Are you going to tell Ash? Can't have gone unnoticed here, surely?'

'No, no,' Karen said in alarm. 'They just want attention. I've got paint still, so I'm going to erase it fast and forget about it.'

'Are you sure that's a good idea?'

'Yes. Please don't say anything. It's hard enough for me here with my job without the extra attention.'

Peta couldn't argue with that, and when they returned to the centre, Karen seemed more relaxed. They found Craig counting piggies on Ned's toes. Ned, who Peta had only seen be so quiet, was still giggling.

'You're awfully good with him,' Peta commented.

Craig shrugged. 'Gemma's ten years younger than me. I'm well versed in all the nursery rhymes . . . plus a few adaptations to keep it interesting.'

'Like what?'

'Oh you know, Mary had a little lamb, its fleece was black as charcoal, whenever it jumped a fence sparks flew out its—'

'Craig!' Peta said in shock. Karen was laughing, and Ned gave her a grin that said he knew this was both naughty, and fun.

Craig raised his eyebrows with perfect innocence. 'And we haven't even gotten to "Ask your mother for sixpence" . . .'

'I'm going,' said Karen, extracting Ned. 'Bye Craig. And thanks, Peta.'

After she'd gone, Craig dusted his hat. 'I'd better get going, too. I just wondered . . .'

'Yes?'

'If you'd thought any more about coming to the class.'

'Oh, I—' Peta, in fact, hadn't. But now the idea had a lure about it, one that she had to admit was all to do with the man in front of her. 'I hadn't thought about it.'

'Well, if you do, let me know.'

Peta said she would. Then, as he went through the door, he looked back once, that same look on his face she'd seen before Karen arrived. And so Peta remembered what he'd said. *Even if it's only temporary.* And she wondered if the wish was for the town to have its facility working again, or if it was more specific to herself.

Chapter 11

Craig lay awake most of the night with nagging thoughts of Peta that would not leave him alone. However much he told himself that she wasn't his type – she was from *Melbourne*, she was stubborn, *and* she knew nothing about the high country – he knew his attraction had inexplicably set in like the wet-year rains. To make matters worse, she looked right in that medical centre, and Craig dearly wished the place would open again. After what had happened to Charlie, he was grateful to her, but he was also finding her skill absurdly sexy. The way she decisively went about her examinations, and ordered people about . . . he imagined many pleasant scenarios involving her doctor's couch, and kept them all firmly to himself. Why he'd thought inviting her to the horsemanship class was a good idea, he didn't know.

It was a relief when the first birds called from the trees, and light began its slow spread across the sky. Pulling on an old sheepskin coat against the chill, he crossed the dozen paces from his cottage to the feed shed and breathed in the air. The horses were always up. Pack animals needed to be on alert for predators, only dozing when they were in the pasture. Candle was the worst; as a former brumby who'd been caught in a trapping muster as a two-year-old, he'd never lost the vigilance of a wild animal. Bel, on the other hand, he could see lying down in the straw-filled loose box that joined her yard. Her ears were turned in his direction; she knew he was there, but was relaxed enough not to get up. The filly's darker head rested near her rump. Craig paused to watch them; there was something lovely about the two of them, and it lifted his heart to see Bel so calm and trusting. She'd come to him in such a different way to all the others.

Candle whickered at him, as if to say, hey, I'm here too! Craig rubbed his nose. 'I know, big man,' he said. 'I'm taking you out today.'

Candle needed a steady, long ride to stretch him out again after his race recovery. And then, there were two yearlings he would spend time with down the field, preparing them eventually for saddle. He began scratching a list into a notepad tacked to the wall: after that, a quick feed inventory, and he wanted to think through the class he was running next week – the applications were still up at the big house. He'd need to read them again, see what the issues were. Inevitably, the real problem would be different. He knew that usually people came with difficult horses and then found they were the problem, not the animal.

When the list was done, he had tasks to last the whole day and beyond, but many of them required the sun to be up. So while a late moth spun itself around the ceiling light, he took down a saddle and started cleaning.

Much later in the morning, as he was returning to the feed shed from the lower field, he heard a car coming down the top drive. Craig grabbed Candle's saddle, wondering if it was Ash coming to see Gemma on some made-up reason. But the tyre crunch didn't stop by the big house; it kept coming all the way down the hill. When Craig peered out the window, all he could see was the white corner of an unfamiliar four-wheel drive.

He was ducking out from Candle's yard when a shadow darkened the doorway. Craig's body stiffened, a moment before he'd even registered who it was.

'Place looks great,' said Wade Masters, glancing around the shed. 'Hasn't changed that much, has it?'

Craig absorbed Wade's profile with a memory of his teenage years flashing across his eyes like an afterimage. Wade's presence then had been no surprise, and they'd enjoyed their time together. Now, Craig shifted himself so he was between Wade and Bel's yard. 'What are you doing here?'

'Look, I wanted to talk to you after the meeting the other night.' Wade wore an earnest expression Craig hadn't seen for a long time. 'I regret some of the things I said. We're neighbours and I'm serious about running for office.'

Craig narrowed his eyes. What the hell was going on here? He reached for Candle's bridle. 'What do you want?'

'I'm not unaware of the change in dynamics over the last four years.' Wade advanced a few steps inside the shed, looking around. Gypsy, the stable cat, gave him the evil eye from her perch on the hay bales. 'You're the go-to man in the district now. People look to you for guidance. Once, that was my father, and I guess it might have been me. But business took him elsewhere and alienated people. I've been away a while, so that's how it is. I'm looking for your support.'

'What?' Craig forgot the bridle.

'Your support,' Wade pressed. 'I know we've had our differences of opinion in the past—'

'Differences of opinion? Is that what you call it?'

'Yes. But we should let bygones be bygones.'

'Should we?' Craig could hardly believe it. Wade must have had a politician's brain implant.

Wade put his hand on the top of a feed barrel and looked at his feet. 'I've made mistakes, I know that. But it doesn't help anyone to hold a grudge. This is about bigger things – it's about everyone's future up here.'

When Craig had first seen Wade show up, he'd been worried again about his temper. Now he was just confused. He'd cut off with Masters after what had happened with Bel, convinced that was the end of any association. But was it possible Masters had changed? Craig frowned as he asked Candle to open his mouth for the bit, and slipped the bridle over his ears.

'What sort of support?'

'Well, endorsement, eventually. Before then, maybe some campaigning. Or a good word with people.'

Craig shook his head. 'Don't get ahead of yourself. If you're serious, prove it in the owners' meetings. Then I might think about it.'

Wade spread his hands. 'That's all I'm asking.' And with that he left. Ten seconds later, Craig heard the diesel engine start up.

He turned back to Candle's saddle, a frown etching deeper. He'd never expected that in a million years. Maybe Masters was drunk. Just thinking about other possible motivations made Craig's head sore. A long ride was just the thing he needed right now.

Then he heard scuffling. Expecting to find Masters returning, he instead found Gemma hanging through the doorway.

'What was Wade doing here?' There was colour on her cheeks, her expression astonished.

'Acting funny,' he said. 'I'm taking Candle out.'

'What kind of funny?'

Craig sighed. 'Politician funny. Looking for votes,' he added, pushing Candle's gate open. He swung himself up into the saddle.

'He didn't say anything else?'

'Like what, Gem?'

She shrugged in an exaggerated way. 'I dunno. Stuff about the town, or the dance, or something like that.'

'No.'

But Gemma followed him as he rode out, chasing him like a puppy. 'Which way you heading?'

'Out to the north trail, see if it's dried out, then across to Charlie's. I want to keep an eye on the place, see if Seb needs a hand.'

'How long are you going to be?'

'All day if I can help it.'

She finally stopped following. 'Okay. If I go out, you'll have to get your own dinner!'

Craig waved over his shoulder, keen to ride away from these problems. Weird must be in the water. He laughed to himself – Karen Waters could probably test for it.

⌁

'I can't thank you enough for doing this.'

Diane perched on her executive chair in the back room of her shop, pen poised over a notepad, glasses down her nose, giving Peta the impression of an expensive psychiatrist. Peta sat opposite, her foot elevated on a cushion, but only on Diane's insistence. She planned to be fully off the crutches and starting proper rehab walks soon. Diane had arranged a plate of enticements on a stool by her elbow – another pie, two kinds of gourmet sausage roll, a scone and a lime milkshake with extra ice-cream. Diane had also later promised clothes, since Peta only had two sets and they were best suited for trekking.

Peta could well believe that Diane could produce anything from the tardis of the shop. The small back room was crammed from floor to ceiling with shelves bearing boxes with hand-marked cryptic labels, such as *YF accts 1989*. On the back wall, a desk held a surprisingly new computer, its wide screen dark.

The two other walls were bookcases, brimming with novels and more document boxes. The most striking item, however, was an antique writing desk in warm wood with an elaborate locked cover, set against the dividing wall to the shop. Rather than use it, however, Diane had balanced the notepad on her knee, her steaming tea mug resting on a pot-plant stand.

'So if I wanted a character to kill someone and make it look like a suicide, how would I do it?' Diane began.

'Gee, Diane, that's really a question for a pathologist.' Then Peta saw the disappointment on Diane's face. 'Does the character have any medical knowledge?'

Diane became thoughtful. 'That's a good question. Maybe I can make them an ex-nurse with a grudge! Oh, oh, the victim could have killed a patient she cared about.' She scribbled furiously. 'So the victim could be a doctor. That's perfect. The nurse would be trustworthy in the beginning. And no one would think the doctor would be murdered. Everyone would be thrown off. So, now, tell me. If *you* were going to kill someone, how would you do it?'

The air in Peta's chest turned to jelly, her next breath thick and cloying. 'I, ah, I've never thought about it. I mean, it would be difficult to get away with. If you used a drug, the stocks would be missed, and most of them would turn up in pathology.'

Yes, that was right. All those direct methods were obvious. Peta's own guilt was something altogether different. She regretted agreeing to this.

'Hmmm,' Diane said, tapping her pen. 'But the pathologist could be in on it. Oh! Or better yet, the pathologist is the victim, because he covered for a doc who was knocking people off. Yes! Then I'd have a sequel, where the nurse goes after him.'

Diane grilled Peta for a long while about what kinds of drugs could be fatal, and in what sorts of doses.

'Would any of those things be in a small-town medical centre like ours?' she asked eventually.

'Some of them,' Peta said. 'Not that the medical centre really has any at the moment.'

Diane made an unhappy sound in her throat. 'Our town's been forgotten. Pains me to see it. You lose things like the medical centre, and everyone's life suffers. That's what we really need – services, and investment to bring local businesses back.'

'You sound like Wade Masters.'

'Ish. Most of the pollies don't get it because they don't live here, and Wade's been away a while. What we need is something like a trade school, and to keep the primary school open. Those things help people to stay. I'm not sure Wade's in that business from what I hear.'

Peta raised her eyebrows.

'Oh, you know,' Diane said. 'There are rumours he drives hard bargains, that sort of thing, bad as those big businesses fishing around up here for land. I see their cars come past, and I'm sure it must be one of them that's bought Harry's place. Anyway, Wade's a big-business man, and places like this thrive on small ones, like mine. We need more help because we're remote. Farms are expensive, and with the greenies wanting conservation, that costs money, too.'

'You should talk to Karen,' Peta said. 'Sounds like something she'd be interested in.'

'Oh no, there's a can of worms. It's just not like the city. I mean, look at poor Old Charlie being shot. He's going to recover, but Ash said they're cold on leads for who did it.'

'I guess we don't have hunting accidents in Melbourne.'

'*Illegal* hunting, if it was even that. But it's worrying, now Harry's sold. Once one goes, it spreads like an infection. Maybe Charlie'll do the same. At least I've taken steps to protect myself here.'

Peta glanced around the room. 'Like what?'

'Ah, I'll show you when it arrives. In the meantime, it's a good thing to have you here, and the centre back in some order again. Karen Waters must be very glad. Poor little Ned – that must have been frightening.'

Peta remembered Craig saying Diane had found out about that. 'News travels fast.'

'It does when you need to look out for people. He is an adorable little boy, whatever people think about her.'

'Gorgeous,' Peta agreed.

Diane acquired a thoughtful look, her eyes becoming animated again. 'It's a great mystery who his father is. I've been trying to work it out for years.'

Peta felt instant sympathy for Karen. She hadn't thought to pry into Ned's father's whereabouts. She'd assumed they'd split, not that it was some kind of secret. 'Jeez, Diane, isn't that a bit much?'

'Oh, I don't *say* anything to anyone. Well, not much. I just keep my ears open, and think about it in the idle moments. Most people think it's someone in Melbourne – she used to travel down there a bit – but I don't.'

'Why's that?'

'Because she stays here, despite all the conflict with the farmers. I figure it's to keep the father close by. I've often wondered if it's Craig Munroe, actually.'

Peta had been taking a sip of milkshake, and almost found herself choking. Abruptly, she thought of how good Craig had been with Ned. But surely, if he was the father, there'd have been some kind of awkwardness with Karen?

'Of course, if it were Craig, then why wouldn't he want to claim him? It's not the scandal it was years ago. Speaking of which, are you bringing Craig to the dance this week? It follows the festival. Because if you're not, I want to impose on you to help sell raffle tickets. The kids at the school need new desks, and everyone knows you've helped out for nothing. Might make them more generous.'

Peta pressed her fingers into her temple. 'I guess I could,' she said, trying to keep track. These details expanded the dimensions of Craig beyond what she knew of him, and it gave her an odd feeling. She shouldn't care about any of it; she was just passing through. But now she found she did care. About Karen and Ned. About whether anything Diane had just said might be true. 'I won't be dancing, will I?'

Diane laughed. 'I don't know, at the rate you're going, you'll be back up on that trail again before you know it.'

There was that odd feeling again. Peta frowned. It was all she wanted, to get back up there. But now, coming from Diane, it almost felt like being pushed out, and she didn't like it.

Diane had put down her notebook, and was digging under a desk in the far corner. 'Before I forget,' she said, as she pulled out a beaten cardboard box with a screech of dust on the tiles, 'I promised clothes.'

Peta investigated, finding shirts that could fetch a tidy price in a Melbourne vintage store. She extracted a pale blue polo. 'Snowy River Festival 2003,' she read on the embroidered pocket.

'Good year, that one. Seb Rusty won the cattle class, and Gemma Munroe fell in a mud puddle so big she couldn't get out again,' Diane said with a laugh. 'She was only seven, but it was priceless. Kept telling Craig to go bring her horse to pull her out.'

'How do you remember all this stuff?' Peta asked, stacking the best of the shirts.

'Good memory,' Diane said. 'Did I mention my late husband used to be the policeman? I helped with all his cases. Now, you take whatever you want, Peta. You help me out, I'll help you.'

⌒

Two days later, the hot days had again disappeared behind a blanket of soft grey cloud, and Peta was making her second trip out to test her ankle. She'd brought only a single crutch this time, her foot strapped with some old tape she'd found in the medical centre.

She'd planned to walk the town road out to the highway and back. The surface was even, and she couldn't possibly get lost. Quickly, however, she realised that the road had no shoulder, and so many blind bends that she was afraid of being scrubbed by a random car at any moment.

Instead, she followed a faded walking track marker in the public park, not far from where the Yarraman River tumbled over the weir. The track was hard-packed dirt that had dried rapidly after the rain, wide enough for a car, and wound beneath a close canopy of tea-trees and wattles. A bed of lush grasses grew alongside. She could hear the low roar of the river always to her left, but she couldn't see the water through the scrub. Then after ten minutes she rounded a bend and the canopy opened before a towering rock wall. Over the lip tumbled a frothing white waterfall, which poured into a green pool before flowing away to rejoin the river. On either side, the wall's red and white rocks were echoed in the pale and red trunks of candle barks and stringybarks. A beautiful harmony of earth and trees.

An old wooden sign, leaning on one broken leg at the curve of the path, simply said *Yarraman Falls*. Feeling adventurous, Peta picked her way past the falls and along the base of the sheer cliff, which eventually tapered as the track turned uphill. Here, sensing she was entering uncharted territory, she turned back. No sense in wandering too far, but she was curious to know why there was a cliff in the middle of the forest, and thought to ask Diane on her way back to the pub.

But as she approached the store, Peta could hear a commotion inside – scuffling and whooshing and honking.

Honking?

Peta stuck her head through the clear plastic door guards. She caught a new, pungent smell, and a white blur streaked across the gap in the counter. She heard Diane muttering.

'Diane?'

The shopkeeper appeared behind the counter, a stiff-bristled witch's broom in her hand. 'Oh, Peta. Come in and see my new security!'

Perplexed, Peta crept into the back of the shop to find Diane near the rear door, facing off with a large, and rather resplendent, white bird. Its yellow beak and broad wings were raised, its eye beadily fixed on Diane.

'Is that a goose?'

'Emden goose, yes. Shoo! Outside!' Diane commanded with a stroke of her broom.

The goose hissed but eventually decided that the backyard was preferable, and shot out the door with a flurry of white feathers. Diane dusted her hands. 'Bugger got my scone,' she complained, indicating an upended plate on the edge of the antique writing desk. 'And they're not supposed to eat white flour. I'd better call Erica and see if it's a problem.'

'What are you doing with a goose?'

'Geese,' corrected Diane.

When Peta looked through the back door she indeed saw a small flock of white geese milling about the yard. Some gave her a wary eye, as the others foraged in the grass.

'So, what do you think? We're in the middle of a crime spree, and what with Craig's class this week and the dance on Friday, there'll be people coming in from out of town. Not going to let one of them clean me out.'

'So, geese?'

'Of course. They're excellent guarders. Especially that one – he's the gander,' she said, pointing out the thieving goose. 'I'm going to call him Monty.'

Diane leaned on the doorframe, arms crossed in satisfaction. The geese circled the fence, bounded on two sides by the store and Diane's house, as if trying to establish their territory. One of them seemed especially interested in the police station over the back fence.

'You couldn't have just got a dog?' Peta asked.

'Can't stand the smell,' Diane said. 'Besides, dogs need looking after, and walking. Once these fellows know this is home, they can just take care of themselves: wander on down to the river in the day and come back at night.'

Peta chuckled, watching the flock strut around, their beaks held high, as if dissatisfied with their new digs. She wondered at them ever doing guard duty. 'Diane, you don't think you should maybe go a bit easier on the crime novels? Mix it up with something else?'

Diane gave her a thoughtful expression. 'What are the kids into these days?'

'To be honest, I don't know. But the last intern in the A&E was reading something called *Divergent*.'

Diane sighed. 'My niece talks about that one. Characters didn't even have real names! Think I'll stick to Agatha Christie. Now, that's a name. Agatha. So distinguished.'

'Like Monty?'

'Exactly.' Diane grinned as the geese finally settled in a corner.

'And how does Ash feel about having a private security detail over his fence?'

Diane waved the broom as she shooed Peta back inside. 'Don't worry, Ash has always had to contend with a bit of usurping. It's tradition up here.'

Peta raised her eyebrows. 'It is?'

'You ever hear about the Wonnangatta murders?'

Diane was doing her excited, eyes-wide thing again. Peta sat in the chair, put her foot up and said, 'Fine. Go ahead.'

'You won't have that look when I tell you about it. Happened a hundred years ago, around Wonnangatta Valley, which isn't too far from here. Two people were murdered, and the case has never been solved.' Diane punctuated the last three words with a pointed finger gesture.

'Okay—'

'One of the victims was the manager of the station, who was well respected. They found his body in a shallow grave on the property; he'd been shot in the back. There was a cook on the station that had a reputation for having a violent temper, and he was missing, as was the manager's horse. So, the assumption is that the cook killed the manager, disposed of the body, then took his horse and rode hell for leather out of there.'

'Did they find him?'

'This is where it gets interesting. A manhunt was on for the cook, but then a little while later the manager's horse turned up, running wild on Mt Howitt, no saddle or bridle. And then, a search party finally found the *cook's* body beside a creek, near one of the mountain huts.'

'Wait . . . so he died trying to get away?'

'Sort of, if you call it dying when someone shoots you in the head. And that's the mystery, because no one really knows what happened, and no one was ever charged.'

Peta found herself sitting forward. 'But there must be a theory?'

'Of course. Most people think that a friend of the manager's came across the murder, knew the cook's reputation and saw the horse missing, and went after him. A mountain man like that on a mountain horse, he could have ridden all night and caught up. The cook stays in the hut overnight, not knowing he's being pursued. The next day, he's riding down the creek and the mountain man comes alongside and *Boom!*, blows him right off the horse. That's Charlie Lovick's theory anyway, and his family know a thing or two about the high country. It's the sort of way things were done up here then – not bothering with the law. Mountain justice, if you like.'

Peta leaned back, considering. 'They must have had a candidate for the cook's murder, though.'

'Sure. But it didn't quite fit. For one, why would a friend of the manager leave the manager's body to the elements? It had been there several weeks before it was found.'

Peta shrugged. 'I guess someone smart would realise that if they moved it, it might give them away.'

Diane grinned. 'Exactly. Mind you, there are other theories. Like that both of the men were killed by stock rustlers. It was wartime and there was quite an industry in stealing horses to sell to the war effort.'

'There's a happy thought,' Peta said, thinking of the thefts around the valley.

'Anyway, my point is, people up here defend their own. That's why Charlie didn't want to leave his place. My husband understood that, and Ash will learn it. So, you let me know if you see anything suspicious with those out-of-towners turning up at the Munroes' on Wednesday so I can warn Monty.'

Chapter 12

Two days later, Peta watched the horse trailers roll in to the Munroe farm. Dawn hadn't long passed when Gemma picked her up from the pub, and now the early bush chorus had given way to engines, whinnies and the odd plaintive cow lowing somewhere down the hill.

Despite Diane's fears, nothing looked suspicious. The boxes were directed into a neat line with plenty of space between, all coordinated by Gemma, who trekked around in jeans and gumboots, balancing a mug dangling two blue teabags.

And then, out came the horses.

Some pranced and some shuffled, and they were bay and black and flea-bitten grey, and were soon all tugging on hay nets or being walked around the clear space in the top paddock. Overwhelmed, Peta slipped into the feed shed, walking carefully with one crutch. Bel and her foal hovered at the fence, the filly cutely imitating the way the mare rested her soft muzzle on the rail.

Peta was most surprised to find Craig, not outside in the action, but sitting on a hay bale, sipping his own mug of strong black tea. He had on a pair of worn buckskin chaps, and a shirt as pale as his face.

'Morning,' he said, sounding hoarse, then lifting the mug, 'Want one?'

Peta shook her head. 'You coming down with a cold?'

'Nope. Just preparing myself.' He flicked his blue eyes in her direction. 'Would you believe I'm a little shy?'

'Shy?'

'Not a fan of public speaking. There's a reason I work with horses.'

Peta laughed. 'So you're going to hide in here all day? I think the crowd will be disappointed.'

He tossed the tea and stood. 'No, I'm going. Just don't laugh.'

'Only if it's funny.'

He chuckled. She liked hearing him laugh like that; he seemed a man who didn't laugh often, so when he did it was full of warmth and meaning. And with him in the shed, and the smells of feed and leather, and Buck hanging his grey head over the fence with eyes that wanted breakfast, it all felt oddly pleasing.

When the class began in one of the yards attached to the feed shed, Peta hung back at first, feeling like an outsider. The fence was lined with thirty people, all of them in jeans and shirts, most with akubras and oilskins. No one spoke; all attention was on what was going on in the ring, where ten horses in halters lined up with their owners.

Peta craned her neck. Craig wasn't in the centre, but moving from person to person, taking time to talk to them before he started. From this distance, she couldn't hear, but he was soon demonstrating with Candle, having the horse walk around him in a circle, then turning to go in the reverse direction. His touch on the rope was so light, Peta wondered how he was doing it, especially as most of the other horses stubbornly refused. But steadily, Craig worked his way around, and Peta found herself hanging on the fence, too, just as he called all the participants together.

'Might be a surprise to you all how sensitive they can be,' he was saying, 'but maybe also that they're not as smart as you think. You have to give to them as soon as they start to do what you want. You wait, and they don't associate – they aren't like us. But I can use the lightest touch on a lead—' he barely shifted the rope in his hand, and Candle began stepping back '—and he knows exactly what I'm after. It's never ever about brute strength. The touch means something to him because he wasn't confused when he was learning it. So we're going to practise giving now, and by the end of tomorrow, we'll aim to have this light touch going on.'

Peta watched as he demonstrated with each person, giving them a length of rope and asking them to give when he did. 'Good,' he said, after a teenage boy got the technique down. 'Just remember it's harder with the horse. If you're in a habit of holding on, you'll have to be disciplined to change your own pattern. But it's worth it, because that's the only way he'll change his.'

Peta sat, enraptured, marvelling at how Craig could coax even the touchy horses into calm manoeuvres with his gentleness and respect. Having grown up on a stud, she'd seen her fair share of breaking and training. Horses beaten and tied up in bindings, with harsh bits in their mouths and still without any changes as dramatic as what Craig was demonstrating with just a few minutes' work, using nothing more than a halter. For such a large, strong man, his deft touch was as surprising as his absolute patience.

'There's no point in getting angry with them,' Craig was saying now. 'That doesn't do anything except make you stiff, and they don't understand it. Pain doesn't teach them anything except to be afraid of you. What you want is a partnership.'

By the time the group broke for lunch, Peta almost wished she'd brought a notepad, as so many others had done. Gemma had a barbecue going, but Peta wasn't hungry. She sat on the fence instead, watching as Craig was kept busy through the break.

'He's amazing, isn't he?' asked a woman sliding in alongside her on the rail. 'I tell you, the first time I saw him at a show, I thought it was a trick. I'm so glad he's decided to start teaching.'

'I've never seen anything like it,' Peta admitted. 'I grew up with horses and it was all about posture and leg signals and keeping the horse on the right leg and on the bit. It seemed to take ages to get anywhere. Now I think I can see why.'

The woman was nodding. 'I know, that was me, too. I didn't understand how their minds worked until I met Craig. Apparently his granny started him off. She was a real tough old lady but such a touch with horses. I met her once at a show, years ago, and I remember so clearly – riding a horse without a bridle, and she was eighty! Craig takes after her. I'm Mandy by the way – I have a stud down near Mansfield.'

Peta watched as the afternoon became evening, and the steady improvement bound the group together in quiet satisfaction. Even the appearance of Ash in uniform, who casually made his way through the crowd, shaking hands and chatting, failed to alter the mood. As darkness fell, they all sat around a fire pit, swapping stories and laughing, occasionally accompanied by the distant crashes of falling stringybark.

When Peta ended up alone on a log seat, Craig sat down beside her. She smiled, suddenly shy. Seeing him work through the day had changed him in her mind. She appreciated the depth of his skill, and despite her first impressions after seeing him with Masters, the extent of his patience. It hinted at hidden dimensions in his life, of time and experience that rendered him far more complex than the man who'd rescued her up on the ridge.

'Need something to drink?' he asked.

She shook her head. His proximity was sending unexpected thrills through her chest.

'What did you think?'

'It was incredible. You seemed to recover pretty quickly from the stage fright.'

A satisfied smile. 'Yeah. Imagining it is worse than doing it.'

'I find it hard to believe you could be shy about something you're so good at.'

He shrugged. 'I've always been like that, I just learn how to hide it better as time goes on. It helps I believe in this stuff.'

'You're not the only one,' Peta said, looking around the crowd. About twenty people had stayed up, talking amongst themselves. But Craig was the one who had her attention. Every time he moved his mug to his lips, and his arm brushed past hers, the desire to touch him made her legs weak. She bit her lip, aware she could easily make a fool of herself. She wasn't sure what to do with how she felt about him, so she looked away.

Gemma sat across the large circle, on a camping chair next to Ash, who Peta assumed was now off-duty. 'Ash seems to be staying a while,' she said.

If Craig wondered at the change in subject, he said nothing. 'He likes her if that's what you're wondering. But he doesn't act on it. It's almost painful to watch.'

'Maybe Ash is scared of you,' Peta said.

Craig grunted.

'Or maybe he's just got other things on his mind. It's the middle of a crime spree according to Diane,' Peta said, swirling the dregs around her cup. 'Did you know she bought geese to protect the store?'

'Gemma mentioned it. Sounds like the kind of crazy thing she would do.' He shook his head.

'Diane's all right.'

Craig looked up. 'I don't mean it like that. She's one of our biggest supporters. When I started talking about this class, she drove all around the high country posting flyers in other stores for me. And when I thought no one would come, she tapped her network and pushed the word out.'

'Don't say that – I'll feel bad.'

'Why?'

Peta pulled a face. 'Because I promised to go to this dance on Friday to sell raffle tickets, and I was thinking of not turning up.'

'Ah.' Now he was looking at her with keen interest. 'So . . . are you going to go?'

The question hung in the air, glittering with promise. 'Maybe,' she said. He was still looking, and the smile in his eyes made her feel all light and fluffy. The feeling then shifted, until she thought she was about to tumble into some strange place from which escape would be uncertain. She stood abruptly. 'Excuse me . . . I just . . . need more tea.'

Craig watched Peta picking her way carefully over the uneven, shadowed ground, her limp still noticeable. His leg muscles bunched to go after her, but he caught himself before he did – what was he hoping for, exactly? For a moment, he thought that she was returning his interest; now, doubt surfaced. He could be wrong.

But he hoped she was coming back.

His thoughts were interrupted as Erica sat down beside him, blowing on a hot mug, her expression less harried than usual. 'Good day,' she said. 'You keep this up, you'll get a reputation and you'll have to go on the road.'

Craig sighed. Erica had been on his case for a while about this. He couldn't run big classes at home; large horse floats had trouble with the road, especially if they'd had rain. And people would only travel so far. 'I hear you,' he said. 'I just . . .'

'Don't want to leave home?'

'Not exactly—'

'Don't want to leave Gemma to the wolves?'

Craig eyed Ash across the circle. 'That's not a wolf.'

'It's painful is what it is,' Erica said, echoing Craig from a minute before.

'Peta thinks Ash might be scared of me,' Craig mused, as much to say her name as to make the statement. 'He's the one with a gun and handcuffs.'

Erica raised an eyebrow. 'Maybe he doesn't want to go up against a man who'd pull a rifle on his own father. I wouldn't.'

Craig winced. Most people knew some version of how his family had come to live in Yarraman. 'That was a long time ago,' he said.

'All right, let's change to a short time ago. How's things with the doctor? She seems very capable.'

'Seems like it.' Craig knew his lips moved into a giveaway smile, and that he'd involuntarily glanced around, looking for where Peta had gone. The nice thing about Erica was she didn't press for things you didn't want to talk about. She thrust her point out there and if you didn't engage, she moved on.

'Must say it's a relief not getting the calls myself when the ambulance is out of town. You always know it's a cattle farmer when they think a vet is as good as a doctor. Speaking of which, I went out to Charlie's to look over those escaped cows. Did you know he's thinking of selling?'

Craig's eyes snapped up. 'What did he say?'

'Nothing explicit,' Erica said. 'But the way he's looking around the place, asking me about what I think the herd would go for, I tell you, he's thinking about it. I don't blame him, but be a shame to lose two so close together.'

'Maybe it's Harry deciding to go that tipped him. They'd got close this last year,' Craig said. He regretted having passed on this week's meeting on account of the class; it would have given him an opportunity to talk to Charlie quietly about what was going on.

Erica stood up. 'Anyway, I'm off. Had to get a brew in before looking at an abscess. Good luck tomorrow.' And with a wave, she disappeared up the hill to her truck.

Craig threw out his tea and rose, wanting to find Peta. Casually, he skirted the circle, but she wasn't there.

When he finally found her, it was in the feed shed, where Buck, Candle and three other horses were all standing at the rail, looking hopeful. But Peta sat on a straw bale she'd dragged up to the end fence, her fingers worrying the end of her necklace, her other hand supporting her head. Bel had her head down level with Peta's, snuffling, and Craig knew she was listening to whatever it was Peta was saying. One look at the slump in her shoulders and Craig backed up silently.

He knew when he wasn't needed. Whatever was troubling her, the horses would be better for her right now than he was.

Chapter 13

The kid was called Felix and he was eight, with freckles across his nose and a tooth missing at the edge of his smile. He stood by the medical centre's leftmost bed as Diane, her cheeks flushed, followed Peta inside.

'So, as I said, Felix was doing so well at the working bee. The school always helps get the hall ready for the dance. But Monty's taken to hanging out down that part of the river, and – and I swear, Peta – I had no idea he would bite anyone.'

'Where did he get you?' Peta asked Felix. It was Thursday afternoon, and Peta had been called to the clinic after a frantic Diane had found her walking the main road towards the falls path.

Felix pointed at his pants. 'On the bum. I was running away,' he added.

'I imagine you were.' Peta judged that Felix wouldn't be much bigger than Monty. 'And where's your mum and dad today?'

'Oh, they're back at the working bee,' Diane said. 'They weren't worried, but I couldn't live with myself and they said I could bring him over.'

'Okay. Is it sore?'

'Only when I sit down.'

'Would you mind showing me?'

Felix obediently pulled down the waist of his shorts, showing an impressive blue bruise along the margin of his backside. It looked as though Monty had grabbed a good chunk of the soft tissue, but no skin was broken.

'Well, Felix, I think you'll live. It's just a bruise and it'll start fading in a few days. In the meantime, we can put a cold pack on it.'

As Peta got Felix set up with some ice, she asked him what they were doing at the working bee. Felix shrugged. 'Painting. But it was boring so me and Alex were chasing the birds!'

'I see! Is that what happened?' Diane was now indignant.

Felix looked bashful. 'It was Alex's idea,' he said.

'You shouldn't chase them. They're guard geese,' Diane scolded, her concern resolved. 'And Peta, while you're here, the school is doing a job talk day for the year sixes tomorrow. Ash and Karen are going. Would be fabulous to have a doctor, don't you think, Felix?'

Felix was playing with the ice pack, squishing the blue gel where it stuck out from underneath his pants. He looked up and grinned. 'She can see the pictures we drew for the dance!'

Peta looked into the gap-toothed grin and felt oddly . . . needed. And not in the way that people needed a doctor; the way that people needed each other. The sensation was so surprising, she didn't know what to say. Diane was making expectant eyebrows.

'I guess I could,' Peta managed.

The Yarraman Falls primary school occupied a converted weatherboard house on the banks of the Yarraman River, its front wall painted a blinding shade of yellow and its walls rimmed with impressive vegetable patches.

'The students do all the work,' Diane explained as they walked over the next morning, which Peta had insisted on as her foot had improved so much. 'Most of them live on farms, but Miss Jenkins likes them to have practical things to do even if it's familiar.'

Miss Jenkins herself was a woman of Diane's vintage, with tight steel-grey curls, a wiry body encased in blue jeans, a white blouse and waistcoat, and an expression that told Peta she didn't tolerate fools. But she also had a warm voice and an inviting smile.

'Come in, come in, we've never had a doctor before, though you'll have to forgive the children if they find Ash the most interesting. It's hard to compete with a man in a uniform who rolls up in a police car.'

Peta was ushered into a neat classroom where a dozen children's seats had already been set in a semicircle. It seemed a very small class.

'How many students are there?' Peta asked.

'Fifteen, but that's from year one all the way to year six. It's just five in year six, and they're the ones who'll come. They're all learning about fish with my aide, down by the river. The older ones will come back shortly.'

A few minutes later, the students came running, a whirlwind of arms and legs and bags before they tumbled into their seats. At the same time, Ash and Karen arrived, and the children rushed to the window to ogle the police four-wheel drive.

'Wow, what a reception!' said Karen as she came through the door, instantly warming to her role and making a show of some kind of test kit that she'd brought along. 'Peta, hello. Diane told me you were coming.' Then she whispered, 'I have to get in early, before they realise what I do doesn't have flashing lights or a stethoscope.'

Peta suppressed a smile, and soon they were all seated and Miss Jenkins was introducing them. 'None of you have to decide for a long time what you might like to do with your lives, but it doesn't hurt to think about it. Would each of our guests like to say something about what you do?'

Ash cleared his throat. 'I'm a police officer, I guess the uniform gives it away. And my job is to help keep everyone safe by enforcing the law. But that can be a whole bunch of things – looking out for dangerous driving—'

'Catching thieves!' interjected a boy in the group. The girl next to him gave him an elbow.

'That too,' Ash finished.

'And I'm an environmental scientist,' Karen began, with enthusiasm, 'which means I look after water, the land and all the wild animals. I get to work all over the high country.'

The children looked distinctly unimpressed. 'Told you,' Karen said under her breath as everyone turned to Peta.

'I'm Peta, and I'm a doctor,' she began.

'What happened to your foot?' asked a girl.

'I was hiking and I fell and twisted it, but it's getting better.'

'What sort of doctor are you? My mum says there are different types.'

'I work in a hospital, in accident and emergency,' Peta explained. 'So I help people when they first arrive.'

'Peta saw Felix's bum when he got bitten yesterday,' the girl announced to the room.

After that, there were a lot of questions about geese and being bitten, then about other things that could bite, such as snakes and spiders. The discussion then derailed as each student tried to outdo each other with stories of the snakes on their farms.

'All right,' interjected Miss Jenkins. 'Let's refocus. Any questions for Ash or Karen?'

'Can we go for a ride in your car?' asked one boy hopefully.

'Sorry,' Ash said. 'But you can come out and look at the lights and the siren when we're done.'

'When are you going to catch the rustlers? And the people who shot Charlie?'

Ash glanced at Miss Jenkins. 'We're still looking for the cows, and the people.'

'So you don't know who did it?

'Miss Jenkins, can we see the car now?'

Peta admired their enthusiasm until, as they were going outside, one of the girls tapped her on the arm and said, 'Are you going to marry Craig Munroe?'

Peta was caught in alarm, having no idea what to say. Not only from the evidence of gossip, but also because the idea made her blush.

'Just say yes,' Karen whispered, saving her. 'It'll be entertaining to see how long it takes to make it back to Diane.'

―

Buoyed by the school visit, in the late afternoon Peta took a fist of change to the pub residents' phone and discovered an out-of-order sign taped to the receiver. So, muttering about being cut-off from the outside world one avenue at a time, she retrieved her crutch, took a deep breath and made for the phone box outside the store. Moments later, the chirpy receptionist from Turner and Decon picked up.

'Mr Turner's not in the office at present,' she told Peta. 'Can I have one of the associates speak with you?'

'No. I mean, I guess so.'

Peta was quickly connected to one of the more junior lawyers, whose name she completely missed.

'Yes, we've received the developer's offer in writing,' he said in a bland voice that made her think he did tax returns for fun. 'It's more than sufficient to discharge the debts and leave you with a substantial cash inheritance. When would you be able to come in and discuss?'

'Didn't Mr Turner tell you I'm in the high country?'

'Well, he mentioned you were travelling.' The man sounded uncomfortable. Probably, Peta thought unkindly, because their fee might be in jeopardy. 'But I really think it's best you think about an interim trip home, perhaps. The developer has put a thirty-day limit on their offer. If you wait, it could be off the table, with no guarantee of another buyer. The debtors would have reason to protest the opportunity loss – we've already received one communication to that effect.'

Peta squeezed her eyes shut. She understood, now, what Diane had meant when she'd said that Charlie didn't want to leave his land. The place where she'd grown up was tied into her soul with laces that were both love and aching loss. She couldn't see it divided and buried under new roads and rooftops. But if the debtors took her to court . . . then maybe someone else would make that decision for her.

'Miss Woodward?'

'Yes, I'm still here. Tell Mr Turner that I need to think about it.'

'I really think—'

'You're talking about my home,' she snapped. 'The place where I grew up and my parents built. Don't act like this is some dispassionate sale. I'm thinking about it.'

'Fine. I'll—'

'And it's *Dr* Woodward,' she fired as she hung up. Fine tremors shook her fingers. She leaned against the outside of the phone box, her injured foot aching in time with the pulse in her chest. She lifted her eyes, trying not to cry. It was one of those alpine days where the sky was clear blue and the sun through the trees splashed dappled patterns across the road.

Peta wondered how the world could look like that on the same day it brought her such news. Stacey had died on a day like this, too. A perfect blue day, the colour of beauty and misery.

Next thing, the shop's door flaps flicked aside and Diane's head poked out, one hand on her broom. 'Peta! Oh, you haven't overdone it?'

Peta sniffed back the tears and avoided Diane's eye. 'No, I was just making a call.'

'You're upset.' A statement, rather than a question, and put across in a protective way. Peta could imagine Diane going after the beige solicitor from Turner and Decon with her broom. The idea actually put a drop of balm on the hurt.

'I'm fine.'

'You didn't meet one of those black cars out on the road?'

'What black cars?'

Diane beckoned. Peta slowly followed inside and through to the back of the shop, where Diane had her computer booted up, showing a webpage. 'I found it.'

'What?'

'The company that bought Harry's place. See?'

Peta looked. There was a simple site with a masthead showing a grain field, with the name *Great Golden Ag*. 'So?'

Diane pointed towards the road. 'There's been some big companies sniffing round for months up here, wanting to buy land. I've seen the cars. Oh, they try to fit in, driving four-wheel drives, but they're too new and shiny. Most of them are hired, but some are from big overseas outfits.'

'How do you know that?'

Diane smiled. 'It's not important. The point is, all those companies are big, easy to find things out about, especially if they're on the share market. But the one that bought Harry's place is different. Something's not right about it.'

'Like what?'

'Hard to find any information. Looks like it used to be a big company, but it doesn't really operate anymore. That's strange, don't you think?'

'I don't really know,' Peta said, wrung out after the conversation with the lawyer. 'Maybe they're just starting up again?'

'Hmmm.' Diane's lips tugged. 'I haven't finished with it yet. Someone's got to check these things.'

Peta left her to it. 'I'll just head down to the river and stretch.'

'If you see Monty, tell him he's got to be back here before dark!'

Peta picked her way down to the weir, and sat staring at the tumbling water. There was no sign of Monty, and it was no good; she couldn't think sitting still.

So instead of going back to the room in the pub, Peta wandered down the riverbank before turning for the medical centre. She pushed in the door and stood in the foyer. The place had become familiar – her balance board was set up in the old plaster room. The bathroom was clean again, the equipment restored to function, and the cupboards ordered with what little stock had been left behind. Before she knew it, Peta was standing by the exam bed in the office. Its surface was soft enough for her weariness. She put her head down and slept.

Chapter 14

Peta woke late the next morning, still at the centre. She hadn't slept so dreamlessly in a long time, despite the chill in the air. Her necklace, too, seemed colder than usual, heavier than the silver it was, as if it had absorbed the weight of yesterday's phone call.

But today was Friday, the night of the dance, and Diane wanted her to drop by and discuss the ticket-selling. Before setting off, Peta remade the exam bed, and had just walked into reception with her single crutch when she saw a man-sized shape darkening the doorway. She felt a bolt of fear; one hand was pressed against the frosted glass, peering in. The fear dissolved when the voice that called out was vaguely familiar.

'Hello?'

Peta opened the door and to her surprise, found Wade Masters, sophisticated in a grey suit, a textured shirt and, fashionably, no tie. Despite his rugby player physique with burly shoulders, heavy jaw and a nose that had been broken long ago, the tailoring made him seem dapper and refined. Peta thought he would have looked at home in a trendy Melbourne bar. Then she saw the boots under the pant legs.

He gave her a very white smile. 'You're Peta Woodward, right? The doctor? I thought I might find you here.'

He extended a hand and, wondering if she was in trouble for having taken over the centre, Peta hesitantly took it.

'Wade Masters. I'm running for office in the next election for this district, and I wanted to thank you personally for all the work you've done for us the past two weeks. It was lucky you showed up when you did.'

'Well, lucky for everyone but me, I guess,' she said, offering her injured ankle as evidence.

'Of course!' He laughed. 'Easy to forget that you're not here by choice. So, Peta, do you think you'll be staying long?'

He used her name a little too eagerly, like a salesman, and his face had the hopeful expression of someone about to ask a favour. But Peta knew she was technically trespassing when it came to the medical centre. It wouldn't really do to be dismissive.

'Only until the foot's better,' she said. 'I saw your speech at the festival.'

'Oh, good, then you'll know what kind of challenges we have up here. Can I come in and talk with you?'

Peta pushed the door open and pulled a chair from the front desk, intending to offer it to him. But when she turned, he'd dragged another one over from beside the gurneys and sat, blocking the exit to the reception.

'Please, you take the comfortable chair,' he said, gesturing for her to sit. 'Right now, I'll cut straight to the chase. I'm developing the policy for my platform. Medical services can be really limited out here, as you can see. I'm wondering if I can steal some of your time to go through some issues.'

Peta made a face. 'I'd hate to disappoint you, Mr Masters—'

'Call me Wade, please.'

'—I've got very little experience in places like this. I work mostly in Melbourne.'

'That's better. I need someone with big city experience, too.' Wade rubbed his face. 'Look, I understand it's an imposition. I don't mean to come on strong, it's just your input would really help steer my direction.'

Peta hesitated. 'What do you want to know?'

'Well, let me set the scene a bit. You can see the state of the med centre here. The ambos and fire crews are all volunteers. People supply their own water out of the river. We're self-sufficient because we have to be, but everyone pays their taxes, and they do it hard in dry years, worse in fire years. All that and they can't expect decent facilities? I want to know how we could get a full-time doctor here.'

Peta chewed her lip, wondering if he could accept the truth, because she'd actually thought about it on her rehab walks.

'Honestly, a full-time doc would have trouble filling their time here,' she said. 'There are just not enough patients. It would probably kill a private practice. People would have to be willing to come in from other towns to make up the numbers. And from what I've heard, the roads in aren't always the best. The town's being bypassed for a reason. Maybe your problem isn't just a doctor.'

'See? This is what I'm talking about,' he said, grabbing a piece of paper and pen off the desk.

Peta rubbed her forehead, wondering if Wade would be the sort of person to care about the details. 'A practice needs a certain number of patients to be sustainable,' she went on. 'The insurance is expensive and you have to maintain all the equipment and stocks. If it's a publicly funded clinic, those things aren't such an issue, but it would be harder to make a case for it.'

Masters was scribbling notes. 'How many patients per doctor are we talking?'

Peta shrugged. 'I work in a tertiary hospital, usually. I don't know without looking it up. A one-doctor town I did a placement in years ago covered about fifteen-hundred people, but don't quote me on that.'

More scribbling. 'Don't suppose I could employ you as an advisor? Pay you to do some research for me?'

Peta almost said yes, because his charm tugged her like an undertow. But she'd never get back to the trail that way. 'I'm not staying much longer. I don't think it would be a good idea.'

'That's a shame. I'm sure I could make it worth your while.'

Peta wasn't sure what drove her to look up at that moment, but when she did, she saw another figure in the centre's doorway. This time it was Craig. And the look on his face . . . Peta read danger in those curiously still features.

Wade glanced over. 'Think about it,' he said quickly, buttoning his jacket as he stood. 'And I hope to see you tonight.'

Peta could have bounced a ball off the tension that had strung between the two men in that instant. Craig was so different to how he'd been with the horses, muscles rigid, eyes following Wade until he was out of sight. She wondered what was going on, even as Craig's presence sent an unexpected peal of nerves through her.

'What did he want?' Craig asked.

'Just to talk about health policy.' She grabbed her crutch and pushed herself up, trying to move her thoughts beyond the giddiness in her stomach. 'How can I help? The geese aren't on the warpath again?'

'I actually came to see if you were still going to the dance tonight.'

Such a simple sentence, but Peta couldn't remember what she had been about to say. Finally, she recovered, trying to be funny to disarm her nerves. 'Yes, but if you're not careful,

Diane will have you selling raffle tickets, too. I wasn't quick enough, what with the foot. Run while you can.'

A slow smile. It transformed the edges of him, gave him just enough softness to be inviting.

'Good advice,' he said. 'I'll dodge and see you there.'

Then he was gone, leaving a trail of anticipation behind.

If the night at Craig's class had been relaxed and gentle, the dance started out looking like someone had opened the box marked big and brash, and shaken out every last item. The Yarraman Hall blazed with rows of coloured lights. Every spare inch of real estate between there and the pub was covered in vehicles, and the music had been audible even through the concrete walls of the pub bathroom.

'I'm thinking it's safer out here,' Peta said to Gemma. 'My ankle's only just up to walking – don't want to get trodden on.' She was sitting with Gemma and Diane at the raffle table just outside the eastern door. They had a view of the hall and the lawn, and full access to the pockets of everyone entering.

'You might be right about that, actually,' Gemma admitted. 'Last year, someone broke their arm in a particularly violent dosido.'

'I think that was the year before,' Diane said, with a grin that said she was making it up. 'Last year, it was a fight outside.'

Peta cast an eye around the crowd, wondering who would be the first of them to require the meagre resources of the med centre. But the idea couldn't dent the expectant quality of the evening, as if fun might actually really be waiting at the small-town bush dance. The crowd was mostly polished, with women in jewelled jeans and shiny boots, men with impressive belt buckles and both with their best western hats. Some were already dancing, others spilling out the doors to talk in groups on the riverbank or between the cars. In deference to the occasion, Peta had pulled on her vintage Snowy River Festival t-shirt and her hiking pants, but now looking at the efforts everyone had gone to she realised a full skirt wouldn't have been out of place. Gemma herself was looking more sophisticated than usual in jet black jeans and a tailored white shirt, her fawn hair piled high above a pair of silver drop earrings.

Kids in smaller versions of their parents' outfits screamed around in packs, or were lofted on shoulders above the dance floor, or shuffled past with full attention on a loaded sausage in their small hands. Another group was being shown how to crack a whip out on the floodlit lawn, and the smell of barbecue and leather soaked everything. Peta spotted Wade Masters looking the part in gleaming cowboy boots, a crisp white shirt and bruised blue jeans. He worked the crowd inside, shaking hands and laughing.

Gemma had spotted him, too. 'Where's Craig?' she asked.

Peta didn't need to look because she knew exactly; she'd been surreptitiously watching him for half an hour. But she made a show of scanning around. 'Over there, behind the whip crackers. Talking to one of the horsemanship class students, I think.'

Gemma appeared to assess the distance between Craig and Wade. Next moment, she was off inside, leaving Peta and Diane to the ticket books. Before the dancing crowd wheeled and cut off her view, Peta saw Wade in Gemma's sights.

'Something interesting?' asked Diane, craning her neck to follow Peta's gaze.

'Just general mayhem,' Peta said quickly. 'Hoping I'm not going to end up with an eye injury in the clinic later.' She squinted across the lawn at a boy of about eight casting a whip around in a highly cavalier fashion.

'Is that why you keep looking over there? Don't worry, we only had three lost eyes last year. What are the odds of one tonight? Raffle ticket?' Diane finished, brandishing the book at the latest arrivals. 'All proceeds to the local school. Win the biggest meat tray in the highlands, or a free horsemanship consult with Craig Munroe.'

So Craig hadn't dodged hard enough.

Peta watched him across the gathering, his akubra tipped down as he listened to the student describing what was undoubtedly a problem horse. He was so still, a sculpture in clean jeans and a blue check shirt; then he would come alive as he spoke, his gestures firm and deliberate as he talked through the problem, as if he were riding the horse as he spoke. And every so often, he would turn and glance in her direction, and Peta would look away.

Then someone blocked her view.

'Dr Woodward, doing more for the community, I see?'

Wade Masters had appeared before her again, large and charming. With Diane making suggestive eyebrows towards the cash box, Peta pushed a ticket book forward. 'How many can I put you down for?' she asked, then whispered, 'Please buy some before Diane refuses me dinner.'

'Can't have that,' he said with a smile. 'I'll buy the whole book – if you'll come and dance. How about that?'

Peta laughed. 'Not sure it's a good idea with my ankle.'

'I'll take the utmost care of you, don't worry,' Wade assured her. He pulled out his wallet and pretended to inspect the contents.

'Yes, she will,' Diane chipped in. Then, when Peta gave her an exasperated look, said, 'You're the one who said you needed rehabilitating. Do you good. And Wade, if you want to buy two books, I'll dance with you, too.'

Wade roared with laughter. 'How can I turn that down?'

So Peta found herself being guided under her elbow towards the dance floor. Fortunately, the band had dispensed with the energetic numbers for the moment – Peta absolutely refused to do the Bus Stop, the Nutbush, 'Cotton-eye Joe' or anything else that involved too much twisting – and were starting up 'Rhinestone Cowboy'.

'Bit clichéd, isn't it?' she asked, as Wade took her up in a dance hold.

'We like to own the cliché a little,' he said. 'Besides, who cares when you dance with a beautiful woman?'

Peta felt a peal of discomfort, not least because dressed as she was in her t-shirt and hiking pants, his comment couldn't be genuine. 'Can hardly call this dancing,' she said, sticking out her foot, trying to deflect him and push some space between them.

'I also wanted to thank you for the information you gave me earlier. Have you had a chance to consider my offer?'

Wade had leaned in as the chorus swelled, which Peta knew wasn't necessary. His hand on her back was proprietary now. That was when she noticed Gemma, watching them from the side of the dance floor, her arms crossed, her face like a cat's bum.

Peta dropped her hands; this wasn't worth making Gemma jealous. Peta knew Wade's type – the kind of man who was comfortable being touchy-feely if he thought it would help him get his way. Gemma was probably too young to know that. All she would see was him getting close to another woman. Peta didn't know what was going on between them, but it was clearly something.

'I haven't,' she said quickly, trying to step away.

'Don't go yet,' Wade said, with a little squeeze. 'I'd like to ask you about a plan I have for the clinic.'

'Later,' she said.

Wade hovered. Perhaps being brushed off was a new experience, but Peta saw him gathering for a new appeal.

Then suddenly Craig had appeared beside her, his face as tight as Gemma's. 'I was coming to find you about that dance,' he said.

His hand slid into hers, his lead gentle but compelling. Peta read the silent request with the speed of intuition. *Come, and come now.*

'Cutting in, Munroe?' Wade said, his voice teasing. The band wound down with the final chords. A few beats of silence at the song's end filled with cheers, and the hostility between the two men.

Craig said nothing, but she could feel the heat of his anger burning through his skin as she limped after him to the exit. Just outside the door, she disengaged her hand. Even her attraction to him wasn't enough to excuse being man-handled. 'What was all that about? And what dance?'

He didn't seem to know what to say now.

'Come on, Craig. What's with you and Masters?'

He frowned. 'It's complicated.'

'So, what, you don't like him so I can't speak to him either?'

There was a different emotion in Craig's face now. He glanced back to the hall, as if making sure that Wade wasn't pursuing them. 'You can do what you want,' he said softly. 'But I don't like you talking to him.'

'Why not?' she asked softly as her stomach tingled with butterflies.

He looked into her eyes, and this time saw the desire in him, unmistakable. Her heart bumped against her breastbone and her breath held. For she also saw his uncertainty, and that she could equally start something, or stop him in this instant. The words tumbled from her. 'How about that dance?'

His smile was slow, accentuating the curve of his lips, his hand warm around hers. And when she thought he'd lead her back into the hall, he instead turned for the floodlit lawn, past the kids and their whip cracking, and down the gentle slope to the riverbank. The strains of a lively country number floated down across the darkness of the water.

'Thought you might like a slower pace with your ankle,' Craig said softly, as his arms came around her. Peta felt so safe with him, she rested her cheek on his chest.

'Mmmm,' he said. 'I can hum the music, if you like.'

'Are you any good?' she asked.

He chuckled. 'Tone deaf, I'm told. And I only know "Rhinestone Cowboy".'

She laughed. 'That's not true.'

'No, it's not, but I wanted to hear you laugh.'

Peta fingered the strong muscles in his back. 'Actually, my ankle's doing much better.'

'Good enough for a trip?'

She looked up at him. His lips were in her vision, and suddenly she very badly wanted him to kiss her. 'What kind?'

'To get your pack back from the trail. We can leave tomorrow morning, head up there nice and easy. Maybe stay up one night, if you wanted. I know you enjoy the hiking.'

'Camp out?'

'Yeah. Been a while since I did.'

Peta laughed. 'You don't think people will talk?'

'I don't know. Don't really care. Has time with Diane made you sensitive to talk?' Craig's eyes flared in a way that warmed Peta's cheeks, and she stumbled over a reply.

Then, as if he'd invoked the devil, torchlight struck Peta in the eyes and a voice came down from the rise.

'Who's there?' it accused.

'Craig and Peta, Diane,' Craig said, holding his hand up against the light. 'Want to stop blinding me?'

'Sorry.' Diane pointed the torch down at the grass. 'I thought you might be thieves. And that damn Monty isn't in the shop yard like he's supposed to be. Reckon he's off down the riverbank somewhere.'

Peta was trying not to laugh, but her shoulders were shaking, even when she could see the gleeful gossipy glint in Diane's eyes – finding her down here with Craig must have made the shopkeeper's night.

'Who's Monty?' Craig asked in confusion.

'The guard goose,' Peta said. 'He's very important.'

'Yes, he is!' Diane was indignant.

'Fine,' Craig said. 'Let me see Peta up the hill, and I'll come help look. I've got a good spotlight in the car.'

But as he took her elbow up the hill, he whispered, 'So what do you say about tomorrow?'

Peta could only squeeze his arm and tell him she would go.

Chapter 15

'Turned out he'd hunkered down in a nice little nook by the weir,' Craig said the next morning, stifling a yawn. 'Crafty bugger – he kept really quiet until I'd actually seen him. Whatever possessed her to buy geese?'

'She said they were good at guarding, and less work than a dog.'

'Not sure about that,' Craig muttered, as they turned out of the farm drive.

It had been dark when he'd picked her up, and mist was still hanging under the gums. The soft tinking calls of early morning birds fell down from above like glitter. The only other sound was the crunch of Buck and Candle's hooves, and even that silenced once they were led onto the grass.

Peta had spent the night anticipating riding with a mix of dread and excitement; she hadn't been on a horse since Stacey's accident, except when Craig had brought her down from the mountain. That had been a necessity, and she'd hardly been in her right mind. Now she wondered if it would bring thoughts of Stacey crashing down on her.

'How's the ankle doing?'

'Fine.'

In fact, the joint was aching but Peta was more concerned with keeping her breakfast down as she gazed at Buck's saddle. Leather, horse and tea-tree scented every breath. She didn't know if she could do this. Then Craig's hands came, warm on her arms. 'Give you a leg up?'

Her overthinking abruptly ended as he shifted his grip under her left knee, and easily boosted her up. Peta swung her right leg over with pure muscle memory. Buck stood solid beneath her, his sparse grey mane swapping sides halfway down his neck. He turned his head to regard her with one placid brown eye. Peta's churning stomach settled. She glanced back to the shed, where Bel and the foal stood at the rail, watching their departure. Clearly, everyone else was okay with this. It was normal. Natural. And slowly, as Craig led the way past the big house and turned onto the trail, soft with its leafy carpet and towering stringybarks, the old rhythm came back, the cadence of moving with a horse as intimate as love.

Peta relaxed, realising what going to collect her pack meant: one step closer to being back on track. Buoyed, she followed Candle uphill through undergrowth on the weaving forest path until the trees began to thin and Craig dropped Candle back to walk alongside her.

The daylight had tempered the tension of the night before, but the memory of it kept warmth in her cheeks as they rode without speaking into the cooling air. Craig seemed at ease with the silence, barely moving with Candle's steps, his face relaxed, akubra shedding the dew. Peta eventually found she needed to say something.

'Tell me about Wade,' she said.

Craig glanced in her direction, his eyes assessing. 'What is it you want to know?'

'Well, I get he's got the politician routine going on, but he doesn't seem that bad. Yet you obviously loathe him. Where did that come from?'

Craig looked away. Peta watched his shoulders move with the reins, and the golden glint of stubble along his cheek. For all the calm collection in the way he rode, as home as he looked on the mountain, this topic was clearly uncomfortable.

'I'm not going to tell anyone,' she added. 'Does it have to do with Bel?'

'What did you hear?'

Peta shrugged. 'Just that Bel used to be Wade's, and you won some big race on her. Was Wade pissed about it?'

Another pause, until Peta thought he wouldn't answer. They began riding past fire-blackened snow gums, the soft grass greens lustrous against the dark trunks. Peta counted them, reaching twenty before Craig finally spoke.

'I'd have to start at the beginning,' he said.

'Okay.'

Craig's hands rested on Candle's neck. 'Wade and I used to be friends. We met just after my family came to Yarraman. Two years later, we were riding the bus out to the high school every day. It was ninety minutes each way, so we knew each other pretty well. He was fun. We did a lot of riding together, exploring down the river, helping out on the properties.

'Wade's father was working on his business, so he was away more and more. Wade would come round pretty often. By the time school was nearing the end, we were both competing in the local rodeos and meets, cattle cutting, roping, and we were getting started on endurance.'

Craig paused, as if he didn't know quite how to phrase the next part. 'But I had this sense that Wade could be . . . mean.'

They reached a blockage, where one fire-damaged snow gum had crashed across the path, its trunk ripped nearly in two.

The conversation derailed as they moved in single file around the fallen timber, and never re-started.

Another five minutes and they broke from the edge of the bush, the undergrowth fading into scruffy ground cover, while the land opened up to show them a view across the high country. Even with haze across the horizon, Peta's heart soared at the lofty sense of space, and they weren't even at the top yet. She tipped back her head, closing her eyes, soaking in the silence. When she opened them again, Craig was watching her with a small smile.

'Yeah, good isn't it? Come on.'

For the next half-hour, they picked their way along the ridge, enjoying the view and the fresh air. The horses seemed electrified with the altitude; Buck carried his head higher, his ears pricked, pausing occasionally to snuffle at the ground.

'Scouting for wombats,' said Craig. 'See there?' He pointed to a flat rock, where a neat dropping sat on top. 'That's them marking territory.' He took the opportunity to stop for a break, and helped Peta down.

'I didn't know they did that,' she said, passing back his water canteen and examining the marker. Nearby was a fractured rock pile, the trail only a suggested indentation in the silver grass cover, at which Candle and Buck were twitching their noses. The view off the edge of the track stretched hundreds of metres to the blue-green sides of the neighbouring valleys.

'I don't recognise any of this trail. Are you sure we're going the right way?'

Craig affected a hurt expression. 'We're going a different way. The grade's easier, and there's less likely to be landslips. Besides, I'd doubt you remembered anything from when we came down.'

'Too busy trying to take over?' Peta asked wryly, as she found a flat rock to sit on, and stretched her leg out, massaging the ankle above her boot.

Craig actually laughed. 'Yes, that. But you did seem to be out of your mind. You said some pretty peculiar things.'

'I did not.'

Craig gave her a challenging stare. 'At one stage you asked me to pass you an artery clamp. Explain that one?'

'It's, um, an instrument for stopping bleeding,' she said quickly. Perhaps her memory wasn't that good. Peta put a hand over her face. 'Anything else?'

'A few times you insisted I take you back up to your pack, which was loopy, you have to admit. And then there was something about an escaped horse.'

'Oh, that one's true. I met some trekkers the day before. One of theirs came tearing down the path. See? Not crazy.'

'You also apologised to Stacey a few times. Who's that?'

Silence. Peta almost heard the clouds rushing overhead. Next, it was the breeze in the grass tips, then the soft click as she opened her mouth for a breath.

'That's my sister.'

'I figured,' Craig said slowly. 'And Emerald?'

Emerald. Peta found herself abruptly upright again, her fingers shaking as she reached for Buck's reins. He came eagerly, but his face was a blur before her. Peta smelled turned earth, felt the sting of splinters in her hand. She rubbed at the skin, but found nothing there.

'Peta?'

'I'm fine.'

She focused on moving air in and out of her lungs, then forced herself to register her surroundings. The fractured rocks in the pile nearby had red in their faces, and Buck's saddle leather was stamped with small triangles on the outer rim.

The mindfulness broke the train, and brought her back to the present. She hadn't relived that day in a while. She shook the remnants off like raindrops.

Craig had come up by her side. Gently, he reached out. Peta then saw her necklace had escaped again. He tucked it inside her collar without a word, the space between them pressurised with her obvious and unexplained pain. It demanded some relief.

So, when Craig pushed Peta up into the saddle again, she said, 'Emerald was my horse.' Their eyes locked for just the length of time it took Craig to sense all the guilt and sorrow in her tone, then she pushed Buck forward.

The disclosure had an unanticipated effect. Peta found not awkwardness, but understanding. They were on equal terms, both holding something back. And as they rode on, Peta found herself wondering ever more intently about what Craig wouldn't say about Wade, and if he was thinking the same about her.

They reached the Ridgeback trail just after lunchtime, the sun beaming down on the endless peaks receding to the horizons all around them. Peta began to recognise the terrain; she'd definitely walked this way. And there, finally, were the burnt-out remains of the hut, and her worn blue pack, stoically waiting.

She tumbled down from Buck, just managing to avoid twisting her ankle again as she fondled the familiar fabric, checking over all the pockets. Relief made her dizzy. All would be fine. Her ankle was nearly mended, and soon she'd bring this pack back up to the trail and continue on.

Craig spoke for the first time since the mention of Emerald. 'You said you'd met people trekking with horses, but the Ridgeback's not a horse trail.'

'No. I came this way to avoid them. I was going to join back up after I skirted round this ridge, down through the saddle somewhere.' She sat on a fallen beam and pulled out her map pack. The waterproof bag had done its work; everything was still dry.

Craig bent over the map with her. 'I see what you mean. You'll have to take care on this part, down near the creek. Gets really boggy with the rain, and it misses the hot winds, so it dries slowly. Plus the creek crossing there is pretty deep. And this doesn't look right.' He frowned, his finger tracing the trail she was planning to use to rejoin her original route. 'Yeah, if that's where I think it is, the track actually runs more north, then there's a steep section, really steep, after it crosses this creek. Difficult to walk up there. Even Candle treats it with some respect. With your ankle, might be better to go back the way you came, and pick up the original trail that way.'

Peta glanced at him. They were sitting close now, hip to hip, the map between them. His eyes were drawn down, his fingers light on the page. Something shifted. He turned his head, and Peta felt him stroke the backs of her fingers. Deliberately, he caught her hand, drawing it across so she had to face him.

Then he kissed her.

Blood rushed through her body, heated by his warmth and strength. A passion she'd kept so restrained broke free, their lips bruising together. She heard his hat fall to the ground, his arms lifting her until she sat across his thighs. He pressed her to him, his interest as much a shock as the depths of her desire to return it. They were primal beings, consumed in fresh air and earth, and a kiss. When they finally broke, Peta's cheeks were incandescent, her lips and cheeks roughed on his stubble, but every other pain had vanished.

He brushed a scrap of her hair away, his thumbs grazing her lips, gaze intense, as if he was sorry he had stopped. The map was crumpled between them.

'So, is there another way through?' she asked softly.

Craig's voice was gruff. 'Always is.'

'I thought I was just some crazy person from the city.'

'You are.'

She whacked him on the arm.

'Doesn't mean I don't want this.'

He kissed her again before he went back to the map, then again after she'd stowed it away in her pack. They spent the afternoon walking the trail in slow bounds, Buck and Candle following behind, while he talked about the mountains. Craig pointed out where trails rose up across the next valley, barely visible as scratches in the trees; told her about a disastrous creek crossing he'd made as a young man, chasing some wayward cattle, in which he'd lost both his saddle and his pants.

'Lesson is,' he finished, 'if you take it off, tie it down, because the water will take it all and you'll never find it again downriver. I know, I looked.'

Peta laughed until he stopped to kiss her again, standing at the highest point, the altitude dizzying her senses. The afternoon was delicious. She had never in her life enjoyed such companionship. Melbourne had been a continuous haze of work, in which she skimmed across the rest of her life. She had few friends, and none whom she would confide in. She tended to know people shallowly – as co-workers, exercise buddies at the gym or the running club. She was practised in meaningless small talk at conference functions, and hated it when seminar presenters brought out 'getting to know you' exercises. She'd dated men who preferred not to talk, telling herself it was all she had time for, but secretly knowing she hated having anyone close. Now, as if she had transformed in the mountains, she found herself quite uncharacteristically indulging Craig's interest, even liking it, and enjoyed finding things to make him laugh.

'I had a map blow off the side of the mountain once, down in Tassie,' she said. 'And in Milford Sound, my tent collapsed under the rain one night. I thought I was going to freeze to death.' Then she went on to how she'd forgotten half her food pack near Cooktown, and had to backtrack for half a day, finally finding it being demolished by zealous scrub turkeys.

'Wonder you ever make it back from these trips at all,' Craig said, teasing.

'At least I don't have any stories about losing my pants.'

'No, falling down an old wombat hole and busting your ankle is much better.'

Peta threw a rock at him, which he neatly ducked.

'On the upside, I guess it means you've already got the story for this trip.'

Then he pulled her towards him for another kiss.

Later, they made a camp in a sheltered lee of the ridge, leaning up against the saddles as Buck and Candle grazed nearby. The last of the enchanted afternoon slipped away with the sun, and then night settled over them with its cool veil. They ate bread and cheese and beef as the stars pricked the last of twilight.

Craig pulled Peta against him. 'Clear night. Going to be cold,' he said.

Peta felt the thrill of knowing she'd be close to him all night. After his kisses, she wanted to draw him closer. She felt his stubble catch her hair. Cocooned in the warmth of his affection, she needed him to trust her.

'You didn't finish the story earlier.'

'I know.'

'You said Wade could be mean.'

'I did.' Craig pressed his lips into Peta's hair. 'Okay, so Bel was Wade's horse, you know that already. He bought her for endurance – her mother was a highland horse, and her father's a champion stockhorse who won lots of prizes. Breeding's always a bit hit and miss but she was a hit from the start. She was only three when Wade was winning comps on her.'

Craig paused and glanced up at the sky, which was now deepening indigo, Venus alone shining above the mountains. 'It was love at first sight for me. I thought she was the most marvellous thing on earth – the way she moved, I was just lost. I'd sneak down to her yard if we were at a comp and just sit with her at night, and she'd be there blowing her breath into my hands. She was some kind of magic. My grandmother taught me most of what I know, and she would have loved Bel.'

'She sounds like quite a woman.'

Peta could hear the smile in Craig's voice. 'Oh, yeah. She'd say the way you ride the horse is deeper than what you want the horse to do. That the connection between you matters. And they can fill in those parts of you that other things can't. Bel was like that for me.'

Peta nodded slowly, though his words were bittersweet.

'But Wade didn't see her like that. Over time, she fell out of favour with him. He's not patient, and you have to be with horses. Bigger bit, bigger spurs, that was Wade's method. And she was never going to go well like that. She lost confidence, and that only made Wade mad. I thought I understood Wade, and I hoped he'd keep a lid on it.

'Then, one show, down on the flat, she had a stumble, and it lost Wade a win. He took it out on her. I found her boxed in the trailer with whip marks down her back, and I don't think it was the first time.'

Craig's hands had clenched into fists. Peta slipped her hand over one of them and he slowly released and blew out a long breath.

'I've only felt that kind of rage twice in my life, and it makes me sick to my guts. I can't be like that around the horses. But it got the better of me that time. I pulled Wade out of bed. He apologised profusely, said he hadn't meant to do it, and he knew it had been a bad call. I believed him, so I backed off. But once we were back in town, we were at the pub one night and he made a joke about her, really cruel. And I lost it.'

Craig's skin was blue in the last of the light, and he glanced at the ground as if embarrassed. Peta sensed he was leaving something out.

'What did you do?'

'Dragged him outside and knocked him senseless. Ash had to pull me off. God knows what would have happened if he hadn't. Spent an hour in the station cooling off. I was lucky not to get charged, really. I never told Mum. She'd have been horrified.'

Craig's jaw worked unhappily, and Peta could feel the regret in the air.

'What happened then?' Peta asked softly.

'He sold her. It took me a month to track her down, out west on someone's property, where she was already behaving badly. Wade ruined her. Once I had her back here, it took a long time to work out the problems.'

'You'd never think she'd gone through that now,' Peta said, thinking of how calm Bel seemed, how confident she was with her foal.

Craig's fingers stroked Peta's neck as he spoke. 'Warms me to see it, really does. And she's changed more since the filly was born. I think maybe she's accepted that my place is home, that she isn't going anywhere else.'

Peta nodded slowly. 'I get now why you don't like him.'

'I can't forgive him for doing that to her. I see him with a horse now ... or with anyone, really, and it sets off that feeling again. I wish I didn't have to deal with him, and now he's running for office, I worry about what that means for

everyone. Though Wade actually came up to the farm after
the last meeting, offering peace.'

'Yeah?'

'Mmmm. I don't think I was that good about it. Hard to
forget. We ask horses for a lot of trust ... what he did was
unforgivable.'

They sat in silence for a while, a light breeze bringing a chill
in off the mountain peaks as the sky became truly black. Peta
shivered, until Craig pulled his coat over both of them. Her
own problems seemed like the mist in the valleys, insubstantial
and far below. Finally, it was Craig who spoke.

'That night at the farm, you said your father had died, and
you were walking the trail to figure something out.'

Peta was momentarily brave. 'I'm the executor for his will.
The stud owed debts that need paying, and so it will have to
be sold. But the value isn't enough to meet the debt, unless I
sell it to a developer.'

'I'm guessing you don't want to do that?' Craig asked.

'I don't want to sell it at all.' That was the truth, and it
prompted more. 'My sister, she died when we were teenagers.
She was only a year younger than me, and we did everything
together, but she was the one that really sparkled.'

'Sparkled?'

Peta smiled, pointing at a few bright points that had now
joined Venus. 'Yes, like one of those stars. She caught attention,
people really noticed her. Before she died, there was an accident
and she was in a coma for a while. My parents thought that
she would wake up, because how could she not? But she didn't.
I think that made it worse. Mum never recovered. When she
passed away, too, Dad said she died of a broken heart.'

Peta had to pause through a wave of guilt, then she rushed
on. 'Dad was never the same either, and the stud went into
decline. After I left, I could never go back, but I still don't

want to sell the place that we last lived all together. So yeah, *solvitur ambulando.*'

'Come again?'

'It's Latin. It means "problems are solved by walking". That's what I do. If things get too much, I walk and I think. After a day at work, I used to walk an hour home instead of driving, and I'd go running on the weekend to de-stress. It's just how I am.'

Craig gave a low laugh. 'Lucky the ankle's improving then.'

'But I'm not sure there's a solution this time. I can't afford to pay the debtors if I don't sell, but that feels like cutting off my own arm.'

Craig's own arms were strong around her. He blew a breath out through his nose. 'What a thing to deal with,' he said. 'I'd feel the same, if I had to sell our place. And I understand the walking part. Just for me it would be riding, and you did pick the best part of the world for it.'

Peta let her head lean against his chest. For all the aches she carried, here she had simple comfort – mountains and sky, air and skin.

'It is amazing,' she said.

'Mmm,' he said, distracted, his fingers brushing along her jaw, his face close enough so that they could make each other out in the starlight. She wondered at the things she'd told him. He was so unlike any of the self-interested men she'd been with in Melbourne: physically strong, unhurried, and those qualities he put to best use now, holding her in his arms as he kissed her mouth, her throat, and found the buttons on her shirt. Peta had never been with anyone she'd felt close to like this, and her own fingers ventured over the smooth skin of his side, then across the curls on his chest, even while she wondered if this was a huge mistake.

'We only met three weeks ago,' she said, breathless against his mouth, his body pressed against her.

'Mmm,' he said, his attention unbroken. 'I know.'

'Do you think . . .'

He paused. 'I think I want you,' he said simply.

She offered no more objections. The part she hadn't mentioned was the truth about Stacey's accident. Her father had forgiven her, but Peta struggled to remove her mother's face from her mind. She'd never laughed again after Stacey had died.

Peta packed that part down tight inside her, and let Craig's warmth carry her through the night.

—

Craig woke with a sense of peace, just as the sun was sliding over the horizon. No haze marred the mountains this morning – the air was icy-clear but dry, the sky cloudless. He rested, enjoying the spreading blush of day and the sensation of being so alone. Just his two horses, and Peta still sleeping against his side.

It had been a long time since he'd woken up like this. Between the horses and the farm, he'd had little time for women. But Peta . . . well, he would like to know her better. Much better. There wasn't a lot of wisdom in pursuing someone who was leaving town again, but wisdom didn't seem to have much to do with it. All he could think about was riding trails with her, sleeping out under the stars like this again.

He kissed her forehead, watching her eyelids flutter, her hair all messed about her head. She opened her eyes, and registered where she was, smiled. And it warmed places inside him that had never been touched.

'Morning,' she said, then, 'Oh, wow.' The sun was an orb above the horizon, and everything was bathed in gold. The cool cleansed the air around them. All the tension Craig had sensed in Peta before the journey yesterday was gone. He took it as a very good sign.

They ate a quick breakfast of muesli bars and tea, and spent the morning making their way back down to the farm. Buck carried Peta's pack, and sometimes Craig walked while Peta rode Candle, and sometimes they doubled, and the synergy Craig felt with Candle seemed amplified with Peta before him. By the time they'd reached the farm, Craig had extracted a good many stories of Peta's time working in Melbourne hospitals, and was of the firm opinion being sick was best avoided.

'It does change your mindset,' she admitted. 'You start thinking the whole world is sick. Must be like being a cop and thinking everyone's up to no good.'

'Speaking of which, I'm just going to check in with Gemma, make sure everything was fine overnight,' Craig said, as they reached the house.

It took a bare minute to swing down from Candle and reach for the front door. Uncharacteristically, he found it locked. Maybe Gemma had taken security to heart.

He knocked. 'Gem?'

Silence. Craig dug for his keys and unlocked, calling down the hall as he walked in, not bothering to take off his boots. No one home. Gemma's bed was crisply made. Craig retreated.

'Not there?' Peta called from Buck's back as he re-emerged. The car was still under the awning.

'Seems like it. Must be down the shed.'

But Craig knew that was odd. Gem was routine as clockwork, and at this time of day, she would be at the big table in the kitchen, working on the latest orders. He helped Peta take her pack to the cottage and then went looking. Gem wasn't in the feed barn, or the big shed, and the quad bike was still there; she wouldn't have gone out of sight without it.

He'd just walked back up the hill and into the big house, thinking he'd check if she'd left a note, when he heard a diesel engine coming up the drive. Craig ducked into the lounge and, through the window, saw a familiar white four-wheel drive pulling in.

His skin prickled on instinct. As he went out the front door, he realised why. With the car facing the house, Craig had an excellent view of Gemma in the passenger seat, leaning across to kiss Wade goodbye.

Craig supposed later that his shock must have propagated all the way across the space between them, because Gemma looked out and saw him standing there. He saw her mouth wordlessly form *shit* before she pushed the door open. Wade, bloody Wade, waved gaily as he turned the car around, heading out before Craig could do anything about it. Gemma slunk towards the house.

'What the fuck are you doing?'

'Hello to you, too,' Gemma said. She crossed her arms. Her hair was uncharacteristically uneven in its ponytail, her lips pursed together, her eyes darting away.

'Well?' Craig could hear the danger in his voice, the white-hot energy burning in the centre of his chest.

'I don't have to say anything. I'm an adult and entitled to my privacy.'

And with that, she swept past him and into the house. Craig followed and with immense difficulty, forced himself to be calm. Gemma had buried herself in the hall cupboard and was busy pulling out her jewellery supplies. Her face was hidden behind the door.

'Don't blow me off, Gemma. He's ten years older than you, and an arsehole. What the hell are you thinking?'

A tub of silver clasps hit the table, followed by a card of horsehair, graded by colour from pale flaxen to deep black.

Craig tried again. 'He's a bad guy.'

'Good!' she yelled, closing the cupboard. 'You know what, Craig, I'm sick of sneaking around just because you don't like him. I'm not a stupid kid. I know what I'm doing, all right?'

Craig loved Gem with all his soul, but his memories of her as a toddler, trailing after him in the feed shed and the tack room, demanding to be put up on his grandmother's horse, were all still fresh. He realised he frequently thought of her as still a child, not the grown woman she was, who had the right to her own choices. He couldn't stand back and say nothing about her pursuing a relationship with a cruel man like Wade, but he also knew he'd make no gains through being hot about it.

He put up a hand. 'I'm sorry I swore at you. But you don't know him, Gem.'

'Maybe I know him better than you do. You haven't seen him in four years, Craig. Four. Years. So what are you going to do about it?'

'Get the shotgun out and tell him he's got the count of three to piss off.'

Gemma abruptly laughed, then covered her mouth with her hand. 'It's not funny.'

'You're telling me.'

'You wouldn't do that.'

Craig didn't want to scare her, and he knew she could be right – maybe Wade had changed. He could hope. 'I don't like it, Gem. I'd like you to stay away from him.'

She folded her arms again. 'It's none of your business.'

The house phone rang. Craig ignored it, searching for some sign that she might be listening to him. But Gemma took his silence as a victory.

'If you're done interfering, I'd like to answer that.'

As his boots carried him down the hill to the feed shed, Craig's insides were a tangle. He'd known about Gemma's crush, but never imagined it could really develop. Gemma was right; he couldn't make her do anything. He had an urgent need to find Peta, to pull her against him, to tell her everything that worried him.

He heard steps behind him, and for a brief moment, he thought Gemma was coming to apologise. To tell him she'd made a mistake. But when he turned, no one was there.

Craig shook his head. Clearly, wishing it wasn't enough.

Chapter 16

Peta spent the rest of the afternoon going through her pack. Craig had been quiet when he'd driven her back to the pub. He'd only provided the barest details and apologised, saying that he needed a day to cool down. Peta was more than happy to give it to him; she daren't mention that she'd known about Gemma and Wade, and she bet the atmosphere at the farm would be awkward for a while.

With no space in the pub, she took the pack to the med centre, sweating under the load during the short, careful walk. She really was out of shape. With her ankle so good now, she needed to step up retraining. So before full dark, with her sleeping bag, tent, cooking tin, canteens, maps, dried food, wet gear and dry bags spread out in the old plaster room, she went out for a session.

For the first time, she decided not to take a crutch, and to go along the river path, behind the pub and up past the weir. Oh, how liberating not to hear the constant click of the metal with each step. She covered the distance to the path's end in record time, raising a sweat, even as the sun was already making the surrounding hills into silhouettes. Looking up into the blushing sky, Peta thought of Craig. The last two days weren't something she'd gone looking for, and she was trying to rationalise what would happen now. Would they write when she was back in Melbourne? Or would it just peter out when she left, a nice memory to take with her and nothing more? The idea sat like a bad meal, but she brushed the queasy feeling aside; it would be another thing she could solve as she finished the trek. At least her confidence to do that was back.

As she turned for home, the weir misted cool drops across her burning cheeks. She trailed a hand around a wet trunk at the bend in the river, her fingers coming away slick with something brown and green and sweet smelling. She rubbed it between her fingers. Everything seemed coated in magic these last two days; a mountain essence that was fresh and cleansing. With no one around, Peta dragged a finger down her nose like war paint, then she touched her fingers lightly to her chest, feeling the necklace against her skin. She could feel the answers waiting, just out ahead of her footsteps. All she had to do was walk for long enough, and she would catch them up.

She almost went straight to the pub; even the prospect of a shower in the body-origami-inducing pub bathroom was no longer daunting. But then she wondered . . . had she locked the med centre door? She couldn't remember.

She stopped, chewing her lip. Probably, she had. But if she hadn't . . . the equipment in there was worth good money, not to mention her pack. She remembered the graffiti. She couldn't risk it.

So she turned the corner into the street, pushing on to see how much her ankle could really take. When she pulled up in front of the centre, she had a stitch, but a massive grin on her face. Her foot was really good. The balance work had paid off. And testing the door, she had locked up. Of course she had.

She stood on the footpath, fanning her face. A white four-wheel drive had parked on the kerb. Peta walked around it to peer at Karen's wall in the fading light. The bins had been moved, and the graffiti was gone. Peta strode up the path. She'd just call in to say hello, ask after Ned.

Then she heard raised voices.

'. . . out of my house—' This was Karen, her voice trembling.

'I'm not leaving until you agree.' A man, who Peta heard clearly now she was standing outside the door. She shouldn't pry, but the fear in Karen's voice kept Peta rooted.

'You must think I'm an idiot. You got more than you deserved, you agreed and here you still are. So piss off and go.'

Karen's reply was too soft to hear this time. What the hell was going on?

'I don't care if the whole department's here. We had a deal. And if you don't stick by it, there's bad things coming to you. Hear me?'

Hastily, Peta pushed the doorbell. A deathly silence followed the chime. Then Karen called out, her voice unnaturally high. 'Who is it?'

'Peta. You all right, Karen?'

'Fine. Just not a good time. Can you come back tomorrow?'

Less convincing words had never been spoken. Peta only hesitated a second before she tried the door, and found it open. She pushed inside and met Karen hastily coming into the hall, her eyes pinched, the pale skin of her neck all blotchy. 'Sorry, Peta, not now, okay?'

'What's going on?'

'Nothing.'

But it was a weak protest, because Peta had already seen into the kitchen, where Wade Masters stood with his meaty hands on the back of a chair.

'Dr Woodward,' he tried, 'nice to see you again. I'd appreciate it if you could give us a minute.'

But Peta's internal gears had shifted. She was back in the emergency room in Melbourne, at two am on a Saturday, her antennae finely tuned for violence, whether physical or verbal. 'No, I don't think I will. I heard Karen ask you to leave.'

Wade didn't budge. 'This doesn't concern you, and you've interrupted a private conversation.'

'Well, I'm here to check on Ned, so I'd say it does concern me. I'm sure as a prospective politician, you can respect a pre-existing appointment, especially a medical one. So you'll need to come back another time yourself.'

Peta watched the blood move in Wade's hands as he squeezed the chair, then he released it and straightened up. She could feel how wide her own eyes were, how her heart was thumping against her ribs. He was a big guy, and right now he exuded some invisible signal that said *danger.*

He prowled into the hall, leaning into Peta's personal space with a smile that was cold and burred. 'Nice to see you again, Dr Woodward.' As he brushed past her, Peta could smell sweat under some kind of expensive cologne.

He leaned in and kissed Karen goodbye on the cheek, but Peta saw him squeeze her wrist at the same time, how she closed her eyes in an effort not to recoil.

They both waited, Karen with her lower lip held in her teeth, until they heard the sound of a diesel engine turning over, and the car on the kerb pulled away.

'Karen?'

'It's nothing,' she said weakly, rubbing her wrist. 'Would you like to wash your face? Bathroom's down the hall.'

Peta glanced at herself in the hall mirror; she still had tree mud down her nose. Her hair was wild from the exercise. Wade Masters must have thought she was insane. *Good.*

'Sorry. I was out walking,' she said, batting at her nose with her hand.

Karen gave her a crooked smile. 'I'll make some tea.'

Peta let Karen put the kettle on and fumble for some mugs before she put a gentle hand on the young mother's shoulder. One of the things Peta had seen too often working in emergency was women struggling with the men in their lives. Peta remembered one in particular, a mother of only twenty who'd brought her one-year-old daughter in, supposedly with vomiting. But after the child seemed to have nothing more than a bad cold, and no further sign of the vomits, Peta had spotted the old bruises on the woman's wrists under her long sleeves. She'd been able to help that time.

'I heard a fair bit from outside,' she said now. 'I'm not very politically minded, but I'm sure he wasn't here looking for votes. Sounded like he was threatening you. What's going on?'

Karen's body sagged, and she pressed her body into the corner of the bench, her voice a whisper. 'I can't tell you.'

'You're safe with me,' Peta said. 'I'll respect whatever you want to say. Maybe I can help.'

Karen gave a short laugh. 'No, you can't.' A sigh. 'Listen, could you go down the hall and look in on Ned? We went for a big walk at lunch and he missed his usual nap and conked out. My legs are a bit shaky.'

So Peta went, and found Ned curled into the corner of his bed, a stuffed cow clutched to his chest, tiny snores evidence of an ability to sleep through a thunderstorm. When she came back to the kitchen Karen had sat at the table with the two mugs and a resigned look on her face.

'You've been in town a while now, right?' she asked, turning a coaster in her fingertips.

'Four weeks nearly.'

'And you're acquainted with Diane?'

'Of course,' Peta said, confused as she sank into a chair opposite.

'Right. So by now you must have heard the rumour that Craig is Ned's father.'

The bottom fell from Peta's stomach. She wasn't sure she wanted to know.

Karen sighed. 'I certainly wish he *was* Ned's dad.'

'You mean he's not?'

'No.'

'Then who— Oh, it's Wade.' Peta knew it with such certainty that she didn't need Karen to nod. 'That's tough. And things have gone sour between you?'

Karen laughed. 'They were never that sweet. I can't claim good judgement.'

'You know you could take out an AVO or something. You don't need to put up with him acting like that.'

'No, I can't.'

'I know it's difficult—'

'No, not because it's difficult. I can't.' Karen glanced away. 'If I tell you this, you have to promise not to tell anyone. I shouldn't even have told you about Wade.'

Peta shut her mouth and waited.

'When I found out I was having Ned, he paid me a stack of money to disappear.'

'What do you mean, "disappear"?'

'He said he didn't care where I went, but Perth might be good. Just as long as it was far away from the district. An abortion clinic would have been even better. See, he was off to Melbourne to build his business connections and with this plan to go into politics. He was never going to marry me – not that I wanted to be with him anyway, after he was always so secretive about seeing me – and who wants an illegitimate kid in the closet when you're going to parliament?'

'What a slimy bastard,' Peta said. Her voice choked with indignation. 'But you didn't go?'

'No way. This is my home, and all the work I love is here, whatever people think of me. I want Ned to grow up by the Yarraman River and love the high country like I do. So I kept enough to pay for Ned's schooling and care and all that, and I put the rest in trust for him. I was all shaky brave back then. I hoped Wade would just cool off; he was away for a few years. Ha, who was I kidding?'

'So now he's back and you're not gone, he's been putting the pressure on?'

Karen took a slug of tea and made a face. 'He doesn't trust me not to say anything, especially now he's a nominee.' Her voice became very quiet. 'He scares me, Peta. More than he did back then. I've seen him lose his temper with his horses. I honestly don't know what he'll do.'

She stared out the window, where the light was the golden glow of late afternoon, a ridiculously lovely counterpoint to the grim atmosphere in the kitchen. Peta's mind was racing. If she'd been in Melbourne there were services she could have recommended, places Karen could have gone to be safe. But here, there was only one thing she could think of.

'What about telling Ash?'

Karen put a hand out to stop Peta. 'No. It'll only make things worse.'

'But if he's going to—'

'I didn't tell you everything.' Now Karen looked embarrassed. 'To get the money, Wade made me sign a non-disclosure agreement. I'm not supposed to tell anyone he gave me money, or that he's Ned's father. I should *not* have said anything, and you must promise me that you'll keep it to yourself. If I break the agreement, he'll come after me, and if it ruins his political career he'll do it savagely. He operates like the mob.'

Peta pressed her lips together. 'This is a really bad idea, Karen. If he's making threats . . .'

'No. If I keep quiet, if he learns he can trust me not to say anything, then I have a chance of staying. Promise me.'

In the end, Peta did, feeling helpless. 'Look, I'll leave if you won't open the door again for him, and if he does come back that you'll call Ash straight away. Deal?'

'Okay.'

'And I'm going to check on you tomorrow morning.'

Peta left reluctantly, the sun having just tucked itself under the horizon, and wandered towards the pub, circling the idea of telling Craig about Wade and Karen. She couldn't go back and sit in her room. Finally, she went as quickly as she dared to the store and asked Diane for Craig's cottage number. Evading the storekeeper's pointedly raised eyebrows, Peta had him on the phone in less than two minutes.

'Hi,' she said, suddenly bashful at hearing the depth of his voice on the phone. 'Can you possibly come down and pick me up? I've just been at Karen's and there's something I need to talk to you about.'

He arrived in fifteen minutes, the sides of the car coated in dust, but it was long enough for Peta to have second thoughts. Karen had asked her not to say anything. Emphatically. Peta was not so blinded by righteousness to realise that she might not understand what Karen was dealing with. Besides, Gemma was the one she really wanted to talk to, and things between Craig and his sister were strained at the moment. So Peta opened the car door expecting to have to back out of a conversation.

It didn't become necessary, because they barely said a word the whole way back to the farm. So much so that by the time they pulled up near the cottage, Peta's heart was thumping in her chest for an entirely different reason. It was as though they were perfect strangers. Craig didn't even attempt to touch her.

'Is something wrong?' she asked as he avoided looking at her, killing the engine. She hated the little tremble that crept into her voice.

He shook his head, his voice gruff. 'Come on.'

She tipped herself out of the car onto her good foot, and followed him to the cottage. The atmosphere between them only charged further as she stepped across the threshold. The cottage was a single large space with a kitchen on her left, a bathroom partitioned off beyond it, a wood stove ringed by a sofa and a cowhide rug on the far wall, facing a bed that pulled down from the wall.

Peta had been inside before, but only to wait. She rubbed her arms and they ended up staring at each other, stiff and unfamiliar, as if the night on the ridge had never happened. Finally Craig said, 'This is stupid. We need to talk about things. I have no idea where to start.'

'Me either,' Peta admitted. The bed loomed as though it was the only furniture in the room. Peta looked around for a safer space.

In the end, they sat on the steps in the cottage doorway. They tried holding hands, but Peta couldn't find the ease in his touch that she had on the night away. Craig was all restless energy, his gaze sliding away from hers.

'I'm off today, the horses know it,' he admitted. 'I gave up working with the young ones. I can't focus.' He blew a breath out.

'Is it me?'

'I don't know what it is,' he said, and Peta couldn't help feeling hurt. 'Gemma and Wade ... that was a real shock yesterday.'

'Was this all too fast?' she asked.

'Maybe. I don't know.' A long pause. 'When you finish your journey, are you coming back here?'

Pressure squeezed Peta, like a giant weight on her sternum. 'I don't know,' she hedged. She hadn't thought about it.

'Maybe there's nothing to talk about then,' he said, and Peta then felt the desperation that the night on the ridge would never happen again.

The only consolation was that the great tide of their attraction was still lurking beyond all the awkwardness. It was just that neither of them seemed to be able to bridge it. He was right – it was ridiculous. They were adults. But both of them had said things that were deeply personal, that perhaps they hadn't been ready for. Besides, she wanted to finish the trail and he was adding a complication she hadn't bargained for.

Peta was trying to form these ideas into sentences when she heard the crunch of tyres up the hill. A second later, Ash's police four-wheel drive came rolling in fast. He spun the wheel to come parallel, hanging out the driver's window.

Peta's mouth had parched, thinking Ash was about to say that something bad had happened to Karen, and why the hell hadn't Peta stayed with her? But instead, the cop's strained voice was for Craig.

'There's a situation on the road. Need your help, mate. Erica's already heading there.'

Craig was on his feet. The men seemed to share an understanding, because without a word, Craig strode down into the feed shed, his footsteps hollow on the floor. When he came back, he had a rifle slung under his arm. 'Stay here until I get back?'

All Peta could do was nod as he swung into the passenger seat, and the car was gone, but for a dull roar receding through the trees. The moment was a lens of perfect clarity, reminding her who she was, and where. She was temporarily marooned in this small mountain town. Craig was the big man about the place, who understood the issues everyone here faced. As Karen did, as Diane did. She didn't fit amongst them.

And yet, some kernel of belonging had set tendril roots down here, ones that would hurt to pull out. She soon had the cottage phone in her hand.

'Yes, really, I'm fine,' Karen said a moment later. 'In fact, Diane's just turned up wanting to know if she could read Ned a story, and with some Agatha Christie movie she wants me to watch. This has to be the weirdest evening for a while.'

'Well, I'm glad you're not alone,' Peta said.

After she put down the phone, the words seemed to haunt her. The cottage was silent and empty. The lights were off in the big house up the hill.

So Peta slipped inside the feed shed. Bel pricked her ears, the filly asleep at her feet. Peta rubbed her arms, her emotions naked under that calm brown gaze. She was scared, and lonely, and achingly sad, and underneath it all . . . lost. She closed her hands on the wooden rail, fighting these feelings back down where they belonged.

Bel stretched out her nose, breaths soft gushes of warm air. The velvety muzzle sought Peta's cheek, a gentle touch that eased the struggle. Momentarily, she was brave and soothed and found, as if time had evaporated and the bad things had never happened. And in that instant, she understood what Bel was to Craig.

Chapter 17

Ash drove with grim intensity. The twisting road was quiet on a Monday evening, the deep greens of the forest either side blending into the long shadows of the valley.

'Driver called it in maybe half an hour ago,' Ash was saying. 'Apparently the horse was on the road as he came round a bend. He swerved but couldn't miss it, then ran the car into the cutting, so it's cactus. Guy walked out. Ambos were up there within fifteen to cart him off anyway, and they called Erica. Apparently the horse is still there.'

Craig rubbed his fingers over his forehead. This was the kind of thing he dreaded. The wild horses were a symbol of the high country, though not without controversy. They wore trails and damaged vegetation, affected the water coming down the rivers. He acknowledged all that. Their numbers needed managing, and the voices of argument were always loudest when that had to be done.

But they were also vulnerable. A hard winter could leave them half-starved by the time spring came, and nothing undid Craig more than seeing a wild horse with sunken ribs and bony hindquarters. And they were attracted to the roads, for the salt spread in the winter. It wasn't the first time this had happened.

He saw Erica's car first, a grey Landcruiser pulled far onto the shoulder, the vet herself leaning on the bonnet with her arms folded. Beyond, a passenger car was crumpled into the low cutting off the road shoulder. A slew of black rubber marked the pavement.

Ash swung in behind Erica. 'I'm going to set a roadblock, then I'll come back.'

That left Craig to follow Erica's gaze. He leaned in beside her. 'Where are we looking?'

'There,' she said, pointing off into the trees on the other side of the road. 'A grey, in front of the tree with the fork.'

She handed him a pair of binoculars. Craig squinted into the shadows, trying to make the horse out. He lifted the binoculars and focused.

The horse was standing, motionless but for the heaving breaths, its head lowered. Craig's eyes assessed almost as quickly as Erica, his stomach sinking even as he spoke. 'Not that old,' he said, 'but in bad condition.'

'Yes,' agreed Erica. 'Been on a poor pasture, probably. Or maybe there's a conformation problem, who knows? You see how he's leaning on the tree?'

Craig looked again. The animal did seem to be leaning against the tree, its near forefoot tipped onto the toe. 'Using it for support?'

'I'd say so. He's managed to move a long way into the scrub, but it was probably in the shock after the impact. From what I've seen in the last minutes, his shoulder's shattered. Maybe the leg, too.'

Erica rubbed at her mouth, her voice catching. Craig felt the dreadful certainty of what was about to happen as Ash came back from the roadblock.

Craig tried to be detached, but he couldn't help imagining what this would be like if that were Candle or Buck out there;

every horse was different, but that desire to connect and do good by them was something he always felt. 'What about a tranq?'

'If we dart him, he'll probably run, which will be agony. That's just cruel,' she said. 'I'd love to be able to put a nice line in his neck and dose him to the eyeballs with morphine. But I can't do that unless you think you can get close without him moving.'

'Not a chance,' Craig said. He knew his limits, they were losing the light and he couldn't bear watching the animal suffer. The way it held itself proudly upright, dismayed by what had happened, yet there was nothing anyone could do. The despair of that broke him, like a piece of his chest was being torn away with no relief.

Ash had Craig's rifle in his hands. Craig reached for it, and steadied his elbow against the bonnet. The horse was a ghostly outline in the sights.

'Both of you, step back please,' he said.

He needed absolute focus. He wouldn't have two shots; he could do that much. He willed the horse to stay where it was, to rest just a moment longer while he drew his breath, lined up. Hands steady. One last breath.

Sorry, he whispered.

Then a crack.

❧

Peta heard Craig's car come back to the farm an hour after full dark. Heard his boots on the path. But he didn't come into the cottage. Instead, she saw the single yellow square of the tack room window.

After an hour, Peta pulled the blanket from the couch around her shoulders and silently moved down the path in her socks. The moon was stark, the air loaded. Something had happened.

She paused at the door to the feed shed, and through the opening she could see all the way into Bel's stall. Craig sat with his back against the wall, legs across the straw, cradling Bel's face as she lay alongside him, the foal curled by her flanks. Her nose pressed into his chest, and his hands stroked her neck. Peta could see Craig's lips moving, wear and anguish written in his face.

Bel gently butted him in the stomach, and a smile crossed his lips, before the gloom returned. Bel was undeterred, her nose moving north again to breathe on his face and neck, and twitch her whiskers across his shirt.

Peta knew she was intruding on a private moment. She was again the outsider, who knew so little about him. She reminded herself she was here only by an accident of circumstance. However sweet the momentary thoughts were that they could have something together, she knew she was imagining someone else's life. Someone who hadn't made her mistakes. Just when she had resolved to leave, Craig looked up over Bel's head and found her standing there.

Peta's chest crumpled, imagining how he must feel being watched. Apologies were on her tongue, but he just held her eye for the longest time before he beckoned.

On halting feet, Peta crept inside, her heart thumping until she reached the open rail into Bel's stall. The mare watched her with one liquid brown eye.

'I don't want to disturb you,' she whispered.

Craig patted the straw beside him.

So Peta crept into the stall and slid down beside him. Craig's arm came around her and he rested his cheek against her hair. Easy and simple, the way it had been up on the trail. Bel stretched her nose across to nudge at Peta's side, and Peta stroked the velvet nose, the comfort of the mare's and Craig's touch soothing her heart.

'What happened with Ash?' she asked, voice soft as the straw. 'Was something else stolen?'

'No.' Craig blew out a long breath. 'There was a horse hit up on the road. A wild horse. Badly injured.'

Peta had heard those words before, once, such a long time ago. She swallowed. 'How badly?'

'We didn't want him to run and Erica couldn't get close enough to put a line in.'

Peta could almost picture it, knew what had happened. She'd seen horses put down on her parents' stud, old friends who became too ill. The vets had always made it easy and calm, and she'd still been a mess afterwards. That was why Emerald hadn't been put down. Not when he was still so young and vibrant.

She squeezed Craig's hand. 'That's why you took the rifle?'

He lifted his empty hand, as if he wanted to erase what he'd had to do. 'Other people when they hold a gun on a target, they tremble, but I don't. I wonder if that means I don't care.'

Peta stroked Bel's nose, thinking of how she'd thought he was stubbornly interfering when she'd first met him. 'Maybe you're just sure of what you're doing.'

Craig grunted and turning his head, tipped her chin up towards him. His eyes traced her lips and cheeks. Peta saw an intensity of emotion in his face that hadn't been there before. So when he kissed her, full of soul and seeking, she melted against him and nothing else mattered.

When they broke away, Peta caught the foal watching them from over Bel's back, his tiny ears pricked.

Craig's voice was hot in her ear. 'Come to bed?'

Peta didn't have to think about it, only stand and follow him, both her ankles suddenly weak. His hand was warm against her back as he brushed the straw from her clothes. The walk to his door vanished in seconds, and then Peta was inside his embrace, his hands removing her clothes and her doubts.

Peta got as far as undoing his buttons, breathing in the lingering scent of soap on his skin, before in one move he scooped her up and carried her towards the bed. She shrieked in surprise.

'Shhh, you'll scare the horses,' he murmured.

Peta giggled, but then found her hands trembling as she undid his belt, sliding her hands down the length of his legs. He was built like no man she'd ever been with – all muscle and strength, and a will to please her above all else. With other men, she'd always been aware they were disappointed in her body, which was thin, almost bony. But Craig never made her feel anything but desirable. As he laid her on the sheets, loving her with his hands and lips, she thought how unlikely it was that they had ever met, and yet, how much he had changed her. She could not imagine being without him, now.

He had woken some part of her that had been buried underneath the front she played to everyone else. It mattered to her that he knew her, that he wanted to know her. As his cheeks pleasantly roughed the skin across her belly, she tangled her hands in his hair, and there was nothing but the two of them and the night through the window.

It was long past midnight when Peta finally lay quiet, Craig's hand moving lazily over her side, still raising goosebumps on her skin.

'You should come with a warning label,' she told him.

'Mmmm. Why's that?'

'Magic hands. I might be persuaded to anything.'

He chuckled. All the tension had left them. In fact, she reflected, it was far more than his hands. He was the most amazing man she had ever met. Peta let her fingers play with the soft hair behind his ear, then trace the stubble down his jaw. His body was all sensations: rough calluses and soft skin, firm and giving, warmth and cool. He caught her hand and tucked her against him.

'Come with us to the Bright show next week,' he said. 'It's a couple of hours' drive. I'm giving a demo there.'

'Sounds good,' Peta said happily. Another week should be fine. It wouldn't hurt to give her ankle extra time.

'And then maybe I could persuade you to come to Yarraman for an extended break.'

Peta turned. His eyes were dark in the soft light of the fire. 'What do you mean?'

'The town could really use your skills. You said you'd taken a long leave from Melbourne and it didn't sound like you were particularly happy there. Why don't you stay?'

Peta silently tried to imagine it. She could see, perhaps, another short stint here ... a working holiday maybe. But she suspected Craig meant something else entirely, and the truth was that she'd always imagined she would go back to Melbourne – once she finished the trek and everything was sorted out.

'What about you coming south?' she said. 'I mean, when you travel with your classes.'

Craig made a sound in his throat. 'I don't know if that's going to happen. This Bright thing's a one-off.'

'Oh.' That avenue of possibility withered, and the dreamy quality of the evening began to lose its soft edges. Thinking about practicalities was less sexy than throwing caution out the window. 'Well, you never know.'

'Could you imagine basing yourself here? You've done such a great job with the clinic.'

'Aren't we getting a bit ahead of ourselves? I still have things to sort out.' But his hands were moving on her skin again, and ripples of pleasure ran across her back, making her think impossible things just might not be.

'I know you still have the executor thing to see through,' he admitted.

'Mmmm,' she said, screwing her eyes shut, as if she was a little girl again, scared of the night beyond the light Craig had brought into her life. She burrowed into his chest. 'Can we leave reality alone right now?'

He chuckled, turning her in his arms with the unspoken agreement it was time to sleep, and softly kissed her neck. 'I could do this every night,' he said.

So Peta slept, comforted by his voice and touch, allowing herself to believe for the moment that he was the only thing she needed.

—

Craig lay awake for more than an hour, listening to Peta's breaths quieten as the night came alive outside. Normally, after a day like this, he'd have trouble sleeping but that wasn't the reason for his wakefulness now. The cause was far more pleasant.

He brushed a strand of straw from Peta's pillow and smiled to himself. For all the proverbial rolling in the hay he might have done in his life, he'd never found a woman like her. Physically, they clicked, no doubt about that. But he also confided in her, and found himself opening up in a way he didn't with other people, not even Gem. She seemed to understand him, and Bel was easy around her, which he took to be a sign.

Craig lifted his eyes to the open window, where the moon had now moved into view. The light that had been so stark earlier now had a tender quality. Peta had done that for him, too. Tasks that he had been dreading, like promoting himself for these classes, seemed palatable in her presence. Craig was surprised; he hadn't known her very long, and his experience had been to discover less to like about someone as time went on. Maybe the fact she hadn't impressed him at first had allowed him to appreciate her more. Regardless of the reason, he didn't question it. But he hoped for more, and he hoped that she did, too.

Chapter 18

Peta never went back to the pub. A week later, her pack had been collected from the clinic and brought up to the farm, and she spent every night in Craig's bed. During the day she occupied herself watching him training or feeding the horses, and she herself walked in radial directions off the farm, recovering her strength and endurance. On one occasion, she took an overgrown four-wheel-drive track off the top paddock, and after a long trek downhill, emerged under the familiar highwall of the old mine, just where she'd turned back the first time she'd seen it. So the path led back to the Munroe farm. It seemed right.

In these days, the world was quieter and full of slow promise, reflecting the state of her heart. Her ankle was almost normal again, with only stiffness after sleep, which was improving as Craig gently massaged it in the mornings before he got up.

'You don't have to do that,' she would say, still nestled in the warm sheets. And he would smile and keep working his thumbs.

'I thought you liked it,' he said, letting his fingers stroke up her calf and past her knee. And Peta would protest that she did, and then that led to kissing and touching, and both of them being late out of bed down to the feed shed, where all the horses gave them maligned looks at being made to wait for breakfast.

She hadn't realised how much work went on at the farm – the fences that needed checking, vaccinations for the herd, moving them from pasture to pasture; chickens that needed feeding and eggs collecting; feed stocks that needed ordering, monitoring the weather and the market; fixing equipment. Craig spent all the remaining hours in the yard with the horses in his care, starting them under saddle, or ironing out problems. Twice during the week floats arrived with owners asking for his help. Peta could watch him work all day.

'People can ruin horses,' he said one day in answer to her question about a troubled colt who stood by himself down the paddock, refusing to come to the feed shed. 'That one's been taught not to trust anyone. But he's young. We'll get there.'

Gemma helped with the farm work, and spent a similarly dedicated number of hours filling jewellery orders. As a consequence of the icy distance between her and Craig at present, Gemma enlisted Peta to gather strands of tail and mane hair in shades required for particular designs.

'Buck's not going to have a tail left soon,' Peta said as she delivered a handful of pale grey strands for a choker Gemma was expertly weaving.

'That's what Craig used to say, too, but there's always more,' she said dismissively. Gemma seemed to have accepted that Peta was spending her time in Craig's cottage. Peta tried many times to gently broach the subject of Gemma's relationship with Wade, and convey her worries without betraying Karen. But it became apparent that Gemma thought Peta was simply siding with Craig, and Peta stopped before it drove a wedge between them, too. Besides, the relationship between Wade and Karen was obviously sour; she couldn't assume that Gemma was in the same situation. The only thing Peta found she missed was the daily visits to Diane's store.

On Wednesday morning, the cottage phone rang early while they were still asleep. Craig hauled himself up and across the cabin, rubbing his eyes.

'Ash,' she heard him say. 'What?' A long pause, then, 'Yeah, she's here. Be down soon.'

He replaced the receiver. 'Peta? They need you down at the clinic. There's been another theft and Wally's been hurt.'

'Who's Wally?' Peta asked five minutes later as she was pushing her fingers through her hair in the passenger seat of Craig's car.

'Cattleman from up the other side of the valley,' Craig supplied as he nosed the car onto the road. 'He's a feisty sort in his forties, brings his dog to pub meetings. Wife is Rita. Two sons, both at Ag college. Ash said something about him catching some men trying to make off with his tractor, and they tried to run him over.'

'In the tractor?' Peta had an image in her mind – tractors didn't go particularly fast, did they?

Craig laughed. 'No, in a truck they'd brought to cart it off. Ash reckons Wally got a good look at them.'

'And why didn't the ambos just take him down to the hospital?'

Craig shrugged, a small smile on his lips. 'He's asking to see you.'

Wally, in fact, turned out to be more than feisty, and well-organised. He'd set himself up on a gurney in the now sparkling emergency bay at the clinic, his arm already in a sling, gesticulating with the other hand to Ash, who had pulled up a chair and was taking notes. A woman leaned against the wall on the other side, her strong arms folded over a faded blue polo shirt. When she saw Peta, she touched Wally's arm.

'Doctor's here, Wal.'

Wally looked up. 'Ah.'

Peta introduced herself, but then wasted no time. 'Want to tell me what happened?'

'They clipped me with the truck,' said Wally, pointing to his shoulder in the sling. 'Didn't get the tractor, the bastards. But poor Sally . . .' He shook his head, as though he might cry.

'Sally?' Peta enquired, pulling out a stethoscope and shooting an enquiring eyebrow at the woman she assumed was Rita.

'Our dog. They ran her down, too,' Rita said, a hard glint in her eye. 'Reckon they were trying to stop us chasing them. Guess it worked.'

'You call Erica?' Craig asked from the end of the bed.

Rita shook her head. 'Of course. Wal insisted on it, and calling Ash, before he'd come here, stupid man. Looks like she'll make it.'

Wally had pulled himself together at this point, and Ash stood up. 'I'll let Dr Woodward check you out, Wal. We can come back to the details when you're done, and I'm going to put the call out on that truck. Craig, can I have a word?'

Peta turned to Wally's injuries. At first, she thought perhaps he'd been lucky – but then she eased the sling off his arm. *Jesus.*

'What's your pain like, Wally, out of ten?' she asked curiously. The humerus was clearly fractured, and the shoulder itself suspiciously shaped, the collarbone resting lower than it should have been. A subluxation, maybe. Or a dislocation. Or both.

'Probably a six,' he said.

She whipped through the rest of her survey. His lungs sounded clear and his blood pressure was good. Heart rate was rapid, but the pain could probably explain that. He said he hadn't been knocked out, and that he hadn't realised his arm was damaged at first because he'd been trying to rouse Sally.

'Poor old dog,' Rita said. 'She was supposed to have been at Erica's last night because she's been losing weight, but Erica got caught up in some other thing. But if Sally hadn't been there we might not have heard them.'

'What did they look like?' Peta asked, pulling out a flashlight to check Wally's pupils, then turning her attention to his arm.

'It was still pretty dark. I know there was two of them, young blokes, but didn't recognise 'em. Got a really good look at the truck though. Ash already called the coppers down the hill.'

Peta glanced behind her where Ash and Craig were talking in low voices, the policeman with the phone to his ear. She turned back to Wally.

'I hope they get them. But in the meantime, good news and bad news for you. Good news is you're walking around. Bad is that your arm will probably need surgery. At the very least, you need X-rays before and after someone sets it. So I'm going to set you up with a drip and then get the ambos in to take you down to the hospital.'

'I'll follow in the car,' Rita said.

'Who's going to watch the farm?' demanded Wally. 'I've got two drums of urea coming in this morning.'

'I'll do that,' Craig said, stepping away from conferring with Ash. 'Just tell me where you want it.'

While Wally gave his convoluted directions about where to put the delivery in his shed, Rita pulled Peta aside. 'Thank you,' she said. 'I was really worried about his arm, but he was so adamant about giving Ash the details first. And I knew if he saw you, you'd make the right call.'

'Happy to help,' Peta said, feeling pleased.

'Now, we better get those ambos here before Diane catches wind of any of this,' Rita said under her breath. 'Otherwise she'll be offering us that damned goose while Sally recovers.'

Craig and Ash had only been gone a few minutes when Peta heard the clinic door. Expecting the ambulance, she was instead surprised to see Wade Masters in the doorway.

'I heard what happened,' he said. 'You all right, Wally?'

'Nothing a beer wouldn't fix,' the farmer answered, then with a concessional nod in Peta's direction. 'All right, and maybe a surgeon. Going to be down on the flats to sort it out.'

'Shit, eh?' Masters slid onto the edge of Wally's bed with a nod to Rita. He avoided Peta's eyes. 'Don't suppose you saw the bastards?'

'I did,' said Wally proudly. 'Was just telling Ash about their truck. Didn't get a look at their faces, though.'

'Mmm,' Masters returned. 'And your arm?'

'Broken,' supplied Wally. 'Listen, Wade, while you're here. I've got some ideas about your campaign.'

'Oh, Wally, for god's sake,' said Rita.

Masters put a hand on Wally's good arm. 'She's right, Wal. Get your arm sorted and we'll talk about it then. You, too, Peta – I still want to hear your ideas about this clinic.'

And like an oversized ninja, he was gone.

Peta stared after him. The man certainly had gall, acting as though she'd never seen him at Karen's house. At least Craig had left, otherwise Peta might be sending Masters for an appointment with the surgeons himself.

Half an hour later, when she was finally closing after Wally and Rita had left, she heard another car pull up and found Diane tumbling out of her Volvo. 'Oh, Peta, did I miss him?'

'Wally's just gone,' Peta said wearily. 'It'll take them about a couple of hours, so maybe wait a bit before you try to call down. How does everyone find out about these things so fast?'

'And are you fine? Did Wade come back?'

'No.' Then Peta paused. This was weird, even for Diane. 'Did he tell you about it or did you tell him?'

A pause. 'He came into the shop. I just wanted to make sure everything was good.'

'It is.'

'And you're right for a lift?'

'Craig's coming back after he sorts out some delivery at Wally's. I'm going to test my foot down on the river path again.'

'Good, good. All right. Better get back.'

And she sped off. Peta cocked her head, thinking she must be missing something. Then again, Diane had a direct view of the police station; she probably saw whenever Ash left. But how she knew about Wally ... ? Maybe she'd fashioned a roadblock. Or maybe Karen had seen from across the street and called Diane. Not that that was something she'd have imagined Karen doing.

Peta shook herself. She was just speculating, becoming embroiled in community politics, and it wasn't exactly something that mattered, not when you didn't really know these people. But as she turned the key in the clinic's door, she stood looking at the little centre with its limited supplies, the street with its sweet houses built for the winter cold. It had all become familiar. Perhaps she knew more than she thought.

Chapter 19

The Bright Classic was a two-day show that ran out of a property near Bright itself, a town in the lee of the mountains with wide, tree-lined streets and a bustling commercial centre. After an early start on Saturday morning, Craig drove them into town just after nine.

In the passenger seat, Peta watched the activity with the window down, enraptured. Even Craig had to admit that after the weeks in the sleepy surrounds of Yarraman Falls, every car coming down the road was a curiosity. If he started trying to teach, there'd be more days like this. Craig didn't know quite how he felt about that.

'There's a chocolate factory, too,' Gemma said, her head poking through between the two front seats.

'You can get chocolate at home.'

'Not this kind of chocolate. The factory's right there. Pull over.'

'Not a chance.'

'Aw, come on, Craig!'

'Do you see parking for a four-wheel drive towing a horse float? Thought so,' he said, when Gemma sat back. Craig saw Peta suppress a smile. He loved that she'd agreed to come, even though her ankle was better and she could have been heading to the Ridgeback. Maybe she was considering what he'd said about staying in Yarraman. She hadn't even brought the crutches. In fact, with the exception of Candle and Buck in the trailer, they'd left everything behind in Yarraman, even the tension with Gemma over Wade. Craig relaxed, knowing the two of them would be separated for the duration.

After the two-and-a-half-hour journey, Craig was glad to finally see event signs, and soon they pulled into a large meadow, reminiscent of the Yarraman festival a few weeks before. Only this time, the grass was dotted with yellow flowers, any mud held off by the week of solid sunshine. From the smell in the air, Craig knew there were no cows, just row after row of horse floats.

When Candle and Buck had been unloaded and were happily pulling at a hay net, Craig was off to find the organiser's tent.

'Best leave him to it,' he heard Gemma say. 'He gets a bit stroppy before classes. We can organise food.'

Craig actually felt remarkably good, with his usual apprehension of performing in front of a crowd on mute. That was, until he spotted the first *Vote 1 Wade Masters* banner, flapping gaily on the roof of a tent two down from registration. He did his best to ignore it. He had the demonstration on his mind.

His stomach finally curdled as the stewards showed him towards the demo ring, which was thick with spectators. His name was in the program for an hour's time, so he tried to calm himself by fetching Candle down. He rarely needed another horse when breaking, but he was always prepared. Candle anchored him as he watched the end of the previous demonstration. The current demonstrator had the horse roped and was attempting to put a halter on. But the horse was spooked by the crowd, his young ears rotating, and the man wasn't responding fast enough to avoid confusing him. The time ended before the demonstrator had made much progress.

Craig had seen it before; things that worked at home sometimes didn't under the pressure of an unfamiliar place.

He kept the thought in mind when his turn came. He left Candle standing outside, and fixed his attention on the young horse who'd been ushered in the opposite gate. The PA must have announced him but he didn't hear it. He draped his halter and lead rope on the fence and took only a long stick topped with a flag. The crowd was quiet as he approached the animal, a wave of compassion travelling through him; the colt was just a baby, with small fluffy ears and nervous, willing eyes.

For the next fifteen minutes, the action followed a familiar pattern. Craig would touch the flag to the horse's rump or withers, and it would dance away, flicking its ears backwards in alarm. Craig maintained the position of the flag, and whenever the colt stopped, he instantly removed it. And then, the colt caught on and he gave up on running, realising that the flag disappeared as soon as he stopped. Craig was then able to approach.

Little by little, Craig showed the animal he meant no harm, that his rules were simple. His signals were clear and firm but never abrupt. He asked; didn't punish. And trust grew with such natural ease. A tide of immense satisfaction and gratitude flooded through Craig. The halter went on smoothly, then he started lunging with the rope, the horse walking circles around him. By the end of the hour the horse was walking a calm circle in each direction, ears angled for Craig's voice. The crowd gave enthusiastic applause as Craig led the colt back to its owner. It was a monumental amount to have achieved in an hour. Craig looked longingly over his shoulder; that was going to be a good horse – he'd learned to respond to feel in no time. Maybe he should ask the owner if he would sell.

Immediately out of the ring, several people descended, wanting to shake his hand and ask questions. He did his best to field them while leading Candle away, eager to find Peta. In his concentration he hadn't looked for her in the crowd, but he knew she'd been there. As short as their relationship had been, he took solace in hearing what she thought when she watched him work with the horses.

As he finished with the questions, he began to see election material everywhere. Vote 1 buttons and bumper stickers, some with Wade's face staring out, looking bullish and hardworking. Every ten paces he seemed to pass someone handing out a pamphlet or inviting him to a 'community consultation' that Wade was evidently conducting in every town from here to Wangaratta.

Finally, he spotted Peta, like an oasis in the desert, loaded down with steak sandwiches and tornado potatoes.

'If someone else tries to give me one of those damn buttons I'm going to do my nut,' he said, stopping himself hugging her before she dropped the food.

'They are rather prolific,' she said. 'You were amazing!'

'Was it all right?'

'All right? I just watched you answer questions for half an hour. I hope you're hungry.'

'Starving. Where's Gemma?'

'Don't know, to be honest. She seems to know everyone. She ran into a girl before and said she'd be back later.'

'Some of her school friends live in town.'

Craig had hoped that the trip might repair some of the damage between Gemma and himself. But it would be good for her to catch up with people she hadn't seen for a while, and it meant he could have time alone with Peta.

'Excuse me, Craig?'

Craig turned to find a man with a crooked nose and a chunk out of his akubra brim, offering his hand.

'Marvellous demo. I'm Eric Halliday. I run a brumby relocation service. Can I have a word? Maybe buy you lunch?'

'Go,' Peta said, before he could apologise. 'I'll see you back at the float.'

—

They finally climbed into their tent near midnight, after watching from the sidelines as the energetic showgoers danced to a local band. Well, Peta had watched. Craig had been occupied with many new fans, all wanting to ask him about his techniques. Under the canvas, Craig pulled Peta to him.

'What a day. I've never spoken to so many people.'

'You made a big impression,' she told him. 'They'll be lining up to take your classes now.'

'Maybe.' He sounded unenthused.

'You don't want to do it?'

'It's not that.' He glanced across at her. 'It would mean a lot of travelling, and further afield than this. I'm in it for the horses, that's a given. But it means being away from home. Gemma's still so young. She needs help with the property, plus everyone in the valley depends on each other. Doesn't feel right to take off.'

Peta fixed on the ceiling of the tent and tried to be tactful. 'You sure this mood doesn't have something to do with a certain future political figure who's splashed his banner all over the place?'

Craig grunted. 'Maybe. I can't stand the idea he'll be the voice of the district.'

'Do you think it will come to that?' Peta thought about Karen. 'I mean, how does a guy like that stay on the good side of people?'

Craig moved the dim lantern to see better, and gave her an appraising look. 'What did he do to you?'

'Nothing,' she said quickly. 'I only mean from what you've told me. And he gives me that heeby vibe.'

'Heeby vibe?'

'Makes me uneasy. Woman's intuition.'

Craig accepted that. 'Given what I've seen, he can't lose. He says all the things people want to hear, and everyone's sick of the last guy. It's just that I know him better than most people.'

'Maybe you need to find someone better to run, then,' Peta said. 'You need someone who actually cares about the world up here, right?'

'Mmmm,' Craig said. He was silent a long while. 'It's funny you say that.'

'Why?'

'Because Eric, that guy who came to talk to me after the demo? He said something similar, asked me if I would ever run. I thought he was joking but it turns out he's the election manager, too. We had a chat by the lunch truck, and he gave me some kind of handbook.'

'Handbook?'

'For candidates. I think it's still in my jeans.' He paused. 'How did we end up talking politics in bed?'

'It's not really a bed, more of a squeaky bag of air. You realise,' she went on, admiring his skin as he pulled his shirt off, 'that this mattress is obligated to be flat by morning?'

'I can think of some ways to help it out.'

Craig bounced a few times.

'Stop it. Gemma's right in the next tent.'

'She's not. She hasn't come back yet. So come here, Dr Woodward.'

⌒

Craig rose early the next morning while Peta was still dozing. He kissed her cheek, but as soon as he was gone she felt his absence in the tent, even though she could hear him moving around the trailer, talking softly to Buck and Candle. Strange

that only a few weeks ago she'd never felt lonely in her tent.
Never needed anyone else there.

Well, she'd get back to that again. It was just that this tent
was so much bigger; the one in her pack was a cosy single.

After dozing another hour, she emerged into the early
morning event ground, with the sky pale grey. Gemma's tent
was still zipped, and Craig was yawning as he boiled a billy
over a camp stove in the back of the float.

Buck whickered and stretched his neck to nudge her, which
nearly sent Peta stumbling. 'I'll get your breakfast in a second,'
she told him.

'He's just trying his luck,' Craig said. 'They already wolfed it.'

Peta stretched her back. The air mattress had actually stayed
inflated, and she'd slept wonderfully, obviously much better
than many at the ground, who were now staggering out of
floats and caravans to begin the day. The cloudless morning
promised a warm day that would chase away this crisp air and
make an easy drive home.

Craig's arms enveloped her. 'What do you say, when you
finish your trek, you come back and meet my mum? They're
planning to be back in a few weeks.'

'Your mother?'

'Sure.'

Peta hardly knew what to say but Craig looked so happy
about the idea. She raked her hands through her hair, smoothing
the worst of the tangles, thinking it was all too much too soon.
Her fingers met bare flesh at the back of her neck. Reflexively
she groped for the necklace at her throat.

It wasn't there. She checked again. No, it really wasn't.

The supports under her heart fell away. She dived back
into the tent, shaking out the sleeping bags and upending the
mattress. No necklace.

'Shit!'

On her hands and knees she made a complete circuit inside the tent's bottom seam. It had to be here somewhere. Perhaps wedged in the fold of fabric? But nothing. Her fingers flew to her neck again, patting around. It really wasn't there. She ripped her shirt up, her hair falling forward, sticking to her hot forehead, and checked the waistband of her pants.

'I know it wasn't the best mattress, but maybe punishment's a bit overboard.'

Craig had lifted the tent flap with an amused tone that Peta ignored. She was thinking furiously. When was the last time she remembered having it on?

'You all right in there, Peta?'

'I lost my necklace.' She squeezed the words out past the steel ring of anguish around her throat. Her last connection to Stacey; it couldn't be gone.

'Just now?'

'I'm not sure. Shit!'

Peta could feel the panic rising, building a pressure behind the constriction in her throat. She had to think.

'When did you last have it?'

She clambered out of the tent, pacing, her hands shaking. 'I don't know. Did you see me wearing it last night?'

'I don't remember. Did you even bring it?'

Peta ran to the car and pulled the passenger door open. 'I'm sure I still had it when we drove in yesterday . . . I think.' The necklace was such an automatic part of her, she struggled to remember. As she tried to find an image in her memory of touching it, her fingers darted under the seat, frisking the upholstery like airport security. 'It's not there!'

She pressed her head against the door rim in despair, taking in the huge area of tents and show rings around them. 'I walked all over the ground yesterday. It could be anywhere!'

'Peta. Peta. Calm down. Gemma and I will help you look. We'll check the car properly first.'

But all Peta could see was the endless green grass. Finding it in all that would be impossible, even if there weren't people and horses everywhere mushing things into the turf. She barely registered Craig lifting the flap on Gemma's tent, a look of surprise on his face.

'She's not here,' he said. Lines of concern rippled across his forehead, and he seemed frozen in indecision, which resolved a minute later when Gemma appeared.

'Looking for me?' she asked brightly. 'The breakfast tent's doing a great roll.'

Even in her distress, Peta noted Gemma was still in yesterday's clothes.

'I lost my necklace,' she said quickly, before Craig could notice.

'What's it look like?'

A broken heart. 'It's one of those hearts in two halves, on a silver chain.'

Gemma's eyes brightened. 'Oh, the Italian one? That says *Divisi ma sempre uni*?'

'Yeah.'

But though they searched everywhere, the necklace remained lost. An hour later, as Gemma was making circles out from the tents, her eyes on the grass, and Peta was checking inside the car again, Craig put a hand on her shoulder.

'Honey, it's not here.'

'It must be, somewhere.' She didn't look at him. Her eyes were stinging with pooled tears. How could she have been so mindless not to notice the instant the necklace had come off?

'We need to leave soon.'

'I'm going to find it.' By now, the vinyl in the footwells was polished from her efforts, all the dust transferred onto Peta's hands and shirt. She was dimly aware of how much she was losing a grip on herself.

'You can easily get another one,' Gemma said. 'Those things are pretty common. I could even order you one through the business.'

Later, Peta realised this was the moment when she lost the plot. She rounded on Gemma before Craig could gently correct his sister's assumption. 'No, I can't just *get another one*,' she said.

Then the grass and floats and horse after horse went rushing past as she ran towards the marquees. She needed to ask in the registration tent again – someone might have turned it in. But then she looked at her watch and realised it was only ten minutes since she'd last asked.

Off-balance, her foot struck a dry clump of manure and fresh pain flashed in her ankle. Peta pulled up in no-man's land, halfway between the coloured show marquees and the float. Then Craig was firmly taking her hand, making her lean on him as he steered her to an over-wheel shelf of an unattended float.

'Here, sit. Let me look.'

Peta stared into space as he eased her boot off and gently rotated the ankle. It wasn't painful but tears escaped anyway, wetting the smudges on her shirt. Her nose started to run. All of the light fluffy feelings of the day before had bloated and sunk. In some part of her mind, she knew she was hysterical and acting like a maniac. But the shame only intensified her grief.

Craig had crouched on his heels, taking her hands. 'It means a lot to you, I know that.'

'I can't replace it,' she croaked. 'I don't have anything else of Stacey.'

He hugged her. 'Peta, I'm really sorry, but I don't know what else we can do. The organisers have my address. We can keep looking as long as you want, but I'm not sure we'll find it. And I've got Erica coming in tomorrow to look over the herd – have to get them up from the lower pasture.'

He was right. Peta gave up, but as they rolled out of the ground, her heart twisted so hard she could hardly breathe. She was leaving her connection to Stacey out there, somewhere unmarked in the endless grass. She was a fool, allowing herself to be waylaid in Yarraman Falls. She'd lost focus on the reasons she'd started her journey. She'd forgotten Stacey, forgotten what she owed to her family.

Numbly, she checked her phone so she didn't have to watch the showground receding in the distance. After so long without reception, she had five voicemails waiting, and more than two hundred emails. She wasn't ready for this. She wasn't supposed to have reception again until the end of the trail, when she would know what to do.

It was all a very bad omen.

By the time the familiar Yarraman Pub appeared at the curve in the road, inside her head felt bruised with grief. They pulled into the fuel bowser in front of the shop, but Peta stayed in the car while Craig pumped and Gemma went in to pay. Across the road, she could see the belligerent geese patrolling the bank, but even this failed to raise a smile. She closed her eyes, aching to touch the necklace that was no longer there.

Craig gave her a lot of room. His only assumption was to drive them all back to the farm, and to apologise that he had to go and bring up the herd.

After he had gone, Peta slid into the feed shed. Having come up the field to greet Craig, Bel now lay in the straw in her box, the filly dozing. Peta slipped between the fence rails and sank down against the straw. The mare flicked her ears in Peta's direction, extending her nose with an inquisitive breath. So Peta inched forward. Another nose stretch, another few inches, until she was close enough for the mare to rest her muzzle in Peta's lap.

Such trust. Peta twined her fingers through the mane and rested her head against the soft coat, tears still sliding down her face. The day rapidly ran into night. Craig must have known where she was, but he didn't demand she come inside.

So Peta found herself still curled on the straw when the first morning birds were calling. Bel was still next to her, eyes half-open, her warmth keeping Peta from the cold air. Peta dragged herself up and put all the horses' feeds together before she went back to the cottage.

She found Craig collapsed on the couch in his clothes, as if he'd been waiting all night for her to come back. Peta bit her lip as she longingly examined his features, peaceful with sleep. She shifted her gaze to the contents of her pack – neatly stacked but abandoned against the long wall of the cabin. Before she'd come to Yarraman, she would never have allowed herself to forget what she was doing, to become so distracted. And now she'd paid the price: Stacey's necklace was gone forever and she was no closer to resolving the problems she'd begun the trail with.

All thoughts of staying in Yarraman vanished. She'd been caught in a fantasy, and it was time to wake up.

Chapter 20

When Peta was finishing a shower fifteen minutes later, she heard the cottage phone ringing and emerged to find Craig rubbing his face and holding out the receiver.

'So, I'm cooking tonight,' she heard, 'and I need your opinion on something. How about dinner at seven?'

Through her brain fog, all Peta could identify was the caller was female and she had a momentary regression. 'Mum?'

'It's Diane. Are you free?'

Peta wondered if Gemma had blabbed about the necklace; the last thing she wanted was Diane's questions. Besides, her back ached and her legs felt as though she'd done a full day's hike without any practice.

'I don't know,' Peta said, pressing her fingers into her eyes. 'I don't feel that great.'

'Do you good, what I'm cooking. And the other thing's important. See you at seven?' Diane hung up.

When Peta put down the phone, Craig was pulling on his boots, his shirt still undone. 'I have to go meet Erica about the herd. Do you want to—'

'Are you using the car today?'

Craig paused as one heel thunked into place. He sat back, and with difficulty Peta looked away from the expanse of chest his open shirt showed. 'You need it?'

'I want to get my pack in order. Pick up a few things.'

Craig dug for his keys without a word but when he handed them over, Peta could tell he had read into her request. He knew she was close to leaving. She avoided his gaze, and he kissed her on the head. 'See you later, then.'

Peta sucked a breath. The pain of keeping things from him had the searing intensity of a hot pan. But once he was gone, she threw herself into activity, and it ebbed away. She felt cowardly for not telling him how she was feeling, but her distress over her forgotten objective was far worse.

So Peta spent the day driving down from the valley to larger stores in the lower towns, restocking her pack. She ate lunch sitting on the bonnet by the side of the road, going over her maps. She felt vaguely guilty for bypassing Yarraman's store, which only intensified when Diane opened her door at quarter to seven that evening.

'What's this I hear about you buying goods at places down the valley?'

'You really do have spies everywhere.'

'The CWA keeps in touch. One of them spotted you driving Craig's car and called me in case it was stolen.'

'Why wouldn't they just call the police?'

'They've got enough to do. Anyway, I'll forgive you. Come in, come in.'

Diane ushered Peta inside. The hall was spartan, with a narrow table growing two doilies either side of a phone and an old-school answering machine. Nothing hung on the walls but the air was thick with the rich smell of roasting meat. The kitchen turned out to be a cosy space with orange tiles from the seventies, a rustic pine table set for two, and a sink beneath a window that looked out on the police station. Through the window of another room to the left, Peta could see the yard behind the store in the dim post-sundown light, white goose-shaped blobs nestled against the fence.

'Coffee?'

Peta hedged. 'If I have one now, I probably won't sleep.'

'Are you sure? I borrowed this stuff from Karen. She's been educating me on proper coffee and I wrote it all down. I'm thinking of making one of my book characters from Melbourne.'

Peta sniffed the offered packet of beans. Oh god, heaven mixed with caffeine. 'All right.'

Satisfied, Diane set to work, reading instructions off a scrap of paper. 'So, I hear you lost a necklace at the show in Bright.'

Dammit, Gemma. Peta sighed. 'Yes.'

'Your sister's?'

'Not exactly. I had one half, she had the other.'

'I see. And—'

'I'd rather not talk about it.' Peta slid into a seat at the table, pressing her palm to her forehead. Diane made an apologetic noise and moved on smoothly as she fiddled with the moka pot.

'You know, I didn't realise you were *that* Woodward. The Woodward stud is quite famous. Some of the competitors in the local shows used to have horses out of the Woodward place.'

'I did used to live there.'

'What's it like?'

Peta didn't even need to close her eyes. 'Green fields as far as you can see, forested hills and farms . . . a bit like here, I guess.' She didn't mention abandoned, run-down and hugely in debt.

'Must be hard to be in Melbourne after that. Terrible thing to have to sell. I can't imagine living anywhere else but here.'

This all seemed to be slowly leading somewhere, and Peta was impatient. 'You said there was something you wanted to ask me?'

Diane set down Peta's coffee. 'Yes. Just wait there.'

She disappeared as Peta took a sip; not half bad. But even the familiar taste brought no comfort. When Diane re-emerged, she put down a plastic zip-lock bag with a triumphant flourish.

'There.'

Peta peered at what seemed to be a scrap of red and black flannel. 'What's this?'

'Evidence. That's why I put it in the bag. Monty came back with it last night.'

'Evidence of what?'

'The thieves, of course. Wally said one of them was wearing a shirt like this.'

Peta inspected the bag with a flare of irritation. 'Diane, Monty could have got this anywhere. There's probably some poor person who went for a walk along the river missing a part of their shirt.'

'Who walks along the river after dark? Only someone up to no good, that's who.'

'And everyone around here wears shirts like this.'

'Monty wouldn't have done this to just anyone. He's got a good sense of right and wrong.'

Peta wondered if Diane was joking, and obviously it showed on her face. Diane sank into her seat and carefully folded her hands in front of her. A serious expression Peta had never seen before crossed the storekeeper's features; the energy in her eyes focused. 'Peta. Hypothetically, what would you do if you'd overheard something important, but you couldn't say how?'

'I don't follow.'

'Let's say the way you overheard it could get you in trouble.'

'What sort of trouble?'

There was a long pause. Then, Diane waved her hand. 'It doesn't matter. It's just for the book, and it's not working yet. Let me think about it some more. Now, we should eat.'

Peta tried to wrap her head around the question as Diane opened the oven. Did Diane know something about Peta's father, and the stud? Was that why she'd asked about it earlier? She certainly had spies everywhere else; why not in the law firm in Adelaide, too?

Then a plate of carved meat landed on the table, brimming with gravy and smelling like Christmas morning. Peta was momentarily lifted out of her funk.

'That smells amazing.' And a moment later when she tasted it, she groaned in appreciation. 'What is this? Turkey?'

'Goose,' supplied Diane primly, producing wine glasses and a bottle.

Peta nearly choked, her eyes darting to the white shapes in the yard outside. 'What?'

'Well, what was I supposed to do? I ordered too many. And this one had a bad attitude, not like Monty. I figured she couldn't be sweet in life, but she could certainly be tasty. Don't you agree?'

Peta found herself laughing. 'What was her name?'

'Didn't deserve one with an attitude like that.' Diane sniffed.

'Poor goose. She is tasty though.'

And so, with the ice temporarily melted, they ate and talked of innocuous things, beginning with Karen's instructions about good coffee, then moving to a critique of the eligible bachelors Diane knew in the district, and who she thought they should end up with.

'Do you really think about them all like that?' Peta asked, trying to think if she'd had one glass or two already, as Diane filled her up again.

'Nothing wrong with a little window shopping, especially at my age, though I'd never have anyone else after my Gregory. We should get something back for being feminists.'

'I don't know if that's how feminism works.' Peta took another gulp of wine.

'Well, you're the city girl,' Diane said, her own words starting to slur. 'But it's given me an idea for a fundraiser. Blokes round here look pretty good with their kit off. We should do a calendar. Put the proceeds towards catching the thieves.'

Peta swallowed another mouthful, the warmth spreading into her cheeks. The room was starting to have wibbles, and her tongue was loose. She squinted at Diane. 'Diane, really? You're still on this?'

'It's important.' She leaned forward and pseudo-whispered. 'I'm pretty sure I know what's going on.'

'Tell me then.' Peta didn't much care; right now, the pattern on her wine glass rim seemed fascinating. The rational part of her mind, which was rapidly shutting down, realised she must have had way too much.

Diane winked. 'You remember that company who bought Harry's place – Great Golden Ag? It's a shell company, doesn't really do any business anymore, but it's owned – through a few steps, mind – by Wade Masters. At least, I'm pretty sure it is.'

Peta blinked, feeling how sluggishly her lids responded. She was having trouble keeping up. 'What's this got to do with the thefts?'

'Pressure. People round here don't want to sell, but make it hard enough and they will. Janice down the valley says her son saw off some people that came by their place to cause trouble a while back, when her husband was having chemo. See, the thieves are going for the weak ones, like Harry and Old Charlie.'

'"Pretty sure" sounds a bit tenuous,' Peta said, struggling to pronounce 'tenuous'. Her tongue seemed overly thick.

'I have good instincts, trust me. I always helped my Gregory with cases. I know there's more to it. Especially after what I heard about that truck Wally saw.' Diane grinned and clumsily pressed her fingers to her mouth, like she shouldn't have said anything.

'What about it?'

An exaggerated shrug. 'It has to be found.'

Peta swirled the wine around her mouth, which had turned sour. Her necklace had to be found, too, and yet nothing could be done about that. Diane, with her crim obsession, was clearly enjoying beating up the story. And a restraint that should have held broke loose.

'Diane, look at you. You run a successful business. You know everyone in town, and just about everyone else in a hundred k radius from what I can tell. You're the reason the school's still open. Do you really want to spend your life fixated on conspiracies and gossip? Imagine what you could do with all that extra time. Maybe finish your book. Or do something really useful.' Peta pulled up as her better judgement finally caught up. 'What I mean is—'

'No, no, that's all right,' Diane said, sitting back with an expression that was abruptly sober and thoughtful. 'I am aware of myself, you know. I know how I sound. I see it on your face. Thing is, I can't seem to get a handle on it. I love the intrigue.'

Peta nodded. 'Maybe it would be a good idea to stay off the internet, let Ash do his job. And off the gossip mags, too.'

'Tricky, in my work,' Diane said, gesturing towards the store. 'Endless supply of both when it's not busy. Funny, I never really thought this is what I'd be doing when Gregory died.'

'Well, what did you want to do?'

'Something with people, I suppose. That's what I really enjoy.'

'You could be a doctor.' Jesus, Peta thought, I must be very drunk.

Diane laughed. 'Oh, god no, my worst nightmare. But the fundraising things, I love that. Especially for the school.'

'And knowing everyone's business.'

Diane gave a coy smile and tapped her nose. 'That's what happens coming from a big family. Hard to imagine now I'm here by myself.'

Peta pushed her wine away and reached for another slice of goose. 'How so?'

'I came here with my husband. That's what we did back then. Well, most of us, except Theresa Munroe.'

'Mmmm?'

'Well, you'd have heard the story already.'

'No.' Peta licked her finger. The meat really was delicious.

'Really? I thought Craig would have told you.' Diane paused, as if to be dramatic. 'The circumstances were exceptional. I can't imagine Craig doing what he did – that's beyond any boy I've ever known.'

Peta felt a cool wedge of clarity cut through the wine. 'What did he do?'

'Well, they came from further north, nearer New South Wales. Old Munroe was a harsh man. Used to beat on Theresa. Maybe Craig, too. Anyway, one night when Gemma was just a baby, Munroe came home drunk as a skunk and started in on the same old rubbish. And Craig – he was ten, I think – he runs out into the shed. Next thing, just as Munroe's getting started, he finds his own gun pointed in his face. Can you imagine?'

The cool wedge of clarity had become a heavy ice brick sitting in Peta's stomach. 'Craig?'

'Yep. Tired of seeing his mother being abused. So he points the gun at his father and he tells him that they're leaving, and that he's not to follow or ever try to see them again. Stood right there while Theresa put a bag together and got the baby into the car. They drove all night to Yarraman, got here some time right around dawn, and Granny Munroe took them in.

She's the one Craig calls his grandmother – but she's actually his great-aunt on the father's side, the only family they had. Wonderful horsewoman. She got Craig started.'

'How do you know all this?' Peta whispered.

Diane shrugged. 'My husband was the cop before Ash. I was here when they first came in, looking for directions to Granny Munroe's farm. It was an awful sight. Theresa still had bruises on her face, Gemma wailing to be fed, and Craig had his little fingers in a death grip on the rifle. I still remember my husband coaxing him to let it go, and unloading it right at that table, there. We fed them a cooked breakfast and hot tea before they went up to the farm. I was so much more naive back then – I was twenty-three and just married to a small-town policeman – but I remember Craig. You never forget something like that. Terribly quiet kid, but extraordinary presence. The story got around, but most people don't talk about it nowadays. Out of respect.'

Peta sat back in her chair, stunned. She was having trouble coming to terms with the picture in her mind, which had been painted all too easily: Craig as a young boy, standing protectively over his own mother and baby sister, staring down a full-grown man. She was back in Bel's stable, listening to him say that his hands never shake. Understanding what he must feel about Wade and Gemma after his experience, the responsibility he must carry.

And then all she could think about was Stacey. She would never forgive herself for losing the necklace. Could never forgive herself if she failed to follow through with her own last responsibilities.

She rose unsteadily and grabbed her keys. 'I should go.'

'Don't be silly, you can't drive like this,' Diane said, taking back the keys. 'Besides, I've still crème brûlée to come. And I ordered the blowtorch specially.'

The next morning, Peta had three hangovers to deal with – one from the wine, one from Diane's couch, and another – lingering and insidious – of shame. And not two minutes after she'd woken, another one descended in the form of Diane, shaking her shoulder.

'Peta? Ash needs to see you.'

Ten minutes later she was clutching a black instant coffee in the Yarraman police station, looking at a man through the bars of the single cell, which took up nearly a quarter of the watchhouse's floor space.

'Apparently he was hitchhiking out on the highway. Threatened the guy who picked him up, but the driver managed to stay in one piece until he could boot him out here. Hasn't said much since. My money's on ice. I've called the ambos, but wanted to know what you thought.'

Peta made a quick assessment through the feather down in her head. The guy was skinny, throat sticking out like a drainpipe as he tipped his head back against the wall, and he had a good growth of grubby stubble over his chin. Blotchy skin, wheezy breaths, heartbeat almost visible through his paper-thin shirt.

'How do you feel about me taking his blood pressure?'

'I'd prefer you didn't go in there,' Ash said. 'He's already socked the guy who picked him up. But I'd appreciate you staying in case he keels over.'

'Don't worry, I'm not keen to go in there. But he doesn't look good. When the ambos get here we'd better all make a plan to have a line in before he goes to the hospital. Could need resus on the way, or even have a seizure. And they'll need to do bloodwork to check his heart, kidneys and a tox screen.'

When the ambulance arrived, the man was compliant at first, almost sleepy, until he registered the uniforms and the

ECG, and decided hospital was definitely not for him. What followed was an intense two minutes where Peta and one of the ambos both tried for a line in the man's arms, while Ash held him in a body lock. Despite her pounding headache and cold sweats, Peta managed to site the cannula and give him a sedative. The drama alleviated, they monitored vital signs for the next ten minutes.

'Blood pressure's come down,' said the ambo.

When they were finally happy to transport him, Peta leaned on the edge of Ash's desk, watching them manoeuvre the stretcher towards the front door. Through the side window, she could see Diane peering through her kitchen window.

Peta caught Ash's eye, who followed her gaze and gave her a wry grin. 'Ah, Diane,' he said with genuine affection. 'She's harmless, and I had huge respect for her husband. He was a good bloke. Sometimes the hijinks are entertaining when there's not much going on, though that goose of hers likes to run at my car.'

'She's going to think this ice guy is somehow connected to the thefts. Monty came back with some kind of fabric recently, and she's convinced it's related.'

Ash's mouth pulled into a quizzical shape. 'Not the worst theory. Drug habits being funded by theft wouldn't be anything new. We've even had people hunting deer illegally and selling the heads for drugs.'

'Seriously?'

Ash shrugged. 'People around here have hunting skills. If you've got a habit to fund, you use what you've got. Can't fault them for being enterprising. However,' he added, 'given the choice between petty suburban theft and men in flannel with hunting rifles, I know which I'd prefer on a dark night.'

'I hope that's the worst of it.'

'You'd think, wouldn't you? Sometimes it's like *The X-Files*.'

He had a cute smile, especially when he folded his arms like that in his uniform, so his biceps stood out. Peta couldn't quite understand why Gemma would go for Wade when Ash was around.

Now Ash was scratching his head. 'Like these thefts. Every lead goes dead. We've never found any trace of those yards. One of the missing cows turned up out west at a sale – but the guy with her swears he just brought his herd in, no idea how the animal ended up in it. I'm starting to think Charlie *was* hit by hunters, though that's weird too. Deer hunters would use much larger bullets than he was hit with – ones that probably would have killed him. So, maybe they were hunting rabbits, which is just nuts. And there's no trace of that truck they hit Wally with. I thought we'd get somewhere with that, for sure. I mean, we had a good description soon after it happened, and the vehicle's damaged – Wally said they clipped the gate on the way out. There are not many main roads around here. The other stations have all been notified, plus we had posters put up in all the stores and pubs. Nothing. Makes me mad I can't do better for everyone.'

'I'm sorry.'

'Don't be. It's like this sometimes. But thanks for your help. It's been invaluable. I tell you, people are really excited the med centre's seen some use again. They like having a doc in town.'

Peta shifted uncomfortably, then dug in her pocket. 'Here,' she said, pushing the centre's key across the desk. 'I need to give this back.'

The disappointment in Ash's face was plain. 'I was kind of hoping you might stick around.'

'Sorry,' she said. 'I've already stayed too long.'

When Peta arrived back at the farm, her hangover was fading, but not the sense that the last two days had changed the world around her. Her stomach whirled as the car cleared the big house and she spotted Craig riding Buck up from the lower paddock. Clearly, he'd been waiting. She would have to face him.

'Sorry I didn't call,' she said, trying to be on the front foot as he swung down near the cottage door.

'Don't worry, Diane did. Good dinner?'

He kissed her on the cheek, trying to draw her into a hug, clearly ignoring the last few days. Such inane, basic things. Such simple gestures. Peta could barely tolerate it. She should never have become involved with him.

'I need a shower,' she said, wriggling away. 'I had to go over to the station. Ash had a drugged-up guy in the cell.'

'Yeah?'

'He was pretty out of it. Glad Ash got to him first. He went off with the ambos.' She wasn't looking at Craig as she pushed the cottage door open. He paused in the doorway, and she felt his eyes on her, watching in that intense way that made her crazy with desire.

'Then what's going on?'

'Nothing. Just need a shower.'

'Peta. Stop.'

Her body obeyed him, stilling before she could disappear into the bathroom. She pretended to sit on the end of the couch to undo her shoes. Slowly, he came inside and rested on his heels on front of her, taking her hands. He was so warm, she felt all the mental preparation she'd been doing to go back to the trail, all that ice she'd packed around her heart melting, and threatening to flow over into tears she couldn't stop.

'Look at me,' he said gently. Peta looked. Blue eyes, so blue. 'This has to do with your necklace, but I don't understand it. Help me out.'

'It's ... nothing.' She couldn't explain how she cared so much for him and yet how much she loathed herself for indulging her time in Yarraman. Her guilt at having forgotten her responsibilities was a deep and unforgiving current in her mind, and now she was caught in it, there was only one way she could swim. She stepped around him, strode into the kitchen, and poured a glass of water. 'Want one?' she asked brightly.

Craig pushed off his heels and sat on the couch where she'd been, broad shoulders rounded, hands relaxed. She'd seen him do this with the horses. Waiting, just waiting. Well, she wasn't a bloody horse. Braver, she shook the glass, a non-verbal repetition of her question.

'No, I want you to come here so I can kiss you,' he said. His lips turned up just at the edges. He'd let her lie to him if that's what she wanted, but Peta saw what would happen – if she went to his embrace, he would try to convince her to stay, and she couldn't afford to be swayed off course again.

'I'm leaving, Craig,' she said, trying to mask her pain. Her chest felt as though it were caving in. But she pushed on with the determination she'd had when she was first injured, that she should have found again long before now. 'My ankle's good. Soon as I can get repacked, I'm heading back up. I have to finish it.'

His eyes flickered. 'Are you coming back?'

A tear dislodged as she shook her head. 'I don't know. I'll have to go back to Melbourne, sort things out. I probably won't have time.'

'What if I don't want you to go?'

She glimpsed the truth, then. That he was holding himself back with cables of pure will, and underneath he wanted her with a passion that was nearly beyond his control, one that wanted to demand she stay. His knuckles were white against the couch, the pain obvious in his eyes.

He came to her, running his hands down her arms, asking her with everything that he was, not to go, not now.

'I won't say it,' he said, his lips moving in her hair, 'because I know I'll sound insane. But this is good. Much too early to throw it in.'

For a second, she let herself rest against him, savouring this one last time. Then she pulled a mental gate down, terrified of how safe and wonderful he felt.

'I'm not sure,' she said, wavering.

'Will you wait, at least? Even just a few days?'

Peta bit her lip. 'Maybe. Just a few days.'

Chapter 21

Craig left the cottage with his heart flattened on the soles of his boots. He'd always known that Peta would want to finish the trail. That was obvious from their first meeting. But he'd truly thought they had something, and that she would see if they could pursue it. All right, he hadn't given much thought to the *how* exactly; he was a practical man. You had a problem, you found a way.

Now he had just a few days to find one.

He swung onto Buck's back, about to head to the southern yard where Erica would be waiting. After that he still had acres of work to do; the pump for the stock water was cutting out now, and he had to find somewhere to put a three-year-old problem colt who was coming in from Bright tomorrow. But then he spotted Gemma, frantically waving at him from the big house. Maybe the water had shut off again. He pushed Buck into a canter up the slope.

'What's up?' he called as he came within earshot.

'Come inside. We need to talk to you,' she said, and she disappeared without a backwards glance.

'We?' That didn't sound like the water.

For a horrible moment, Craig expected 'we' might be Wade and Gemma. But when he pushed open the back door, he found his sister leaning on the kitchen bench, with phone in hand.

'Mum's on speaker,' she said.

'Hello, Craig,' Theresa said, an unusually forceful tone in her voice.

Craig wondered if she was going to deliver some kind of bad news, like Grant had been injured, or something like that. He braced.

'What's this about you running in the election against Wade?'

Craig cursed. 'For Christ's sake.'

'Language,' scolded Theresa. 'But I take it that it's not a false report?'

Craig dropped his hat on the floor and sank into a kitchen chair, stretching back to loosen the frustration from his muscles. 'I had one conversation with the Election Manager in Bright over lunch. How the hell does that become "I'm running" and get back to you? You weren't even there, Gemma.'

Gemma shrugged. 'Diane's cousin Rita was working in Wade's booth, handing out electoral nominations. She saw the manager give you a candidate handbook. I won't need to lay out how it came to me from there.'

Craig rolled his eyes; Diane could run some kind of secret police. 'Look, I haven't decided anything. I just got the information. I didn't even know the guy was the Electoral Manager at first – he asked me about a horse.'

'But you hate public speaking,' Theresa argued. 'You've been saying you wanted to expand the horsemanship classes for years. What's happened to that?'

'And what about having to go to Melbourne for months out of the year?' said Gemma.

Irrationally, Craig's first thought was that time in Melbourne would mean the possibility of seeing Peta, though chasing it was the horror of leaving behind the horses.

'Masters' stuff was slapped all over the place, and I can't stand the idea of *that man* being our rep,' Craig argued. 'He doesn't care about people. And he'll cave the first time he's confronted with something where he has to do the right thing. His allegiance is to his business, whatever he says.'

'He's not *that* bad,' Gemma said.

'He didn't even show up in Bright.'

'He did so, he was just meeting with the local business owners in town—' Gemma broke off, her voice buckling.

'Oh really,' Craig said softly. 'That explains your enthusiasm in coming with us.'

'That's not fair. I would have come anyway.'

Theresa's voice came tinny down the line. 'What are you talking about?'

Craig pushed his chair back, and replaced his hat. He locked eyes with Gemma, hers silently appealing to keep his mouth shut. Craig pressed his lips together. So, she hadn't mentioned Wade to her mother. That set off alarms.

'Gemma's seeing Wade,' he said.

'What?'

'Craig!' Gemma gave him a face like she'd drunk sour milk.

Craig shook his head. 'You don't know anything about him, Gem, and we don't keep secrets from Mum. I'm not covering for you.' But as soon as he'd said it, he wondered if he was doing the wrong thing. Horses wouldn't trust you if you betrayed them. Why did he think Gemma would be any different?

Theresa paused. 'Didn't you tell her about Bel?'

'She knows,' Craig said. He hadn't told her every gory detail, but enough. It was just that she hadn't lived it like he had.

'So he's done something bad in the past,' Gemma argued. 'That's not a reason to give up on someone. This is just because you don't like him.'

'Gemma, he's so much older than you,' Theresa said. 'What about Ash?'

'What about him? He's older than me, too. And every time he sees me he looks the other way,' Gemma said. 'How did this become about me and not Craig? He's the one supposed to be getting the hard time. Running for office, remember?'

Theresa chuckled. 'She's not wrong about that.'

'Thanks a lot, Mum.'

'I can't pretend this is a good idea for you,' she said. 'But if you're serious, people know you. You could give Wade a good race.'

The idea glimmered in Craig's mind. Maybe he could do it.

'But you'll need a plan,' she went on. 'Grant told me he helped his brother run for mayor once, up north. Even that sounded pretty involved.'

'Fundraising, too,' put in Gemma. 'Wade does heaps of that.'

Craig was less keen on those things. But with the reminder of Gemma's dalliance with Wade, which she'd declined to discuss any further, Craig considered. If he agreed to run, maybe it would put something between the two of them.

'What about helping me out?' Craig said to his sister.

Gemma made a face. 'I suppose I could talk to Diane about fundraising . . .'

She didn't sound keen, but Craig took her up on the offer, kissing her head and thanking her while saying he needed, for the moment at least, to get back to real work.

He hadn't reached the bottom of the paddock before he saw Gemma's car turn out onto the main drive. With Diane in the loop, the whole valley would know about it by sundown.

Craig sighed. A large part of him knew that he could never pull off the slick politician that Wade could summon; he wasn't that man. He was better with practical work – he still had to meet Erica, fix that pump.

And work out how to approach things with Peta.

After Erica had signed off on the cows, he took the tool roll down to the river, but his repair took ages, most of his mind wrestling on the issue of Peta. Maybe he'd gone about it all wrong. He'd tried for too much certainty. If his work taught him anything, it was that you had to go with things as they happened, be prepared to change your approach.

So when the pump was fixed and Buck was enthusiastically pulling back up the paddock, Craig had decided that simple honesty might be best. He'd admit that he didn't have the answers. He would give her all the room she needed to finish the trail, ask if they could meet up again afterwards, even if it meant him coming to the big smoke.

Still, his stomach was full of butterflies by the time he'd sorted out all the feeds and it was getting too dark to work outside. The cottage was dim, but for a single lamp in cheerful yellow, burning through the window. The sight unwound the knots in his shoulders. He wasn't ready for her to turn him down, but he was ready to face her.

He opened the door and found the cottage neat and tidy . . . and empty.

All Peta's gear was gone. The bed had been neatly made, the kitchen scrubbed, a key he'd given her lying on the bench. Just that single lamp was burning, the only evidence she'd been here at all. Craig felt the air leave his lungs, like he'd been punched.

'Craig!' Gemma's voice caught him from behind. 'So, Diane's in quite a state but I think we've got—what is it?'

And then it was real. His mouth was sticky, his blood flooding with despair. He was too late.

'She's gone,' he said.

As Peta put one foot in front of the other up the mountain, the weight in her chest grew, and the little hiccups in her breath threatened to erupt into tears. Whenever that happened, she snatched at her maps and studied them. She wasn't entirely sure where she was. On her chart, the area between the Munroe farm and the Ridgeback showed no trails; she was relying on her memory of some of her rehab walks, and the trip up with Craig over two weeks ago.

Craig.

She sucked a shaky breath, sniffing with her head tipped back to the sky. She shoved the map away and plodded on. She was leaving for the right reasons. She'd forgotten herself, forgotten what mattered. Losing the necklace had shown her that. She had no choice but to go and finish what she'd started.

Oh, but it hurt, deep in her chest, as if someone was grinding her lungs to dust.

She didn't want Craig coming after her and making it any harder, so for the first few hours, she took detours off the trail when she could. But this tactic slowed her down and, she had to admit, increased the chance she'd end up in another accident. A falling snow gum, or another bloody wombat hole.

The weight of her pack was monstrous after several weeks without carrying it, except on a few of her last walks, and the uphill route made her breaths burn. By the time the light was fading, her ankle ached as badly as her heart.

She set her tent off the trail and away from any overhanging branches, desperate to feel the satisfaction she yearned for in recommencing the journey. But as she threaded the thin tent poles into their keepers, the forest rustled and creaked around her, and doubt lingered with the last of the light.

She knew she'd been a coward, leaving without goodbyes or explanations. But finishing the trek was more important, for herself, for Stacey, even if Craig became another memory she tried not to feel.

As the darkness gathered, she reached for the absent necklace. She sank onto her heels and put her hands over her face. She was alone now, the only person for miles.

She crawled into her sleeping bag, not even bothering with a torch, but she couldn't settle. When she started to drift off, the rustling that had always soothed her would startle her awake. Some of the noises were light, small creatures – perhaps native mice. But some crashed like boulders down the hillside, and others sounded like horses, thundering through distant trees.

She finally woke, gritty-eyed, just after dawn and packed up in a daze, the chill of the first light never thawing from her fingers. Her ankle was stiff and cold, just like her heart. She struggled on uphill until she finally saw the edge of the trees. From there, it was probably another half-day at a good pace to reach the ridge.

Mist lingered in the trunks like smoke, and déjà vu washed over her. It was just like the day Patch had come tearing down the trail, when this whole episode had started. Abruptly, a quiet fell over the forest, until all Peta could hear was her breaths. The hairs rose on her arms, and gooseflesh crawled down her neck. She froze, twenty metres short of the tree line. There, against the pale trunks, loomed a dark shape. She registered the curve of a neck and head, the pricked ears, the flared nostrils. A wild horse, its breath a metronomic huff in the foggy air.

They weren't supposed to be in this part of the park. They ran on the other side of the highest peak to the north, and then all the way to the New South Wales border. Its shoulder was a wall of muscle, and Peta knew enough from her childhood on the stud to guess that it was a stallion guarding a herd.

The ears pinned against its neck, and a flash of teeth showed as it raised a hoof.

Peta was aware of the vulnerable softness of her body. She was no match for half a tonne of animal. Silently, she unhooked her pack and let it slip to the undergrowth. Her legs refused to move; there was nowhere to run. She was at the mercy of a horse, just as Stacey had been. And Stacey was gone. The necklace was gone. Soon, her childhood home, her last connection to her family – that would be lost, too.

She sank down amongst the dead leaves as the horse danced towards her, an angry, black silhouette. Her heart thundered and the air set hard in her lungs. Was she about to die?

With the thought came regret. She'd left Craig behind. Against every fibre of her soul, she'd left him rather than take the chance of being happy. Rather than telling him she loved him. Stacey would never have done that – she'd had the courage to take risks. Peta wished in this last moment that she had never left.

The horse flicked its head, and vanished.

Peta blinked. The forest was as still as a painting, her gasping breaths the only sound. A single low branch rocked, as if by a ghostly hand. She gripped her pack with her fingers, twisting her body, searching. No horse.

Several long minutes passed as she sat in contemplation, and the forest transformed. The mist burned away, leaving only the sky at the edge of the trees, the mountains rising like beacons towards the blue.

Peta stood, leaving streaks of mud on her pants, and stumbled to the tree line. She'd told herself walking the trail had been about deciding what to do about the stud, and processing her father's death ... but was leaving Craig for that just about punishing herself over Stacey?

She didn't want him to be only a memory, didn't want to risk it being too late if she waited to go back. But the idea of the trail had been with her so long . . .

She stared back down the mountain, caught in indecision. Up, or down?

Finally, she shouldered the pack and took a step.

Chapter 22

Craig had spent the night nursing the hollow space in his chest, which refused to fill even when he sat with Bel until long after sunset. He'd thought about going after Peta, but he knew that would be a dumb move. He remembered too well what she'd been like the first time they'd met, and he knew when he wasn't wanted. That's why she'd cleared off in secret. It hurt to think he'd read the situation wrongly between them, and of all the things he'd do, he wouldn't beg.

So, instead, he was 'impossible' as Gemma described it, sullenly attending to the farm work while brushing off her attempts to engage him. Whenever she began on the issue of Peta, Craig bit her head off. Hoping that would be the end of it, he instead found it only induced Gemma to stay, and now she was perched on a straw bale in the feed shed, silently observing him as he beat a new shoe for Buck on the portable anvil. At least the hammering helped him manage his mood, and he could escape to the pub meeting later on.

'You could ride to Omeo faster than she can walk,' Gemma said now. 'Why don't you meet her at the end?'

Craig bashed the shoe, ignoring her. He couldn't tell her that the bright pain of Peta leaving was quickly dissolving into despair. He'd thought that the hurt would cure him of her, but it only seemed to make it worse. In fact, the idea of meeting her at the end had occurred to him, but he worried what kind of scene he'd create if he wasn't welcome. Without an answer, he wished Gemma would push off to do the mail run.

'Would make a good promotion,' Gemma said idly. 'Launch your campaign.'

Craig gave her the dirtiest look he could muster. 'Out.'

'I'm just *saying*.'

'Out!'

The sound of crunching tyres announced a car passing the big house. Gemma went to the window.

'It's Ash,' she said. A minute later, the cop walked in wearing a cautious expression.

'Came to see if it was true, or if Diane really has lost it this time,' he began. 'You really running for office?'

Craig sighed. 'Maybe.' He stuck five nails between his lips and lifted Buck's hoof to check the shoe's fit. Perfect.

'Masters know yet?'

'Don't know. Don't care,' he mumbled, plucking the first nail and driving it through shoe and hoof. Beyond informing Diane and asking him the occasional question, Gemma had shown little enthusiasm for helping him, and her perceived lack of allegiance only stoked his temper.

'What he means is, he welcomes spirited debate and competition,' Gemma coached from the hay bales.

'"Don't know, don't care" might fly better with the locals around here.' Ash chuckled. 'Seriously, though. You? Wearing a suit in Melbourne?'

'Diane agreed he should stick to chaps and akubras,' Gemma said. 'Although, are you still interested in appearing at the cattlemen's get-together in a few weeks? Wade's going too.'

'I go every year,' Craig protested, throwing tools back in the farrier bucket. 'Wade's the one who's missed it four years running.'

'But you haven't been to stand on a podium and give a speech. It's not you. Talk to him, Ash, he's been impossible since Peta up and left on Monday.'

'She's really gone?' Ash's forehead wrinkled. He rubbed his mouth. 'I'd got used to having her around to help. Diane obviously doesn't know yet. She'll be beside herself. She's been planning a surprise farewell party.'

'Uh oh,' Gemma said.

'So you're not going to do this horsemanship thing, Craig?'

A static crackle and a faint distorted voice drifted through the feed shed door. 'That's the car radio,' Ash said, ducking out.

Craig gratefully went back to Buck. His head was full of premonitions – having these conversations with everyone in town over the next few months. The idea was already wearing.

'You could help a bit more,' he said to Gemma. 'You're my sister.'

Her cheeks reddened. 'I can't exactly do that, can I? I mean, Wade said it would be a conflict of interest.'

'What? When?'

Gemma backed up a step. 'Don't get weird. Yesterday, after I spoke to Diane.'

So it was all still going on. Craig was struggling to find civil words when Ash reappeared. 'Sorry, Craig? Just got a radio call – apparently there's been another horse hit on the road. A tree down, too, apparently. Can I use your phone? Need to call Erica. My mobile doesn't work here.'

Craig showed Ash to the cottage phone, his insides moving like midnight-chilled lead. 'How can there be another one so soon?' he asked.

Ash's fingers were stiff as he dialled. 'Must be bad luck,' he said.

Craig didn't need to be told that; he felt like he was swimming in it, especially as he went down to the feed shed for the rifle.

'What are you going to do?' Gemma asked, her voice trembling as he unlocked the weapon. The idea of animals being hurt had given her nightmares since she was a little girl. Craig hadn't told her about the last horse for that reason.

'Just going to help Ash, that's all,' Craig said, trying to spare her. 'Why don't you come for a drink at the pub after? I've got to go to the meeting, but we could have dinner.'

Gemma seemed reassured and for a moment she was his little sister again, convinced that if he was suggesting they eat, nothing bad was about to happen. 'Okay. You want to invite Diane?'

'As long as you let me get a beer in first.'

He jogged across to the shed to retrieve the chainsaw, then met Ash descending the cottage stairs. 'Erica's going to be delayed,' the cop said.

Craig said nothing, just stowed his tools and piled into his Rover and followed Ash out of the drive. Fifteen minutes saw them down the valley to the town road, where they turned left, heading for the lower highway. After another fifteen minutes, they met a few cars coming back towards them. One in the column slowed and wound down a window, revealing Jack Rusty.

'Keep going,' he said, 'you'll be there in two minutes. Want me to bring a chainsaw?'

'Got one,' called Ash.

And true enough, a few minutes later they pulled up in front of a blockage, waiting while another car performed an awkward U-turn on the narrow highway. Craig threw his door open and came up beside Ash.

'Well, there's something you don't see every day.'

The tree across the road was hefty, a scribbly gum that had a trunk two feet across, and was tall enough to block both lanes.

'Where the hell's the accident?' Ash said, pacing the length of the tree and peering down the road.

Craig was already scanning around. He noticed the end of the trunk. The tree had clearly been felled, the stump showing neatly cut surfaces, and piles of wood shavings on either side. Someone had thrown some branches over it but quickly, with not enough leaves to cover the evidence.

Ash had vaulted the trunk and was pacing down the road, searching the brush to either side. He came back as Craig was peeling off the branches.

'What did they say on the radio?' he called across.

'That someone at the scene called in a car accident, which had struck a horse and knocked down a tree. They weren't still on the line, so they had no idea if anyone was injured.'

They both heard sirens in the distance. 'That's the ambos,' Ash said.

Craig felt a cold sweat gather between his shoulder blades. 'This isn't an accident. Look.'

He pointed out the chainsaw marks, feeling like he was missing something important.

Ash's face wore a frown of confusion. 'Okay, so someone cut it down. But there are no tyre marks, no evidence I can see of a collision. Most cars have ABS these days but if they'd hit an animal . . .'

'Why would someone call in an accident?'

'Could be a bunch of kids in the bush, laughing their heads off because we're standing around with our thumbs up our arses . . . I'd better call dispatch back.'

Craig saw the familiar forest on either side of the road – gum trunks receding through a sub-forest of shrubs and grass. The towns and farm were carved from that forest, and it sheltered the tracks and trails that were as familiar to him as breathing. But what was normally home felt suddenly sinister. And he remembered all the conversations at the farmers' meetings, that tonight that's where he was headed, regular as clockwork.

A chill crawled down his neck. He didn't like it.

Ash was looking up the mountain as he spoke into the radio, but Craig was already striding for his car. Something told him he had to get back to the farm, right now. Everything else faded, even Ash yelling to the ambos.

Craig spun the wheel and headed back to town. Metal clicked on metal as he planted his right foot to the floor. He snatched a glance at his watch. He'd been away for twenty-five minutes already; it was another fifteen back. Forty minutes. They had two tractors in the shed, and two quad bikes that wouldn't be hard to put on a truck.

And Gemma was there by herself.

The Land Rover's rear end slid as Craig rounded into the drive. He squinted at the big house. Gemma's car was gone.

He pulled up with a squeal of brakes and tumbled out.

'Gem?'

No response, and when he pushed the door open, he found a note on the kitchen bench. *Gone for drive. Meet you at pub.*

Craig turned the paper in his fingers. Gemma had ripped it from her invoice book, the rest of her jewellery making supplies still on the table. Gemma was ordinarily so neat, it was an odd sight. But maybe he was just imagining things.

Ten seconds later he was back in the Rover and angel-gearing down the hill to the cottage. Everything looked in order, and the doors of the big shed were still closed. Craig pulled up outside, threw on his headlights for illumination, then jumped down and hauled the door open. In the twin beams, he could see both tractors were still there, both quad bikes, too. The work bench, full of tools, was undisturbed, and the portable forge was in its usual place. He breathed out.

More slowly, he walked around the shed and looked out on the herd, still in the middle paddock. Even from this distance, he could tell there were none missing. He was just being paranoid. He'd call Ash, see if he still needed help with the tree, then meet Gemma at the pub and suck up his misjudgement like a man.

He turned back for the cottage, counting the horses off in the yards as he went. Everyone was there; Buck was hovering under the shady awning near the feed shed, enjoying a scratching from Candle, who paused to prick his ears. Craig plucked his shirt from his chest; he'd sweated through it. He pulled it over his head and into a ball he could throw in the hamper.

Then a glance towards the rear of the cottage made him pause. There was a dark mark in the grass, one that hadn't been there this morning. Jogging over, he found twin rows of dark earth pushed up beneath the grass. They only showed where the ground was always a little soft, courtesy of the septic tank, but they were unmistakably tyre marks.

Craig followed the indentations, his gut turning in a sick circle. Someone *had* been here. The tracks were no longer visible after the boggy ground, but the grass was still folded over in places. He reached the edge of the field at a run, catching himself on the fence post as his eyes roamed where the tracks disappeared under the boundary. There. The fence wire had been clipped and retied. Beyond, through the scrub, was a disused four-wheel-drive track. He knew it well; it was the original drive to the farm and it led down through the forest to where the falls crossed the old mine wall, eventually connecting to the highway heading north. It hadn't been used since the new, more direct and less-prone-to-flooding track had been cut, but it was still passable.

But what had they taken?

And then, with an arrow of horror, Craig realised.

He ran to the feed shed. The world turned slowly as he rounded the corner and looked into Bel's box. Empty. He ducked through the fence, facing the long field, calling her.

All that returned was silence.

He called again, expecting to see her elegant head with its pricked ears appear at the rise, the foal in tow, or around the corner from the box.

Still nothing.

Craig's insides were on fire, driving his blood and bones into overdrive. Candle came at a trot, his ears whipping back and forth at the panic in Craig's call. The saddle went on in a blur, the bridle in a half-second. Craig's hands moved the girth and throat strap buckles in precise movements. His only hesitation was when he ran back to his car for the rifle. He'd only picked up a gun intending to point it at someone once before in his life.

Guess it was going to be twice.

He stowed the gun in its saddle sheath. His last action was to pick up the cottage phone and put in a call to Ash; all he got was the copper's voicemail.

Candle pranced as Craig threw the gate open and swung his leg over. They wouldn't be getting away, not this time. Not from a man who knew the mountain better than they did.

He pointed Candle up the paddock, straight at the tracks. The horse never hesitated. He galloped like he was a thoroughbred on the home straight at Flemington, then tucked his feet up to clear the fence. Craig copped a branch across his bare shoulder but the sting barely registered. All he could see were the signs of where the thieves' truck had passed through – the broken branches, the cracked ridges in the path – and all he could think about was how many minutes it would be until he had her back.

Chapter 23

Peta's back was slick with sweat, but her soul lifted the moment the cluster of buildings winked into view through the trees. All the ache ebbed from her chest; Craig's cottage and the stables, with their silver-grey shingles, seemed to anchor the green fields, promising the comfort and permanence of home. This was the right decision. She knew it was.

She stepped off the trail and onto the driveway, shifting her heavy pack. She'd been thinking about what she would say the whole way back, and now she wondered if Craig would be here, or if she'd have to wait.

The farm was quiet, but for far-off lowing. Gemma's car was gone. And Craig's seemed to be, too. No, wait, there it was, parked by the big shed beyond the cottage, whose doors were open. Craig must be in there.

But, besides the tractors, quad bikes, tools and drums of stores, the shed was empty.

'Craig?' she called, hesitant, unsure of her reception.

He couldn't be far away; the Rover's driver door was still open, the headlights on. She strode back to the cottage door, found it open, and called again.

No response.

Peta dropped the pack, fear sparking between her ribs. Once, when she'd been a young doctor out on a visit to a remote house, she'd found a front door open like this. The woman in the house had collapsed and broken her hip, lying on the floor for two days unable to move. The thought drove her inside. But Craig wasn't there. Her next move was the feed shed.

A t-shirt was crumpled in the dirt to the side of the door. Peta knew it well; it was one of Craig's favourites. That in itself was unsettling; Craig was attentive and neat, especially in the feed shed.

She heard a car coming down the drive.

Sticking her head out, she saw the police four-wheel drive dragging a plume of dust past the big house. Ash drove straight down the hill and, seeing her, pulled up beside the cottage.

'Peta! I thought you'd gone.'

She blushed. 'I did.'

'Craig here?' Ash's brow was so furrowed the skin between the lines had gone white.

'No. I was just looking for him.'

'He left a message that he'd seen tracks, that someone had taken Bel.'

The sweat on Peta's back chilled. 'Oh, no.' She ran for the feed shed. Ash was faster, and he was already inside by the time Peta reached the doorway. The first thing she saw was the open rifle cabinet. Then the open rails on Candle's yard. Buck spotted them and came trotting up, hopeful for a feed.

But no Bel.

Peta ducked around the corner. Candle's tack was missing from the racks.

She heard the shed door bounce as Ash went back outside. Peta leaned her hands on the yard rails scanning down the paddock. Bel and the foal weren't in sight. A gate in the side of their paddock was open; acid burned Peta's throat. Not Bel.

When she ran back out she found Ash in a crouch, inspecting the ground behind the cottage.

'They came across here,' he said. 'And I can't see Craig's rifle in the car. He had it down on the road earlier.'

'Candle's gone, and all his tack,' Peta said. 'So he must be riding. Why didn't he just drive?'

Ash's feet tore the grass as he twisted around, following the line of the tracks. A minute later, they were at the fence. 'Sneaky buggers,' he said. 'The fence was clipped and fixed, and there are broken branches. Craig must have gone that way. I can see an old track, but where does it go?'

Peta didn't even have to think. 'It's a really steep spur,' she said. 'I walked it once, getting my ankle right. It comes out at the falls.'

—

Craig had taken every shortcut he could remember on the winding track, Candle cutting downhill between the switchbacks, dodging trees like barrels at a rodeo. Craig's shoulders were raw from copping the branches, and stringybark fell on him in cascades, but he kept his focus on Candle. The ground was treacherously steep off the track, and he had to shift his weight just right so Candle could find his footing.

The horse seemed to be enjoying himself. Craig never allowed him to run like this in races; too quick for long distance – and now he seemed to relish the opportunity to show off, as if he longed for the time when he'd roamed wild in the mountains.

Craig was doing mental calculations. He'd been away forty-five minutes. Even if they'd been waiting for him to leave, it would have taken them some time to drive in and load Bel. Maybe fifteen minutes if she'd been down in the field. And they'd be slow going on this drive with a truck. It would maybe take them half an hour to negotiate all the switchbacks and the overgrown sections. Craig could do it in a fraction of the time. Still, he wasn't sure he could catch them before they reached the highway.

As the ground finally levelled out and the track began to run beside the old mine's highwall, he found a rockfall across the track. Craig pulled up, Candle's breath snorting into the air. Fresh, boggy vehicle tracks marked several attempts to go around into the nearby scrub. That would have slowed them down.

Craig pushed on. He steered Candle around and into the floor of the old mine, cutting a path straight across the uneven, overgrown mounds of tailings, Candle placing his feet like a mountain goat. Eventually this track would rejoin the highway above the village, and the truck would pull away.

But finally, through the tea-tree he spotted them. The truck lumbered on the track beneath the red and cream scarred rockface. They were picking up speed now they were on the flat, the whine and rumble as they changed gears echoing through the bush. The sight stoked the fire in Craig's blood. It wasn't a proper horse truck, just a covered van. Candle sprang towards it through the scrub, and a shot of tea-tree filled Craig's senses. The bottom of the old mine was dense with regrowth, and he had to keep to the edge of it, hoping the thieves would be too focused ahead to spot him. He could see only the shadow of whoever was in the cab, and he was burning to hurt them.

As he closed in on them from behind, he knotted the reins and pulled the rifle from the saddle case. Candle kept up the chase as Craig cocked the weapon. His vision was filled with the ochre red streak of the highwall's dirt face. It flashed in the space between the truck's cab and the back, and then through the cab window as he drew alongside.

The man sitting in the passenger seat had a tattooed arm up on the window, his attention inward as he fiddled with the radio, a lit cigarette dangling from his mouth. He straightened and glanced out, straight into the barrel of Craig's rifle.

'Pull up,' Craig yelled.

The driver saw what was going on in the same instant. A squeal of brakes, and the truck slipped back as Candle overtook them. Craig saw Yarraman Falls rushing towards him, its pool a deep green. Candle skidded to a halt two feet before the water. For a second, all Craig could hear was a roar, and he wasn't certain if it was the falls, the truck's engine, or his own blood. He spun Candle on his hind legs.

The truck had stopped, the two men still inside. Craig advanced on them, rifle raised.

'Out,' he shouted.

Very slowly the doors opened. Craig didn't recognise either of them, but they didn't have the look of locals. They were youngish, maybe in their twenties, with scruffy hair and sun-kissed faces, tattoos, and dark sunglasses. Both of them stood behind their open doors.

Now what?

Craig hadn't thought this far ahead. The men waited, hands raised, though the passenger rested one on the truck's door frame. Craig wanted them to open the back of the truck so he could see Bel was in there, but if he did that, he might lose sight of one of them.

'You, driver, walk around the front,' he called.

A shot cracked the air. Craig had a microsecond to realise that the passenger had a handgun. Instinctively, he threw himself down and the earth rushed up to meet him. He tasted blood and earth, then heard dirt scratch and hiss under boots as the men ran. Then a punch landed on the back of his head and he blacked out.

He came round in what must have been only a few seconds. Fervent discussion was going on above him, and he could hear the click, click of a safety being played with. On and off. He couldn't see Candle, but he could see two sets of boots.

He launched himself off the ground and drove his shoulder into the nearest legs, knocking the man flat. Grabbing hands came from over his right shoulder, so he twisted, kicking out a leg that tripped one of the men. He then spun and caught the other man in the kidney with a ripping punch. Craig lurched to his feet. The first man was stretching for his gun, so Craig kicked it off the road, then braced his hands on his knees, winded and dizzy. His own rifle was nowhere to be seen. And he had a hell of a headache.

Something bumped him in the back and he spun with his fists up, only to find Candle, nostrils flared, ears swivelling in distress. In relief, Craig grabbed rope off the saddle and trussed the first man like a calf. The second was moaning about his back, but he seemed to still have use of his arms and legs, so Craig tied him up as well. Then he checked Candle over twice, making sure he hadn't been hit.

Job done, he leaned against the saddle, his whole body aching. Then slowly, he paced around until he found his rifle, fallen into the ditch on the side of the track. His headache pounded as he bent to retrieve it by the stock. It was then he heard vehicles.

Fearful it might be accomplices arriving at some rendezvous, Craig fought the aches to pace down to the back of the truck, rifle raised. The long shadows of the sinking sun made the highwall into dark bars. He could hear Bel snuffling inside the back of the truck, and he was ready to defend her. As he stood there, the first tremor came into his fingers. Hold still, he told himself.

He saw the strobes first, then the familiar four-wheel drive covered in stripped foliage came bouncing down the track and skidded to a halt. Ash. Thank Christ. Craig dropped his aim. It was probably an offence to point a gun at an officer of the law.

Ash came running and Craig sagged against the rifle. He pointed a thumb over his shoulder. 'They're back that way.'

Then he saw an apparition. Peta, hauling a first-aid kit from Ash's car.

He had no words, only a spark of confused relief. He'd thought she'd gone, so this made no sense. He must have been wrong. Her expression seemed oddly concerned and professional, and it was then he realised blood was running down his face. He almost laughed; the sight of blood must have that effect on her.

Her fingers were moving over his skin, assessing, before he'd had a chance to ask her any questions. 'What happened?'

'You should see the other guys,' he tried, and was rewarded with small smile flitting over her lips. His mind cleared and he stopped her hands. 'It can wait. I need to open the truck.'

He fumbled with the latches. Finally, the doors creaked open and in the dark interior, he could see the outline of Bel's pale coat. She'd wedged herself right up against the end. Down the road he could hear Ash calling out, and the crunch of another vehicle's approach. He recognised Erica's voice yelling back.

Talking softly to Bel, he climbed inside. She had clearly been terrified, the pink of her nostrils showing, her head held high where her halter rope had been tied off short. He approached, projecting a calm he didn't feel. She would pick up on how fast his heart was racing, so he tried to breathe easy, push his fears away. It was okay, now. It was all okay.

Finally, he was close enough to touch. The heat radiated off her skin, her muscles trembling. 'There,' he said, stroking her neck as he untied the rope. 'It's all right.'

It occurred to him that the foal wasn't here, and that could only be making it worse. He must have missed the filly in the paddock, or maybe she'd escaped somewhere on the farm. Either way, Bel would be the best one to find her baby. He just had to take her home.

'How's things in here?' Erica's voice came from the light outside.

'Shaken up,' Craig said. 'Is Candle really all right? One of them fired a shot.'

'Seems to be. He's just tried to eat my ponytail. What about Bel?'

Craig was running a hand down her front legs, then across her back. 'So far, all right. Wait a second.' When he reached the back legs, he could tell she had shifted her weight. The near leg was fine, but the off she'd tipped up on her toe.

By now, Erica had crawled into the back and was shadowing Craig's movements. He felt the change in her body when she looked at Bel's leg. She twisted back around.

'Peta? Can you see if Ash has a good flashlight? There's one in my truck if not.'

While they waited, Craig tried to swallow the fear that was growing inside him like an insidious weed. Erica was gently feeling the leg. By the time Peta had brought a lantern back, she'd finished her survey by feel. She straightened with the light, running it all over the mare before switching it off.

'Craig, come with me a second.'

'Why?'

'Not far. Just to the end of the truck.'

⚊

'Where's the foal?' Erica asked when they'd reached the square of light. Craig could see Peta rummaging in the back of Ash's car, the first-aid box at her feet. He had an awful sense of foreboding.

'Back at the farm, I think,' he said tightly.

Erica turned to him then, and he saw the tears in her eyes. 'Craig. Her leg's broken. Do you understand what I'm saying?'

Erica's face had receded into some kind of grey mist. He could barely hear what she was saying.

'Craig. Craig?'

'Can't you fix it?' he asked. His voice was distant and strange. A small boy's.

She shook her head sadly. Her hands pulled on his shoulders. 'Listen to what I'm saying. It's bad. We don't have a way to transport her from here. Even if we solved that, it would be hours of pain for her, and little chance surgery would work. You want to do all that and have her get laminitis? Look at her. She knows.'

Craig dragged his eyes around. Bel's attention was fixed on him, her ears swivelling, her head dipped. He didn't know if Erica was right; but Bel was certainly waiting on him. He felt a great sinking weight. He'd failed her. Since he'd first taken her away from Masters, she'd been his responsibility. And now look at what had happened. He couldn't bear that he had to tell her she wouldn't be leaving this shitty trailer. He didn't want to think about what she'd gone through being put into it. Maybe she'd broken the leg during the drive. But maybe she'd kicked out before they'd even got her up the stock loader. They were bastards; they deserved to be lying out there on the road, trussed up and hurting.

Craig had to shove that all down. 'No guns,' he said.

'No. Sedative and phenobarb. Then we can take her home.'

'Give me some time with her first,' he said softly.

Erica patted his arm. From anyone else, Craig would have found it patronising. But he knew the wiry vet was distressed, too. She wiped her eyes on her sleeve cuff. 'Of course. I'm going back to the truck for my gear. I'll hold everyone else off, too.'

And so Craig had to go back to Bel. This time, the horse pressed her nose into his chest, then laid her head heavily against him. She blew out a breath.

'I know,' he said, his fingers running through her mane. He tried to apologise, to tell her he was sorry he hadn't done a better job at keeping her safe, but the words were jammed up behind his eyeballs. All he could do was hold her while the tears slipped down his face.

'I'm sorry,' he whispered finally, as Erica reappeared. He knew this couldn't be avoided, but he felt as though he was still on the chase with Candle; the scenery going by too fast and no way to pull up. Erica saved him. She did nothing until he said she could, and her sure hands placed a line quickly and painlessly, while Bel breathed into his hands.

And so Bel died in the back of the thieves' truck, in the holding cup of the old mine, her head resting in Craig's lap. Erica knew her work well. Bel simply closed her eyes and folded, her breath drifting, until her head was heavy and still. Craig knew when Erica pulled her stethoscope away from Bel's side that the horse was gone.

And then came the grief, shattering and heavy, like a boulder tumbling down from above. As it crashed through him, Craig felt all the anger he'd tamped down boil up onto the surface. Bel was gone.

Nothing could hold him back now.

Chapter 24

Peta sat waiting in the open back of Ash's four-wheel drive. Between her, Erica and Ash, they made a miserable trio. Erica had filled them in on what had happened, and Peta was stripped raw at what Craig must be going through. She wanted to go to him, but knew better than to invade the private space. Ash was offering her a Monte Carlo out of a beaten packet. She shook her head, amazed he could eat. Then she realised he was munching like a machine; he probably wouldn't have noticed if he'd been chewing bark.

Erica had no such affectations. She leaned against the open door, arms folded, riding out the silence with clear displeasure. Finally, she turned to Ash.

'What did you do with the two hogties?'

'Cuffed them to a tree once Peta gave them an all clear,' Ash said. 'Not exactly standard procedure, but . . .'

'Enough said. Perfectly good horse ruined through incompetence,' Erica huffed, wiping her eyes again.

'Most thieves are incompetent. That's why they get caught.'

'I don't suppose I can go spit on them?' Peta asked. The idea actually felt like it might be satisfying.

'Can't be seen endorsing behaviour like that,' Ash said. 'But if I was looking the other way – wait a sec. Craig?'

Peta twisted around to see Craig exiting the back of the truck, his face twisted and intent, his bare chest making him seem all the more primal and dangerous. He didn't look at them as he stalked around the side, even as he stumbled and put out a hand to the truck to steady himself.

'Shit,' Ash muttered, throwing down the biscuit packet. 'Craig! You can't touch them!'

Craig didn't reply. He'd obviously spotted where Ash had the two men cuffed to a loop of chain around a tree. Both of them had seen him coming and were huddling against the trunk.

Peta ran after Ash, who had managed to get an arm around Craig's shoulder.

'Let me go,' Craig hissed.

'Can't do that, mate. Now just come and—'

Craig stumbled again. At first, Peta thought that Ash must have pushed him backwards, but then the policeman lunged in an attempt to catch him. Peta watched as Craig's face turned sideways, his gaze unfocused.

Ash barely managed to keep him upright.

Peta didn't need Ash's look of appeal to know something was very wrong. 'Sit down,' she said. But he stayed swaying on his feet. All she could see was the blood clotted at the corner of Craig's eyebrow. She tried to focus his attention. 'Craig. *Craig.* Were you hit?'

'Mmmm.'

His knees buckled. Ash managed to stop him hitting the deck, but even once he was sitting, the grey pallor didn't lift, and he couldn't register anything Peta was saying. Peta felt an old terror come creeping out. She'd seen patients like this, but not someone she knew and cared about. Not since Stacey.

With rapid fingers, Peta felt over Craig's skull, finding a boggy patch behind his left ear that even in his stupor made him wince. She pulled up his eyelids; the left pupil was sluggish.

Ash hovered. 'You need the ambos?'

'Yes. Fast,' she said as she propped her knee behind him to keep him sitting. 'Then get on the radio and organise an airlift. He's going to need a trauma surgeon. Any delay and we need to take him to the med centre ourselves.'

Next moment, the first-aid box landed next to Peta and Erica was kneeling across. The vet threw open the lid. 'What can I do?'

'Put a line in that side while I finish this survey. We need to keep him as stable as possible, and keep the intracranial pressure down.'

'You think he has a bleed?'

Peta didn't want to say what she was thinking. Subdural haematoma. She wanted to be wrong; it was the most lethal of all head-injury complications. What Craig needed was a CT scan, surgery and the best support a hospital could give – and all of that as fast as possible.

But they were in the middle of goddamn nowhere.

In her peripheral vision, she could see Ash gesticulating as he spoke on the police radio. Down the track, the two thieves watched. Let them watch, the bastards. She suspected they'd be waiting a while.

She focused her attention back on Craig. Erica, muttering it was good he had veins like a horse, had managed to insert a sixteen-gauge cannula into his arm, and Peta strained to hear his heartbeat over her own panicked breaths as she took his blood pressure.

Craig's eyes opened, unfocused. 'Hurts,' he said, when she'd pulled the stethoscope from her ears. 'Head hurts.'

'I know,' she said, trying to hold his gaze. 'Stay with me, okay? We need to get you to hospital.'

His lids drooped. Erica caught him as he sagged again. 'How long for those ambos?' she yelled towards Ash.

'Two minutes!'

It felt like two hours, but finally the community ambulance team came tearing in from the town end, faster than she imagined it was probably allowed in the rule book. They pulled up alongside Erica's truck near the creek, and were soon unloading a stretcher. What followed was a tense few minutes, manoeuvring Craig onto it while they waited to hear about an evac.

'There's some bullshit going on in air dispatch,' Ash panted as they felt for slippery rocks near the falls with their feet. 'They're trying to find a pilot who still has enough flying hours left today.'

Peta shook her head. 'Tell me when you've got good news.'

The drive back to the med centre was white-knuckled and completed in ten minutes. Even so, Peta knew he was slipping. On the scale of assessment doctors used for consciousness, he had started out at the best score: fifteen. But during the journey he slipped to eleven.

For a brief moment when they arrived, he opened his eyes again, although this didn't reassure Peta in the slightest. She and the ambos were doing everything they could, but they weren't in a hospital. They worked in the back of the van outside the med centre, hoping to hear about an evac and avoid another transfer. As the minutes ticked by, they had to tube him to help him breathe, and push in fluid to keep his blood pressure up.

Time was running out.

Peta began to contemplate desperate measures. If she had to, could she put a hole in Craig's skull to alleviate the pressure? The med centre had no trephine, she was sure of that. She was about to pick up the phone and do some yelling of her own when Ash came running.

'There's a chopper coming to the airfield now.'

The next fifteen minutes was breath-held madness. Peta remembered only snippets: passing the Yarraman (international) Airport sign, the helicopter settling down on the grass. Craig's eyelids fluttering when the flight doc checked his pulse. Then the bird was in the sky, and Peta was left behind, windblown on the tarmac with the ambos and Ash.

Peta was frozen, listening to the retreating thunder. It sounded like a fading heartbeat. And that was when the truth rose up and struck her deep in the chest. Craig's prognosis was not good. Even at St Ann's Hospital, one of the best trauma centres in Melbourne, it could all turn out the worst possible way.

She had to move when Ash put a hand on her arm. 'I've just reached Gemma. She's coming down to the med centre. You'll need to talk to her.'

Gemma arrived five minutes after they got back, near hysterical with her shirt mis-buttoned and her hair coming out of its ponytail. Ash had to spend two minutes calming her down before she could put a sentence together, then he had to call Theresa in Queensland, because Gemma couldn't manage it.

Twenty seconds later the med centre doors burst open again. 'I saw the chopper,' said Diane, who appeared to have run all the way. She took in their faces. 'Oh, god, who is it?'

'Craig has some kind of head injury. He's on his way to Melbourne,' Peta said quickly, but her voice cracked like shards of broken glass.

'Is he going to be all right?'

Peta hesitated. Social protocol dictated that you said, yes, of course he'll be fine. But she looked into Diane's wide enquiring eyes and couldn't lie. 'I don't know,' she said, sweeping the glass behind her professional armour. 'The air lift was delayed. We just have to wait.'

'Delayed? Why?'

This seemed to snap Gemma out of her mind-block. 'I don't understand how this happened,' she said. 'You said he was fine, then he suddenly collapsed?'

'We won't know anything until they do scans in Melbourne,' Peta said. Her voice caught and she bit the inside of her mouth to stop herself breaking down.

At last Gemma's panic seemed to pass through like a storm cloud, and she shook herself. 'And these two men, you'll be charging them?' she said, turning her shiny-eyed attention on Ash as he cupped the phone receiver.

'They'll be in a world of legal pain. Your mother's saying Grant's driving her to the airport now, and she'll get on the first flight.'

Gemma drew herself up. 'Right. Okay. I'll start driving. Oh wait, I'll need to call Harry—oh, no I forgot he's gone. Maybe Seb, see if he can look after the farm . . .'

'He's down in Mansfield,' Diane said. 'Mother's sick, not due back for another week. What about Charlie?'

'He's just out of hospital himself. The herd needs turning back out to the lower pasture, and there are the horses.'

'Forget it, you go,' Diane said firmly. 'Your mum will get there before you do at this rate. It's only a three-and-a-half-hour flight from Cairns. I'll call who I need to help sort out your place.'

'Are you sure?'

'I might only be a copper's wife, but I've been around this area long enough. I can do it. Charlene will watch the shop.'

Gemma grabbed her keys. 'What about you, Peta? Are you coming?'

By now, Peta had had time to think. And while she had no desire to delay leaving, Craig's family should go first. 'I'm going to show Diane the horse feeds, pick up my pack, and put a bag of clothes together for you.'

'Oh, I didn't even think—'

'Then I'll drive Craig's car to Melbourne,' she rushed on. 'He'll need it when he gets out.'

She had to cling on to that hope.

Diane was already holding the clinic door open. 'Yes, yes, you should take two cars. Don't forget what happened to the Mullers three years ago. Went off the road on the lower highway and they waited a whole day before someone found them. Best to have back-up.'

'Thanks for the thought,' Gemma said, aghast.

Diane was unapologetic. 'You don't want to tempt fate. Now, which hospital are you going to? You must call when you get in safely.'

—

Five minutes later, Diane was driving Peta back up the hill to the Munroe farm, and the conversation had circled to drilling her on the issues with the airlift.

'I don't really know any more about it, just that they didn't have a pilot with enough flying time left today to do it legally,' Peta said, distracted.

Not knowing what was happening with Craig dragged on her thoughts like a heavy, cold stone. Would he even make it to the ED? Who would be on? How soon could they scan him and get him to theatre?

'Well, I'll talk to Ash about it. It's not good enough,' Diane said as they pulled into the drive. Then, as she cruised past the big house, she touched Peta's arm. 'I'm sorry if I'm going on. I'm scared for him, and I ramble. You must be out of your mind. Be sure to drive very, very carefully. It takes five hours and the sun will be down before too long – lots of wildlife on the road. Now, how do I do the feeds? You shouldn't wait for that.'

'There's a board in the shed, all the combinations are written up there. You just don't have to do Bel's.'

Peta's voice cracked again, and then she had to tell Diane about Bel in rapid-fire sentences between blowing her nose. Diane was appalled. 'After here I'm going straight down to the watchhouse. I want to see who the bastards are. Go do what you need to so you can get going. I'll sort things out from this end, and I'll call Erica and find out what's happening with Bel. Craig will want to know where she's buried when he comes round.'

Peta hung onto the assurance in Diane's voice as she strode down the hall to Gemma's bedroom. She'd never been inside, but Gemma's organisation helped. Peta rapidly found an empty backpack hanging from the bedpost, and opening three drawers in the chest under the window, threw in underwear, three shirts, two pairs of jeans and what looked like beaten trackpants. Emerging from the back door, she shuffled down the hill, her ankle aching. Diane had parked by the cottage and disappeared into the feed shed. Peta found her pack still by the cottage door as she went for Craig's Rover, parked outside the big shed, the keys still in the ignition. Thank goodness Ash had turned the headlights off.

She threw the pack and backpack into the back seat. Then, as she climbed in, she caught a flash of movement outside the window. At first, she saw nothing. Then, she made out a tiny chestnut face with its misshapen star peeping around the shed.

'Oh, you're here,' Peta said.

She'd forgotten about Bel's foal in all that had happened. Her heart broke at seeing the little animal, her body pressed against the cottage, her head lowered, ears drooping. She remembered foals being weaned on her parents' stud, the way they looked for their mothers. But Bel would never be coming back for her baby. And there was a more pressing issue – Bel had been gone for much of the day, so who knew what the foal had eaten or drunk in that time. She could see her little legs were covered in burrs; maybe she'd been out looking for Bel and now night was falling, had come back to the familiarity of the yards.

Peta stretched out her fingers gently, and when the foal didn't shy away, she inched towards the shed, stroking its neck and shoulder as she'd seen Craig do. The filly seemed to accept Peta, her coat shivering. She had seen Craig getting the filly used to being handled, including short times with a halter on, but now all she could think was to make sure that the animal was secure and safe. Amazingly, the foal allowed Peta to encourage her towards the feed shed. There, Peta found Diane squinting at the board.

'I thought you'd be gone— Oh,' Diane said, putting down a bucket.

'This is Bel's foal,' Peta said. 'Can you open the gate there?'

The filly went back into the yard with its big loose box, and sniffed at the straw. No doubt, it smelled of Bel. Peta wiped her eyes as she strode off into the paddock and made sure the other gates were shut. When she returned, Diane was coming back out of the cottage.

'I just called, and Erica's on her way up anyway,' Diane said. 'She was organising someone to drive the truck back up here, but she'll come and see the foal now. She said it was a good thing we found her.'

So Peta waited. She could do nothing but stroke the little animal's neck, trying to imitate how Craig had behaved. Otherwise, she had no idea what to do with a foal – it had been too long since she'd lived at home, and she'd been too young to know the ins and outs of situations like this. She could only remember orphaned foals being fed with bottles. When Bel's filly was still shaking, she had Diane find a blanket to throw over her.

Erica rumbled into the yard a few minutes later.

'Well, seems in good enough health. Bit dehydrated, and she'll be pining. I've got Jack Rusty bringing Candle back up. He and Buck are the only other horses she knows, so that might help for now. We'll try some fluids, then I need to get on the phone and see what I can find in the way of a foster mother. I don't like my chances.'

'I'll help,' Diane put in, pulling a peacock-blue address book from her jeans pocket. 'What are you looking for, exactly?'

So two hours after Craig's flight, when Peta finally drove away from the farm, she was assured that Bel's filly would have the best chance anyone could hope for.

But what about Craig?

The roads down became black long before Peta reached the motorway. All she had during that time were the headlights lighting up the pale trunks of the trees in an endless black expanse as she turned the car, left, right, left, right, down the switchbacks. She'd had dreams like this once, when Stacey was first injured, and then again when she'd been in the exam hell before graduating medicine. She was lost in a forest, always at night, and she could hear her sister's voice. Not the words . . . there were never words, but she knew it was Stacey. And then the hoof beats. They would come from all around and drown out anything else. In the dream there was no escape. The forest stretched forever, the night was endless, and she never emerged. She would never hear Stacey's voice again, only the hoof beats.

Peta pressed her fingers into her temple. They had been only dreams. But now, driving through it, she couldn't deny that what waited in Melbourne was very, very real.

Chapter 25

The forest, of course, did not last forever. Just after eight pm, the road straightened and widened, and she rattled across the flats to an on-ramp for three more painful hours on the motorway. Peta surfed the radio stations. Music seemed a poor choice, sending her emotional rollercoaster to vertigo highs and subterranean lows. When Shakespeare's Sister came on, she punched the button angrily and found a dry program about artwork on Radio National, and turned up the volume.

But even the mind-numbing drone of the art professor had no effect on her heart rate once she cleared the city limits. No one had called, her mobile silent on the passenger seat. That could mean good news . . . or no news. But did anyone in Yarraman even have her number? That could mean all the bad news in the world was waiting for her to catch up.

It was after eleven-thirty when she found a park and entered the cool clinical air of the emergency department. She spotted Gemma immediately, slumped in a chair in the far corner of the waiting area with another, older woman alongside. Peta approached with terror making her breaths into short little gasps.

'Oh my god, Peta, we were worried,' Gemma said, leaping up. 'Mum, this is Peta.'

'Theresa,' the woman said, her voice steady. Peta had to double-take. Theresa was a photocopy of Gemma, but for the glasses pushed up over her greying hair, the length of which was twisted into a plait. The touches of age were only noticeable up close – Theresa's cheeks were no longer as rounded as Gemma's, and lines creased her eyes. But she looked out from the same blue eyes, the ones she had no doubt also given to Craig. Such a strong family resemblance underlined the strength of the emotion, and that she was only an outsider. She held her elbows awkwardly.

But then Theresa was pulling Peta down into a seat, holding onto her hand, squeezing with warm fingers. 'I only just got here, and there's no news yet,' she said quickly. 'The nurse said the surgery finished ten minutes ago, and the surgeon would come down to see us. Gemma told me you helped Craig in Yarraman.'

'What I could,' Peta stammered.

Theresa searched her face. Then Peta realised the woman was just as scared as she was, and was probably holding herself together for Gemma. Conversation was a dam to hold in their hope.

'Craig's told me so much about you,' she went on.

'He did?'

A brief smile, but so very warm it showed the cracks in her calm. 'I think he was looking forward to us meeting. I'm sorry we didn't, under happier circumstances.'

Theresa's hands were still around Peta's. Normally Peta would have pulled away, but there was something steady and comforting in the touch. 'I don't know much about hospitals,' Theresa said. 'Do you know what they're doing?'

Peta swallowed. 'I would guess they're making sure there's no pressure build-up in his head,' she said. Then she looked at Gemma's distraught face. 'But it's better not to guess. Why don't you tell me about your trip? Craig said you were in Queensland.'

With a grateful look, Theresa talked, about her partner Grant, and the long journey they were both on now their children were all grown, the old friends and family they were visiting along the way. Then she talked about Grant's farm, the orchards and sheep they were running, about the reservations she'd had leaving the Munroe place, but how well Gemma and Craig had done. So there was no silence as they waited, but each passing minute kicked Peta's anxiety into a higher gear. If it was taking the surgeon this long, he hadn't seen fit to leave the post-op area, which might mean things weren't going well.

Eventually, however, a woman in green scrubs appeared from the elevators. Her glasses had slipped on her nose and grey hair escaped from her theatre cap. Peta recognised her as Dr Garret, one of the premier trauma surgeons, a woman who'd blowtorched a trail through the male-dominated specialty. She'd been someone Peta admired in med school, and she'd seen her presentations over the years. Was this a good omen? Or the most horrible taunt?

Now the doctor marched straight across. 'Mrs Munroe?' she asked Theresa.

'Yes, and Gemma, Craig's sister, and Peta,' Theresa said quickly.

'I'm Dr Garret. I need to lay out a few things right at the start,' she began.

Peta clenched the plastic arms of her chair.

'The scans showed a bleed between Craig's brain and the skull, which was causing an increased pressure. The surgery was able to relieve that pressure and stop the bleeding. He's in ICU now, and for the time being we're using medication to keep him unconscious. This is just to give everything time to settle.'

The doctor held a long pause, waiting for this news to register. Gemma's face was a mask of misery. Thoughts of Stacey bloomed across Peta's mind.

Theresa was pragmatic. 'Are there any good signs?'

A single curt nod. 'He's young, and he's fit. He came through the surgery well, and from what I understand, he received good care in the time before he could reach us. Given how far he had to come, that could have made the difference.'

'That's Peta's doing,' Theresa said, reaching over to squeeze Peta's hand.

Peta hardly felt the contact. She knew she had barely been able to do anything. All she could think was that she should have made him sit down when she'd first seen him, examined him then. Then maybe, maybe, it might not have come to this.

Dr Garret raised her greying brows. 'Have we met?'

'Dr Peta Woodward,' Peta said wearily, offering her hand. 'I worked in the ED at Royal Melbourne. I've seen you speak at grand rounds. I was in Yarraman on holiday.'

'She's Craig's girlfriend,' added Gemma, in a defiant tone that Peta guessed was heading off any suggestion that Peta shouldn't be there.

Dr Garret swiftly moved on. 'Having laid out those positives, this is still extremely serious, and there's a long way to go. We'll be monitoring him very closely.'

'I'd like to see him now, please,' Theresa said, already on her feet. Her tone said she wouldn't be stopped, the unshakable bond between mother and child desperate to reconnect.

As they rode up the lift, Peta couldn't help think how her own mother must have felt when Stacey was injured. How the despair must have undone her. No wonder her mother had never recovered. No wonder none of them had.

⤙

Peta could have described in detail what she expected to find in the ICU. She could have found words to explain it to a patient's family; confronting, that was one word, scary was another. They would see someone they cared about crowded with equipment, reduced to a chart documenting their heart rate, blood pressure, blood gases and medication. She'd seen families go through it countless times, and the experience with Stacey was still indelibly etched in her memory.

But still, nothing prepared her.

Craig wasn't like Stacey – she knew that the moment she saw him against the hospital blankets, the tube taped in the corner of his mouth, his head swaddled in bandages. Stacey had been her sister, but the accident had happened when Peta was still young and optimistic.

But Craig . . . Peta's memories of him were vivid – his voice, his touch, his eyes – and the sight of all that equipment broke some illusion that Peta had been holding in her mind.

Oh god, this really was real.

She couldn't do it again; couldn't watch another person she loved die, and their family wither around them. The idea froze her.

Theresa and Gemma had no such problem. They immediately pulled up chairs and took his hand, talking to him about all kinds of things – Gemma the most animated, brave now there was something to do. Theresa was drawn and worried, her voice low, but she was no less engaged. Both of them seemed to take heart in just being able to be here, as if they could force him better by sheer will. From their lips flowed good-natured remonstrations for worrying them, questions about what had happened, or comments about all the equipment, how he looked, that this really wouldn't do ... nothing seemed off limits, all delivered with a tearful mocking that spoke of their strength as women, that this was how they handled things. They expected him to come back to them.

Peta couldn't do it, the inclusion she'd felt in their family moments before dashed. She hung back, gripping the edge of the bed curtain, even when Gemma made room for her, ashamed by how easy it seemed for Gemma and Theresa.

'Can I have a word?'

Peta hadn't noticed Dr Garret standing quietly behind her. 'How are you doing?'

Peta had to drop her head so Dr Garret wouldn't see the emotion that misted her eyes.

'It must be very confronting to see your boyfriend in this situation, especially when you were there at the start.'

Peta nodded numbly, not able to meet Dr Garret's eye.

'Don't feel pressured to react a certain way,' the doctor said. 'You've had a high-pressure day and you're personally involved. Your knowledge might work against you here. If you want to speak to someone on the staff, I can organise it. Otherwise, maybe you should try to get some sleep? He's stable for now. I can let you know if anything changes.'

Peta agreed, but she couldn't sleep. Her fears were a great pressure behind her breastbone that ached when she lay down, even on the more padded waiting room chairs near the ICU. Instead, she paced. She was desperate to talk to someone, to lance the pressure by letting it out, but who could she call at three in the morning?

On TV shows, women always had friends they could call any time of the day or night, but Peta didn't have people like that. She had co-workers and training partners at her running club, people she might socialise with in a group, but never more than that. If she called, they'd have to remember who she was first. Peta? Oh, Peta from training, right!

She walked great circles around the hospital floor, until there was a lightening blush in the sky. Twice, she brought coffees from the vending machine for Theresa and Gemma. Otherwise, she would peer in once a circuit, checking only that nothing seemed to have changed before she went on. Neither of them questioned why she didn't stay.

Then, as the sky paled, she passed the paediatric ward and saw a nurse walking with a sleeping child on her shoulder. Probably only two, he had a nasogastric tube and a head of soft curls. Peta immediately thought of Ned.

Suddenly, she was dialling Karen's number.

'Peta!' Karen exclaimed the moment Peta hurriedly tried to apologise for calling so early. 'Don't be silly. I'm always up early, and besides I couldn't sleep. Diane told me what happened. How is he?'

Peta sagged against the wall. For a moment, she couldn't start. Then all the details came out, first a trickle, then a torrent. Karen didn't interrupt, simply made noises at the appropriate times.

'My god,' she said eventually in a choked voice. 'You must be beside yourself. How horrible. Ash must have called every cop he knows – there's been police cars down the street all night. And Diane's already started some kind of fundraiser.' She gave a slight pause. 'But I know none of that will really mean anything. Peta – is there anything we can do to help?'

'I don't know,' Peta said. That weight behind her breastbone was still there. Words seemed too weak to move it.

'Let us know if there is, and call as often as you need. And let Theresa and Gemma know the same? We're all thinking of you.'

Peta put down the phone, the offered support so unfamiliar. The pressure was still in her chest. She put her hand up to her neck and found it empty. She needed the necklace. If she'd had that, if she hadn't failed so completely, she could have said it.

I'm so scared ... of ... of ... of ... everything.

Chapter 26

Peta expected resolution, but none came. One day became two, then three, then a week. Craig's progress was satisfactory, and the doctors said that he had every sign of waking.

And yet, he didn't.

Peta returned to her flat and shuffled around, opening windows to clear the stale air. But no matter how many blinds she tweaked, the light falling on the blank walls and dusty flatpack furniture was dim and grey. Arid and soulless, even a sad cactus had turned brown on the kitchen windowsill. After the warmth of Craig's cabin, she couldn't understand how she'd ever lived here.

Over the next days, Peta existed in a kind of twilight, shuttling between her flat, where she couldn't sleep, and the hospital, where she sat for hours in the despair of waiting. As each day passed, the fears mounted on each other, building a cairn in her mind that overshadowed everything else.

She couldn't face calling Turner and Decon to tell them she was back in Melbourne, and she stopped calling Karen after a few days when there was nothing new to report. Instead, Karen took to calling Peta, often with Diane firing questions in the background. Peta never discussed her fears with Theresa or Gemma; they were listening to the doctors, and expected Craig to wake any day. And though they were clearly distressed, Peta knew they had the comfort of blind trust – faith that the doctors were right. Theresa especially tried to draw Peta out.

For a few hours, she absorbed Craig's mother's optimism, until she overheard a chance conversation. She was curled in a chair, tucked in the corner of the bed curtain, when two nurses came to re-make the next bed – the previous occupant had spent three days there after a car accident, and was now happily back on the ward, his leg in plaster. As the nurses stripped the linen, one of them said,

'You ever see something like this before?'

'Once,' said the other. 'Passed away eventually, but weeks and weeks after the initial injury. When you expect them to wake up and they don't . . . there must be something else wrong.'

Peta sat rigid as those words fed the hungry wolves inside her. She couldn't bear to watch Craig diminish, become less than the amazing man he'd been, only to lose him at the end.

When Karen called ten minutes later, Peta was in a state. 'I can't talk today.'

'Why, what's happened?'

Only the thread of their connection kept Peta on the line. 'I don't think he's ever going to wake up,' she said finally. 'They say signs look good but they don't really know. We're all talking to him, well, I'm trying, but I know it's not enough.'

A short pause. 'What *would* be enough?'

The question had never occurred to Peta. Craig's biological functions were being met. His body was warm and fed, his blood pressure solid, his heart rate steady. The latest scans showed minimal issues in his brain, the surgical site healing well, his hair growing back. And yet . . . something was missing. Her hand grasped for the necklace that wasn't there. She had no answers.

'I don't know.'

The line muffled as Karen spoke to someone in the background; probably Diane. Then the line cleared.

'Listen, Peta, can you give me some details about the hospital? His doctor's name, the address, all that stuff? We're just tossing around some ideas. Diane's saying she knows someone who was in a coma.'

A tiny smile creased Peta's lips. Of course Diane did. Diane knew some of everyone. So she gave the details, and then had to face Gemma, who'd arrived for her turn at the vigil. Tucked under her arm were two books.

'I went to the library,' she said. 'He used to read me these stories when I was little. I thought I'd try them out.'

'Good idea,' Peta said, but her voice was hollow. She didn't believe anything anymore. The world was cruel and indifferent. Good luck happened to other people.

Which was why she was so unprepared for the next day.

—

The day began the same as any other. Peta arrived early to find Theresa flipping through the news on her phone and relaying it to Craig, like he was just sitting down to breakfast. Peta took over, but her heart wasn't in it, her voice flat and croaky.

At lunchtime, she went home and tried to sleep. Her bedspread was barely wrinkled by her attempts over the last week, but she lay down anyway, curled around her empty stomach. She wasn't eating anymore. The sense of dread was enough to fill her.

So when Gemma called in the early afternoon and told Peta she needed to come back to the hospital, Peta assumed the worst.

'Has something happened?' *Has he died?*

'Not yet,' Gemma said with a note of excitement. 'But I thought you'd want to be here.'

'Tell me now.' Peta couldn't bear anticipation; it bound her lungs until she felt she was suffocating.

'Diane called. She's bringing some kind of surprise, but wouldn't say what.'

Peta exhaled. Probably it would be the proceeds of a fundraiser, or maybe a blanket, crocheted by the CWA's finest. But when she arrived at the hospital, she found the ward in upheaval, with groups of excited staff rushing around.

'What's going on?' she asked a passing nurse.

'I don't know, but apparently the doctor's okayed something unconventional.'

Unconventional?

'What are you doing?' she demanded a moment later, when two orderlies unlocked Craig's bed, and prepared to roll him away.

'We're taking him downstairs,' said one.

'To X-ray?'

'No, to the parking lot.'

'What?'

'Peta!' Gemma and Theresa appeared around the corner, drawing her out into the hall. 'Come on, quick!'

Peta was tugged along as Craig's bed went into the elevators, and then down, down, past the emergency entrance, to the service car park at the rear of the building. And there waiting was a jubilant-looking Diane, with a white float and Candle and Buck tied to the outside.

The scene had gathered a crowd of onlookers, and more peered down from the glass windows above. Peta spotted Karen, too, dressed for her role in gumboots, jeans and a check shirt.

'I can't believe you did this,' Peta said, breathless.

'Diane's idea. She'd said the two of them were pining for Craig anyway. Next thing, she's on the phone to the staff down here organising permission.'

'Not exactly standard therapy.' Dr Garret had appeared outside, dressed in scrubs, her wiry arms folded. 'But exceptions do need to be made.'

Theresa was hugging her. 'This is wonderful. Just what he needs.'

Peta glanced down at Craig. Outside in the natural light, his pallor was shocking. She'd heard people say that coma patients looked as if they were sleeping; but she knew better. When Craig slept, his face relaxed, his eyelashes brushed his cheeks; and when he dreamed, she could watch those dreams unfolding in the movements of his eyes. Now, he didn't dream, and his face was blank and unfamiliar.

Candle and Buck didn't care. From the moment they realised it was Craig in the bed, they refused anyone's directions. Candle half-dragged Diane across the car park before gently, unbelievingly, snuffling over Craig's chest. The nurses jumped forward, scared that he would disrupt a drip line, but Candle was delicate, feeling with his whiskers, twitching at the blanket with his top lip. Buck held back, his ears swivelling, before he took to investigating Craig's left arm, pressing his velvet nose into Craig's unmoving fingers.

A sob escaped Peta to see Buck confused, as if he couldn't understand why no pat was forthcoming. But he waited, patiently, gently nudging the hand into a cup shape, while Candle rested his muzzle against Craig's cheek.

All the staff were in tears. Even Diane was dabbing at her eyes. But as moving as it was, Peta couldn't help feel all the more devastated. Was it cruel to have brought the two horses, then send them home without Craig ever coming back? It was unbearable, especially when Candle gave his soft, deep whicker – Peta had only ever heard him do that for Craig. She was afraid for them, too, of what would befall them if she never woke up.

If *he* never woke up. That was what she meant.

Peta couldn't take it anymore; she needed to run until she wore herself to collapse and had left this ache far behind. But as she looked for a path out through the crowd, a jerk in Buck's neck muscles stopped her.

Craig's fingers had moved. Buck held his nose very still, as if he'd had a taste of something amazing and was waiting for more. Peta held her breath. She realised Dr Garret beside her was doing the same. Then, a tiny movement, just the fingertips of the outer three fingers. Peta couldn't believe it. She searched Craig's face. His eyes flickered behind his lids.

And for the first time since she'd seen him in the ICU, Peta saw life.

Diane explained later that the deal had been for fifteen minutes with the horses. But in the end, they stayed in the car park over an hour. There was no miracle awakening; Peta knew that only happened in the movies, but the positive signs were undeniable. The horses had managed something no one else could, and a faint streak of hope appeared in her heart like the first light of dawn.

Diane packed Candle and Buck away reluctantly, after accepting hugs from Theresa. 'I'm taking them to my sister's – she's got a property just outside town. Then we can come back if we need to.'

'Thank you. So much.' Peta actually hugged Diane. She must have been completely overcome.

'Karen helped,' Diane said, waving away the thanks. 'It's the least I can do really. Considering.' Diane almost sounded guilty. 'Besides,' she went on, 'we help each other out, right?'

'Have you heard anything about the foal?' Peta asked, bracing herself for bad news.

Diane's face warmed. 'Cute little thing! Erica's brilliant. She found a nursing mare at Mandy's down near Mansfield. The mare's apparently taken an orphan before, and she's adopted Bel's foal. Apparently Craig trained the mare, too, a few years back, so Mandy was only too happy to try it out. Erica said she didn't have much hope, but the filly's showing interest in soaked pellets too, whatever that means. Here, I've got a photo.'

Diane produced a snapshot on her phone, showing the chestnut filly standing shoulder to shoulder with a darker colt, the mare a spirited-looking bay who was keeping a beady watch on the photographer.

Diane put the photo away. 'Listen, Peta, can I ask you something? The two men who did this to Craig, they've been charged and they were in court last week. Ash thinks they've got no chance of getting off, given they were caught red-handed.'

'Good.'

Diane looked away. 'The thing is, the truck they were in was stolen so there was nothing to trace. They've been cagey about why they did it. Said someone hired them, but claim that they don't know who. Ash said he didn't believe it, but they were adamant.'

'Okay . . .' Peta inspected Diane's face. The woman was definitely hiding something. 'Are you saying you know who?' Peta now dimly remembered Diane saying something about this at the goose dinner.

'Shhh.' Diane looked around, furtive, as if they were in a detective movie, not the parking lot of a city hospital. 'I have to be careful.'

Peta thought Diane had lost her mind. She really had watched one too many movies, spent too many hours alone in the shop.

'Well, I'll leave it up to you,' Peta said. 'I'm sure you'll do the right thing.'

Diane's lips twitched, then she drew her shoulders straight. 'Right. Yes.' A pause. 'There's one more thing, and I hesitate to raise it, but the deadline for the candidate entry is coming up.'

Peta gave Diane a withering eyebrow.

'That's what I thought. Now, off you go and see to Craig. Let me know if the horses can come back.'

Chapter 27

Craig had no sense of time passing, only the order in which things happened. Firstly, the sense of being tired, so very tired. He could smell horses, as if he'd fallen asleep in the feed shed. But he didn't remember what horses were, not exactly. Only that the smell was familiar, warm and comforting. Awareness of his body trickled back. At first, his skin was simply a pressure against a softness. Then he remembered his hands, his face.

When he heard sounds again, it was voices first, but he couldn't make sense of them. Words came slowest of all, as unnamed pictures in his mind gradually reacquired their labels.

When his eyes first opened, he had a sense of how important it was. He hadn't known how to do that for such a long time. He saw shapes, but he didn't recognise them. His eyelids were heavy. He closed them again, and more time passed.

The second time, the things he saw had more meaning. People, familiar people. Not their names, not yet. But faces, yes. He felt pressure on his hand, a light weight against his hair. He could flex his fingers, squeeze against someone else's.

Little by little, this was how it went. Craig didn't have a concept of how long it took. Only that he slept between awarenesses, and when he woke, the same people were always there. Mother. Gemma . . . and Peta.

He said their names, and then they were crying. Three other women he didn't know were smiling. He recognised two of their voices. They were explaining they were the nurses, and the other woman was the doctor. He was in a hospital. He'd been very sick.

Craig tried to process this before he next woke. And that time, the world was clearer, sharper. He finally saw evidence to support what he'd been told – the tubes and monitors, the unfamiliar bed. He tried to clear his throat, his voice cracking like a dry creek bed he'd once trod across out west.

Only one thing confused him.

'Can't be in hospital,' he said, blinking slowly. 'I remember the horses.'

He didn't understand why they laughed. Not until they asked him if he wanted to see Candle and Buck. Then later that day, they took him downstairs to the car park. And there were the two of them, nudging people away in their delight to get to him. He stroked their noses. Candle tried to peel off Craig's blanket with his teeth.

Then Craig remembered Bel.

All the lightness went out of him. He loved Candle and Buck, but Bel had her own place in his mind, one that had now collapsed. He would never see her again, his heart stiff at the thought. By the time they were back up in the ward, the heaviness had spread into his chest. He caught Peta's arm.

'What did they do with Bel? And what about the filly?'

She pulled a chair in close, her voice soft. 'Erica buried her on the farm. We found the filly the same day, and Erica sourced a mare down the valley, at Mandy's, who came to your class. Erica says she's doing well so far.'

He let his head fall back on the pillow. This was something, but nothing could remove the pain of knowing Bel was gone. However foggy and slow his faculties were in returning, that was a constant.

Her death had also shifted something inside him. He'd been eager to leave the hospital, but now he wasn't sure what home would be like, as if fundamentals like sunrise and sunset might not happen anymore.

But there was one thing that gave him hope, and that was Peta.

For Peta, watching Craig's recovery was equal parts torture and marvel. His initial confusion, and the slowness of regaining memory and speech was painful to watch, even when she knew that was how it would be. The progress he made seemed most rapid after the horses were allowed to visit. A local journalist caught wind of the unusual therapy and came down to interview everyone involved, even managing to have Dr Garret appear on camera.

Diane was only too happy to pose for photos with Candle and Buck, in her element as she answered questions, raised the issue of evacuation services in rural towns, and promoted both the CWA and Yarraman Falls in emphatic style.

Peta was happy to leave her to it. She was struggling with decisions. The idea of completing the trail hung in her mind like a distant star. She'd willingly abandoned it to come back to Craig, but their future was unresolved, just as the issue of the stud still was. And on the latter, she was just as stuck as before.

To avoid her dingy flat, and to try forcing some normalcy, she picked up some casual work, but her concentration was frayed. The frantic pace of work in emergency was part of the life she'd left behind. She didn't fit there anymore; she didn't fit anywhere.

Then one night, after the first time Craig had been up walking and visiting hours were nearly over, he stopped her leaving. 'I don't remember a lot about the accident,' he said slowly. 'But I do remember you'd left. I thought you'd gone to finish the trail. Why did you come back?'

Peta decided against telling him about the ghost horse; instead, she tried to remember the tentative hope she'd held when she'd been walking back to the farm.

'I didn't want to regret leaving,' she said simply.

'And did you?'

Hope in his voice. She nodded, and was rewarded with a slow smile that set off sparkles of joy in her heart. They stared at each other a long while, the silence fanning the sparks. She knew he wanted it to work, and she edged her hand forward and took his, his skin as warm as she remembered. Only the issue of the stud remained wedged between them.

After a while, he squeezed her hand and his head sank back against the pillows. Peta thought he must be tired, until he said, 'You're still looking for your necklace.'

Peta snatched her searching hand away from her throat. 'I just had an itch,' she lied.

'You know, I might have had a brain injury, but I'm not that thick,' he said. His wry smile turned sympathetic. 'I know it meant a lot to you.'

And with her hand still in his, Peta found herself telling him. 'Stacey was the one who bought it. I told you she was the one who really shone. Our birthdays were two days apart, and a year between us. I was older, but she was the adventurer – always getting into scrapes. By the time she was thirteen she'd broken more bones than any other kid I knew. She was fearless. We spent a lot of time in emergency. I actually think that's where I got the idea of becoming a doctor. I tried to look after her.'

Peta glanced down. The lino floor was grey with flecks of green. 'Anyway, she made me promise to never take it off. She was dramatic like that. That was a week before the accident. Like she knew.'

Craig's face wore a tiny frown now. 'Do you want to tell me what happened to her?'

Peta pulled her hand away and stood. 'I need a coffee. Do you want one?'

'I'm pretty sure caffeine's off the menu.'

'Right. Sorry.'

'You don't have to tell me.'

She met his eye, part of her curious if this extraordinary man, who'd rescued his family, who'd survived a serious brain injury, could see her guilt. She couldn't bring herself to explain that it was her fault.

Finally Craig said, 'Peta, I know that I'm here thanks to you. If you hadn't come back, then this would have been a story with a different ending. I think that means something.'

Later, Peta didn't know why that had such an effect on her. Maybe it was the simplicity that they were, indeed, both still there. Survivors of one sort or another, and that there was a bond between them they could choose to explore. She hadn't considered that if things had gone more smoothly and she was never injured, then she wouldn't have met him.

Hope surfaced again.

Craig took a breath. 'Diane's taking the horses back to the farm tomorrow. She said Charlene's bankrupting her store.'

Peta smiled. 'I heard.'

'The physio's been going pretty hard with me because I told them I need to be able to ride again, but they're happy. The doc is talking about letting me go home this week.'

'I heard that, too.'

'Come back with me?'

The request tingled with anticipation, and Peta wanted it to be that simple. But later, as she paced around the hospital, she noticed herself still feeling for the lost necklace. She hadn't accepted that it was gone. That her family were gone.

Would she ever?

She stopped in front of a dark window that looked out across Melbourne. The city was a dark expanse, dotted with lights. This had been home, once, but her heart had never left the place in the Adelaide Hills where everything had started.

That was where she had to go.

The idea struck her like a blow, and Peta jerked away from the window. No, she wasn't ready for that. And besides, she had to make a go of things with Craig, first.

But a part of her wondered: would she ever be brave enough to do it?

Chapter 28

Peta found it easy to avoid the issue as another week passed and Craig gained strength. He was clearly impatient, and was ready to go by six am on the day of discharge, sitting on the edge of the bed in his old jeans even while the staff were still organising paperwork.

'You'll be lucky to get out by ten,' Peta warned him.

Gemma was worse. Even Theresa, normally so easygoing, told her to calm down. 'You'll be on your way soon enough.'

Gemma wasn't placated. 'It'll be dark before we're back at this rate. Diane's been looking after the horses for ages. Plus there's no food at home.'

That was how Gemma argued to start the journey back without them. She would stop in at the big supermarket at the edge of the flats so that Craig and Peta could head straight to the farm and not need to go out again. Theresa was heading to the airport to rejoin Grant, who had stayed with the caravan, before they made the journey back home.

'She doesn't get it from me,' Theresa said, shaking her head at the stubbornness. Peta saw Craig's expression darken, and he was distracted for a long while afterwards. Only stepping into the car finally at eleven seemed to cure him. He gave the hospital a long backwards glance. 'Can't say I'm going to miss it,' he said. 'Let's go home.'

Theresa said her goodbyes before the drive and drew Peta aside. 'I know this has been really hard on you,' she said. 'But take your time. We'll be a couple of weeks bringing the van back, and then I'll drop in to make sure all is well. Call anytime.'

Craig obviously found the return both wonderful, and bitter. Peta walked with him around the farm, letting him check out how everything was, making comments about what Diane had moved in the feed shed, which paddock Seb had chosen for the cows, and how Buck and Candle fared after their long road trip. He made no comment about Bel's empty yard, or about Gemma, who had left five bags of groceries on the bench in the big house with a note saying that she'd do the mail and check in with Diane and Seb, and be back later.

Finally, without a word, Craig stopped what he was doing and turned for where Bel was buried. It was just down from the cottage, under a sprawling candle bark, the ground carpeted with tiny yellow flowers. He removed his hat, silent, as a light breeze blew with the scent of hay and cows.

'Do you want me to leave you for a bit?'

He nodded. 'Please.'

'I'll take the car down to the village. It needs fuel and I didn't see any milk in Gemma's haul.'

So Peta drove the Rover down the valley and filled it outside the store. The village looked the same as ever – the white-walled pub perched on the high ground above the Yarraman River, the schoolhouse just visible down the side street. She was going to miss all of it when she eventually had to leave. She made a mental note to call on Karen as soon as Craig was settled in.

Diane was drumming her fingers behind the counter, watching political coverage on the ABC.

'Peta! I heard you were back. How's Craig?'

'Adjusting,' Peta said. 'It's probably going to take a while. What on earth are you watching?'

'Oh, just research,' Diane said, flicking the TV off. She seemed to want to say something more and couldn't find the words. Instead, she rang up the fuel. 'Anything else?'

'Did Gemma happen to get milk when she was here?'

'Haven't seen her. But I'm sure you'll get through it with Craig home.'

'Oh. Maybe she was going to drop by on her way back. She's probably gone to Seb's.'

'I doubt it. Seb drove down to his mother's again yesterday afternoon.'

'But she's been gone all day.'

Diane gave her a shrewd look. 'Then I'd guess she's at Wade's.'

Peta blinked. 'Is that still going on? She hasn't said anything since . . .' Peta thought. She couldn't remember. 'And she's been in Melbourne for four weeks.'

Diane shrugged. 'Guess there's some reacquainting to do, then.'

Peta, of course, mentioned none of this to Craig, even when Gemma didn't come back until it was nearing dark. Peta was busy heating the oven for pies when she saw the headlights pull in up the hill. Craig was setting the fire in the cottage grate. The days were drawing in, and with the sky so clear, the night was going to be cold. Even so, Peta knew he wouldn't usually have lit it. But he knew that she liked it, and he probably wanted to reconnect with home.

He saw the lights go on in the big house as he came to wash the soot from his hands.

'About time,' he said. 'I'd better go and see if she wants to come down to eat.'

'No, I'll go,' Peta said. 'I want that fire roaring by the time we get back.'

'Gemma?' she called two minutes later as she pushed inside the back door. Twilight had washed the sky in ink and turquoise, the only shadows now cast by the dim yellow bulb in the kitchen.

'Oh, Peta!' Gemma emerged from the bathroom, shutting off the light. She was wearing a sloppy jersey and a soft head band around her forehead. 'You scared me. I didn't hear you.'

'Sorry. You coming down to eat? Pies and chips.'

Gemma yawned. 'I ate at Seb's, and I'm knackered after all the driving. I'm going to turn in.'

It was obviously a lie, but Peta let it go. 'You want help setting the fire?'

'Not going to bother. I'm just going to put the blanket on. Night!'

As Peta carefully stepped down the hill towards the cottage, she was certain Gemma had been to see Wade. Craig might not approve, but being secretive about a relationship wasn't really a good idea. That was why the next morning, when Craig had gone into the feed shed to see to the horses, Peta resolved to try to talk to Gemma. When she reached the big house, she found Gemma making toast in the kitchen.

'Morning,' Peta said, then paused. In the brightness of daylight, Gemma's face looked oddly smooth, her freckles in retreat. 'Are you ... wearing make-up?'

Gemma's glance out the window was furtive, and she looked down at the toast so Peta couldn't see her face properly. 'Don't make a deal out of it. I'm just off down to the village.'

Peta's stomach contracted like a fist. Gemma was behaving very oddly, in a way she'd seen before in the A&E. It didn't take getting too close to confirm her suspicions. Gemma had tried to cover it over with foundation, but it couldn't hide the puffy eyelid or the deep hue of purple around her eye. Peta felt a triple wave of sympathy, anger and exasperation break within her. 'Oh, Gemma.'

'It's just something stupid. I hit my head on the car wheel. Seb's driveway is terrible.'

'Diane already told me Seb's away. Did Wade do this?'

Gemma's face crumpled, but she swiftly sucked a breath and pulled herself together. A look of terror crossed her features, her voice pale. 'Where's Craig?'

'In the feed shed.'

'You can't tell him.'

Peta nodded in the way she would have if she'd been at work. 'What happened?'

Gemma pressed the back of her hand to her forehead, as if she could still not believe it. Her voice was faint. 'I don't even know who she was. I overreacted. I know I've been away a while but I didn't expect to find . . .'

Gemma's jaw compressed angrily. Peta saw the muscle bunch in her cheek. But her lip quivered. 'I thought he really liked me. Then I find him with this woman – skirt as high as her armpits. Wade said she was his campaign manager, but I know what I saw. We got into a fight after she left. That's when he grabbed me.'

Gemma wrung her hands around her wrists lightly. 'I tried to pull away. He wouldn't let go. He was . . . squeezing, really hard, then he released, really suddenly. And I fell and I hit my face on the coffee table.'

Peta winced, leading Gemma to a chair and gently examining the eye, making sure there were no fractures in the surrounding bones. 'Then what happened?'

Gemma shook her head. 'I think I was in shock, because I stayed a while. He was so apologetic. He went and got ice from the freezer, said it was a misunderstanding. That it wouldn't happen again, and he wasn't like that. But I didn't believe him. I remembered what Craig had said about Bel, so I felt weird and I came home. I feel like an idiot.'

'It's not your fault,' Peta said quickly.

But Gemma had taken her lip in her teeth, shaking her head as she picked up a bag, her toast forgotten. 'Craig will go insane.'

'What are you going to do? You can't hide your face.'

'I'll stay with Charlene for a few days or something.'

Peta was just opening her mouth to try tactfully encouraging Gemma not to hide, and to tell Ash, perhaps, when the back door suddenly opened and Craig appeared.

Gemma had no time to escape, and Craig's radar for his sister's state of mind was clearly keener than Peta's, because he didn't need to look twice. Peta watched as he took in Gemma's face, and his own set rigid. He left his boots on, and in three steps, he'd crossed the threshold.

'Stand up,' he said.

Gemma complied, her expression now terrified. Craig very gently tipped her chin up.

'Show me your arms,' he said softly.

After a moment's pause, Gemma pushed up her sleeves. Her wrists were a mess of bruises, some of them clearly finger-shaped. Peta saw the tremor in Craig's hands, the way his breath hitched, as if he'd known exactly what to expect. Then he pushed the fabric back down and took Gemma in his arms.

He stood there, protective around her, and after a moment's shock, Gemma pushed her face into his chest.

'Anything else?' he asked, his voice husky.

She shook her head.

'Anything broken?'

Peta spoke. 'Doesn't look like it.'

He gave one curt nod and released Gemma. His face still seemed chipped out of marble, his lips tight, eyes hard. He strode into the kitchen and looked out the window, his profile a black silhouette against the green field beyond. Then he carefully manoeuvred around the bench and out the door.

⟶

'Craig, don't!'

Craig heard Gemma and Peta, too, imploring him to call Ash, but he paid them no attention. This was personal. His psyche had been jerked back to his childhood home as soon as he'd seen the bruises. He'd been a boy back then, the bruises on his mother, and he counted their escape from his father as lucky.

Well, he was a goddamn man now, and no one was going to touch Gem like that.

The rage infected him. He snatched the shotgun down from the cabinet. Thank god Candle was already saddled, anticipating heading down to the herd.

'Jesus, Craig, no!' Gemma's voice was a wail.

'Craig, you just got home from hospital! The doc said take it easy!'

Heedless, he pulled himself into the saddle. Candle picked up on the tension, his body coiled under Craig's touch. He didn't even bother with the gate. Instead, he took off down the field, towards the river. As the slope levelled out, he reined south, heading for the lower gate that would take him on to town. It was ten minutes to the village at this pace, another twenty beyond to reach Masters' place, if he took the forest shortcut over the next ridge.

Over the gate Candle sailed, though Craig felt the landing as a shock in his lungs. His body wasn't back to condition yet, his movements off-balance. He pushed himself forward in the saddle, giving Candle his head as the brave horse opened up across the flat ground.

As Candle's hooves thundered across packed earth near the road, Craig couldn't help remembering going after Bel, and how that had turned out. He tried to temper his emotions but the sense of unfinished business, and thoughts of Gem, pushed him on.

By the time they met the main road, lather had gathered under Candle's breastplate and Craig was sore in the back from balancing his weight. The shop and pub went by in a blur, and then Candle clattered across the bridge over the river, jumped a ditch, and pushed uphill into the forest. The air under the canopy was a cool shock, and Candle's hooves scattered fallen stringybark in every stride.

When he finally reached the old side gate of Masters' property, Craig forced himself to pull up and tumble down. Candle was blowing hard. Craig's own breaths were great sucks of air, and he had to brace his hands on his knees. Rehab at the hospital hadn't prepared him for riding across country, and he felt as though he'd been hours in the saddle. It took five minutes to pull himself together, and feel as though all his muscles were back under his control.

The gate's chain was cold in his fingers. The eucalypts towered overhead, the ground an inch deep in leaf litter. His boots crunched the undergrowth, sending tiny creatures fleeing before him, and yet Craig experienced a rare sensation, of feeling small in the grandeur of the land around him. He could remember the exact time he'd last felt that way – the first time his grandmother had taken him into the mountain trails. The swing of her grey plait down her back had been ahead the whole time, until suddenly it wasn't. He'd fallen behind, and it was just him and the horse under the towering gums. Gooseflesh had crawled over his skin, and he could still smell that rich scent of earth and greenness in his nose, then unfamiliar and frightening . . . until his grandmother's voice had called to him through the forest.

He heard a voice in his mind like that, now. He could still back out, it said. He didn't have to do this. An image of Gemma tried to force the anger back into his mind, but he held onto the calm in that voice, and thought. What if this went bad again, like it had with Bel? Would he put Gemma and Peta through another ordeal?

He gripped the saddle, clenching his hands into the leather. He thought about turning around.

That was when a patch of the downhill forest over Candle's back caught his eye. The shrubs and ferns were thick all around the old access track, but something was odd about the shape and colour just there. Was there some pest plant growing? The caretakers might not be good at spotting such things. Leaving Candle on the trail, the sweat cooling on his back and throat, Craig struck off towards it.

Within ten metres, he caught glimpses of white and silver behind a wide candle bark, and realised he was looking at cut branches covering a bulky shape. A little closer and he saw the camouflage net under the branches. As Craig rounded the tree, his heart was double-stepping in his chest. He knew what this was.

A truck. A white truck. With damage to the front bumper.

Craig remembered the description Wally had given to Ash. It had to be the same one. Craig straightened, an emotion deeper than anger welling in his chest. Masters was an arse, a man with a cruel streak, but Craig had never imagined he'd rip off his own neighbours. Then he remembered what Diane had said about a big consortium looking for properties in the area, and a different picture clicked into place.

Craig stood in the cool of the canopy for a long moment, making a different plan. Then he vaulted onto Candle's back, his feet falling into the stirrups as the horse sprang away.

—

They cleared the tree line a minute later, and in the distance, tucked against the hill, the Masters place came into view. It was a sprawling house, an architectural investment that appeared to shimmy down the hillside, dragging its collection of stables and sheds with it. Craig spotted cars in the port, and another sportier number resting in the drive. And there was Masters, helping a shapely woman in a black suit into the car.

Masters saw him coming, and his face registered a moment's surprise. As Candle pulled up, Craig saw only a stranger, no trace remaining of the friend Masters had once been. The woman in the driver's seat craned her head around to see what was going on.

'Well, Craig,' Masters said, spreading his hands magnanimously, 'you didn't have to come all this way. You won't have met my campaign manager, Jocelyn?'

Craig ignored the woman, a tight burning ball of disbelief in the centre of his chest. He fixed his gaze on Wade. 'We need to have a chat about Gemma. And about that truck dumped by your north gate.' His voice sounded strange: cool and controlled, like Ash.

'Is everything all right, Wade?' Jocelyn asked.

'You go,' Masters said, patting the car's roof. 'Craig and I are old friends, aren't we?'

The woman looked dubious, but she started the car and pulled out of the drive, which gave Craig plenty of time to swing down from Candle.

Masters seemed controlled, but for his eyes, which were wide with fury. As soon as the car disappeared behind the trees, he spoke. 'Get on that horse and go home, Munroe. You've got nothing.'

'The hell I don't.'

'What are you going to do about it? Come on then, big guy. Take a swing. Or is that head of yours too soft for it now?'

Craig had enough control to see only two ways this would go. Either he'd knock Wade down and throw him over Candle, or Wade would admit defeat.

'Ash must be on his way by now,' Craig tried, praying that Peta or Gemma would have called him. 'So I think I'll just—'

Something wet hit him in the face, and he was momentarily blind as a searing sting bit his eyeballs. He smelled bitter coffee as his surprised breath sucked droplets into his nose, which punched at his cough reflex. He hadn't even seen the cup. He stumbled back, and felt a weight rush past his cheek.

Shit, Masters had taken a swing.

Craig wove on instinct, his heart thundering like Candle's hooves, and took Wade's next punch on his shoulder. He blinked, the world a blur. Masters was coming for him again, and the next blow glanced off his ear.

An ache sprang up where his stitches had been. Panic gripped him; he couldn't let Masters land a head shot. So he dropped his shoulder and shoved forward. His collarbone met Wade's solid middle, and Craig drove him backwards into the earth.

He heard the air rush from Masters's lungs as they hit the dirt. But then Wade's hands pressed on Craig's ears, thumbs diving for his eyes. Craig ripped away, only to cop a knee in the side. Winded, he rolled, scrambling up before Wade could loose another blow. He got his first good look, then. Masters was lurching up, expression brutal and intent.

Craig had the piercing realisation that Wade could put him down permanently, then easily claim he was only defending himself. Craig was on his property, and their history would do the rest. Time to get out.

Craig searched for Candle, and found the horse dancing on his toes at the edge of the action. He had to get to the saddle. Masters was already on him. Craig ducked as Masters took a shot, then he swung from underneath, his fist mashing into Wade's ribs. But the power had gone out of Craig's arms, and his lungs were a furnace. He dodged the next blow, copping it on his chest, then managed to land one on Wade's cheek. The shock felt like his hand had broken in half. Wade reeled, and Craig spun for Candle.

As he got a hand onto the saddle, Wade grabbed him from behind. Craig snatched the nearest thing, which was the rope around the pommel. He whipped it backwards, and heard the stiff fibre connect with skin. As Wade's hands loosened, Craig had a single second to unclip the pouch. Don't fumble . . .

Then the shotgun was in his hands.

He swung the barrels, and Masters pulled up like a Mack truck meeting a concrete wall. Craig held his aim, his chest heaving, nostrils flared, eyes painfully wide. As he sucked hot breaths, liquid dripped from his cheek to his neck; he hoped it was sweat.

Wade's hands pushed skywards, a pink mark from the rope visible across his cheek. 'Calm down, Craig, just—'

Craig heard the distant grumble of tyres on the drive, and a quick glance revealed Ash's police four-wheel drive flying out from the forest below, heading right for them.

Wade saw it too, with obvious relief. 'Don't want to do anything stupid, Craig, not like last time. Not with the law watching.'

Craig shook his head, thinking of Bel, and Gemma. 'You piece of shit.'

And he pulled the trigger.

Wade recoiled as the hammer clicked. But click was all it did; Craig cracked the barrel open and, giving Wade a cold smile, showed him the empty breech. 'I don't make mistakes twice, not like you.'

Ash was skidding to a stop, his door already open. Craig raised a hand to tell him he didn't have to worry.

Masters chose that moment to bolt.

He went straight for one of the big sheds, where a trail bike was propped on its stand outside. Craig didn't know where Wade was planning on running to, but he had a simple solution. With a last pump of adrenaline, he snatched the rope from the ground and flung himself onto Candle, who took off as if he were chasing a cow. Wade might have had a good head start, but he was no match for Candle, who ate up the ground between them.

As Wade went to throw his leg over the bike, Craig cast the loop over Wade's head. The rope snapped tight around his arms, and the aspiring member for Yarraman keeled sideways like a felled tree. Candle, ever the perfect mount, pulled up on his haunches to keep the rope taut. Wade thrashed about, his arms pinned, a tiny trickle of blood from the side of his eyebrow collecting bits of grass.

Ash came panting over a moment later, the unloaded shotgun in his hands. 'Christ, Craig,' he began. 'You'd better let him up.'

Craig tumbled down from Candle, sensing this was finally over. His legs would no longer hold him up, and he dropped unceremoniously into the dirt, reaching a hand to Candle's fetlock to steady himself. His whole body ached, but the relief was as refreshing as cool mountain water. Not only was Wade sorted, but Craig had pulled himself back. The silent fear that he carried – that his father dwelled within him – eased. For the first time, he felt his own man, one who could trust himself.

'Craig?'

Ash was standing over him with a look of concern that made Craig give an exhausted laugh. 'Go take a look down the side gate before you let him go, Ash. I think I found that truck.'

Chapter 29

Despite the relief, a few hours later, Craig was squarely back in fevered frustration as he sat on a hard metal chair in the corner of the tiny Yarraman police station. On the other side of the room, Masters sat behind a grey desk with another man, who had a distinguished rake to his greying hair despite his casual polo shirt and bone-coloured, knee-length shorts. Craig sourly thought the lawyer must have left a golf course somewhere in a hurry.

'So, you're not even going to charge him?' Craig demanded of Ash.

'I didn't say that. But they're arguing that Wade didn't know anything about the truck. It's right near an unlocked gate on his property, well out of sight of the house.'

'You can't be serious.'

Craig's mood was not improved by the impact of the whole incident on his body. He'd managed to avoid being hit in the head, but his thighs and back ached from riding, and every joint was stiff and sore. More than this, he was concerned about what Peta thought, because right now she was looking Masters over at Ash's request. They hadn't had a chance to talk about things, and while her sticking around and coming back with him were positive signs, he didn't want her thinking twice about that. At least she looked as though she wasn't being gentle with Wade's eyebrow. Now she straightened, slung her stethoscope around her neck and stood back with her arms folded.

The lawyer rose. 'Excuse me, Senior Constable? My client's answered your questions and in view of the sensitivity of his public profile with the coming election, we'd like to leave.'

Craig flicked his eyes across to Wade. The bastard was so smooth. His only consolation was that with Diane stickybeaking from her kitchen window, the story would be around the district anyway.

'What about Gemma?' he asked.

Ash's eyes flared with a fire Craig recognised in himself. But Gemma had refused to come down with Peta, which Craig could not understand. Ash rubbed his face. 'I need to call OPP. If she's not willing to make a statement . . . I don't know.'

'She's got a black eye!'

Ash's jaw contracted, and he dropped his voice, a menacing tone Craig had never heard before. 'Don't think for a second that I'm not bruising to hurt him, too. But I have to do my job. And in of itself, it doesn't prove anything. I have to get advice on this.'

'She told Peta.'

'Might I remind you,' said the lawyer, 'that my client was subject to vicious treatment, and that it isn't the first time.'

'Masters swung first,' Craig growled, but he was losing heart. He was filthy; his shirt smelled of stale coffee and sweat, and he ached so much he'd rather have been lying down.

The lawyer ignored him. 'Senior Constable, this man *pulled a gun* on my client, and I'd like to know why he isn't in the lock-up for assault. This isn't the wild west.'

Craig glowered. It nearly was, sometimes, but he kept quiet. He knew what it looked like, especially after the fight four years ago. The idea his own actions might have jeopardised justice being done filled him with the hot burn of remorse.

'Moreover,' continued the lawyer, 'given my client's social standing, and his campaign, if accusations are made that turn out to be false, it could very seriously affect him. It wouldn't be out of the question to sue for defamation.'

Ash held up a hand, and Craig could see he was struggling to remain professional. 'Look, everyone can calm down. These are serious allegations on both sides, and I am going to call OPP. This isn't done. If you're worried about image, then go down to the pub and have some lunch. I'm putting it on you to make sure that your client doesn't go anywhere else, and stay off the beer. The tension in here isn't helping anyone, and I want a word with Peta.'

Masters didn't need a gilded card. He sauntered out of the station with the lawyer alongside, giving Craig a cheery wave.

'You're letting him go?'

Ash lost his cool. 'Craig, shut it. I'm doing the best I can. He's not going anywhere – he's too sure he's got nothing to answer. But I need that lawyer off my arse while I talk to prosecutions, and work out if I can get some detectives onto that truck. If he starts swinging his dick around claiming we're damaging Masters's reputation, it's not going to help. Now, stay here and let me work.'

⟶

Peta had hardly believed the story when she arrived at the station. Now the cop's face was grim as he spoke.

'Is there any chance he'll end up with a head bleed thing, like Craig did?'

'Unlikely. Craig said he landed one hit, but that it didn't have much power in it. It's been hours and I see no focal signs. He's got a few bruises around his arms from the rope, and some very superficial scratches, plus the welt on his cheek. All in all, though, he doesn't look too bad. I'm amazed,' she added. 'After Craig left, I thought you'd find a body.'

'Gun wasn't loaded,' Ash said.

'Oh.' Peta glanced at Craig. He'd leaned back against the wall, with his head tipped up, black shadows under his closed eyes and hollows in his cheeks. She wasn't surprised he was exhausted, and even after her initial terror that he'd sustained another serious injury had been soothed, she was keen to take him home. 'Is Craig going to be charged?'

'Not if I can help it. I believe him, and that truck is a smoking gun. Proving it, though, is a different matter.' He paused, chewing his lip. 'Why wouldn't Gemma want to say anything? It's not like her.'

'I think she's embarrassed. She knows it'll be all over town in five seconds flat. She was so sure she knew what she was doing, even after what Craig said. She seems a bit shocked that it turned out like this.'

Ash grunted. 'All right. I have to make this call.'

Peta excused herself with the purpose of collecting coffees for Ash and Craig, but really she wanted to get out of the station and clear her head. She was carrying her own shame. With what she knew about Karen, she regretted not trying harder to talk to Gemma about Wade before this had happened. She felt a keen need to absolve herself but Gemma wasn't answering the phone.

In desperation, she stepped into the call box and dialled Karen's number, but despite it being Sunday afternoon, it went to voicemail. She left a message saying simply that she wanted to talk to Karen about Gemma and that Karen would know why.

Peta found the shop counter empty, and had to ring the bell twice. Diane finally appeared, then came running when she saw it was Peta.

'Oh, what's going on?' she said. 'I saw Craig and Wade in the station, and Wade's got that hot-shot lawyer who has that country escape house down the valley.'

Peta winced. 'They had a little personal disagreement. About Gemma.'

'Really? It isn't about the thefts?'

Peta cocked her head, remembering Diane's behaviour in Melbourne. 'Diane, what do you know about it?'

The older woman hesitated. 'Is he going to be charged? I just saw him head for the pub.'

'Doesn't look hopeful. Gemma doesn't want to make a statement, and Wade's lawyer's pretty good. He's saying he didn't know anything about the truck.' Briefly she explained about Craig finding it on Wade's property.

Diane collapsed dramatically into a chair. 'He's claiming he doesn't know about it? Isn't Ash going to have it fingerprinted?'

'He's making phone calls. But I gather there's a gate nearby, so someone could have just dumped it there.'

Diane was silent a long time. It was so uncharacteristic Peta felt the urge to snap her fingers in front of the storekeeper's face.

Finally, Diane sighed. 'You remember I told you about the men who took Bel being cagey about what had happened? In my years as a policeman's wife, that's pretty odd.' Diane dramatically removed her green apron, and smoothed the front of her jeans as if she was wearing a skirt. 'This won't do. I need to talk to Ash.'

Peta followed Diane to the station, wondering what was going on. Craig was still there, his elbows on his knees. Ash was just putting down the phone, and spotted her coming. He held up a hand.

'Now's not a good time, Diane. I'm in the middle of something.' Ash had the pinched look of someone who'd just had bad news. Peta was willing to bet that Masters would be celebrating tonight.

Diane seemed to have other ideas. 'That's what I'm here about,' she said. 'I have information about Wade's involvement in those thefts.'

Ash paused with his pen hovering over his notebook. 'All right, you have my attention,' he said carefully.

Diane nodded, and cleared her throat. 'So I understand Craig found the truck that was involved at Wally's?'

'We're still needing to confirm that—'

'Well, Wade Masters told the men to put it there.'

Ash frowned. 'What do you mean?'

'I mean he called the men who did the job and told them to stash the truck. Of course, they didn't discuss *where* on the phone. But he definitely said it would need waiting out, because someone had identified it.'

Peta stared at Diane, completely amazed.

Ash slowly flipped to a new page in his notebook. 'How about you sit down and tell me how you came by this information?'

Diane slid into a chair across the small table. 'That's simple. I overheard the conversation. It was after Wade had been down to see Wally at the clinic. He came back to the store and used the phone box to call the men. He was annoyed that Wally had seen enough to identify the truck, and of course he wouldn't want to make a call like that from his mobile.'

Son of a bitch, thought Peta, remembering how Masters had acted so concerned for Wally.

Ash frowned. 'Diane, that phone box has glass walls. Why would Masters have said anything if you were standing there?'

Diane took a deep breath. 'Because I wasn't. I was listening from the back of the shop. There's a little device in the phone box, see. Oh, I made a recording, too.'

Ash nearly dropped his pen, and the notebook closed in a flurry of pages. 'Jesus, Diane.'

'I know it's illegal, of course I do. I was married to a policeman,' she rushed out. 'But quite a few years back, there was a big operation going on with some detectives from Mansfield over a drug-crop problem. It was supposed to be covert, but Gregory knew about it – they put the mike in the shop phone and wired it back to the writing desk so that someone could listen. I guess they forgot about it when it was all over. Gregory showed me how it worked. That was just before he died, and I just got into the habit of listening to people, like the radio.

'I know I should have said something, but I knew it wasn't admissible, and I didn't want to end up with any threats. Those big corporates probably have legions of bully boys, and we'd had enough incidents around here.'

'What?'

'Well, that's what this is all about, isn't it? That big foreign investment venture is looking for farms to buy up in this area. Wade knows it, so he's buying them first to onsell at a profit.'

Ash leaned back, tugging at his hair so hard it lifted his lids off his eyeballs. 'How do you figure that?'

'Well, a few months ago, some of those big conglomerate investors sent a scout crew through town. They stopped at the shop.'

'What, were they wearing name tags?'

'No. I overheard them talking about the area while they were pumping fuel, and I saw the logo on a folder in their front seat when I cleaned their windshield.' Diane seemed quite pleased with herself. 'I also took their number plate and had it traced to a rental company. I still have some contacts, you know.'

Ash had put his hands over his face. 'Oh my god. I am not hearing this. Is there any one of you who hasn't committed a crime today?'

'Hey,' Peta said. 'I'm pretty clean over here.'

Diane ploughed on, more animated. 'Then my cousin Rita told me she'd overheard a real estate agent complaining about missing out on deals because some company was going direct to owners. So when Harry sold his place, I found the company is owned through a bunch of others that connect to Wade.'

'How did you figure that?'

Diane shrugged. 'I learned how to read through company records for my novel research. Seemed a good way to use it. I even went to the company address in Melbourne and found just an empty office, to confirm it was a shell. And Wade's clearly behind Bel being taken, too. I mean, Craig says he's going to run against him in the election, and so Wade takes a swipe.'

Peta glanced at Craig, who, from the lack of surprise on his face, had already considered this possibility.

'Christ, Diane. Let's be careful with the allegations you're throwing around,' Ash said. 'The two guys Craig caught claim they don't know who hired them. Have you got any proof?'

Diane's face fell. 'Not exactly. And of course they wouldn't. Wade would be too smart for that, wouldn't he? I know how these things work.'

Ash held up his hands. 'Look. Let's stop there and take a step back. Your tape's not admissible. Any lawyer would see to that. Everything else is circumstantial and I don't see a clear connection between the company and the thefts anyway. Even working with your tape to find some other evidence, it'll take time to build a case for a warrant, and we might not get it even then.'

They were all silent a long time. Finally, Diane said, 'So that's it, then? We just wait and see what comes of the truck?'

Before Ash could answer, Peta heard the chime of the station's outer door opening behind her. Ash gave them all a warning look. 'Now, behave yourselves. I don't want Masters to have any more arguments about this not going by the book.'

But when the inner door opened, the expression on Ash's face lost all the warning. Peta twisted in her seat. Gemma stood in the doorway in a pair of faded jeans and a grey hoodie zipped up to the chin. Her hair was pulled back in a ponytail, and she'd left the make-up off her face, the colour around her right eye a floral shade of purple. Beside her was Karen, offering silent encouragement, her own gaze searching the room – probably for signs of Wade.

Gemma's gaze flitted around them all, but it landed on one person in particular.

'Ash,' she said. 'I'd like to make a statement.'

Chapter 30

It was several hours later by the time the uproar in the station died down, and Craig could finally get a word in with Gemma. They'd retreated to the benches in the station's foyer, avoiding the tension in the main room where Wade Masters was awaiting transport to Mansfield. Two other cops had turned up a half-hour ago from other centres, and the room was a storm of phone calls and discussion.

'It might be a bit difficult, but we're sending him there so he can be charged with assault and bailed through the courthouse,' Ash had told them. 'That means we can put conditions on him, like not coming near you. I'm talking to the detectives about that truck. We could get lucky with fingerprints, but they'll turn it upside down looking for anything else, too.'

Now Craig put an arm around Gemma's shoulders. Her bones seemed so frail under her skin, her cheeks still pink from talking through what had happened with Ash.

'You did a brave thing,' he said. 'But what changed your mind? Karen?'

Gemma looked up at him with her big eyes misty with tears. 'Yeah, she came to talk to me. And while she was talking I remembered something about the day that Bel went missing.

Wade called me just after you left and asked me to come over. When I got there, he was acting distracted. He said it was because of the campaign, and I said I'd come back later, but he kept saying no, stay a while. I realised he probably did it deliberately so no one would be at the farm.'

She hesitated. 'I was the one who told him about you running,' she blurted. 'I could tell he was mad about it. But I couldn't shut my mouth. If I hadn't done that, he wouldn't have taken Bel. And if I hadn't gone that day, they couldn't have taken her. I should have listened to you.'

Craig gently shook her. 'Shush, Gem. It's *not* your fault.' He hadn't realised the extent of her relationship with Wade and that she'd kept it quiet because he'd been so disapproving.

Craig understood that now Gemma had made a statement, she was worried what would happen. He could take care of that. He reassured her, telling her about what would need to be done at the farm to ensure she felt secure. Maybe she could go and stay with their mother for a while. Only when Gemma twisted around and he saw her face did he realise something was wrong.

'Craig, I'm not skulking off to Mum's place. And I don't want you hanging around because you think I need your protection.'

'What's that supposed to mean?'

She shook her head. 'You know, when I found out you were talking to that election official, I thought it was nuts, but I also thought *finally*. You're doing something about getting off the farm. You've got this gift with horses, and it's stuck in Yarraman Falls.'

'That's not true—'

'One demo at a show and a few classes here isn't enough. People were falling over themselves after that demo, but you haven't done anything about it.'

'I've kind of had other problems,' he argued. 'Besides, you need help.'

'You taught me to drive the tractor, remember? The herd's small and I've got the business, too. If Karen can stay here when people give her a hard time, I'm not going anywhere. Let me handle it and go do your thing.'

Gemma had gone completely mad. Running the farm was hard even with two of them – no way could she cope on her own. Besides, he enjoyed it. Even when he was elbow deep in mud or baking in the dry summer winds, his soul belonged here. He couldn't leave.

'And what are you going to do in the winter?' he said now. 'I can't be off on the road, somewhere in Western Australia or goddamn Queensland while you're trying to work out how to fix a pump in the freezing river! You can't do it on your own.'

'Excuse me. What about Charlie?'

'He's barely coping, and he relies on everyone.'

'Sure. But that's what we all do. I've got Mum and Grant, and the Rusty brothers, and Diane and everyone else in the valley. I can work it out, Craig.' She dropped her voice. 'You need to go and find how to make your thing work. You know, with the little bit of brain you have left.'

She gave him a cheeky grin, but Craig didn't miss seeing how serious she was. Even so, all he could think was that nothing could bring Bel back. 'If something happened again, I'd never forgive myself.'

Gemma hugged him, low around his waist. 'Poor Bel,' she said. 'Do you think Diane's right? About why he did it?'

Craig glanced towards the station's main room. Peta was in there still, wanted for her medical opinion.

'Ash said we might not find out for sure,' he said, 'but I think she's right. Harry sold. And I believe he'd do it.'

The inner door swung open and Peta slipped out, rolling her eyes, an exasperated look on her face. 'They've decided now that I'm biased and they want another doctor's opinion before he gets transported anywhere. So they're trying to find one. Suits me. I don't want anything to do with him.'

'Do you think he'll still run?' Gemma asked.

Peta scoffed. 'I can't see how he can. Even if he wasn't convicted, it wouldn't look good.'

The station's outer door opened then and Diane appeared, bearing a tray of coffee and cakes.

'You're not seriously feeding him?' Peta asked.

'Of course not. These are for Ernie and Chris,' she said, meaning the two out-of-town coppers. 'They drove all this way, and my Gregory knew both their fathers.'

'And it's a great opportunity for a look,' Gemma said after Diane had disappeared through the door.

'I caught her watching Parliament Question Time when I went in to the shop earlier,' Peta said. 'Maybe she's planning on joining the interrogation?'

But when Diane emerged a minute later, the tray now empty, she turned and gave them her full attention, including a pause for dramatic effect. 'Well,' she began, 'I'm glad you're all here. I wanted to talk to you about the campaign.'

'I thought you said the nominations had closed,' Peta said.

'Yes, they did.'

'You didn't put one in for me, did you?' Craig asked with a shiver of horror.

Diane surprised him by laughing. 'Oh, heavens, no. You'd be awful at it, wouldn't you? No offence, Craig, but there aren't any horses in parliament. Buck and Candle and I had good chats about that. But Peta said some things to me that gave me an idea.'

'Oh, about that, Diane—'

'No, let me finish. I thought I was going to die running that shop, and they'd find me keeled over in the bain-marie one day! But when the date was coming up for nominations, I found myself filling one out.'

'Wait, you mean—'

'That's right. I'm running. And I must say I'm disappointed that Wade will probably drop out. I was looking forward to a good contest.'

Craig was suddenly laughing. 'Diane, if anyone can win it, it's you.' Not only was she the district's best fundraiser, she knew everyone's secrets. She'd be right at home in parliament.

⟵

With Diane still excitedly outlining her plan to Craig and Gemma, Peta excused herself. Outside, the late afternoon sun was streaming the last of its warmth through the treetops. The air was full of scents and sounds – a sweet floral perfume mixed with coffee drifting from the shop, the distant gurgle of the river weir, and the calls of birds overhead.

She exhaled slowly.

Everyone seemed to be bringing their lives to a new place – Gemma had found the courage to stand up to Wade. Craig was moving on without Bel. Diane in particular had surprised her. But all this highlighted what Peta had not yet done. The reason she'd started the trail in the first place was still unresolved, and her future with Craig couldn't happen without it.

Now, standing at the corner of the Yarraman Falls Road, with the little white pub and Diane's shop facing each other across the bitumen, she knew finishing the trail had never been the answer. She couldn't walk away from her problems. And the idea that she'd had that last night in Melbourne about going back to the stud – she knew she couldn't wait for courage. She would have to act, to finally face Stacey and what had happened.

The idea settled in her chest like a wind-borne seed come to ground. And over the next few hours, as they finished with Ash and headed back to the farm, it grew in the twilight and the deepening night into a plan, fully formed.

Craig had insisted on setting the fire in the cottage, moving slowly and painfully, but refusing all help. So Peta eased herself onto the couch behind him and sat with her hands pressed between her knees.

'I need to talk to you,' she said finally, when he struck the match.

Craig eased around onto his knees, dusting his hands. 'I know. I'm sorry for acting like an idiot. I'm lucky I'm not in the lock-up. Ash knocked it into me pretty well, but I'll take it from you, too.'

Peta smiled. He didn't know that she'd found it incredibly sexy that he'd reacted like that to protect his sister. There was something comforting about knowing your man could lasso his enemies, but she'd never have said it out loud. 'I'm amazed you managed it after all that time in hospital.'

'If it makes you feel better, I feel like I've been trampled,' Craig said.

'It was probably the adrenaline,' Peta said, but she looked away, trying to stay on track. 'But it's not about that, Craig. I need to go back to Adelaide.'

A flash of disappointment knotted his brows. 'That's it, then?'

'Oh, no! I don't mean for good, at least I don't think so. It's the stud. I need to go and see it. I have to decide about selling it to the developer. I can't avoid it anymore.'

Craig looked out the window, his eyes moving in a way that told Peta he was thinking about something important. Then he gave a single nod. 'When do we leave?'

Chapter 31

Three days later they drove to Albury, caught a flight to Adelaide and in a hired car, turned north into the hills.

Peta hadn't been home since she'd left after high school. As she drove the last long country road, she tried to quiet the thundering in her heart, wiping away the sweat that kept appearing on her top lip. Craig said little, watching the scenery slipping by, but he kept his hand on her thigh, a silent reassuring presence.

Peta was glad of it. When finally the familiar drive at the top of a rise came into view, flanked with the same wooden fences, Peta thought she would be sick. She lurched the car to the shoulder and jammed on the brake.

Craig's hand tightened. 'You all right?'

'Fine,' she said quickly, taking two long breaths. She tried to focus on specific details. The grass was the same shade of green that grew along the Yarraman riverbank. But there were no horses in the fields anymore.

Other things had changed, too. The trees along the drive were shaggy. The fences were missing rails. She knew her father had let it run down before his death, but the evidence of it was confronting. Needing to know what she would find allowed her to pull back onto the road.

'Lovely place,' Craig said as they crunched into the drive, and bounced down towards the dark brick house, which sat behind a sizable turning circle. The stables were down a short bank on the right, their white walls now grey, the red roof faded. Weeds grew up between the bricks paving the path down, and the house was silent, the carport empty.

Peta found it hard to process. In her memories, a few horse floats were always pulled into the side of the house. There should have been a climbing rose over the archway near the house door, but the trellis was bare. Someone had come and slashed the fields, but they'd missed the borders so that the grass stood high against the buildings.

The nerves in Peta's stomach were smothered by loss. She opened the car door and crunched across the stones to the house, her footsteps too loud in the silence. No distant neighs or feed bins banging against a fence. No hiss of water troughs filling. No horses at all.

She fingered the key in her pocket, but she didn't want to go inside. Instead, Peta slid past the windows. The first two had closed curtains, but the third were open a crack. Past them, she saw nothing. Bare carpets, empty walls. Her father had removed everything.

But it wasn't the house that kept her from wanting to sell; it was the fields, rolling away until they met the dark line of distant trees, the fences like vanishing lines to the horizon. Stacey's ashes were spread over those fields. They were the places they'd played together, the backdrop to almost every childhood memory Peta had.

Could she give that up?

She felt a warm hand on her shoulder. 'Peta?' Craig put his arm around her. 'Are you going to go inside?'

'No,' she said. 'Out here is where we spent all our time.'

She told him about riding with Stacey to the edge of every field, and then when they'd been allowed to go out into the forest beyond. How they'd propped fallen logs against the trees to make jumps, and stopped by a stream to eat biscuits snuck from the kitchen.

'It was all Stacey's ideas, though, she was the conspirator,' Peta said. Then her insides crumpled like cellophane. 'It's all my fault,' she whispered.

'What is?'

'Everything.' She looked around at the abandoned property. 'All this happened because of me.'

'What are you talking about?'

Peta grabbed his hand and dragged him back around the house to the turning circle, then across the stones and down the path to the stables. Inside the barn, she pushed the gate and it crashed from the hinges, the post rotten. Craig stood it up again, while Peta faced the long line of silent loose boxes. Some of the half-doors hung open, and cobwebs gathered in the rafters. A flurry of dust came down when a disturbed pigeon took flight.

Her shoes scuffed on the concrete floor with each step, down the long row until she reached the end where a single holding yard and sheltered feed bay joined the stables.

This was the place. Craig was a touchstone beside her, holding her steady. She leaned against the railing and closed her eyes.

'This is where it happened,' she said. 'Where Stacey . . .'

She could still smell the barn from that day, the mix of hay and horses and terror. Could still hear it; the leather-heeled boots running across the concrete, the bite of splinters in her hand from the broken rail. The shouts of the groom. Her mother screaming. But nothing from Stacey. Peta never heard her voice again. Her guilt pushed her words out like a piston.

'We'd both had horses since we were five. Ponies at first, but horses once we were teenagers. That's when I got Emerald.'

'You mentioned him once before.'

She nodded. 'He was my horse. Stacey named him Emerald because he was a palomino, and always rolling in the grass and coming in with green flanks. She thought it was cute – but she wasn't the one who had to spend hours grooming him.'

Peta felt a tug at the corners of her mouth, almost a smile. Stacey's horse had been black and called Sooty.

Craig's weight made the rail creak. 'What happened?'

'Emerald, apart from his rolling, was also a bit of a trickster. He'd work out how to get the latches undone on gates. Loved coming up to the house and surprising people, sticking his head in through windows. Stacey thought that was a riot, particularly when she had friends over from school. My parents were on me to make sure Emerald couldn't get out. I tried, but I didn't realise how clever he was. One day he got out when we'd gone to a play at school. I still don't know how – the gate was closed. But I guess when he couldn't find us up at the house, he wandered down to the road.'

Craig squeezed her shoulder, as if he knew what was coming next. Peta couldn't remember anything for a moment; all she could see was the emergency vehicle strobes flashing in the dark as they'd neared home. Someone had hit a horse on the road; that was all she and Stacey understood at first. Then she had found out it was Emerald.

'The people in the car were pretty badly injured. They'd swerved to try to avoid him. The vet found Emerald down in the ditch. He was shaken up but hadn't broken any bones and he seemed fine at first, just a few cuts. One on his neck needed stitches. The vet was amazed. It seemed a lucky escape, but I was in a world of trouble.'

Peta opened her eyes, trying to fill her mind with the empty yard, rather than her father's face, raving about how she'd been irresponsible. Two people had been injured. Peta had cried all night, horrified at what she'd done.

'Emerald never got out again. I chained the gate with a padlock. But problems started showing. He wouldn't let anyone touch him. And when a car came down the drive, he'd go nuts. If he was turned out in the field, he'd charge the fence. So I put him back in this yard, where he couldn't see the drive.'

'Head injury?' Craig asked.

Peta nodded grimly, her eyes catching the tufts of horse hair still caught in the timbers around the yard. 'That's what the vet thought after he saw Emerald again. I was distraught about it. He'd been this lovely cheeky horse, but he'd become something I didn't even recognise. I hoped he'd get better but he just developed other problems. He'd eat the dirt in the yard, probably because he was bored. Out in the field he was a menace. No one could go and catch another horse because he'd be there, being aggressive. My father said we had to put him down. I begged him to wait. I was hoping for a miracle.'

Peta's cheeks were hot at the memory.

'Stacey comforted me crying about Emerald all that night. And the next morning, when I slept in, she went into Emerald's yard.'

Peta pushed away from the fence, hugging herself. 'I still don't understand why. Our father had told everyone to stay away until the vet came back. But Stacey was the brave one – when I was dying of nerves at a gymkhana, looking at the height of the jumps, she would complain they weren't high enough. She probably thought she was saying goodbye, giving Emerald a treat, something like that. And I should have realised she might do that.

'Anyway, Emerald pinned her up against the fence. One of the stable hands saw it happen, but he couldn't stop it. My father shot Emerald on the spot, but Stacey was badly hurt. She never woke up again.'

Peta paused as the strength went out of her body. Her arms dropped, and she had to lean against the rough timber post that held the roof up. 'My parents were devastated. My father was angry at first, because that was how he dealt with most things. I remember him saying "I told you this would happen".' Peta's voice cracked and she had to wrestle her emotions to go on. 'Eventually he forgave me, but Mum never recovered.'

'How old were you?' Craig asked.

'Fifteen,' Peta said quickly. 'Stacey was fourteen. She'll always be fourteen. I limped through two more years here until school finished, then I left. Went to Melbourne and got a job making coffee and put myself through uni. I think I lived on the stale muffins from the shop where I worked. When I got into med, I worked in a lab. I was too much of a coward to come back home. Mum moved away soon after I left, and Dad got into financial trouble. Everything broke because of me.'

Craig turned to Peta, the lines on his forehead bunching. 'You know that's not true.'

'But if I had—'

'What? If you'd decided to put him down that day? You were still a child, and that's an adult's decision. Hell, an adult would struggle to make it.'

'You did, with that horse in Yarraman.'

Craig laughed as if she'd gone crazy. 'Right. An animal I had no connection to, and who was horribly injured, and I still found it hard. Jesus, Peta. Did you hear me beg Erica over Bel? If your parents were angry, it was at themselves. Everyone wants the miracle. It wasn't anyone's fault, least of all yours.'

Peta shook her head. 'What about with your father?' she whispered. 'You had to make a hard decision too and you were younger than I was. If you could, why couldn't I?'

Craig frowned. 'Oh. So you did hear that.'

'Diane told me.'

'Hmm,' Craig said. His face held a strange expression. He looked around the yard, and the empty barn. 'Is that what you've been thinking about?'

Peta nodded numbly. She hugged herself, goosebumps running up her arms. She couldn't forgive herself, no matter what he said. She couldn't control anything that her parents had done; but *she* could have made different decisions, and Stacey would still have been here.

But Craig wouldn't accept her stepping away. He pried her hand off her arm and took it in his. 'Come on. We need to talk about this.'

He led her away from the stables and around the house, to the green patch of grass overlooking the big back paddock. He sat on the edge of the back deck, and pulled Peta down beside him. 'All right. First thing is, I don't know what Diane told you, but I've heard enough of the rumours around town to get the general idea. And some of it's true. But people tell it like it's some kind of heroic act, and it really wasn't.'

He put his arm around her, hugging her as if he needed the comfort. So Peta released the hold she had on herself and buried her face in the muscle of his chest.

At length, Craig spoke. 'My father was a violent man,' Craig began. 'Very good with strangers, very charming, but in private he could be a monster. And Mum was the one who bore the brunt of it. That's the thing I remember most about my childhood – Mum and me both being scared. She'd shield me from him, and he never touched me – well, only once. And somehow that made it worse. I hated that he hit her and I was too afraid to do anything about it. It was when Gem was born that things changed. I was getting older and thinking about how life could be better for us. Maybe then my father wouldn't be like that anymore. Maybe he would mean it when he said it would never happen again.

'When Gem was still really tiny, something happened one evening. I don't know how it started – something about dinner. Mum could hardly move she was so exhausted – Gem cried a lot and Mum had been up all night with Dad yelling to keep the baby quiet. Then my father started on with his usual bullshit, and she couldn't fight him off. He was just this big bully, picking on her. I can see him now, towering over her, this big bear of a man, and her face turned away, just waiting for him to hit her again. I couldn't stand it.'

Craig blew out a breath, moving his feet. 'I remember like it was yesterday. Dad didn't keep his rifle locked away. I knew where it was. I can remember pushing those rounds in like I'd seen him do if he was going rabbit shooting. Next thing I was pointing it at him and I was telling him that we were leaving and not coming back.'

'That's pretty much what Diane told me,' Peta said.

'Well, when you tell it that way, all dramatic with us rolling into town before dawn and the local cop having to prise a gun out of my hands, yeah, I suppose it makes a good story. But I had nightmares about it for years.'

'You did?'

'Yes. I don't regret what I did. I would lay down everything for Mum and Gemma. But I was ten. My father was a huge man. He could easily have called my bluff and I don't know if I could have pulled the trigger if he'd tried to stop us. It could have ended up with that gun pointing at me, or at Mum. It was just luck. I didn't realise that until later, when I was working with the horses. Even when they seem trained, they're still a big animal. They're letting you do things to them, and it's all based on trust and acceptance. It's not control, nowhere near it.'

He stared off down the field, shredding a dried leaf in his fingers. He gave her a brief, sideways glance. 'I try not to think about that night. I'd say something clichéd, like you can't live in the past, but it is kinda true. I think about other things.'

'Like what?'

'Am I like him?' Craig examined the shredded pieces of the leaf. 'I mean, he's my father. We're blood. Maybe I would have pulled that trigger, and not cared. I don't know.'

Peta snaked her arm around him. 'You were worried about that with Wade?'

'Yeah,' Craig said. Then he chuckled. 'When I went after him, all I could think about was Gem ending up like Mum, and I was going to kill him. But I was so exhausted I had to stop – I've got him to thank about that, I guess, because then I started thinking about what my grandmother would have said. Then I found that truck and I wondered whether what I was doing was any better than Wade. I wanted to be better. So I unloaded the gun. Realised I have it in me to take time to make a better choice. Maybe I'm like my grandmother, not my father. You'd think I'd have worked it out sooner. With horses, the first thing you have to learn is how to control your emotions. You can't work with them when you're angry, or frustrated. I think my grandmother would have approved.'

'Is Wade like your father?'

Craig raised his eyebrows, then shook his head. 'I don't know him anymore. I used to think I did. When we were kids, his own father was away a lot, and I felt we had something in common. But if Wade did set up all those thefts to pressure people to sell, that's calculated. My father was never that. I'm not sure which is worse.'

'Lucky he's not going to be elected.'

Craig laughed, genuinely amused. 'Diane's a terror. She'll know everyone's dirty secrets inside a week.'

Peta laughed too, and the sound reinflated some of the collapsed parts inside her. Finally, she squinted towards the forest on the horizon and faced the biggest question.

'What do I do with this place, Craig? Stacey's ashes are spread over these fields. I don't want a developer to put houses on it.'

'Do you have to sell?'

'The debts are huge. Selling it as a stud won't be enough to cover it – the agents were clear about that.'

'How much is the shortfall?'

'About a hundred grand.'

Craig whistled softly. 'That's more than just change. Makes it hard to suggest this.'

'What?'

'Do you want to live here?'

Peta had thought about it many times. 'No, I couldn't do that. Too hard.'

'What if you could find a buyer who wanted it as a property, and covered the difference on the debt yourself? It's a lot of money, but you're a doctor.'

'I could sell the flat in Melbourne, I guess,' Peta said slowly, not altogether warmed by the idea. 'There would still be money to make up.' But as she looked around the rich carpet of grass, the lovingly cut posts in the fences, she knew which had the greater value.

'If you do, there's always a room for you in Yarraman,' he said.

Peta felt the expanse of the future before them, how wide and uncharted it was. Her old life seemed like a country left far behind, and new land was not yet in sight.

'What are we doing, Craig?' she whispered.

He looked into her eyes, searching, a small smile on his lips. 'I don't know. What are we doing?'

Peta thought about what he'd said in the hospital. Maybe Craig was right; so much was chance, and that was how she'd ended up in Yarraman. In part, why he was still alive beside her. She felt as though she had known him years instead of the weeks that had passed. She didn't know if it could work. But maybe she had to let go of the plan, like she had with the trail, and take the leap first.

'The district could use a good doctor,' he said. 'Or if these workshops work out, there would be a lot of travelling different places. Maybe even in Melbourne sometimes.'

A soft twinkle of light appeared on that distant horizon in Peta's mind. Its precise form was still unclear, but the one thing she knew was that Craig was there. She thought about the clinic in Yarraman; she'd enjoyed setting the place right, being able to help when she was needed. In Melbourne, she was one doctor in a big machine. She'd missed the sense of community she remembered growing up with, no matter what bad memories had later covered it.

'I don't know how it would end up being funded,' she said slowly, thinking about the possibilities. Approach the health department? Run it as a dual practice with another town? Lord, crowdfunding?

But Craig had a grin on his face, realising that she was saying she'd come back with him, that they might find a way to make it work.

'I don't know if it will be that much of a problem,' he said. 'I'm sure Diane would lobby for it.'

Twelve months later

The hall in Yarraman Falls had never seen so much attention, even for a dance. Party lights blazed from the awnings, competing with the spotlights from the news vans jostling for room outside. Peta and Craig crept down the road, wondering where on earth they'd park. The lawn was already occupied with utes and cars of every kind.

'Maybe this was a bad idea,' Peta said, looking at her watch. 'After all, they can only have counted some of it. They won't even know who's won yet.'

Craig was still staring at the hall.

'What?' asked Peta.

'Oh, nothing,' he said with a look of mock terror. 'I'm just counting my lucky escape.'

They ended up sneaking into a space behind the pub, which was already jumping with people who'd decided beer was needed to fortify themselves through the election coverage. As they squeezed past the front doors, Peta spotted a pert blonde reporter trying to interview two men in jeans, singlets and cowboy hats.

'And who's your money on for the election?' she asked.

Being a wag, one of them scratched his head. 'Election? I thought we were here for the footy!'

'If someone sticks a camera in my face,' Craig said, 'I expect a rescue.'

Peta squeezed his hand. They were both exhausted after the long drive, taking a night off from Craig's workshop in rural western Victoria to drive home to Yarraman. Peta had left the medical centre in the care of a part-time registrar. She had been running the practice for eight months now, which, after paying for insurance and stock, was touch-and-go financially. But in the last month, she'd reached an agreement with two universities to make the med centre a rural training hub, especially during winter when the ski trade swelled numbers in the region. Next year, they'd be taking students, and specialist trainees, too. It meant the town would always have a medical presence, and the students got experiences they never had in the city. Plus she'd managed to attract a GP who had a young family, and relished the chance to live in Yarraman, work part time and cover the practice when Peta was away.

Peta loved it when she was at home, but enjoyed taking the mobile clinic with her on the road. Next year, she could even take students along. Opening the practice and making the agreements had been a huge effort, especially with the long hours Craig worked building enough interest in taking his classes. But the sight of the town celebrating washed the fatigue away.

Finally they reached the hall, where Diane's face stared out from the door-sized posters that had been applied like wallpaper. The photo captured a new piercing intensity in her gaze, and a sharp suit that she'd consulted Peta on created the impression of a force to be reckoned with. Her political slogan said simply: *For the high country.*

'Peta!'

Peta turned to find Karen also in a smart suit. With the demise of Wade's political aspirations, Karen was free from pressure and her easy smile attested the fact. Ned walked beside her in a Spiderman costume. 'I tried, but he insisted,' she said with a shrug. 'Diane's just finishing an interview, then I know she'll want to say hello. She's very touched you put the poster on the side of the float.'

Craig laughed, and Peta knew he was thinking of all the times he'd complained that Diane was following them all over Victoria. The complaint was good-natured, though; Diane had enjoyed huge support. She knew the issues everyone faced, remembered names like it was her superpower, and was capable of being diplomatic – Karen had been a consultant on her environmental policy. The coverage she'd enjoyed after Craig's stint in hospital hadn't hurt her public profile, and her years of fundraising was a head start. Overall, though, it was her genuine love for what she was doing that inspired people. No one expected miracles, but in Diane they felt they had someone who cared.

Now, Peta could see her holding court amongst the cameras.

'Keeping people in rural towns is all about quality of life,' she was saying. 'We're clever out here. But farms are expensive to start and run, and so is conservation. No matter which side of the table you're on, we need grant programs for our smart people to run their businesses and keep the young men and women here. Not to mention protection from predatory commercial practices. That's good for every Australian, and what I stand for. Australian businesses for Australian communities.'

Even the hardened journalists had wry grins on their faces, especially with the mention of predatory practices. When the district count came up in the scrolling coverage, projected on a big screen hanging over the stage, everyone paused to look. Cheers erupted as Diane's face with its *independent* subtitle appeared. A hush fell, then the result graphs filled in, with Diane's line outstripping the major parties'.

Karen nodded in satisfaction as Diane turned back to answer more questions, this time spruiking innovation in agriculture, how local farms were embracing technology and trying different business models. She was a machine.

'There you have it.' Karen shook her head in wonder. 'They might only have counted twenty per cent, but I'd say it's going to be a landslide.'

Another half-hour passed before Diane finally shook off the pack and spotted them in the crowd.

'Craig! Peta! I hope you didn't drive straight through. How's the class going?'

She listened with rapt attention as Craig summarised the horses he'd seen that week, prompting him about the owners and ferreting out connections to people she already knew. In between she signed two autographs and lined up another interview.

'When you're back next, let's have a sit-down about the med centre,' Diane said finally. 'I want to do a review of everything we have in the district, find the gaps so that when I run across the health minister, I'm ready to go.'

'Might have to meet you in Melbourne the way you're going,' Peta said.

Diane's smile was broad. 'Who'd have thought, eh? Now, make sure you go past the CWA table before they run out of cake.'

This they duly did before meeting Gemma at the pub for dinner. Craig's sister embraced them both, still dressed in her chaps and with a hat mark across her forehead. 'I was down the field trying to find two stragglers,' she explained. 'Ash wanted to come, but he's fighting a losing battle against driving infringements. I'm not sure he'll make it.'

'Look out,' Craig said, 'if you're not careful you'll replace Diane as the copper's wife in town.'

Gemma threw a coaster at him, but her cheeks were pink with happiness. None of them mentioned the controversies around the election – the press would do enough of that for them. Wade Masters had been charged with assault, but before that could even go to court, detectives found suspicious connections between the truck on his property and one of his companies. It wasn't enough to prosecute him, but then people had begun coming forward. Firstly, it was an accountant in the business who had overheard Wade giving directions to rough up local owners. The two thieves who'd taken Bel had maintained not knowing who'd hired them, but had identified Wade's voice. After that, it had all become messy; Ash said the OPP was still sifting through it all.

Later, after they'd left the bustle of the election party behind for the farm, they sat together in front of the fire in the cottage, luxuriating in the downtime before hitting the road again the next day. When the next class finished up, they were going even further west, into South Australia for the first foray interstate. It was a special trip, one Peta looked forward to, but with apprehension of what she would find.

She had to wait two weeks to find out.

⟿

That day, a sunny Sunday, she and Craig took the car an hour from their workshop ground into the Adelaide Hills, following the same route they had just a year earlier. The old Woodward stud couldn't have looked more different – the grounds were tidy, fences fixed, and the fields full of horses.

Peta opened her car door where they'd pulled over and climbed out, shading her eyes. She could see the cars dotting the turning circle outside the house, a new covered arena in the field beside the stables. She'd decided to sell the property, the buyer an Olympic horseman who was as keen to keep it from developers as she was. It had meant a low price, and she'd taken a loan to cover the difference while she put her Melbourne flat on the market. The new owner had created a hub for training, which regularly brought other horses in. Craig had even been asked to run a workshop there in a few months. Peta could only trust that it wouldn't be developed, but she knew it had been the right thing to do.

Now, Craig came to stand beside her. 'Happy?'

Peta grinned. She could see a bay and a chestnut playing with their feed bin, and a group of children running around the house. It was right that someone else could give the place new life.

'I got you something, too,' Craig said, leading her around the bonnet and easing a white envelope out of his jeans. 'Gemma wants you to know that it was very difficult, but she sends a big kiss anyway. Sorry about the package. There's a box, but it didn't fit in my pocket.'

Peta frowned, curious as he handed it over. The edge of the paper fluttered in a breeze that smelled of summer grass and sweet wildflowers. She unfolded the paper and peered inside.

'Oh, Craig . . .'

From out of the package she pulled a double strand woven from a rainbow of horse hair, finished with a silver horseshoe. Peta slipped the necklace through her fingers; the hair was cream and black, silver and chestnut, but all silky smooth to touch.

'I know it's not the one you lost,' he said. 'Most of it is Candle's, and Buck's, but there's the last of Bel's in there too, and some of her filly's. Plus two strands I picked up from the fence here last year. Gemma said that would be one for you, and one for Stacey. I hope that's okay.'

Peta nodded, speechless. She'd been so upset when she lost Stacey's necklace, but she knew that was only her past. Now, Gemma had made something that was past, present and future.

Peta fumbled to put it on, and when Craig helped slip the catch over the ring near the horseshoe, the strands nested perfectly against her collarbone. Light and right, with the tiny weight of the horseshoe at her throat to remind her of its presence.

'It's perfect,' she said. She ran a hand down his cheek, cupping his jaw before she kissed him. He scooped her up easily, depositing her on the car's hood so he could kiss her back more easily, enthusiastically massaging the seat of her jeans until she squealed. Craig gave her a slow grin, not letting her escape.

'There's just one thing left,' he said. Peta raised her eyebrows. 'Bel's filly. She'll be coming back to us soon, and she needs a name. Can't keep calling her "baby".'

'How about Chance?' said Peta with a smile. 'Good and bad – it's how we're here at all.'

Craig nodded, his arms warm around her. 'I like it. Now all we need is for my courses to sell out, all the patients to come to town, and Diane to do well in parliament.'

Peta grinned, wrapping her arms around Craig's neck. She still found it hard to believe, in just a year, how deep and strong their love had grown in spite of all the challenges. Or maybe it was because of them; they'd seen each other at their worst, learned to forgive themselves and each other. Now they backed each other's dreams, knowing they were stronger together than each of them would have been apart. And while Peta knew they'd had good fortune to find each other, it had been trust and hard work that had allowed them to make a future.

'One thing at a time,' Peta said, kissing him again. 'I want to enjoy tonight. We can do all that tomorrow.'

Acknowledgements

The Horseman as a book began at our writing group's retreat, but it has its origins much deeper in my childhood – with Elyne Mitchell's stories, and every other book I read just because it had a horse on the cover, and my own horse Dellah, with whom I spent so many happy hours. Thank you to my parents for indulging my horsey obsession, and so many years later, to the many fine people I met in Mansfield and at the Mountain Cattlemen's get-together, who talked to me about life in the high country. Very special thanks to JM Peace, who endured many questions about police procedure, and Captain Craig for advice on firearms. Any faults in the rendering of the facts are all mine.

Thank you also to my baby bear Alec, who came with me on that research trip before he was born, and afterwards, was good enough to sleep on my lap while I rewrote and edited; and my husband, who created spaces for more work to be done in what was the most difficult time for editing I can imagine.

To my publisher and editorial team at Hachette – Rebecca Saunders, Karen Ward, Julia Stiles and Chris Kunz – thank you again for another smooth ride, your enthusiasm and advice. Endless gratitude to my writing buddy Rebekah Turner for reading the manuscript, helping me in so many ways, and being a great friend; to Kim Wilkins for advice and support; and to Nicole Cody, Fiona McMillan and Meg Vann for your encouragement, input and ideas. Much owed to you all.